THE SUM OF ALL SINS

Mark Sennen

This novel is a work of fiction.
The names, characters and incidents portrayed in it are
the work of the author's imagination. Any resemblance
to actual persons, events or localities is
entirely coincidental.

First published 2018

Copyright © Mark Sennen 2018

Mark Sennen asserts the moral right to be
identified as the author of this work

All rights reserved. No part of this publication may be
reproduced, stored in a retrieval system, or transmitted
in any form or by any means, electronic, mechanical,
photocopying, recording or otherwise, without the prior
permission of the publisher.

Web: www.marksennen.com
Twitter: @marksennen

The present is the ever moving shadow that divides yesterday from tomorrow. In that lies hope.

FRANK LLOYD WRIGHT

PART ONE

Prologue

Chapter One

Rain. Slatting down in a deluge. The wipers going double speed. Swish-swish, swish-swish, swish-swish. The windscreen clears for a fraction of a second with each sweep, and she is able to catch a glimpse of the way ahead. Water lies in puddles in every dip and torrents crisscross the road. It's as if all the winter's rain has come at once. Forty days and forty nights in a single evening.

The car radio is tuned to a news station and the storm is the lead story, the only story. High winds have knocked down electricity pylons and whole towns are without power. The ports are closed and all flights have been grounded at Heathrow and Gatwick. Two people have been killed in central London by debris blown from a tower block. A man has been crushed by a tree in Manchester. A lorry has ploughed into the rear of a coach on the M1, leaving four dead and twenty injured. The emergency services are struggling to cope. And there's worse on the way, the forecasters predict. The weather becoming colder, the rain turning to snow. It's the kind of night where only the mad or the foolhardy would venture out. The mad, the foolhardy, or the desperate.

She hunches at the steering wheel. Dabs the brake to slow for a corner. On the next straight she urges the car on and rips through a deep tranche of water. The wheels aquaplane and for a moment her heart is in her mouth, sheer terror creeping across her skin, before the wheels grip the road surface and the car forges on.

Not long now. Perhaps fifteen minutes. Perhaps half an hour. Fuck knows to be honest. She's been here once before, but she wasn't driving back then and the roads are unfamiliar. Roads? No, not roads, lanes. Twisting between low walls of stone and climbing over the undulating terrain. Not that she can see much in the darkness and the rain. The occasional road sign picked out in the car's headlights. The pale glowing eyes of sheep on the verges. The glistening granite boulders ready to mangle the car should she stray from the narrow strip of tarmac.

For a second, she loses concentration and almost falls asleep before she jerks back to consciousness and blinks. She cracks the window down a touch and cold air rushes in, reviving her. It's been over six hours since she started out. Two hundred miles, most of it on the motorway, but much of the journey driven at a snail's pace. Only the mad or the foolhardy would drive faster. Not the desperate. The desperate want to make sure they arrive at their destination.

She'd set off from an anonymous street in an anonymous borough. Her house was a non-descript, semi-detached property, with a recent extension out the back. That was a good portrait of her too: non-descript, semi-detached, the add-on to the main event. She'd always been an appendage. To her cleverer siblings, to her more attractive friends, to her larger-than-life husband. The truth was she didn't mind. Not everyone could be centre-stage. There was merit in standing off to the side and providing the occasional prompt. Working the lights. Moving the scenery. Even sweeping up afterwards. For the stars to shine, somebody had to do the dirty work.

The dirty work...

Like clearing the blood from the floor or sweeping away the fragments of bone. Luckily, she wasn't squeamish, so cleaning up hadn't bothered her. Before she'd married she'd been a nurse and vomit and urine and shit were part of the daily routine. If an auxiliary wasn't around, you often found yourself wiping an old man's arse right before your lunch break. No, dealing with the mess hadn't worried her a jot. Especially not since they'd had new tiles put down in the living room. So *easy* to clean. Just *wipe* away the stains. *Erase* the evidence.

'You'll have to do it,' he'd said to her beforehand. 'To make this work.'

'I understand,' she'd said. It was all to do with suspects and alibis. They cancelled each other out. And, of course, her involvement implied she was the star for once. That meant something to her because she now meant something to him. He couldn't do this alone. He needed her. Perhaps, after all, she was moving beyond nondescript.

Water splurges up from a puddle and sluices across the windscreen. The wipers swish the glass clean and she's back staring at the strip of road. The satnav app on her phone flashes up a warning and an insistent female voice tells her to *make a U-turn if possible*. Damn it, she's missed the junction. She slows the car and inches along until she finds a place she can swing round. She eases off the road, but when she tries to go forwards to complete the turn, the car doesn't move. She lowers the window, hearing the engine rev and the wheels spinning on the soft verge.

She wrenches open the door and clambers out, her feet squelching in mud. The wind pulls at her hair and rocks the car as rain slants across in the headlight beams. The light is swallowed by the all-enveloping darkness. She's stuck in a little cone of brilliance, and beyond the cone is a black void. No streetlights, no comforting glow from a town or a village, no stars, no moon. She doesn't think she's ever been so far from another living person in her life. She's utterly alone.

She shudders, but before the anxiety builds, she turns and peers at the rear of the car where the wheels have sunk deep into the grassy verge. She reaches back inside the car and nudges the handbrake off. She goes to the rear and pushes. The car rolls back and forth once, twice, and then she slips and tumbles to the ground.

She cries now, the adrenaline that had fuelled her for the last few hours all used up, her will to go on broken. And without him, that's what she'll be: broken. She sobs as the rain soaks her clothing. She wants to lie there in the mud. Curl into a ball and hibernate. Let the cold take her as she sleeps. She'll just fade away from this world and leave the pain behind.

For a minute she stays still, knees drawn up to her chest as if she's returned to embryonic form. A simple blob, knowing nothing, fearing nothing. The red glow from the taillights heightens the womb-like feeling and the cold slips away. A strange euphoria washes over her. This was meant to be. She'd been born screaming, but she'd die with a whisper on her lips.

'Sweet,' she says quietly, deliriously. 'Lovely.'

She closes her eyes to sleep, but all of a sudden there's a voice in her head. Female. Demanding attention. She scrunches her eyes tight, trying to concentrate. Does the voice belong to her mother? One of her friends? She tries to listen as the rain lashes down, pattering in the dirt and thrumming on the roof of the car. A gust of wind howls and now she's shivering, the euphoria snatched away. She pushes herself upright and stands. She doesn't want to die. The voice may have been in her imagination, but it's a sign. He's sent her a message. He wants her to do this for him, for both of them. If she wants to be with him she must go on. She moves to the car door and bends to climb in. As she does so, the voice calls out once more.

Make a U-turn if possible...

She feels cheated, but then she looks at the display on the satnav. Three miles to go. She can do it.

She pulls the phone from the holder on the dash and thumbs the navigation app off the screen. She brings up her address book and taps an entry. Not far from here a phone is ringing. Not far from here a friend is picking up and answering, the voice quiet and hesitant but profoundly comforting. Now all she has to do is slump down in the seat and speak.

'Help,' she says. 'Please, Catherine, I need your help.'

Chapter Two

The trill from the phone jerked Catherine awake. As she opened her eyes, the surroundings seemed foreign. Even after three months in the new house, the low ceiling and vast stone inglenook hadn't lost their novelty. She pushed herself upright and gazed across the room. She'd fallen asleep watching a movie on TV, but the film had ended and now a news report showed pictures of the storm. Trees down, coastal towns flooded by high tides, the emergency services inundated with calls.

She blinked and reached across for her mobile, thinking it was likely to be her husband, Daniel, but when she looked at the screen the number displayed was unfamiliar.

'Hello?' she said.

'Help. Please, Catherine, I need your help.'

'Who's that?' She didn't recognise the voice. 'Hello, who's there?'

'It's Lisa,' the voice said. 'Lisa Paget.'

'Lisa?' Half asleep, Catherine took the phone from her ear and stared at the display. A bunch of numbers. Caller unknown. Then she had it, blurting out the answer before she realised how it sounded. 'Toby's wife?'

'Yes. You could put it like that.' There was another pause. 'Look, Catherine, I need some help and advice and I don't know who else to turn to. There's no one like you. No one else who I can imagine ever understanding my situation.'

'Lisa. God, love. It's all a bit of a shock. You phoning like this.'

'Sorry, but I didn't know who else to call. When we had lunch at New Year I really felt we connected.'

Connected? Catherine took a deep breath. The only reason she knew Lisa was that Lisa was married to Toby, an old university friend of her husband's she didn't think much of. They'd met a handful of times but were hardly best buddies, and Catherine hadn't remembered their recent gettogether in quite the same way; Lisa and Toby had been subdued, the conversation somewhat pained. 'OK, calm down. Tell me how I can help?'

'I'm in a pickle, Catherine. More than a pickle to be honest. I'm in serious trouble, danger even. If I don't get help, I'm fucked.'

'Look, Lisa, I don't want to be rude, but there's not a lot I can do from down here. This sounds like a matter for the police.'

'No, that's not possible. Not the way things are. When I see you I'll explain, OK?'

'When you *see* me?'

'I had to come. I had to get away from London. It was my only chance. I thought I'd be safe down here with you.'

'Safe down here... where precisely are you?'

'Close. My car's run off the road. The B3212. I missed the lane to your place. I guess I'm about half a mile farther on from the turning.'

'Shit, Lisa, I—'

'Can you come and get me? I'm soaked to the skin. Freezing.'

Catherine glanced at the TV again where a weather forecaster was giving an update. The wind was predicted to get worse and even heavier rain was on the way. The forecaster was talking about snow in the coming hours too. Cold air sweeping down from the north and meeting a second westerly front. A red weather warning. Severe disruption. Danger to life. Remain tuned for further updates.

She felt selfish. People were dying in the storm. Crushed by falling trees, killed in car accidents, swept away by floodwater. Lisa was out there as well. Alone on the moor in the wind and the rain and the dark.

'Stay put,' Catherine said. 'I'm on my way.'

Catherine Ross was thirty-six years old. She was half English, half Irish, her father's family being of Norfolk stock, whereas her mother came from Galway on the Atlantic coast of Ireland. Her father's shock of blond — now grey — hair and angular face had lost in the battle of the genes though, and she bore her mother's dark locks and soft features as well as a hint of her silk-like accent. However, she credited her father for her practical nature. There'd been no hint of gender bias in the way he treated his son and two daughters. All three had been taught to bang in nails and knot ropes, wire up electrical plugs and change car oil filters.

Her father's profession was accountancy, but the minute he arrived home in the evenings he'd change from his pinstripe suit into a blue boilersuit, balancing the drudgery of the spreadsheet with a life-long passion for DIY and woodwork. In a shed at the end of the garden he produced the most beautiful pieces, turning chunks of oak, cherry and walnut into everything from huge items of furniture to delicately carved fruit bowls. She remembered standing watching him at work, seeing the chips fly from the lathe, or marvelling how he could carve perfect dovetails with a chisel. Her father had asked her if she wanted to have a go, but the young Catherine had shaken her head. She didn't want to copy her father and end up second best. She wanted to make her own way.

At secondary school she'd taken art at A Level, and an enthusiastic teacher had introduced her to sculpting, not in wood but in stone. Back home her father partitioned off a section of his workshop for her. 'No half measures,' he said. 'You give it your all or you don't bother.' Soon, the whine of her father's lathe was accompanied by a chip, chip, chip as she experimented with the possibilities of this new medium.

By the time she went to university to read history of art, she knew her eventual career would be far more practical and hands on, and once she'd graduated she supported herself with a number of boring jobs as she learned her trade. Little by little, her sculptures began to sell. There was an intricacy to her work which was distinctive, and the pieces she produced in marble and granite were highly detailed: birds and mammals, the occasional figurine, and her speciality — unique abstract shapes with random holes bored through the stone at precise angles. The novelty of the abstract works brought her to the attention of several top galleries and soon they were taking all she could supply.

Then, when she turned thirty, came the move to London, the acceptance into an artistic circle, the invitations to exhibitions and gallery openings, the parties...

It had been at a party where she'd first met her husband, Daniel. She'd glanced across a crowded room in a top-floor flat in Battersea to find a pair of startling blue eyes staring at her through a forest of bodies. Never one for being shy, she'd sauntered across and flirted and pulled him into the next room where several couples gyrated on a makeshift dance floor. Daniel soon had his arms wrapped round her as if they were already an item, and as they'd danced she'd fallen into those blue eyes, thinking that still waters ran deep. And she'd noticed the way his gaze had wandered to the other girls in the room. A mind never quite settled and a body with passion to spare. But that was part of the attraction. His energy. When he did focus on her, all that energy flowed like a lightning bolt arcing to earth.

There were two sides to Daniel, however, two sides to his passion. On the one hand there was love, on the other an explosive anger that manifested itself in blazing rows. Never in violence though. At least not until Daniel had...

The incident wasn't an event she liked to recall, but it had been the catalyst for their move from London to Devon. They'd wanted to get out and get away. To never have to look back. Only now Catherine found herself looking back all-too-often, because the shift from a terraced property in a busy street to an isolated farmhouse on Dartmoor had been more than a relocation, it had been a dislocation, a shock to the system. That was what they'd wanted, of course. To banish the bad memories and jump start their marriage, but from almost the first day she'd felt uneasy. It was as if they were intruding in a landscape that regarded them as aliens, as if they were invaders who had to be repelled. The sensation was heightened when Daniel had to travel on business and she was left alone. As the darkness fell and the wind picked up, she would double lock the front and back doors and shut herself in her bedroom.

She often wondered how their life might have turned out had they stayed put in London. Would they have been able to solve their problems? She didn't know, but for sure the move hadn't helped in the way she'd prayed it would. In fact, it had eroded their relationship. The trust between them was gone, and perhaps the love was too. She hadn't wanted to admit to it, but now she felt a breakup was all but inevitable. And when Daniel returned from his latest trip, she was going to have it out with him. One way or another.

Catherine opened the front door to a dim circle of white cast by the outside security light. Beyond the circle, black. She still wasn't used to the countryside at night. In London the sky had been a glowing reminder she'd been surrounded by millions of other people. An open window let in the sounds of the city, whether a wail from the siren of an emergency vehicle, a shout of a drunk in the street, or a roar from the last incoming flight of the evening as it passed above. Here, a stream bordering the garden gurgled as the rain spattered down on the muddy yard, and the only voices came from a pair of owls calling to each other in an outbuilding. The roar above her head wasn't a 747, but the sound of the wind as the gale rushed across the surrounding hills.

She stepped outside and slammed the door shut. Droplets of rain glittered as they swirled in the glare from the light, and she ran through the shimmering crystals towards the garage and dashed inside to where there was relative calm. Daniel had taken his car, but parked next to the space was their Toyota pickup. They'd acquired the pickup second hand from a local car sales place which specialised in 4x4s. It was a monster of a vehicle and in a bit of a state. The gearbox rattled like a pocketful of loose change, and the accelerator pedal had a disconcerting tendency to stick halfway down. On the plus side it had chunky snow tyres, four-wheel drive, and a massive truck bed at the rear. For once, she was pleased to see the pickup. It could go anywhere, and a little rain wasn't going to cause it any problems.

The vehicle started up with a throaty chug, belched a puff of smoke, and she was away, out of the garage and bouncing up the track to the lane. Five minutes later, she turned from the lane onto the main road and headed west, slowing down as she looked for Lisa's car. The rain sluiced from above, javelins of water in the 4x4's headlights. As she climbed away from the valley, the rain became sleet. Higher still and the sleet had become snow. Visibility was now down to a couple of car lengths, and the tarmac had all but disappeared in a sheet of white.

Then the headlights sucked a burst of colour from the falling snow, and Catherine saw a bright red Audi sports car sitting beside the road, all four wheels sunk in deep mud. She beeped the horn, pulled over, and lowered the window.

The driver's door of the car opened, and a woman climbed out. Long auburn hair, wet and mattered, fell across her face.

'Lisa?' Catherine said as the woman staggered across.

'Yes.' A smile beneath the bedraggled mop. 'It's me. Sort of.'

Catherine took in the shoes clogged with mud, the dirt spattered jeans, the sodden jacket with a ripped pocket.

'Jesus, Lisa, what happened?'

'I missed the sign to your place and when I tried to turn round I got stuck.' Lisa let out a laugh. 'There's a metaphor if ever I heard one.'

'Get in. Let's get you back to the warm and dry.'

'My car...'

'We'll sort it in the morning when this lot has blown over.'

'NO!' Lisa shouted. 'We need to move it now. I don't want to leave it here.'

'Calm down.' Catherine leaned back from the open window. The outburst had surprised her. Lisa usually played the part of the quiet little wife, sidling along in her husband's shadow. Now she was wild, like a wounded animal trapped in a corner. 'We're not in London. I promise your car will be OK if we leave it here.'

'I *said* we need to move it *now*, right?'

'I don't understand?'

'The police. I don't want them to find it.'

'The *police*? What the hell would the police be doing up here on a night like this?'

'I don't know, but I can't risk the car being found by them or anyone else. I don't want anyone to know I'm here.'

'Lisa, you're going to have—' Catherine paused. Lisa's fists were clenching once more and her arms were locked rigid. Anger. Anger and another emotion too: fear. The cornered animal again, scared for its life. 'Fine, we'll try to tow it out.'

She opened the door, clambered down from the pickup, and flipped down the tailgate. There was a long hank of towing rope lying on the bed of the truck. She pulled the rope out, hooked the loop round the towbar, and went over to the front of Lisa's car. She bent and found the towing eye and looped the rope through.

'Get in and I'll give you a pull.'

Lisa went back to her car. Once she was in, Catherine put the Toyota in gear. She lifted the clutch and the rope tightened. Lisa's car came off the verge and back onto the road. Catherine reversed a touch and got out and released the rope, coiled it, and stuffed it back in the 4x4. She walked over to Lisa's car.

'Follow me, it's not far. Be careful on the snow, OK?'

'Yes,' Lisa said. 'Look, sorry I shouted. I'll explain when we get back to your place.'

'Sure.' The damp was beginning to work its way inside Catherine's clothing. She was tired and it was way past her bedtime. With all her own worries, the last person she wanted to see was Lisa. However, the poor girl was in a state and whatever the problem was, it must be serious. Why else would she drive two hundred miles in a storm to visit someone who, to be honest, wasn't even a proper friend? Catherine smiled and tried to sound reassuring. 'Don't worry. Everything will be fine.'

They headed off and a few minutes later Catherine parked up in the garage. Lisa rolled her vehicle onto the gravel yard.

'Come in,' Catherine said, opening the front door. 'We need to find you some dry clothes and get a warm drink inside you.'

'Yes.' Lisa stumbled across the threshold. She looked half comatose, and as she made it into the hall, Catherine had to catch her as she slumped down at the foot of the stairs. The anger had gone, replaced by worry and fatigue.

'Let's get you cleaned up,' Catherine said. 'And if you can manage to stand, a hot shower would do you the world of good. You reckon you can?'

Lisa mumbled several words and nodded. 'Need to tell you something. Something important.'

'It'll wait ten minutes, won't it?' Catherine led Lisa along the hall to the little shower room tucked in beneath the stairs. 'I'll get you some spare clothes and make a hot drink while you clean yourself up. Then we'll talk.'

Catherine went upstairs and found a pair of tracksuit bottoms, a T-shirt, and a big baggy jumper. She doubted the clothes were what Lisa was used to wearing, but they'd do for now. In the kitchen she made a pot of coffee and opened a packet of biscuits. By the time she'd gathered together cups and milk and sugar and taken the whole lot to the living room, Lisa was sitting on the sofa, legs curled beneath her, just a glimpse of her pink toenails sticking out from the folds of the baggy jumper.

'Dan's up in London,' Catherine said. 'But I expect you realised he's away.'

'London.' Lisa extended her left hand and touched her ring finger with the thumb of the other hand. She rubbed a plain gold band as if it itched. 'Yes.'

Lisa sipped her coffee and Catherine let the silence build. She glanced at the clock on the mantelpiece. Nearly one in the morning. Jesus.

'You didn't say on the phone what this was about. Is it Toby? Are you going through a bad time?'

'I wish it was that simple.'

Catherine waited again. Silence. 'Go on.'

'It's... well...' Tears began to flow down Lisa's face and she started to shake. Catherine shifted to the sofa and took the cup of coffee away and placed it on the table. She put an arm round Lisa and gave her a hug.

'Don't worry. Whatever the problem is we can work it out. I'm sure we can.'

Lisa leaned against Catherine. She tried to speak but her words came out as sobs. Then a yawn, eyelids fluttering closed. She was almost unconscious.

'Come on, let's get you upstairs to bed. The world will seem better tomorrow. It always does.'

Little by little she coaxed Lisa to stand and led her upstairs to the spare bedroom. The bed was made up and she just had to turn back the duvet and help Lisa climb in. Never mind getting her undressed, she could sleep with her clothes on.

As soon as Lisa's head hit the pillow she was gone. Like a baby, Catherine thought. Inconsolable one second and dreaming peacefully the next. She pulled the duvet up and went to the doorway. She switched the light off and went back downstairs. She sent her husband a text message asking him to call, and then cleared up Lisa's wet clothes and put them in the washing machine.

A little later she was in her own bed, but sleep didn't come as easily to her as it had to Lisa. She lay and listened to the wind as it howled outside. She thought about Lisa's wild eyes and how she'd got angry about moving the car. She wondered why Daniel hadn't got back to her. She shivered and wrapped the duvet around herself, now scared to fall asleep, dreading what the next day might bring.

Chapter Three

When she got up in the morning, Catherine poked her head into the spare room. Lisa was out for the count. She made herself breakfast and then took a shower. By the time she'd finished, Lisa had risen, and Catherine found her standing at the sink in the kitchen, nursing a glass of water.

'Couldn't find your bottled stuff,' she said, holding up the glass. 'Had to use the tap.'

'The tap's all there is these days,' Catherine said. 'You want some breakfast? Then we can talk.'

'Yeah, sure.' Lisa clunked the glass down on the drainer and put a hand out to steady herself. 'Some food would be good. I haven't eaten a meal since breakfast yesterday.'

'Do you want to call Toby?' Catherine gestured at the phone stuck on the wall by the door. 'You can use the landline. Sometimes mobile reception's not great in the house, but you could go outside and sit in your car.'

'No thanks.'

'Won't he be worried?'

'I've switched my phone off and I'd prefer to leave it that way.'

'If you're out of battery, you can charge it here.' Catherine indicated an electrical socket with phone charging points. 'I'll get you a lead.'

'I'm not out of fucking battery,' Lisa said, pushing herself away from the sink. Her voice dropped to a whisper. 'Don't you get it? Don't you understand what's going on?'

'Sorry, Lisa, I don't.' Catherine shook her head. 'Look, I rescued you last night. Brought you back here and gave you a bed. I've been, to be honest, a saint, yet all you can do is be rude and ungrateful. We're friends because Toby is a mate of Daniel's, but I'll always try to help somebody in need. However, you're acting as if you're the only one with problems.'

'What the—?'

'No, let me continue. You breeze up here expecting me to be a shoulder to cry on even though we barely know each other. When I rescued you from the lane you shouted at me and now you're doing it again.'

'I'm sorry.' Lisa looked across the room at Catherine, holding her gaze, a hint of contrition in her eyes. 'I told you, I'm stressed. I shouldn't have snapped, but I genuinely didn't have a choice about coming here.'

'There's always a choice. It's making the right one that's sometimes difficult.'

'I couldn't remain in London, I simply couldn't. It was too dangerous.'

'*Dangerous*? Please tell me you're being melodramatic?'

'I'm not.' Lisa lowered her gaze.

'Why don't you go to the police? Surely they could help.'

'They can't, I'm afraid. They really can't.'

'OK.' Catherine glanced at the window where snow brushed the glass and frosted at the sill. Several inches had fallen overnight, and white specks continued to tumble from the sky. She turned back to Lisa. 'Let me make a pot of coffee and some toast. After that we'll talk, right?'

'It would be better if I showed you what this is all about first.'

'Sure. Go ahead.'

'It's in the car.'

'In the car?' Catherine began to protest, but then figured it was easier to go along with whatever Lisa wanted. 'Right, let's go then.'

In the hallway, Catherine found a spare pair of wellington boots for Lisa and gave her one of Daniel's coats. She opened the door and snow swirled in, the door almost snatched from her hand by the wind. Lisa's car stood sheathed in a layer of white. In the daylight the vehicle looked in a right state. A scrape ran along one wing and mud hung frozen on the wheel arches. They walked across and Lisa blipped the locks and went to the rear.

'I don't want you to panic, Catherine,' Lisa said. 'But this is the reason I came.'

Lisa lifted the Audi's rear hatch. A slab of snow slid off and Catherine moved closer. Inside the back of the car, a sheet of translucent plastic had been wrapped round a bulky roll of carpet. The roll of carpet was about six feet long and half curled so it could fit in the confines of the boot. Silver gaffer tape crisscrossed in all directions, parcelling the object and sealing the plastic at each end. Catherine had trouble comprehending.

'What's in there?' she said, shivering as a gust of wind caught the side of her neck. She peered over the lip of the boot, catching a whiff of decay, and tasting iron in her mouth as if she'd bitten her tongue. 'Oh my—'

'Yes,' Lisa said flatly as she slammed the hatch down. 'It's a body.'

'Oh fuck!' Catherine sprang back from the car. She gagged and put her hand to her mouth as she bent double. 'Fuck, fuck, fuck.'

The boot clicked shut and Catherine crouched down, one hand resting on the snowy ground for support. This was a nightmare. She needed to go inside and call Daniel. Get him to cancel whatever he was doing and drive home.

'You understand now why I had to come,' Lisa said. 'I'm in trouble and you're the only person I can turn to. We need to get rid of the body and bury it somewhere it will never be found.' Lisa glanced at the surrounding moorland and gesticulated into the distance. 'It's why I came here. I knew you'd be able to find a solution. I knew you'd help a friend in need.'

'No, I can't!' Catherine felt bile rising at the back of her throat. She swallowed and pushed herself up. She staggered towards the house, hands held up in front of her face as if hiding the scene from view might banish it altogether. 'Leave me alone! Get out of here!'

'I'm not going anywhere.' Lisa stood by the car, her eyes wild but her voice low and determined. 'And unless you help me, neither is the body.'

Catherine stumbled into the porch and went inside the house. She slammed the front door and shot the bolts top and bottom. She ran upstairs and locked herself in the bathroom. She lowered the lid on the toilet and sat with her head between her knees. Nausea washed from the pit of her stomach and she swallowed back saliva and fought the urge to vomit. Even wrapped in carpet and plastic, she'd been able to smell the iron tang of blood rising from the body. She sat motionless for a minute and then stood and went to the basin. She splashed cold water on her face and washed her hands. As she reached for a towel she realised she was shaking. She dropped the towel, sank to the floor, and sat against the side of the bath with her head in her hands.

She wished she hadn't answered the phone when Lisa had called. Wished she'd never got together with Daniel. Wished they hadn't left London. Wished a thousand and one other things hadn't happened along the way.

PART TWO

The Move

Three months earlier...

Chapter Four

Snow. We don't get so much of it these days. Not with this global warming malarkey. Some people might call that a shame but to me, with all my sheep and cattle to worry about, the lack of snow is a blessing. Of course, there are those who say we're due another hard winter and I kinda think they're right. Even so, I doubt it will be as bad as the one in '82. Hell, that was a winter to remember. Cold like I'd never experienced before and the snow lying solid on the ground for several months.

We ran low on coal and wood and Pa said we had to tear down one of our barns and cut up the oak beams to provide fuel for the fire. Without that barn we'd have frozen to death because there was no way out, see? The drifts were so high that many villages on the moor were cut off for weeks. Food wasn't a problem though. We had hay and grain to feed the sheep and once a week we slaughtered one of the older ewes to feed ourselves. We had several tons of swedes in a huge clamp out the back, so mutton and swede pie became our staple. Milk from the cows. Jams and pickles that Ma had put away in the autumn. Bread baked daily. We were well nourished, and with the oak logs on the range, we were cosy too. But we were bored. Once the day's work was done, I'd retreat to the parlour and sit by the fire. I'd whittle a stick or play my fiddle, but mostly I sat and stared out at the snow.

It was magical the way it transformed the moor from a dreary green and brown to a sparkling white. The blanket covered the landscape from the summit of the tors down to the valley bottoms, smoothing harsh edges and deadening loud sounds. It was as if God had poured a cup of bleach over the moor in an attempt to remove the stains. For a while it worked, but bit by bit we made inroads. Round the farm the snow turned to slushy mud as we tramped this way and that. The tractor forged a little farther up the track to the lane each day. Eventually, the big yellow snow plough made it up the valley and there was a snake of black tarmac leading all the way down to the village.

Then the weather changed and the snow thawed. Spring arrived and in a few weeks the hardship we'd endured was just a memory.

Still, these days every time I see a snowflake the events of that winter come back to haunt me. Not the snow and the cold, but what happened at the place down the valley. At World's End Farm. I try to put the memories from my mind, and in the daytime that's easy. There's things to do and plenty to occupy my thoughts. But at night it's another matter. Especially in the long dark nights of winter. Sometimes I lie awake in bed for hours. I tell myself I should have done thinking about the place years ago. The house, I mean. Stones and lime mortar. Dark slates on the roof. Casements of rotten oak and cracked glass. That's all it ever was to me. A load of building materials in a plot of marsh and poor pasture. Honestly. That's all it was.

Then again, I never was much good at lying.

Chapter Five

Catherine slipped across the bare boards in the living room. She stood in the centre. Looked at the plaster cornicing. The stripped-pine floorboards. The fireplace with the original Victorian tiling. She tapped her right foot and the sole of her shoe clicked on the wood, the room empty of furniture and now no more than an echo chamber. Sounds and memories. A house warming party. Glasses chinking. Laughter. Sleepy weekend evenings curled up on the sofa with Daniel, the lights dimmed, the TV on low. Sunday mornings in bed and the rustle of newspapers shoved aside as they fucked. The smell of fresh toast. Late night curry. The crackle of the fire in the winter, the rain drumming on the windows, the wind rattling the sashes. The thud of a heavy object splitting a man's skull.

She shivered and drove the last thought down into her subconscious. She concentrated on the room again and tried not to look upon the absence of all their possessions as some kind of void. She focused on where they'd soon be arriving, not the place they were leaving, but she couldn't help hearing the raised voices. Their arguments had permeated the fabric of the house the way cigarette smoke stains a ceiling. The prelude to a cancer.

You lying bastard. All this time you've been cheating on me.

Cathy, you're being unreasonable, you're—

Unreasonable? Don't make me laugh. You're the one who's the fraud in this relationship. Sliding into that slut at every opportunity. I swear, I'd kill her if I got the chance.

Catherine. You're angry. I get it and I'm sorry. I love you so much and I couldn't bear to lose you. Please let's talk this through. Find out where we went wrong and try to fix things.

Where we *went wrong? Are you fucking—*

A vehicle drove past in the street outside and Catherine strode to the window. She looked out. Daniel stood by their BMW. Thick black hair. Tall but not thin and lanky. Well proportioned, fit and with the stamina to match. Despite what had gone before, she caught herself smiling. He was her extra square of chocolate bar. The oh-so-sweet cocktail drunk at the end of the night. The line of cocaine sniffed with a giggle and a smile at the knowledge of the rush to come. The feeling wasn't one she admitted to her girlfriends. Their husbands had jobs in the city. Talked about rugby and cricket and cars and the next ski trip. Played squash one evening a week. Poker with the lads on another. Thought they were God's gift, even though you could see the disappointment in their wives' eyes every time the husbands cracked a dirty joke.

Her friends had never understood the frisson and the mixture of good and bad she found so intoxicating about Daniel. To them, he wasn't the type of man you could settle down with. Still, until recently, settling down wasn't what she'd wanted either. They'd talked about children, but he'd said they should wait. Kids were a tie and they took over your life. You existed in their circles, rather than the other way round. The emotional intensity of their relationship would be broken, the focus shifted. He wasn't sure if he was ready for that, even if she was.

She hoped he'd change his mind once they'd moved. He was staring down the line of parked cars almost as if he didn't care they were leaving or didn't want to be reminded of what had happened. That was good, wasn't it? A sign he'd left the past behind, something she'd yet to do. She touched the window frame, thought about knocking on the glass. Would he turn, or would he continue to avert his gaze?

She was the one who'd insisted on coming back inside for a final look. Ostensibly it had been to check for bits and pieces they'd forgotten, but they both understood the real reason was because she wanted one last chance to be in the house where their relationship had taken form. To reflect on the highs and lows. Even though those lows had been painful, she felt an almost unbearable agony in leaving. Once she stepped outside and pulled the front door to, she'd never be able to return. Soon, another couple would live in the house. The essence of their relationship would be wiped the instant the new owners put the key in the lock and burst into the hallway, laughing at their good fortune at getting the property cheap, planning the way they would transform the empty shell into a home.

She wished there was some way to bottle what they'd had. She'd thought about asking Daniel to lift a tile from the fireplace or prise a piece of wood from the living room floor, so they had a tangible item to take with them, but he was too rational for that. The house was bricks and mortar. Wood and plaster. Sentiment played no part. Besides, why remember, why look back?

In truth there was no reason to because a man had died in their house and Daniel had killed him.

Hours later they were heading west on the motorway, meeting heavy rain and appalling road conditions somewhere past Swindon. A stream of cars blurred the opposite carriageway, their headlights reflecting on the slick road. Concentration lay etched on Daniel's face as he tried to follow the removal van at a safe distance. He swore every now and then when a vehicle pulled into the gap in front.

'Bloody idiot!' He thumped on the horn. 'Cut me up why don't you?'

'There's no need to worry about keeping so close,' Catherine said. 'The removal guys know where we're going and so do we.'

'Are you sure?' Daniel swung his head and fixed Catherine with a stare, before looking forward again and flicking the windscreen wipers to double speed as if there was a simple mechanical solution to all their problems.

There was more to his question than the three words suggested. A lot more. But she didn't want to be drawn into an argument, so she closed her eyes. She tried to imagine the new house filled with all their possessions. Building a nest from scratch again. A place to rekindle their love. The wipers worked a rhythm and she imagined a ticking clock. Time passing and wounds healing. Daniel was understandably tense. They both were. Bereavement, divorce, and moving house were supposedly the three most stressful events in life. They'd almost split up and now they were moving. Two out of three. Three out of three if you counted the death of the man Daniel had killed as a bereavement, which in a way it was.

She dozed on and off until a bump of the car jerked her wide awake. She peered into the afternoon gloom. A brown mass of moorland rose ahead, the motorway long gone, replaced by a narrow lane cutting up the side of a hill. The removal van crawled beneath the branch of a wizened hawthorn, then lurched off to the right between a pair of stone pillars and headed along a rough track, wheels spinning on the uneven ground, the vehicle swaying with a violent motion. Catherine crossed her fingers that the crew had packed their possessions securely and reached across and grasped her husband's arm.

'Love you,' she whispered.

Daniel gripped the steering wheel and leaned forwards. Catherine followed his gaze. The track shouldered a rise and the valley spread out before them, several fields of rough grass, the house beyond. A chunk of granite rested on a grass bank to the left of the track and three words had been chiselled into the stone: *World's End Farm*. World's End, Catherine had discovered, wasn't quite as an apocalyptic name as it appeared at first sight. *World* had been derived from *wold* which was old English for forest, although sometimes the word was also used for an elevated area of open ground or moorland. World's End was, literally, the place at the edge of the moor.

As they drove closer, she could see the house in more detail. A black slate roof hung over a stone cottage. A chimney stack stood at each end of the roof apex, uneven chunks of rock layered in teetering stacks reaching for the grey sky. At the top of one chimney stack, the mortar hugged a red chimney pot, at the other a cowl of two slates resembled hands steepled in prayer. The upstairs windows were overhung by deep eaves. To the right two small openings, and to the left a larger one. At ground level a window sat to each side of a door adorned with a simple porch of slabs.

The lopsided arrangement of the upstairs windows gave the house a contorted look like a face disfigured, as if one eye had a permanent squint. Inside, there were three bedrooms, a boxroom and a bathroom upstairs, and a large reception, a dining room, a decent-sized kitchen, and an old scullery downstairs.

The building sat plum in the middle of a paddock ringed with a rough wall of granite boulders. To one side stood a new garage constructed from stone salvaged from a tumbled-down stable, to the other a second barn, half of which had been converted into a workspace for her, half left open. At the back a cottage garden was bordered with earth banks. A stream ran past one of the gable ends of the house and dropped away to a modest pond the size of a couple of tennis courts. There'd been ducks when they'd last visited. A trio of wading birds in the shallows. Dragonflies skimming across the surface. Now there was a bed of decaying rushes standing in brown water.

The removal van manoeuvred round in front of the house. Daniel parked up and they got out.

'We're here,' he said. 'Looks different somehow.'

Daniel was right. When they'd come down in early September, she'd felt excited as she'd wandered through the house and explored the land. The stone walls at the front of the house had warmed in the sunshine and the grounds had been bathed in light. Now the grey façade of the building stood cold and damp.

Catherine shivered. The sky was filled with bulbous clouds that scudded in from the west and rushed across the valley, pulling curtains of water behind them. All of a sudden she had second thoughts. The light was fading and within a few hours the removal men would be gone. She'd be left alone with Daniel in the middle of nowhere. The closest village was three miles distant, the nearest town, seven. The cities of Plymouth and Exeter were more than an hour's drive away. Even their neighbours were... she realised she wasn't quite sure. There was a farm a mile or so up the lane, but when they'd called round on their last visit there'd been no one there. Only a barking dog keen to chase them back to their car.

'Best get moving,' Catherine said, trying to break her unease with some action. 'I'll open up.'

Within minutes the minutiae of their lives were being unloaded from the van as the removal men carried dozens of cardboard boxes into the house. Daniel had meticulously labelled each box with a colour-coded system, but the men either didn't understand, ignored the system, or were colour blind. The result was a rainbow of labels in every room.

They had a tea break, and then the furniture came in. Beds, the sofa and armchairs, coffee table, kitchen table, white goods. After another hour, Catherine stared up into the empty van as the foreman tidied away some strapping and dumped it in one corner.

'All done, love,' he said as he came down the ramp. 'And nothing broken 'cept Ned's little toe.'

'It's not?' Catherine felt herself blush, as if she was the one who should feel guilty because their big oak wardrobe had crashed down on the young man's foot.

'No. His pride's bruised, but if he can survive the ribbing on the way home then he'll live.'

'Thank goodness.' Catherine looked at the cavern which had teleported their life from South West London to Devon. She struggled to find a new topic of conversation which might forestall the removal men's departure. 'You'll have another cup of tea before you go?'

'No, thanks.' The man waved out across the nearby fields. The air had cooled and the rain had grown fat and mushy. 'It's sleeting now. I wouldn't like to be driving down from the moor if this turns to snow. We'll be off. If the traffic's not too bad, we'll be back in London in time for a jar.'

'This should buy a round or three.' Daniel stood at the foot of the ramp, an envelope in his hand. 'Perhaps some salve for the lad's toe.'

'I reckon he'll prefer medicine of the liquid kind.' The foreman and one of his colleagues lifted the ramp and secured the doors.

'Well, thanks again.' Catherine and Daniel shook his hand and nodded to the other three men. 'Safe journey.'

'Aye.' The foreman tramped across to the cab. His mates got in, but he stood with his hand on the door. He gazed at the sky and then down at the mud. Catherine almost expected him to shake his head, but he looked up and smiled. 'Oh, and good luck, hey?'

With that, he hauled himself up into the cab and slammed the door. The van drew round and wobbled away up the track, the red taillights soon fading, their warm glow suffocated by the now heavy sleet.

'Good job.' Daniel said. He walked over to the house, his feet leaving prints in the thin layer of slush.

Catherine stood there trying to follow the lights of the van, waiting for the instant when the vehicle turned from the track and onto the road. She thought about running after the removal men. Shouting and screaming that it had all been a big mistake and could they please, *please*, take them back to London.

In the darkness she saw the indicators blink yellow and then came a beep-beep from the van's horn. Not au revoir, but goodbye. Moments later, white light cut across the lane and abruptly vanished. She turned from the black night and went over to Daniel. He stood in the doorway, framed in a golden glow. He smiled as she approached. Then he took her hand and led her into their new home.

Chapter Six

Joe Foster sat behind a stone wall not thirty paces from where the removal van had stood. A thick sleet tumbled from the sky. He was wearing his old parlour suit, but the rubber had grown brittle and every time he changed his position, the suit creaked and crackled. The best you could say about the suit was it was still in one piece. That and the colour. White. Snow white. In the sleet the suit made him near invisible. By rights he needed a new one, but since he'd got rid of his milking cows he didn't have much use for it, and it was keeping him dry enough for now.

He'd brought along a Thermos and a sandwich, but the food had long gone, and the flask held the dregs of a sugary tea. He'd been at the wall from about half an hour after the removal van arrived, but the thrill of watching had subsided as the rain had grown heavier and become sleet. He hadn't expected to be here for so long, but the men had gone from the van to the house, again, and again, and again. Foster had lost count after an hour. How in the blazes could the couple have so much stuff? And the books. Crates of them. A bloody library. Back home, Foster had a Bible which had belonged to his mother, a dictionary, and a single shelf of paperbacks, most of which he'd picked up in the local charity shop. Frederick Forsyth, Alistair MacLean, Hammond Innes, Jeffrey Archer. He was pretty sure the authors were all dead now, the yellowing pages of their fiction serving as their sole legacy.

As the sleet began to turn to snow in the half-light, the men got in the van and drove off while the couple stood and watched. Then they went inside the house and the door clunked shut. Lights shone from every window and now and then a figure came to peer into the darkness, as if they were wondering if there was anyone out there, if anyone was watching. Foster muttered to himself. Another set of fools. They wouldn't stay long, he'd see to that.

He rose from the ground, groaning as his bones creaked in sympathy with the parlour suit. He was too old for this kind of silliness, but when he'd seen the van coming along the lane he'd known he had to go down and take a look.

'Just a gander, Jess,' he'd said to his dog, adding in no uncertain terms that she was to stay put. She'd cocked her head on one side, scepticism in her eyes. The bitch was wise to his ways, wiser than his missus had ever been. 'I want to see what they're up to, right?'

Foster was well used to speaking to himself since he lived on his own, his wife having died a good few years back. One night she'd gone to sleep and the next day she hadn't woken up. They'd had separate bedrooms, so the first he'd known of it was when he'd plodded up the stairs with her breakfast on a tray and found her lying in the bed with her mouth hanging open and not much to say. The doctor said she'd had a brain aneurysm, but Foster was pretty sure she'd died out of pure bloody spite.

He had to admit though, he'd grown tired of caring for her, tired of running her errands, of going up and down the stairs every time she called out. Tea. Coffee. The newspaper. Could he turn the television over to a different channel? What the fuck was wrong with using the remote control? he wanted to say, but he kept quiet. She'd had it bad for months, lying there wasting away in front of his eyes. Father Carmichael had said the end was a blessing, but Foster wasn't sure there was much to be said for dying whatever which way it happened.

He'd loved her once, he supposed. Not the dry, wrinkled corpse with spittle on its pale lips he'd found one spring morning. Rather his wife as the woman he'd wooed and married. Plump and round with hips which could bear him a string of healthy sons. She had a good pair of breasts too. Only nobody had ever suckled on those breasts but him. Their union had been childless, his wife as barren as an old ewe. They'd married late, that was the problem, the doctors had said. Foster knew they were right. He'd been single until a couple of years shy of forty, the marriage as much about convenience as love, but he'd hoped for children, so he'd have somebody to leave the farm to.

He wondered about the woman in the house and whether she'd be having kids. 'Catherine,' he'd heard the man call her. She was in her thirties. Dark hair the colour of black treacle, skin like vanilla ice cream. Sweet as any woman he'd set eyes on since... no, he thought as he emerged from behind the wall, she wasn't like *her* at all. Nobody ever could be.

He traipsed across the yard, his feet squelching in the slush. He went round the house and stood at a window. With the lights on inside, they'd not be able to see him and if they did, so what? He was just a neighbour coming to wish them well.

Joe Foster hadn't wished anyone well, not for a very long time, but they weren't to know that.

He peered into what had once been the old parlour. The builders had hacked the place about and now it had been transformed into a sterile kitchen. A myriad of lights shone down on an expanse of polished granite and there were more cupboards than you could ever need. Cosy was a word long forgotten by the younger generation, Foster thought. As for the worktops, well, granite was best left out on the moor or reserved for marking your span when you were six feet under.

At that moment, the woman came into the room with the man close behind. The man stood near the window. His eyes were the strangest shade of blue, the same colour as the eyes of a merle dog Foster had owned decades ago. The dog had gone bad and savaged three ewes before Foster had reluctantly placed the barrel of a shotgun to its head and put the animal out of its misery. As the couple embraced, he walked away. He'd seen nothing to make him change his mind about the new owners. They didn't belong here and the sooner they realised that, the better.

He trudged back home in the dark. He could barely see to place his feet, but he let himself be guided by the crooked oak at the top of the hill. The distinctive lopsided shape stood like a beacon showing the way to his farm. When he arrived at the gate to the yard, the dog ran over to greet him. The bitch's eyes sparkled with a brightness, as if she'd sprung a hare from a hidden lie. She knew what he'd been up to, he thought. He patted the dog and she scampered over to the back door and waited to be let in.

After he'd peeled off the parlour suit, he fed the dog and shooed her outside. Then he fixed himself dinner. Three bangers, two eggs and some bread. The whole lot fried in a pan on the stove. He ate his food. Drank a mug of tea. Minutes passing. The grandfather clock in the hall ticking. His life was marked by the ticking of that bloody clock and every day he followed the same routine, save for Thursdays, when he drove to the nearest town to do some shopping. He went to the pub and had a pint of Guinness followed by a glass of single malt. A packet of plain crisps. He drove home again having spoken a handful of words to the man who took his money in the shop and the pretty barmaid who served him at the pub.

He took another sip of his tea. 'You daft idiot,' he said, wallowing in a dose of self-pity.

He finished the tea, scowled at the tannin stains in the mug, and dumped it in the sink. Outside, the bitch rushed into the yard, skittering to a stop in front of the kitchen window. She yapped up at Foster, urging him outside.

Sheep to check before you go to bed, she was saying. Hay racks to fill, feed to prepare for the morning. Plenty to do and not much of the day left to do it in.

'Alright, alright,' Foster said and tapped on the glass. He went to the back door and took his big waxed coat from a hook. Opened up and lumbered into the yard. Said what he'd said every time he left the house for as long as he could remember. 'Farming. Bloody farming.'

Chapter Seven

The first day in their new house dawned with an eerie calm. There was the click of a radiator as a thermostat opened. A creak from the bed as Daniel turned over. A drip from a leaking tap in the ensuite. Other than that, silence. No traffic noise, no aircraft overhead, no hustle, no bustle.

Catherine stared up at the ceiling. White plaster and dark brown beams of oak, the ceiling canted here and there, the plaster rough and ready. Their place in London had been period — Victorian — but World's End was entirely different. The neat lines and fancy decorative features were gone, replaced by uneven walls and floors which sloped. Since they'd bought the house, they'd had builders in to renovate, but the idiosyncrasies remained: the staircase which narrowed near the top, a doorframe in their bedroom misshapen, a mullion in the living room window well off-centre, a tiny alcove in the kitchen which served no apparent purpose.

She stole from the bed and moved to the window. She tweaked the curtain aside. Dark fields rose to the surrounding moorland, and above the horizon the sky was the colour of wet slate. The snow from the night before had gone, washed away by an overnight rain, but the day looked wintry. Hardly an auspicious start to their new life. She sighed. In a while she'd prepare breakfast, but first she wanted to go outside and check her workshop.

She dressed and went downstairs where she put on a warm coat and a pair of wellies. She caught sight of herself in the hallway mirror and laughed. If her friends could see her now, she thought. Fashionable her new look wasn't, but that was the point, wasn't it? To leave behind the shallow lives they'd once led and find a deeper and more meaningful existence. To leave behind...

She cursed. She'd promised herself she wouldn't keep thinking about what had happened. Not just the violence and death, but the other things too.

As she stepped outside into the wind, she couldn't help wondering what those friends of hers would be saying if they realised quite how isolated the house was. Catherine turned her head from left to right. Not a dwelling, a car, or another person to be seen in any direction. She pictured her friends sitting and drinking lattes in some trendy café.

I couldn't be with him. Not all alone down there. Just the thought gives me the shakes.

In truth, the fact her husband had killed someone didn't disturb her. More worrying was the way he'd acquired a notoriety that would be with him for the rest of his days. It was an infamy impossible to shake off. Daniel was a composer, and he dearly wished to be recognised for his film and television scores, but it wasn't to be. Once, Catherine had browsed his Wikipedia entry, shocked to have to read through several paragraphs before she came to the bit where Danny Boyle and Wes Anderson were mentioned as directors he'd worked with. She edited the article, switching the order round, but a day later she found her edits undone, the lurid material back in pride of place at the top of the page.

Wherever they went, people stopped and gawped. In restaurants, wives nudged their husbands; in the park, mothers gathered their children; at dinner parties, there was a noticeable hush as they entered. She sometimes wondered if it would be better to cut to the chase and make a formal announcement whenever they arrived somewhere: 'Hi, this is my husband, Daniel. He bludgeoned a man to death. He acted as judge, jury and executioner. The victim had no chance to plead his innocence or mitigating circumstances, no chance to say goodbye to their loved ones. Daniel hit the man over and over and over until he was dead. Still, he's great with animals and children.'

She imagined, if her life were a movie, the director (Wes, not Danny) cutting from a shot of Daniel looking menacing, to a symmetrical frame of pink watermelon arranged on a dish. An elderly woman would faint, there'd be a fade to black, and the inevitable scream in the darkness.

Of course, she never had to introduce Daniel because his face was instantly recognisable from the TV or the newspapers. The dark hair, pale skin, the deep blue eyes. If he'd been more extrovert, she was sure he'd have been a rock star rather than a composer — he certainly had the looks — but he always felt safer behind a mixing desk or a computer screen.

His appearance had helped though, because the press didn't have to pause to think about whose side they were on when someone as handsome as Daniel was in trouble. This wasn't a swarthy immigrant or a bearded religious fanatic or a mindless skinhead yob, God no! Daniel was an Englishman defending his castle, and the newspaper headlines expressed the moral indignation of the masses that the police had even dared to lay a hand on him. As the Mayor of London, the local MP and some minor celebrities from the music and movie industries, took Daniel's side, the pressure built, and the case against him was dropped. No charges, no blame, free to go. Just that stain, a dark memory stuck in almost everybody's mind; a one-word label henceforth to be whispered whenever his name was mentioned.

Killer.

She'd been away for the weekend when it happened, visiting an artists' retreat in the Lake District where she was providing encouragement and tuition for half-a-dozen wannabe sculptors who hadn't progressed much beyond the Play-Doh stage. Daniel was at home in their terraced house in Richmond. In the early hours he awoke to sounds from downstairs. He went to investigate and discovered an intruder in the living room. A struggle ensued, and Daniel ended up clouting the burglar over the head with one of Catherine's abstract pieces. Luckily, the man had been armed with a knife, so there hadn't been any real doubt that Daniel had feared for his life. There was though some concern excessive violence had been used, but Daniel's brief argued that when disturbed by an intruder nobody should be expected to have to calculate how much force to use to protect themselves. Hitting a burglar several times was entirely justified in the circumstances. In the end, thank goodness, media pressure and legalistic logic won out, and the Crown Prosecution Service decided not to proceed with the case.

Catherine looked again at the moor and the empty sweep of hills and ridges and tors. Daniel wasn't a murderer and she couldn't possibly have lived here alone with him if he had been. It would be too easy to imagine his temper turning to violence, his hands clutching at her neck. Too easy to worry about waking in the night to a shadow looming over her, a heavy piece of marble in his hands as he poised to strike. The chunk of smooth rock rising and falling again and again and again.

She shook herself free of the image and strolled across to the barn. Half of the open-fronted building had been converted to a workshop for her. Daniel would work inside the house in a spare room earmarked as a mini recording studio. She hoped he'd be able to return to the creative peak he'd reached before the incident, but she realised it might take time. Sure, he'd had a year and a half already, but the whole affair had shaken him. Not the fact he'd taken a life — he seemed to get over that within a matter of days — it was what went with the act. The arrest and the time he'd spent in custody. The long wait to see if the CPS would go ahead with the case, and the parallel thought of years in prison were he to be convicted. The massive media intrusion. Reporters shouting through their letterbox at all hours. Photographers snapping his picture in the most inappropriate places.

Daniel had confessed to her that he was in danger of cracking up. Catherine had suggested he see a therapist, and for a while his weekly visits seemed to help. After some months though, he seemed no better, in fact he was worse. The therapy appeared to have split open his cool outer mantle and he started to explode at her without warning. He acted like a child with a behaviour problem. He even broke a piece of sculpture she'd been working on.

Then, quite unexpectedly, Daniel returned from one of his regular consultations a changed man. He apologised for the way he'd been behaving and for all the crap he'd come out with. He wanted to start over and leave the past behind. Catherine was touched. They kissed and hugged and went out for dinner. That night they made love and Catherine felt a tingle on her skin at the raw passion. For a while their relationship seemed to return to the days when they'd first met. Perhaps the therapeutic process was akin to climbing a mountain: a long slog uphill until, after an extreme effort, you got to the top. Had that happened to Daniel? Was he taking the final steps to the summit?

It appeared so until, sometime later, she learned the only conquest Daniel had made on the day he'd apologised to her was of a young intern who worked for his agent.

Catherine unlocked the door to the workshop and went inside. The floor was bare concrete and above her head massive oak beams floated across the space. The paint was fresh on the walls and a workbench awaited assembly. All her tools were in a set of boxes along one wall and several commissions she'd been working on sat in wooden transport crates in the centre of the room.

A new start, she thought. Eighteen months had passed since the death of the burglar, nearly a year since she'd discovered Daniel's infidelity. Now was the time to move on from the past. Time to give life another go. Time to forgive and, if at all possible, time to forget.

Back inside she laid the kitchen table for breakfast and set about cooking a fry up. The smell of the bacon must have woken Daniel, because a few minutes later she heard him shuffling down the stairs. He came into the kitchen topless with a towel wrapped round his waist.

'Our new life.' Daniel grinned. 'A fried breakfast every morning. I like it!'

'Not every morning, stupid,' Catherine said. 'Just today. We've a lot to do and we'll need the energy.'

'I know what I'd like to do, and I've certainly got the energy.' Daniel darted across to where Catherine stood and grabbed her from behind. He kissed her on the back of her neck. 'The food will wait, won't it?'

'No, it won't.' Catherine wriggled free and waved a wooden slice at Daniel. 'Now, if you don't behave I'll whack you with this.'

'Sounds promising, but—' Daniel paused midsentence. He cocked his head towards the hallway where a knocking echoed off the bare walls. 'What was that?'

The sound came again. Rap, rap, rap on the front door.

'Our first visitor, I guess,' Catherine said. She glanced down at Daniel's bare chest. 'You're not decent, so I'd better go.'

Catherine handed Daniel the slice, pointed at the frying pan, and went into the hallway. She clicked the latch and opened the door.

'Hello?' she said. A battered Land Rover stood parked at the gateway and the gate itself was ajar, but there was nobody on the doorstep. 'Anyone there?'

Then she spotted him. A lumbering figure over near the barn. He wore a tatty waxed coat bound round with orange string at the waist. The hem of the coat almost touched the top of his green wellington boots, and a black and white Border Collie scampered about at the man's heels. He appeared to be more interested in the barn than Catherine, but after a few seconds he turned and came over.

'You must be the new 'uns,' he said. He gestured at Catherine's workshop. 'Nice job on the barn. Tidy.'

He spoke with a strong West Country accent and was seventy years old if he was a day. Deep lines ran across his face, the skin weathered by sun and wind, the surface like a walnut. A flat cap sat at an angle on his head, tufts of flowing grey hair moving in the wind.

'I...' Catherine was about to speak when she saw what he was carrying.

'Thought you might like these.' He nodded down at his left hand where two pheasants hung limp. One bird was a drab, tan colour, the feathers speckled with black. The second was a deep reddish brown, a beautiful iridescent sheen on the bird's throat glistening with rainbow colours. 'A nice brace. A bit of meat to keep you going until you can get to the shop.'

Catherine couldn't help but gawp at the birds. A wing was half blown off, blood and bone visible. An eye dangled on a length of sinew. She'd never seen anything so revolting in her whole life.

The man seemed to be aware she was uncomfortable. 'They'd been having a good week right up until I shot them. Nothing wrong with them that a spell in the oven won't cure.'

'How much do you want for them?' Catherine tried to remember where she'd put her purse. She could grab a couple of notes and pay the man off. Chuck the birds in the rubbish bin before she was sick.

'Want?' The man shook his head. 'Don't want no money for them, girl. They're a present.'

'A present?' She hadn't been called *girl* for ages. It was faintly comical.

'New house. Moving in. Don't you do that from where you come from? You know, the neighbour coming round with a cup of sugar?'

'Oh gosh! Sorry!' Catherine felt a wave of embarrassment. Despite her revulsion she realised she had to accept the birds with good grace. 'Thank you. Thank you so much.'

'Joe. Joe Foster. I live just round the corner. Head up the lane for a mile or so and take the next track signposted for *The Steddings*.' Foster nodded at the fields. 'Along the old drovers' way if you want to walk it.'

'Nice,' she said without thinking. Then she scolded herself. This wasn't like London where there were dozens of people close at hand. Even if he lived a mile away, Joe Foster was their nearest neighbour. 'I'm Catherine,' she said, smiling. 'Catherine Ross. Look, would you like to come in for a cup of tea?'

'No thanks. Got to get back to feed the sheep.' Foster stepped forwards and held up the pheasants. 'There you go.'

Catherine held out her hand, trying not to flinch as her fingers clasped the yellow bony legs of the birds. Foster let go and they almost fell from her hand. She had to catch them with the other hand and bring them close to her body as if she was cradling a new born baby.

'Keep them outside until you want to prepare them. A few days hanging in the shed will do them some good, but they'll be spoiling if they get too warm.'

Without another word, Foster turned and stomped off across the gravel. He gave a sharp whistle and his dog rose from behind a clump of rushes and bounded after him. He walked over to the gate and climbed into his Land Rover.

'Thank you, Joe! Thank you!' Catherine shouted, feeling elated, as if she'd passed an important test.

Foster started the Land Rover, and the dog barked and leapt up over the tailgate into the rear as the vehicle began to head up the track.

'Cath?' Daniel's voice came from behind her. He'd dressed. Jeans and a Fair Isle sweater. He looked down at the two dead birds. 'What the bloody heck are they?'

'I think,' Catherine said, making a face and trying to hold the birds as far away from her body as she could. 'They're supposed to be Sunday lunch.'

Chapter Eight

Years ago, I used to go there to look at the house. I'd scramble up to the tor which lies high to the north. That way the light was to the south and there was no chance of anybody spotting me silhouetted against the skyline. Not that there was anyone to see me. Not back then. Only the willow the wisps which flitted between the bog plants as dusk fell. When I was a kid, my ma told me the lights were in my imagination. My pa said it was just gas escaping from the marshland. I've got a different take on it now. The lights are fleeting spirits, ghosts, or just bad memories that no amount of time can heal.

Of course, I remember the place from when the Murrin family lived there. There was Mr John Murrin and his wife, the two lads, and the young kid. From the front the house looks much the same as it always did, although there's a new garage built from reclaimed stone and part of the barn has been converted too. Both are eyesores.

Beyond the garden, acres of land lie sunken in a deep valley bordered by dark granite tors. Clumps of bog grass sit beside pools of water and the drier areas are dotted with gorse bushes. The land is enclosed with a mixture of stock fence, scraggly thorn hedges, and some stone and turf banks. A track runs from the house to the bounds where two huge pillars of stone guard the threshold.

For me, those pillars mark something else too. A point in time as painful to me as any I've ever known. Like many tragedies this one started and ended with a woman, although she carried no blame for what happened, and I bear her no grudge. Sadly, I know the reverse isn't true. I'm both guilty and despised and therein lies the real tragedy.

Her name was Helena Hodgson and she lived at the bottom of the valley. There was our place, then World's End Farm where the Murrin family lived, then the Hodgson's smallholding. Helena was fair and lithe. Clever in the way she could turn a phrase. Wise from the books she'd read and full of the knowledge she'd gained from her parents. She was younger than me — just twenty when the Hodgsons relocated from London, whereas I'd turned thirty and was living at home with my parents and elder brother. Pa needed all the help he could get with the farm, and the house was plenty big enough for all of us. Many farming families lived the same way, but it might have seemed odd to an incomer, I guess. Still, Helena showed no sign of wanting to up and leave her own nest. She helped round the smallholding and had a part-time job in the town library.

In my heart I knew she was too clever and too beautiful for me, and her background was so different. The problem was the more I saw of her, the more I ached for her. Just to see her skipping across the fields in a summer dress made me catch my breath. Her smile cut me, her laugh made me dizzy, her words were like birdsong, her scent like blossom carried on a soft breeze. But she knew nothing of this. I was too shy and too inarticulate to say much to her and anyway, my words were those of a shambling country bumpkin.

Helena's father was an architect and as you can imagine that didn't wash with the locals. 'London types' they'd said when the Hodgsons arrived in the summer of 1977. 'Won't stick it for long.' By the January of '82 they'd managed four and a half years, but folks continued to predict disaster. 'Never known a foreigner last more than five years in this part of the world,' said my pa. 'See if I'm not right. This winter will be the end of them.'

He was correct, of course. In the spring following the bad winter the family returned to London. Mrs Hodgson and Helena's two sisters, Helena with them. Not her father though. He stayed. There's a stone in the churchyard with his name on. Two dates, the years *between a long way short of three score and ten. Died suddenly, it says. Taken by the angels.*

Not many folk round here believe that though. The thing about the angels. I certainly don't.

Chapter Nine

Foster always liked to start small. It was the best way. He didn't want to go scaring them too much at the beginning, he wanted subtlety. He wanted a story to develop. In a month or two they'd realise something was wrong. Then he'd hit them full force and after that, once they had discovered the truth about World's End, there was just one possible outcome.

The pheasants, of course, had been a ruse. Act a bit friendly and the couple wouldn't be suspicious of him when odd things started to happen. Couldn't be that nice Joe Foster, could it? No, not him. And if they asked him what was going on he'd shake his head and pretend there was some awful secret he couldn't share. Which was pretty much true.

In a way it was a shame. The woman seemed alright, nice, even. The husband was standoffish though. He'd barely acknowledged Foster when they'd passed in the lane three days ago. Like he was too clever to speak to a mere farmer. Foster had noted the man's eyes again, too. They were a strange colour and shifted every second. They reminded him of bluebottles flitting about in search of a rotting carcass. You could judge people by their eyes, he'd heard. They were windows to the soul apparently.

It was a month after the couple had arrived and he was back behind the wall sitting in the darkness. The place wasn't much of a farm any more, but it had fifteen acres and Foster didn't reckon they'd ventured out onto their land more than a handful of times. He could've sat against the rough stone for a week and they'd have been none the wiser. Still, he hadn't bothered with a flask this time, he didn't intend staying for long. He just had to wait until they'd gone to sleep.

At half ten, Foster snuck a peek round the wall for the umpteenth time. Strewth, he thought, London folk went to bed late. It was as if they had nothing better to do than sit and read all night. He liked a bit of a read himself, but fifteen minutes with Frederick Forsyth was enough. He'd slip in the bookmark and fluff his pillows up before reaching for the light switch. He was out like the light bulb, without a thought; the dreams always came later, not during the witching hour, but the one before dawn, the darkest hour. Often, they woke him, and he struggled to sleep again, his mind full of anguish and regret. He'd lie there and try to divert his thoughts to the present, but that brought more worry.

A light went on in an upstairs window. Likely the couple slept easy. No bad dreams for them. Not yet, at least.

Twenty minutes later and finally the house went dark. Foster waited a while longer before emerging from his hiding place. He slipped through the side gate and into the garden. The brook bubbled over a weir and the noise concealed the crunch of his feet on the gravel path. He edged round to the front door, thinking the one piece of advice he could give the couple — other than getting the hell back to London — would be to get a dog. They weren't animal people though. He'd seen that when the woman had taken the birds. The look in her eyes as she'd held them in her hands was one of revulsion, not gratitude.

Later the same day he'd sneaked back and watched as she'd buried the birds in the back garden. He hadn't known whether to laugh at the absurdity or rage at the waste. The trouble was people these days were separated from nature. Foster recalled a radio programme he'd heard about kids from the inner city. The children hadn't been able to match the meat on display in the supermarket with the animal it came from. They'd have been as repulsed as the woman had they known how the lamb chops they ate for dinner got from farm to plate.

Foster smiled to himself as he hefted down the rucksack he was carrying. Considering the way the woman had reacted to the pheasants, the little stunt he'd planned would go down a treat. He delved into the rucksack and pulled out a bin liner, wrinkling his nose as he undid the knot at the top. The stench was appalling. He tipped the contents onto the front step and prodded the mess with his foot, spreading it out for better effect. Nice, he thought, as he leaned back to admire his handiwork. Then he scrunched up the bin liner, put the rucksack on his back, and set off for home.

Chapter Ten

October became November and the autumn slipped into a period of unseasonably warm weather. Catherine and Daniel worked on the house, finishing off the bits the builders had neglected to do during the renovation. They painted from top to bottom and kitted out Daniel's studio. Next came her workshop. They constructed a workbench and installed new lighting. They bought an old 4x4 pickup and used it to roam across their land, ferrying dead wood down to the house and carting stone from an old sheep pen to the garden so they could create a rockery.

By now Daniel was head down and busting himself crazy to finish a movie score, so Catherine welcomed the chance to get some serious work done herself. By day a chip, chip, chip, could be heard from the studio and, if Daniel had the window to his room open, a wash of violins or the stab of a brass section from the house.

In their downtime they read, went out walking on the nearby moorland, and made love. Their moods ebbed and flowed but always meshed together like cogs inside an intricate time piece. Aside from Joe Foster, who they occasionally saw in the lane, they had no other near neighbours, and yet Catherine didn't feel lonely. It was as if she and Daniel had been transported back to an earlier period in their relationship, to a time when they'd only needed each other.

The first sign of trouble came one morning in the middle of November. Having finished breakfast and cleared away, Catherine headed for her workshop. As she opened the front door and went out, her shoes skidded on the step. She peered down, aware her feet were tangled in a coil of grey and slimy entrails. She gagged as a putrid odour wafted up to her nostrils, but she managed to shout for Daniel before nausea overcame her.

'Dear God,' Daniel said. He pushed past her and closed the front door behind them to prevent the smell entering the house. 'What the hell is this?'

'Intestines,' Catherine said, averting her gaze. She stepped off the porch. The cool air bit at the back of her throat as she breathed in and out, trying to cleanse her lungs of the bad smell. She walked across the gravel to the stone wall and leaned against it. 'Someone must have dumped them in the night.'

'Don't be stupid. Why would they do that?'

'It was bound to happen sooner or later.' Despite his denial, Catherine could tell he was thinking the same way as her, and she felt the tranquillity she'd been experiencing in recent weeks drain away.

'But nobody knows me out here.'

'*Everyone* knows you, Dan.'

'This is crazy. I've done nothing wrong. Anyway, I thought country folk were, you know...?'

'What?'

'More right wing. Not liberal wishy-washy.' He smiled. 'We're the liberals. This lot are supposed to be foxhunting, gun-toting, gin-drinking, Nazis. I thought they'd be all for defending your own property.'

'Could you — *possibly* — be generalising just a little?'

'Moi?' Daniel smiled again. He held out his hands. 'Come on, let's get the mess cleaned up.'

'And then what? Phone the police?'

'No way. After what I experienced up in London, they're the last people I'd trust.'

'But somebody wants to hurt us.'

'No, Catherine. Somebody wants us to feel unsettled, but they only succeed if we let them. We ignore this and get on with our day-to-day lives as if it hasn't fazed us.'

'That's easy for you to say. You're not the one who has to be here alone next week.'

'I told you, it's just for a few days. I have to run through the score with the director now the rough edit's been made. You'll be fine. Lock the doors, draw the curtains and binge out on a box set. Nobody's coming down here so there's nothing to be scared of, and if you do get worried, you can always call our neighbour.'

'Joe Foster?'

'Yeeerrrrssshhh.' Daniel raised his hands, lowered his head, and hunched his back. He started to plod towards her. 'Got some nice pheasants for ya, girl. Ugh, ugh, ugh!'

'Stop it!' Catherine shrieked and tried to dodge away, but he caught her round the waist, his hands clawing at her. 'I'm warning you!'

'Alright.' Daniel let her go. 'I was only joking.'

'Well don't, because it's not funny.' She glanced over at the step where the pile of guts sat in an odious mass. 'And if you think it is, you can clear *that* lot up.'

After Daniel had removed the mess, Catherine mopped the step and sprayed it with some disinfectant to try to sanitise the smell. They ate lunch, but Catherine picked at her food, the memory of the intestines all too recent. Then, to her surprise, Daniel insisted they went to the village. They'd driven through to pop letters in the post box, but as it was some distance away, they'd never felt as if they were part of the community.

'A few miles are as good as next door round here,' Daniel said. 'The locals probably think we're being rude. We've lived at World's End for over a month and I bet they don't even know who we are.'

'Really?' Catherine said. 'I thought it was all twitching curtains and news passed on by smoke signals. I bet they know *exactly* who we are.'

'Look, if people are distrustful, we need to show them we can be trusted. We'll saunter down there and show our faces. They'll see we're not so bad. Perhaps whoever dumped the guts might have second thoughts once they realise we're only human.'

'And if they do recognise you?'

'That might be a good thing. Get the initial wariness out the way and prove I don't match the person in the headlines. That I don't bite the heads off babies.'

They set off mid-afternoon, taking the Toyota because Daniel said it gave the impression they'd embraced the rural lifestyle by buying a proper vehicle rather than a Chelsea Tractor. They wound their way down the valley to where a T-junction provided a choice: right to the nearest town, which was where they went for their basic shopping needs; or left to the village. Daniel swung the 4x4 left and they passed a stone cross surrounded by a patch of immaculate cut grass. Two tight bends later and they arrived at the village centre. To one side sat several large detached houses, while on the other a row of pretty terraced cottages nestled under a long, undulating roof of thatch.

'That's our Christmas cards sorted,' Daniel said. 'Wait for a dusting of snow, take a picture of those cottages, and scrawl a message on the back. Job done.'

'Nobody would believe it wasn't Photoshopped,' Catherine said. 'Christmas card, chocolate box, and period drama all rolled into one cosy scene.'

'Too cosy?'

Catherine looked again, this time paying more attention to the little details. At one end of the terrace a mud-spattered van was parked in the road, while the door of the adjoining property could have done with a lick of paint. A satellite dish poked out from under the overhanging thatch, and a Countryside Alliance poster had been plastered up in a downstairs window. 'No. Real people live here, they're not holiday cottages.'

'For now.' Daniel pulled the 4x4 onto a verge. 'But with all these bloody newcomers...'

'Funny.' Catherine wrinkled her nose at Daniel. 'Anyway, we're contributing to the local economy. We've employed builders and electricians and plumbers, we bought the kitchen from the nearest town and the carpets from Exeter. Plus, I'm going to open a gallery that will attract tourists.'

'But we haven't contributed here, have we?' Daniel clicked open the door and got out. He gestured over to the Post Office which appeared to double as a local café and store. 'And that looks as good a place to start as any.'

They strolled over to the Post Office and a bell clanged out as they entered. To the left there were people sitting at various tables. At one a middle-aged woman was tucking into an iced bun while reading a newspaper. At the next table two young mums breastfed their babies. A man in a dark suit sat at a third table, and he was reaching across and holding an old woman's hand. The woman had tears in her eyes.

The bell seemed to punctuate the room like an explosion and heads turned as one. Catherine smiled while Daniel muttered a 'good afternoon.'

They walked across to the other side of the room where a woman in her fifties stood behind a counter. Half-moon glasses balanced on a pug nose and she wore a striped apron. She'd rolled the sleeves on her shirt up exposing podgy arms.

Catherine had brought a parcel she needed to post, and she plopped it on the counter.

'Hello,' she said. 'First class please.'

'Pop it on the scales,' the postmistress said. She pointed to the right and Catherine put the parcel on the scales. The woman looked at a readout. 'OK, done.'

'Thanks.' Catherine pointed at the parcel. 'I've put the sender's address on the back. It's World's End Farm. We've just moved in.'

'I thought I didn't recognise you.' The postmistress peered over the top of her glasses. 'What happened to the Larwoods?'

'I think they relocated to Wales,' Catherine said. 'Mr Larwood got a new job or something.'

'Or something.'

'Sorry?'

'That'll be three pounds thirty-five please.' As Catherine proffered a card, the woman indicated a terminal. 'How are you finding it up at World's End?'

'Good, thanks. We've had a lot of work done so it's quite cosy now.' Catherine tapped her card on the reader. 'We also converted part of the barn into a studio. I'm a sculptor, you see, and Daniel is—'

'The barn. Right.'

'Yes, Daniel will work—'

'Here's your receipt.' The woman tore off a slip of paper and handed it across. 'Will that be all?'

'Er, yes, thank you.'

Daniel reached out and slipped some money into a RNIB donation box on the counter. 'Goodbye,' he said.

As the door clanged shut behind them, Catherine uttered a sigh. 'Jesus. I thought she was going to yell out, "strangers", at some point. Talk about weird.'

'She's a bit suspicious, that's all. Once she gets to know us, it'll be fine.'

'You mean we have to go in there *again*?'

'You wait, within a month she'll be pushing her homemade chutneys on you and inviting you to join the WI.'

'No way!'

'Now, now, sweetheart.' Daniel wagged a finger in jest. 'We have to make sacrifices in order to become part of the community.'

They strolled back to the 4x4, but as Daniel went to open his door, he stopped. 'The church. Why don't we take a look?'

Catherine followed Daniel's gaze. At the far end of the village, a stone tower poked above a tall yew hedge. A graveyard was visible behind the wizened branches.

'Since when did you turn religious?'

'The pub and the church. They're the cornerstones of any community. You debauch yourself in one and repent in the other.'

'I'm not in the mood for drunken debauchery today.'

'The church it is then.'

They ambled down the road and found the entrance to the churchyard. A path of worn slabs led to a porch where a set of iron gates stood open.

'Shall we go in?' Catherine hesitated at the gates. 'I don't know why, but it just feels strange.'

'Nonsense.' Daniel stepped into the porch. There was a noticeboard. A poster for a Christmas Fayre. The Mother and Toddler group. A leaflet advertising the local history society. 'And you thought there was nothing going on down here? I don't know where we'll find the time.'

'Don't be silly.'

A heavy door led into the church itself, and their footsteps echoed as they entered. A narrow nave with pews crammed on either side led to a small chancel and an altar adorned with a simple wooden cross. They stood for a minute and Daniel walked down the aisle and examined some of the memorial stones set into one wall. Catherine took a postcard from a rack and dropped payment in a box.

'Peaceful,' she said as they emerged from the church into bright sunlight.

'And no sign of a bolt from heaven striking me down.' Daniel took her arm and they strolled through the graveyard. 'But perhaps I spoke too soon.'

Up ahead, the man they'd seen earlier in the Post Office was striding towards them. Dark suit, black shirt, a circle of gleaming white at the collar. As he approached, he stuck out his hand.

'Father Peter Carmichael,' he said. 'I'm the vicar of St Mary's and three other surrounding parishes. Welcome to Dartmoor!'

'Thank you.' Catherine shook first, followed by Daniel. 'You must have overheard us in the Post Office.'

'Gosh, yes.' A tinge of red flushed Carmichael's neck. 'Sorry about that, but it's impossible to be anonymous out here I'm afraid.'

'I can't say we're religious,' Daniel said. 'So if you're trying to recruit us to your flock you're almost certainly wasting your time.'

'Don't worry, I never presume anything with newcomers.' Carmichael tilted his head towards the church. 'But you could do worse than come along one Sunday, perhaps at Christmas. You'd meet some of the locals.'

'Are you sure they want to meet us?'

'Oh yes, I mean... well...' Carmichael threw his hands open in a gesture of resignation. 'Look, they don't realise who you are. Not yet. However, I do, and I just want to say, um, I've no preconceived ideas. Everybody is equal in the eyes of God and all shall be forgiven.'

'You're not talking about forgiveness for my latest movie score?'

'Well, no.' Carmichael shrugged. 'Sorry if I've offended you. I just thought you should know that I'm here and ready to listen. If there's anything bothering you, if you have any problems with anyone, then please do come and see me.'

'We did have a little surprise actually,' Catherine said. Daniel tugged at her arm, but she ignored him. 'This morning somebody left a pile of offal on our front doorstep. A not very Christian moving in present.'

'Oh dear.' Carmichael ran a hand over his forehead and his eyes lifted to the sky as if in search of some divine inspiration. 'I have to say I doubt it was to do with you personally.'

'It felt pretty personal,' Daniel said. 'Like some kind of threat.'

'Awful, simply awful.' The hand again, sweeping his head, but this time his eyes flicking to the right, focusing for a moment on a nearby grave adorned with a bouquet of fresh flowers. 'I'm afraid that's not unusual up at World's End. Over the years I've heard about several minor incidents, but none seem to be directly connected to the occupants of the house. I don't suppose it makes you feel any better, but at least you know the malice is not related to, um... well...'

'Me,' Daniel said.

'So why?' Catherine said. 'Has someone got a long-term grudge or is there a land dispute?'

'Oh, I'm sure it's silly and insignificant. Honestly. You should just ignore it.'

'Ignore—'

'I overheard you say you're a sculptor, was that right?' Carmichael seemed keen to move the subject on. Catherine nodded. 'Perhaps you and your husband would like to come and give a talk in the village hall sometime. Daniel about the famous directors he's written music for, you on your own work. It would be for the church roof repair fund, so you'd be supporting a good cause.' Carmichael smiled. 'Even if you aren't religious.'

'I'm not sure.'

'Everyone would be very interested and it would help you meet some more people.' Carmichael cocked his head again as if waiting for a response, but then he glanced up at the clock tower. 'Right, I must run to an appointment, but you think about it, OK?'

With that he was gone, wheeling on his feet as if on a parade ground and marching off out of the graveyard.

'Jesus!' Catherine said.

'He's you man.' Daniel pointed after Carmichael. 'And we should do that talk. It could even lead to some commissions.'

'I doubt it, but as he said, it might break the ice. Perhaps if people see our faces they might not be quite so predisposed to leaving nasty surprises on our doorstep.'

'Perhaps.' Daniel didn't sound convinced and he looked away, his gaze moving to the grave with the beautiful flowers. He turned back to Catherine and gave a half smile. 'Or perhaps not.'

Chapter Eleven

A warm and sunny weekend meant the incident with the guts slipped to the back of Catherine's mind. On Saturday she worked in the garden repairing a stone terrace, and on Sunday Daniel insisted on a long walk across the moor; they spent the evening in bed with the papers.

Daniel left for London early on Monday. He'd have three whole days in the city and be back Friday afternoon. 'You won't even notice I'm gone,' he said, as he kissed Catherine goodbye and climbed into his car.

In truth, he was correct. At least at first. She had a big commission to finish by Christmas and was way behind. She worked until close to midnight Monday night and went to bed exhausted. She'd been worried about sleeping, fearing that she would lie awake all night listening to every little sound, but as soon as her head hit the pillow, she was gone. A strong sun woke her, the light cresting the ridge opposite the house and pouring in through the curtains which she'd forgotten to close. She showered, breakfasted and got straight down to work. Lunch was eaten standing in the kitchen and, as with the previous day, come evening she was worn out.

She forced herself to cook a healthy dinner instead of grabbing a ready meal from the freezer. After she'd eaten, she retreated to the living room and read a book until she found herself dropping off. Coffee, she thought, and went to the kitchen to fill the kettle. Which was when she noticed something odd about the back door.

She flipped the switch on the kettle and went across to investigate. The door had a cat flap and when they'd moved in the flap had been free to swing. Every time there was a gust of wind it opened, letting a strong draught into the kitchen. She'd screwed a flat piece of wood to the outside of the door and stuffed the gaps with wood filler. At some point they'd need to fit a whole new door, but the bodge worked fine for now.

Only it wasn't working any longer.

Catherine bent to the door. The plastic flap was moving slightly, just as it had before the fix. Had the piece of wood on the outside fallen off? It seemed unlikely as she'd used a powered screwdriver to drive the screws home. She stretched out a hand and touched the flap, pushing it backwards. As she did so, she felt a resistance from the other side, as if an invisible force was trying to push back the other way. She flinched. Silly, she thought, it must be the wind. She berated herself and, remembering Daniel's words about not being scared, lifted the flap.

Which was when she saw the rats.

Not two or three, but six, seven, ten, more. They were crammed together on the far side of the flap as if they were confined in some way.

Catherine screamed, dropped the flap, and jumped back, but it was too late. The rats poured through the opening, falling over themselves as they tumbled to the floor. She froze as the plague heaved in a living mass around her. Furry bodies brushed against her feet and ankles, and there was a collective shriek as they scurried across the tiles, running in all directions. She felt a scratch on her calf and looked down to see a rat clawing at her leg. She screamed again, kicked the rat free, and dashed from the kitchen and along the hallway, pausing to turn back and slam the connecting door. She grabbed her phone from the living room and ran up the stairs, dialling 999 as she went.

A call handler answered in a calm voice and asked her which service she required.

'Police,' she yelled, as she hurried into the bedroom and closed the door.

She waited for what seemed like an age before a second operator came on the line and asked for her name and address and the nature of the emergency.

'Rats!' Catherine said. 'There are dozens of rats in my kitchen!'

'That'll be a matter for the council,' the operator said brusquely. 'It doesn't sound like police business.'

'Somebody must have stuffed them through the cat flap deliberately. That's police business, isn't it?'

The operator didn't answer. Instead he had a barrage of questions. Was the incident ongoing? Was there an intruder on the premises? Was there any danger to life or limb? Was she or anyone present a vulnerable person, or did they identify themselves as a member of a recognised minority?

Catherine's answer to all the questions was 'no' which led to the call handler informing her she didn't require an emergency response. The incident would be recorded and, if it was deemed appropriate, an officer would visit when they could. In the meantime, she should phone the council or call a registered pest controller.

Fuck it! She hung up and threw the phone onto the floor. Then she thought better of it. The kitchen was swarming with rats and a pest controller sounded like a very good idea. A Google search on the phone showed several local companies, but only one had a 24-hour emergency response. She dialled and within a few minutes had given her details and been assured that somebody would be with her in the next couple of hours.

A couple of hours? Catherine slumped on the bed and began to cry.

The pest control company were as good as their word, and she was woken from a light sleep by the beep of a horn a little before midnight. She went outside to find an affable young man removing equipment from the back of a van.

'You've got rats, Ms Ross?' The man said and Catherine's view of him went up a several notches. He'd managed to get her name right and he didn't sound in the least bit condescending.

'Yes,' she said. 'Rather a lot of them, I'm afraid. They're in the kitchen.'

'OK, let me take a look.'

Half an hour later, having told Catherine to wait in the living room, he was finished.

'All done.' He gave her a reassuring smile. 'Luckily your kitchen was built-in with no little hidey-holes. I'm pretty sure I managed to catch them all.'

'*Catch* them?' Catherine said. 'You mean *alive*?'

'Yes.'

'What will you do with them?'

'I'll take them back to base and gas them. It's the best way and the most humane.' He paused before gesturing to the kitchen. 'I'd better show you what I found. There's good news and bad news.'

'Sure.'

The man explained there had been twenty-five rats in total. They were wild rats and from the bite marks on some of them he guessed they'd been caged together and had been fighting.

'But that's not all.' He led the way to the back door. The light from the kitchen shone out on the patio where a wooden box sat next to several bricks. 'The rats were in there. All of them.'

'In that little box?'

'Yes. It has a sliding door on one side and had been positioned up against the cat flap. The bricks were to raise the box to the right level. With the sliding door open, the rats pushed at the flap. It was when you came to look they realised they could escape. That's when they—'

'Don't.' Catherine shivered. 'It's not an experience I want to relive.'

'The good news is you haven't got a rat problem. I've had a look round outside and there are some runs here and there, but that's to be expected considering we're surrounded by moorland.'

'If that's the good news, what's the bad news?'

'Self-evident, isn't it? The bad news is someone released those rats into your kitchen to scare you.'

Chapter Twelve

It had taken Foster three weeks to trap all the rats. There was never a shortage of vermin round the farm, but he only had two live traps and rats were cunning buggers. He put the ones he caught in a cage he constructed from weldmesh and kept his fingers away from the bars when he fed them. There'd been over thirty in there at some point, but they'd begun to fight and several had died. The survivors had turned cannibal and eaten their comrades. Never mind, twenty-five had been a tidy number. Getting them in the box had been tricky, but he'd used a wire funnel with a little swinging trapdoor. He'd attached the funnel to the cage, and using plenty of food to entice them, and a blow torch to scare them, he'd managed get the rats to run into the box.

Down at World's End, he'd hesitated for a minute when he'd realised the woman was alone. He wanted the couple to leave the farm, but he didn't want to scare her to death. Trouble was, he had no idea when the husband would be back, and the rats were already at each other's throats. Either he did it now or he released them and started afresh. No point getting all soft and gooey in your old age, he told himself as he unscrewed the piece of plywood blocking the cat flap and positioned the box in place.

He was walking back across the fields when he heard the fruits of his labours. The scream was loud enough to escape the house and float half a mile up the valley. He smiled, but he wondered if he'd gone too far.

'You daft bugger,' he said. 'You want them out, don't you?'

He did. Out and tomorrow wouldn't be soon enough. The thought of anyone living there was sickening to him, as if they were desecrating holy ground. Every day the couple spent in the house caused him pain. Of course, once they'd gone there'd be someone else and then someone else. He couldn't stop them coming. He'd thought about burning the place to the ground, but that in itself would be awful. Anyway, there'd be a greedy builder along soon after, ready to put up a new dwelling and make a nice little profit. No, this was the best way. Over the decades, the property had been empty for months at a time, years even. He'd found a sort of peace during those periods. As if that was how it was meant to be. As if World's End was supposed to stand dormant for eternity, a monument to evil, stupidity, and cowardice.

Barney Weston, his neighbour over the hill, knew what Foster was up to, but he turned a blind eye. He'd once asked Foster why he didn't buy the place himself.

'You could sell your house with just the buildings and have enough money to purchase World's End. The land's adjoining so it wouldn't make no difference to the farming.' They'd been in The Crown and, when he'd finished his suggestion, Barney had raised his stout to his lips and supped deep before continuing. 'You can't argue with it, Joe. Not if you've got an ounce of sense in that body of yours.'

Well, perhaps he didn't have an ounce of sense, but living at World's End would have been unthinkable after what had happened there. It was better this way. Whether it took weeks or months or years, eventually the couple would leave. Nor would their decision be simply a result of his little tricks, because there were other factors at work down there. Not ghosts or spirits. Not zombies rising from the dead or a portal opening to hell. Not a poltergeist throwing objects around the rooms in the middle of the night. No, none of those.

'Memories,' he said as he entered his farmyard. The dog skittered round the edge of the barn door and ran across to him. He let her nuzzle up to his leg and bent and stroked her under the chin. 'It's the bloody memories, Jess. Gets them every time.'

The dog stared at him with her brown eyes and Foster figured she didn't have a clue what the hell he was talking about. Which, he thought, was probably for the best.

Chapter Thirteen

Catherine couldn't get the vision of the heaving mass of rats from her mind. Snake-like tails curling round, yellow teeth chattering, a myriad of little noses twitching. She felt like calling a builder to come in and rip out the entire kitchen and replace all the units with new ones. She even said as much to Daniel when she managed to get hold of him in the early hours long after the pest controller had gone.

'Calm down,' he said. 'I can understand you were scared, but you're overreacting.'

It was at that point Catherine had exploded and they'd had a massive argument which ended with her hanging up.

As she lay in the bed with the bedside light on, she thought that replacing the kitchen wasn't going to cut it. They needed to get out of here and move back to London. For one thing, Daniel wouldn't have to be away from home. She'd been terrified when she hadn't been able to contact him, even though she realised it was likely because he was working late in the studio or edit suite and didn't have his phone with him. Long ago, he'd told her the technicians had a strict *no phones* policy which meant devices weren't simply switched off, they were left outside. At times though she'd questioned if the policy was genuine or a fiction Daniel had invented to cover his tracks.

She'd never fully trusted him, even before he'd cheated on her with the intern. Not when they'd been younger and totally smitten, lovers at all times of the day and night. Nor later, when their relationship had become a little steadier. Not even when they were married and a ring supposedly marked their lifelong commitment to each other.

Daniel, Jonathon, Young, will you take...
I will.
Catherine, Fiona, Ross, will you take...
I will.

No, marriage hadn't changed their relationship one bit. The happy ever after myth was just an ideal. The gold standard to aim for. And, as she'd found out, gold could be debased.

Even the gold of a wedding ring.

The intern's name was Gemma and she worked for the rights agency that handled Daniel's music. Catherine had coined several alternative names for the girl, some childish, some puerile, none remotely noble. But what Gemma had got up to with Daniel wasn't particularly noble either. Rather perversely though, Catherine was grateful to her. Without Gemma life would have carried on as before. Dozens of milestones passed, but no distance travelled. Everything going on, but not much happening.

As long as you both shall live...

At twenty-three, Gemma was some fifteen years younger than Daniel. She was blonde with a cleavage Catherine could never hope to emulate. She had full lips and eyelashes that fluttered as if she was in a constant state of near orgasm. She wore short skirts which showed off her long legs and rounded bum. Not that Catherine had ever met her. Not face-to-face. Her knowledge of Gemma came almost entirely from thirty seconds of video-selfie shot by Daniel on his phone, a dozen pictures, hundreds of texts, and a miserable hour spent standing in a torrential storm outside a pizza restaurant in the West End while inside Gemma and Daniel ate, kissed and — worst of all — laughed.

The hour of rain-soaked torture had come at the denouement of the affair. Catherine had discovered the video a week earlier, along with the pictures and the texts which Daniel had neglected to delete from his phone. If he'd been cleverer, he could have explained away the video and the pictures as a drunken fumble at the agency's annual Christmas party. Not so the texts. Each one had been a lesson in conciseness. Explicit pornography in under one hundred and sixty characters.

The texts revealed that Daniel was in fact a lying, cheating bastard. He'd fucked Gemma every which way. They'd had sex in the public toilets at Covent Garden. On the train to Brighton. In Daniel's car. Under an oak tree in Hyde Park. Most brazenly of all on the kitchen floor of their house when Catherine had been away for a weekend. The sex hadn't been a drunken fumble at the office at all. It had been both regular and frequent and, from the sound of it, akin to the passion she'd had with Daniel when they'd first met.

He denied the affair at first, but when she confronted him with the hard evidence he confessed. He said he'd been stupid and foolish and had never meant to risk what they had together. He said he should have listened to his therapist, because she'd told him that some kind of stress disorder was quite understandable. Post traumatic. Whatever. After all, it wasn't every day you killed someone. Daniel had held Catherine's hand and looked at her like a lost puppy.

Blue eyes. Deep water. Run or at least grab a lifebuoy.

She knew his words of apology were bullshit. She knew he'd say anything to avoid a scene and to try and rationalise the guilt. Since when did PTSD manifest itself in needing to search out the nearest young woman willing to spread her legs?

In the end she forgave him, but she couldn't forget the deceit. She lived day-by-day, wondering what Daniel was up to when he wasn't home, never trusting his word. She started following him, becoming adept at leaping on and off tube trains as the doors closed, mingling with the crowds round Covent Garden as she waited for him to emerge from his agent's office, hoping he'd come out alone and not with a laughing, flirty Gemma on his arm.

Much to her surprise she didn't catch him with Gemma again, and for a while she was reassured, but the paranoia began to return. What if Daniel realised she was watching him? His casual walks through central London, along the Thames, sometimes stopping for a drink at a riverside café, could all be for her benefit. At other times, when she was working hard on a sculpture at home, he could be at Gemma's place fucking her for all he was worth.

After weeks of fretting, she had it out with Daniel. He'd been away at a movie shoot near Bristol, and Catherine had imagined him shagging the pretty young actresses, the make-up girl, the mature, motherly director, anyone female between the ages of eighteen and sixty.

When he returned she was ready for a fight, but instead he held his hands up. He understood she was unhappy and he agreed they needed to find a solution. The answer, he suggested, was a complete change of scenery. In short, they would move. The sale of their cramped little terraced house in London would allow them to buy a palatial spread somewhere in the West Country. An idyllic artist's residence. He could create a mini studio and Catherine could have a workshop. They'd both have to travel every so often, but that would be true no matter where they lived. They'd also be moving to a low crime area. There wouldn't be any more burglars breaking in.

Initially, she'd been opposed, but the more she thought about it the more a move made sense. Christ, a man had died in their house and Daniel had fucked a woman on the kitchen floor. She wasn't sure which was worse but leaving both memories behind seemed to be a good idea. Anyway, she'd begun to feel claustrophobic in London and the countryside would be different. Just her and Daniel and the wide-open spaces. A breath of fresh air. Back to nature. Authenticity. Time and space to relax and dozens of other clichés.

They began to scan the property websites, make calls, and register their interest with estate agents, but it was Daniel who found World's End Farm. He phoned the estate agency and made an appointment. They drove down one weekend and even as they passed between the stone pillars which marked the boundary to the property, Catherine could see his mind was set. The agent let them in and left them to look round. Daniel was smitten with the house and its three-hundred-year-old beams of oak and beautiful exposed stonework. While there was some renovation and refurbishment to do, the work wouldn't be difficult or costly; the place was almost perfect as it was.

Daniel grinned as he talked about where to put his studio. How Catherine would finally have enough space for all her tools and a good stock of materials. She could even open a gallery, he said. The land would allow them to keep chickens and sheep. They could get a dog, maybe a pony. Catherine found herself bowled along by his enthusiasm and later the very same day they made an offer. She'd argued that they should at least look at some more houses in the area, but Daniel wouldn't listen. Why continue searching when they'd found their dream place? This was fate, he said. The house chose them as much as they chose it. They were meant to live here. Destined.

He'd stared at her with his blue eyes and she'd found herself falling again. Just like she had when they'd first met. Falling and floating. Slipping beneath the waves. Drowning.

Chapter Fourteen

Catherine lay awake for much of the night, thinking alternately about Daniel, the house, and the rats. Eventually her eyelids closed and mercifully she dreamed of city streets chock-full of traffic and people.

In the morning she took a shower. She was rinsing her hair when she heard a loud banging from downstairs.

'Mrs Ross?' The banging came again, followed by a voice calling through the letterbox. 'It's the police, Mrs Ross.'

Shit.

She stepped out of the shower, wrapped a bath robe round herself, and ran down the stairs. She opened the front door to see a uniformed policeman standing out in the yard next to a four-wheel-drive patrol car. For an instant she wondered about slamming the door. The man had a hooked nose and bloodless lips, and on the side of his face there was a patch of pale skin like a scar or a birthmark.

'Constable Jencks,' the officer said, walking towards her with a hand outstretched. 'I believe you had a spot of bother last night?'

'Oh, yes,' Catherine checked her towel wasn't about to drop off. She held out her hand. 'But they said you might not even bother visiting.'

'Did they?' Jencks winced. He shook her hand. His palm felt cold and limp, like the tail of a dead fish. He peered beyond her shoulder and into the house. 'Well, they made a mistake. I try to attend every crime on my patch. I take any lawbreaking as a personal affront. Now, the report says somebody's been scaring you with a whole load of rats?'

'Yes,' Catherine said. 'Could you excuse me while I go and get changed?'

'Sure.' Jencks moved into the doorway and for a second Catherine thought about asking him to wait outside, but it was too late, and the man was in and through to the hallway. 'Nicely done up, Mrs Ross.'

'It's Ms Ross.'

'You live here alone?'

'No. My husband's in London at the moment.' Catherine made for the stairs, regretting she'd said Daniel was away. 'He'll be back later. I won't be a second.'

'You take your time, Mrs Ross,' Jencks said. 'I'll have a look round.'

Catherine hurried to her bedroom and dressed. Back downstairs she found Jencks in the kitchen. The back door stood open and he was crouching down and examining the cat flap.

'There's a box outside,' Catherine said. 'The pest controller said it was placed next to the cat flap.'

'Ingenious.' Jencks bit his lip and stood. He sidled out onto the patio and examined the wooden box. 'Whoever did this must have taken some time setting it up. You didn't hear anything?'

'I was watching TV and then reading. I dozed for a bit. If there was a noise, I didn't hear it.'

'How many rats were there, Mrs Ross?'

'The pest control man said twenty-five.' Catherine pointed to the kitchen table and a pink carbon copy of the invoice she'd been given. 'It's all detailed there. I guess you could phone him to confirm my story.'

'Oh, there's no need to do that.' Jencks came back into the kitchen. He turned his head from side to side. 'What exactly is it you and your husband do, Mrs Ross?'

'My husband's a composer and I'm a sculptor. We converted the barn into a workshop for me, and Daniel uses the spare room as his studio space.'

'I see.' Jencks ran his tongue over the front of his teeth as if he was trying to remove a piece of food from the enamel surface. 'Perhaps I could see the barn?'

'What's the barn got to do with this?'

'Probably nothing, but I'm pretty fastidious. I wouldn't want to discover later on that I'd missed some vital piece of evidence.'

Plain nosey more like, Catherine thought as she led Jencks back outside and round the house. She wanted him gone. He was weird and made her feel uncomfortable.

When they approached the barn, Jencks half turned his head away.

'It's changed,' he said. 'Since I was last here.'

'As I said, we converted it.'

'Of course.' Jencks stopped. His eyes were focused on the open half of the barn — the half which hadn't been converted. He was staring up at the main beam which spanned the entire space. 'Interesting.'

Catherine tried not to look at Jencks. Instead she went across to the door to her workshop and unlocked it. 'There's not much to see.'

'Nothing missing?' Jencks peered into the studio, taking a minute to scan the room. He waved at the sculptures. 'Everything where it should be?'

'Yes. Anyway, the door was locked.'

'Right.' Jencks walked a few steps from the barn. 'You need a security system fitting, Mrs Ross. Cameras, alarms, panic buttons.'

'Panic buttons?'

'Yes.' He smiled, but the smile was more of a leer. 'You see, somebody could pretty much do anything they wanted out here and nobody would be any the wiser. Anything, understand?'

'Do you think we're in danger?'

'No, not as such.' Jencks went across the yard and sniffed the air. 'How long have you been at World's End, Mrs Ross?'

'Since mid-October. We bought the place in early summer, but it needed some work.'

'Converting the barn?'

'Yes, that and a new kitchen and bathroom, some repairs inside.'

'Perhaps someone didn't like what you've done with the house.'

'It went through planning without a hitch. I don't see—'

'No, you wouldn't, but others might.' They'd reached Jencks' patrol car. He put out a hand and drummed his fingers on the roof. 'Did you know much about this place before you bought it?'

'Not really. There was a family here before us, I believe, but it was empty when we viewed it. They'd already relocated.'

'Re-lo-ca-ted.' Jencks articulated each syllable as if he was pronouncing a word he didn't know. 'Yes.'

'What?'

'That would have been Mr and Mrs Larwood, right?' Jencks said. Catherine nodded. 'They were here for three years. Before them it was the Gillards. They managed five. Then there was a lady artist, bit like you, only she painted. A year for her. Before that another family called the Crossfords if I remember correctly. Two years. Before that, well, let me see...'

'What's your point?'

'Nobody stays here long.' Jencks leaned towards Catherine, his nose wrinkling. 'There's something about the place. It's either empty or there's a *For Sale* board at the end of the track.'

'But the solicitor's searches didn't highlight any issues. No mines, no pollution, no flood risk, no radon.'

'Radon? It's not in the ground, love.' Jencks came closer until his nose was almost touching Catherine's face. She could hardly help herself from staring at the scar tissue on the side of his cheek. She wanted to ask if he'd received the scar in the line of duty or if it was a birthmark. 'It's in the air. Can't you smell it?'

'No.' Catherine shifted to one side to put some distance between herself and the policeman. She wanted to get back in the house and lock the door. Once again she fumed that Daniel was away. 'Our neighbour didn't say anything.'

'Your neighbour?'

'Joe Foster, he—'

'*Foster?*' The name came out accompanied by a globule of spittle. If Catherine had been any nearer it would have landed in her face. 'What the fuck was he doing down here?'

'I...' Catherine stepped away again. She'd been suspicious of the police all her life, from long before Daniel's arrest, but Jencks was pushing her reservations to a new level. 'He came by when we moved in. Just being friendly, I guess.'

'There's nobody friendly round here, lass. That's why the others left when they did. A succession of minor events like your rats, like dog shit through the letterbox, a dead crow hung on a post at the top of the track, a rabbit skinned and nailed to the side of the barn.'

'Intestines.'

'What?'

'On the porch.' Catherine motioned towards the front door, remembering the grey viscera spread on the step. 'I forgot to say earlier, but last week somebody left a pile of guts for us to find.'

'That would be par for the course.' Jencks smiled, as if he'd worked the whole thing out. As if he had the combined deductive ability of Holmes, Poirot, Rebus and Bosch. 'For World's End at least.'

'Why didn't the police get involved before?'

'They did, Mrs Ross. Or rather *I* did.' Abruptly, Jencks body seemed to deflate, the tension gone. He dove into a pocket for a business card. He handed it to Catherine and then clicked open the car door and stood there. 'The problem is I've never been able to prove anything.'

'You had a suspect?'

'Oh yes, I had a suspect.' Jencks got into the car and slammed the door. He lowered the window. That smile again. Half a leer, half a more sinister expression. 'If you have any other problems, give me a call, right?'

'Yes.' Catherine wanted to ask Jencks about what precautions she should take, about whether she should be worried, but he'd already started the engine and was off, the car sweeping round on the gravel and shooting up the track. Jencks sat hunched over, his hooked nose almost touching the wheel, his face screwed up in concentration.

Catherine ran back inside the house and locked the door.

Chapter Fifteen

Daniel was sanguine about the rats on his return.

'I wouldn't worry about it,' he said. 'Simply a prank.'

Catherine protested. What had happened with the rats was more than a prank. She couldn't understand Daniel's attitude, why he appeared so unaffected. But then he'd been away, hadn't he? He hadn't had to spend several nights lying awake worrying about crazed nutters stalking round outside.

She broached the subject of moving, but he wouldn't hear of it. They'd just arrived and teething problems were to be expected. It was great here with all the space they had, the moor and the pretty villages, the countryside and the wildlife.

The wildlife? Catherine wondered if her husband had lost his mind, but she bit her lip and kept quiet.

Their first visitors came in early December. Daniel's friend Toby and his wife, Lisa, drove from London on a wet Friday evening and arrived in the dark as the clouds parted to reveal a starry sky.

'Drown us and freeze us, won't you?' Toby said as he got out of his car. The Jaguar F-Type in shocking pink was as ostentatious as Toby. 'Not to mention that trap you set back on the main road. I'm used to knocking pedestrians out the way, but I draw the line at a pony. Bloody animal would have made a right mess of the Jag.'

Daniel bounded over full of enthusiasm and slapped his friend on the back.

'Jeez, Toby, what did you do?' Daniel indicated the car. 'Win a million on the lottery?'

'In a manner of speaking, yes.'

Catherine stood on the front step. Toby wasn't her cup of tea at all. Sure, at first sight he appeared charming with his bumbling, easy manner, wide smile and mop of blond hair. He was a lecturer in English and it was easy to imagine his female students swooning as he read them passages from Wuthering Heights or Jane Eyre. But Catherine knew some of them had done way more than swoon. Daniel had told her the stories with a grin, as if Toby cheating on his wife and deflowering some innocent nineteen-year-old girl was the type of behaviour to be proud of. Lisa wasn't unattractive, but she was approaching forty. Toby liked them younger, although on several occasions his wandering hands under the dinner table had made it clear to Catherine that he was well up for it if she was.

Whenever she mentioned her concerns to Daniel, he just said, 'oh, that's Toby,' as if any misdemeanours his friend committed should be excused. If a sexual harassment case was ever brought against Toby, she could imagine Daniel jumping to his defence: 'I wouldn't really call it *assault*. That's just Toby.'

She'd argued with Daniel on numerous occasions: 'What do you have at the end of it? A dozen pretty young things notched up on your bedpost. He can feel good about that, can he? Feel good about cheating on Lisa?'

'Toby's got papers. A book of poetry. Last time we spoke he mentioned he was going to write a novel.'

'Crap. Toby's always talking about a novel. And did you ever read any of those poems of his?' She'd gestured across the room to where the slim volume Toby had given them sat sandwiched between the voluminous works of G.R.R Martin and an RSPB bird book. 'Popular, informative, and there's Toby's contribution in the middle. The best you can say about it is that at least he hasn't wasted too much paper. It's a vanity project, no more.'

'The collection was reviewed in the *Guardian*.'

'There you go then. Case closed.'

'Catherine, he's a friend. You accept imperfections in your mates. At least I do. I guess all your friends are Stepford Wife perfect, right?'

'I'd call what Toby gets up to more than imperfect. He's not far off a pervert. A paedophile.'

'Don't be ridiculous. He's thirty-nine. His students are in their twenties, they're not children.'

'They're half his age for fuck's sake, plus he's abusing his position.'

'Catherine!' Toby's shout snapped her back to the present. 'How's my favourite sculptor?'

'Fine,' Catherine said. She held out her hands as Lisa emerged meekly from the car and shuffled over. Lisa had flat brown hair and a petite figure and alongside Toby's burning supernova, she appeared as a miniscule and insignificant speck of light. 'You OK?'

'Yes,' Lisa said. She tried to smile as she leaned to kiss Catherine on the cheek and then half glanced back towards the car. 'Good, actually. Toby's—'

'Have you heard the news?' Daniel jogged over. Toby was retrieving luggage from the back of the Jaguar. 'About Toby?'

'I think Lisa might have been about to tell me,' Catherine said.

'I'll let Toby.' Lisa said, getting smaller by the second.

'You're not...?'

'No.' Lisa smiled flatly. Relieved or disappointed, Catherine couldn't tell. 'No, not that.'

'So, Toby,' Catherine said as Toby came over. 'Going to enlighten me?'

'Love to,' Toby said. 'Name a time and place.'

'The news.' Lisa tugged at his arm. 'Tell them, darling.'

'It's a bit hush-hush, so this goes no further, right?' Toby put a finger to his lips and winked. 'I've got an offer for my Young Adult series. There's talk about a movie too. All of which means I'm done with bloody lecturing.'

'Congratulations,' Catherine heard herself say as inwardly she groaned.

'And if the movie deal comes off, I'm determined to do the music,' Daniel said. 'That would be great, hey?'

'Great for our agent.' Toby raised an arm and pulled down on an imaginary one-arm-bandit. 'Double the money. Ka-ching!'

Catherine felt her silent groaning turn to nausea. One of the reasons she detested Toby was that he'd been complicit in Daniel's affair. They shared the same rights agency and not only did Toby know all about Daniel and Gemma, he'd covered for Daniel on numerous occasions. Catherine imagined the three of them in some bar round the corner from the agency. The drinks flowing, Daniel cuddling with Gemma, Toby with a girl of his own on his lap, possibly the head of the agency, Barry Henderson, there too. Henderson was a larger version of Toby. Larger, older, more obnoxious. He employed a succession of interns, invariably pretty, female, and keen to get on. If it hadn't been for Henderson, Daniel would never have met Gemma, and if it hadn't been for Toby, the affair wouldn't have stayed hidden for so long.

'You alright, Catherine?' Toby leered. 'Wondering if you chose the wrong man all of a sudden?'

Catherine shot Daniel a glance and turned and led Lisa inside.

'Sorry about Toby,' Lisa said. 'He's... well, you know?'

Catherine nodded. She sensed telling Lisa her husband was a complete tosser wouldn't add much to the weekend.

In the kitchen, the four of them made small talk while Daniel opened a bottle of fizz. The cork popped, Daniel poured the drinks, and they chinked glasses.

'Congratulations on the move,' Toby said. He turned to Catherine. 'Never thought the old boy would be able to tear himself away from the bright lights and short skirts.'

'Toby!' Lisa touched her husband's elbow. 'It's a beautiful place, you two. Lovely and cosy inside.'

'It was a bit of a wreck, to be honest,' Daniel said. 'But we had a sympathetic builder and he did a great job on the renovation.'

The conversation moved on to how Catherine and Daniel had found the place and how it had been the only property they'd looked at. Then they started to talk about house prices and gazumping and the economy before Catherine intervened.

'Show Lisa and Toby to their room, Dan,' she said. 'I expect they'll want to freshen up.'

'Sure.' Daniel put his glass down on the table. He made a bowing motion. 'I'll take you up to your suite.'

Daniel led the way and the three of them left the kitchen. Catherine shook her head. At least tomorrow the boys were going out on a bike ride. Hopefully they'd come home tired and Toby wouldn't be quite so much of a handful. She just had to entertain Lisa, which wouldn't be so bad.

A few minutes later, she was at the sink washing up a pan, when she heard Daniel come downstairs. Footsteps padded across the kitchen floor and hands fondled her waist. She wriggled and leaned back, expecting Daniel to kiss her on the neck.

'You're bloody gorgeous,' Toby whispered in her ear.

'Get off!' Catherine squirmed away.

'Alright, keep your knickers on.' Toby smiled. 'Although I'd prefer it if you didn't.'

'Grow up, Toby.'

'That's just the problem, I can't. I'm still a randy teenager at heart. I'll fuck anything. Especially a lovely mature bird like you.'

Catherine glared at Toby. Half the time she was sure his behaviour was a wind up. 'Might I remind you that you're married and your wife is upstairs?'

'True.' Toby waved his hands in the air, making an hourglass shape. 'But Lisa's a bit thin. A broomstick, you know. Not like you. You've got curves in all the right places.'

'Who's got curves in all the right places?' Daniel stood in the doorway.

'Your wife, Dan.' Toby repeated his air drawing. 'Curvaceous Catherine. All woman. You're a lucky man, Dan. Very lucky.'

'She can cook too, can't you honey? Talking of which...?'

'It will be thirty minutes if you leave me in peace,' Catherine said. She tried to stay calm. Toby and Lisa were only staying for the weekend and come Sunday afternoon they'd be gone. 'I'll call you.'

'Good girl,' Daniel said, and he turned and left the room. Toby followed but couldn't resist blowing her a kiss as he went.

Over dinner they talked about London and Devon, and surprisingly

Catherine enjoyed herself; it was good to have some intelligent conversation and Toby behaved himself. Catherine and Lisa cleared away while Daniel and Toby got started on a bottle of Cognac.

Later, when Daniel crawled into bed smelling of spirits and cigarettes, Catherine sat up and switched on the light.

'Don't invite him here again,' she said. 'Earlier, he was all over me in the kitchen.'

'That's just Toby,' Daniel said. 'He was mucking around. Can't you take a joke?'

'Jesus, is that all you can say? I don't know how Lisa can put up with it. Why she hasn't left him years ago is beyond me.'

'I'm not sure you understand Toby, darling. There's a lot more to him than the surface fluff.'

'That's what worries me. What lies beneath the veneer.'

'The same artifice didn't worry you when we met.' Daniel slipped a hand under the covers and ran his fingers up Catherine's thigh. He smiled his sexy, boyish smile. 'You wanted to explore the deepest recesses.'

'I *liked* you. I don't like Toby. He's creepy. How any woman can stand to be with him, I just don't know.'

'Look, Toby helped me back in London, didn't he? He was there when I needed a friend to talk to.'

'You had me,' Catherine said, offended the support she'd provided was being overlooked. 'Wasn't I good enough?'

'Of course. I couldn't have got through those months without you, but Toby helped too. Having a beer with him and talking about the old times, joshing about, going for bike rides. That kind of thing really took my mind off the other stuff.'

'Just because he helped you, doesn't make the way he treats Lisa OK.'

'Can we stop talking about Toby?' Daniel's hand wandered higher up Catherine's thigh, fingers probing. 'In fact, can we just stop talking?'

Catherine clicked the light off and the room was plunged into darkness as Daniel snuggled up to her, his breath full of alcohol and tobacco, her thoughts full of Toby's grasping hands.

Chapter Sixteen

I've heard talk that seventy is the new fifty, but now I've reached that age I can tell you it's not. Seventy is seventy. Aching limbs and memories and more pills to take than there are hours in the day. Not much to look forward to neither.

I don't know if I believe in heaven or God or the devil, but I do believe there's something out there. Something good and something evil. Like there's a necessity to have opposites. There's light and there's dark. There's good people and there's wrong 'uns. Of course, it ain't so simple as that. Folks fluctuate. They'll be good in the morning and the afternoon, but right around six o'clock they might get a temper on 'em that'll last for a couple of hours until they calm down. However, you can average it out. Mostly I reckon we're made up of about nine parts good to one part bad. In some it's worse. Eight to two. Maybe seven to three. But circumstances can change a man. Push him one way or another. He might go wrong for a year, but he'll usually come back. Occasionally though you get people right at the extremes. Saints and tyrants or angels and monsters.

I don't know how you deal with the bad ones. Mass murderers. Terrorists. Men who take a life because it turns them on. God says thou shalt not kill, but I'm not sure how you square the sixth commandment with wars and the like.

If you ask me, I'd say them Murrin boys were a mixed-up combination of tyrants and monsters. They got the tyrant gene from their father, but where the monster part of them came from, Lord only knows. They were just bad from inside to out, and evil ran through them like the writing on a stick of pink rock. Doesn't matter whereabouts you break the candy, the same stuff is written there. I don't know if they started bad from the outset or if they became that way. If it weren't from the start, then you couldn't blame it on a lack of intelligence or education, 'cos them boys were clever like their dad. Couldn't be blamed on poverty neither. The Murrins owned half a dozen tenanted farms and several houses in the village, meaning they had money enough to make most folks jealous. That didn't stop them raising hell though, and since Sergeant Jencks was in old Murrin's pocket, the boys did what they liked without fear or consequence.

When it was all over, when the boys were dead and gone, part of me began to wonder if it wasn't to do with the place they lived. With World's End Farm itself. Just as candy bought from a seaside resort has a word written all the way through it, could the same apply to the granite beneath the house? That being the case, I got to reconsidering. Did the Murrin family stand a chance? Perhaps their minds were formed from the outset. They were just going to be bad and there was nothing God or anyone could do about it.

Now, of course, World's End is no longer abandoned and I'm no longer free to wander round and peer in the broken windows. Think about what happened. Harbour those regrets which will stick with me until my last moments. Long ago a builder renovated the place. A couple moved in, had children, moved on. Then another. I've lost count now, but a removal lorry arrives roughly every five years to load up a family's dreams and transport them away. One lot lasted six months, while another managed seven years, but the latter were the exception which proves the rule. Five years at World's End is enough for anyone.

Funny, that. My pa was right all along. About the five years.

Chapter Seventeen

October had promised gales, but they never came. November was usually calm, but the wind blew out of the west for two weeks solid. You could expect the first hard frosts in December, but the weather was a mild as a warm April. A trio of daffodils flowered at the side of the lane and trees budded. A swarm of insects clouded the air above the cattle trough in the top meadow. Foster did his rounds and muttered to himself.

'Something's not right, Jess,' he said as he stomped into the kitchen, sweaty from a bout of knocking in fence posts. 'The weather's fucked. It's a bad omen, I reckon.'

Earlier he'd set a leg of mutton to stew, and at eleven he'd added carrots and potatoes. Now, at lunch time, he stirred the whole lot round and sniffed the stew. Ten minutes later he was using half a spud to mop up the remains from a cracked plate, while Jess sat at the edge of the table with her head raised.

'You'll get the rest,' Foster said, nodding at the pot where the bone lay deep in the soupy sauce. 'And then we'd best finish that fence.'

With the washing up done, Foster went back outside and returned to the top meadow. He spent a couple of hours banging in some more fence posts until there was a neat line running up the hillside towards the lane. A roll of sheep netting lay ready to be uncoiled and stapled to the posts, but first there was a gatepost to dig in and brace. Dang it, Foster thought, why did he always save the worst job till last?

Soon he was wielding a shovel and crowbar, first digging away the thin layer of topsoil and then using the bar to smash down into the underlying rock. Bit by bit the hole deepened until he was lying on his front groping in the bottom for the last bits of shale. Jess lay close by, entranced by Foster's missing arm.

'There.' Foster extracted a handful of dirt and chucked it onto a pile of spoil. Jess snapped at the flying debris. 'We're done.'

He lay on the ground. The afternoon had gone, the light getting dimpsy, but there was just enough time to backfill the hole before it got dark. Foster straightened, placing a hand at the base of his spine as he rose to his feet. He blinked, feeling a giddiness sweep over him.

'Better get that post in, ol' girl,' he said. 'Give me something to lean on.'

The post was an old railway sleeper, thick with weeping tar. He figured it had been bedded on some branch line for thirty years and once in the ground would last another thirty for sure. Foster bent to the post so as to heave it over to the hole. As he did so, he spotted an object out of the corner of his eye. A car in the lane down near World's End Farm. Hideous pink. Like the rear end of a young ewe about to come into season.

'Bloody hell.' Foster abandoned the sleeper and straightened once more, this time the giddiness all but gone, replaced by a sense of wonder at the stupidity of man. 'A vag on wheels. Now I've seen it all. Strewth.'

He watched as the car climbed the hill away from the valley. In the dusk, the taillights glowed red, and when the car crested the ridge he could see the people inside silhouetted against the evening sky. *Four* people. The couple had visitors and were going out for the evening, likely as not to have dinner in Chagford, a little town a few miles away, otherwise known as London on the Moor.

They'd be gone for a while, Foster thought, three or four hours. Filling their faces with overpriced food and talking, talking, talking. Those types of people didn't know the value of silence. They used ten words where one'd do. Most things in life, he'd found, were pretty simple, but there was a class of folk who tried to overcomplicate everything. The vag car was a case in point. What the fuck was wrong with red or blue or white or black?

Foster picked up his tools, took them over to the tractor, and loaded them into the transport box. He'd come back tomorrow to put the post in the ground and hang the gate. Meantime there was the opportunity for some more mischief making down at World's End.

'Scurry on now,' Foster said to himself as he climbed up into the tractor and started it up. 'And enjoy your dinner. Be a surprise waiting for you when you return.'

Back in the farmyard, he parked the tractor and went inside and put on an extra layer of clothing. Despite the warmth of the day, the air was cooling fast. When he emerged from the house again, Jess was at his heels.

'Grand,' he said. He sniffed the air. Cool but dry. Perhaps the weather was beginning to align itself with the correct season. There just might be a frost by morning. 'Come on.'

He'd hung the dead rabbit round the back of an old pigsty. A week ago Foster had spotted the animal grazing on a row of carrot tops in the vegetable garden. He'd crept to within ten paces. Then he'd pulled out his knife, flicked the blade open, and thrown it.

As it flashed in the light, he remembered a summer day by a brook. A patch of moss and his two brothers, Jimmy and Martin. Foster had been eleven or twelve. Roundabouts that. They all took turns throwing their knives at the moss from three paces. Then five. Then ten. The trick was to make sure the knife spun the correct number of times so the blade would dig in. Foster had been the youngest and he'd managed to succeed once at five paces. Martin went out to twenty and tried from there. Foster remembered seeing the knife in Martin's hand and a second later, as if by magic, the bone handle lay poking from the moss.

'Practice,' Martin said. 'Nothing to do with luck, but not much is.'

As a lad, Foster had returned many times to the same spot on the moor. Throw, retrieve, throw, retrieve, throw, retrieve. Eventually he'd matched his eldest brother's feat, but when he'd boasted about it, Martin had dismissed him.

'Moss? Easy. You go and sit in the barn and see if you can stick a rat.'

So Foster had. One rat, two rats, and after a week, more than a dozen. He'd lined the corpses up for his brother's approval and this time Martin had been full of praise for the young Joe.

'Good lad. See what you can do if you put your mind to it?'

A month later, just shy of his nineteenth birthday, Martin was gone. He'd rolled the tractor while harrowing the top field, broken his neck. Sixty years later and Martin wasn't much more than a whisper of memory; but Foster still had his brother's bone-handled flick knife.

As he approached the pigsty, he had to put a hand to his nose. A week hanging in the warm weather had left the rabbit crawling with maggots and the stench was horrendous. It was a perfect present to welcome the four diners home. He dropped the rabbit in a bin liner and put the liner in his rucksack.

He took the old drovers' way to World's End, the dog at his heels. A path cut down between high banks, thin branches looming overhead and curving to form a tunnel. In the summer the leaves blotted out the sky, but now the bare branches were like skeletal fingers linking together. The path dropped down the hill and forged deeper below the landscape. For hundreds of years people had come this way across the moor, heading to the local town with sheep or cattle or geese. Their carts had carved ruts into the stone bedrock, leaving traces that would last for centuries.

'Not your paws, Jess,' Foster grunted. 'Nor my feet. We'll be dead in the ground and not a mark left behind.'

He swished through the leaves that had accumulated in the dip, the dog bounding along beside him. When they emerged from the end of the drovers' track, a moon had risen over the moor to the east. Big and full, the light cast Foster's shadow onto the ground, and when he lifted a hand to his face he could see the hairs and wrinkles clear as day.

As he crossed the final field and arrived at the stone wall surrounding the house, he stopped. There was a glow from a ground-floor window. He inched forwards and put one hand on the gate.

'You stay here,' he said, waving the dog into a 'down' position.

The latch on the gate clanked, and he opened it and walked across to the front of the house until he was a few strides from the window.

The curtains were open, and he could see the light came from a lamp in one corner of the room. A low coffee table stood next to a sofa. Magazines lay in a neat stack, a remote control for the TV beside the magazines. The cushions on the sofa had been plumped up and arranged: blue, white, blue, white, blue.

'Definitely not here, Jess,' Foster said. He made a low whistle and the dog trotted across to him. 'They've gone out, but the daft buggers have left a light on. More money than sense, right?'

He strode over towards the barn. For what he'd come for. Despite what he'd said to the woman, he didn't think much of the conversion. It was a tidy job alright, but it was a job which should never have been done. As with the drovers' track, there were traces in the old barn.

The moonlight bathed the front elevation with white light. There was a large window and to one side a door. He tried the door, but it was locked. Bugger.

'That won't stop us, Jess.' The dog made a little whine, almost as if she didn't approve of what Foster was about to do. 'Sorry, 'tis the only way. I've been meaning to leave a little surprise in here ever since they moved in.'

Foster went to over to where a pile of unused stone had been piled up. He selected a rock the size of a brick and returned to the door. He hefted the rock and the glass shattered, tinkling down onto the floor inside. He reached through, undid the latch, and went in, closing the door behind him.

Then he stopped. There was a pale woman standing in the middle of the room. No, not so much a woman, more a girl. What's more, she was naked, at least her top half. Small, pert breasts, shining like ivory in the wan light from the moon.

'Christ!' Foster staggered to one side, clutching at the wall for support. Nausea washed up from his stomach. He caught his breath, not quite believing what he was seeing. He always expected to find memories at World's End, yes, but ghosts? He sucked in air and straightened. The woman hadn't moved. 'Helena?'

Even as he said her name he realised he was mistaken; this was no ghost. As far as he knew, Helena wasn't dead, but perhaps this was another trace. Helena had left a part of herself behind and now she was going to punish him for what happened all those years ago.

Foster froze, expecting the figure to float across to him, her expression to turn to rage, her fingernails to claw at him like some demented harpy, but the woman remained in the same spot, her eyes blank and empty.

He took another gulp of air and tried to calm himself. He scanned the shadows. Next to the girl there was a large, sphinx-like cat. To one side, perched on a table, an eagle with wings spread wide. On the other side, atop a workbench, a squirrel appeared to be scurrying towards him. Only it wasn't. Like the woman and the other animals, the squirrel didn't move.

Foster scrabbled at the wall, his fingers finding a switch. He flicked it on and the room was flooded with light. Then he began to laugh.

'Statues,' he said, the laugh growing into a full belly ripper. 'Of course, she's a bloody sculptor, isn't she?'

The room was some sort of studio and everywhere he looked there were figures in marble and granite. The workbench contained an array of chisels and mallets, and now the light was on he could see the squirrel's tail was square and angular and had yet to be carved. The woman was a graceful form in marble, her skin smooth, her hair long. Solidified in white stone, there was no way she could be mistaken for Helena.

Outside, Jess gave a yap and Foster came back to his senses. He wasn't here to admire the artworks. He hefted the old haversack from his shoulders, placed it on the floor, and straightened, giddy again. His vision blurred and, when his eyes cleared, what he saw astonished him.

'Oh fuck!' He peered up towards the ceiling where an array of bright spotlights shone amongst the internal beams. Vast pieces of oak spanned the space above his head and locked the A frames in place. A chill crept over his skin. No, it couldn't be.

Foster picked up his rucksack and made for the door. He called for the dog as he stumbled across the gravel driveway and he didn't look back until he was halfway up the hill to home.

Chapter Eighteen

Much to Catherine's relief, Daniel and Toby spent most of Saturday out on the moor on their mountain bikes. While they were gone, she wandered the bounds of World's End with Lisa and showed her the workshop. Lisa was entranced with an abstract piece Catherine had recently completed.

'Totally original,' she said. 'It would look so good in our front room.'

Catherine explained the work had been commissioned and was spoken for.

'Shame,' Lisa said. 'Perhaps when Toby receives his next advance we could get our own commission, yes?'

Catherine muttered a non-committal response; the last thing she wanted was to have any more to do with Toby.

The boys returned home in the middle of the afternoon, splattered with mud and full of tales of biking bravado. After they'd cleaned themselves up, Lisa drove the four of them to Chagford where they'd reserved a table at a well-regarded gastro-pub. An attractive waitress with a nice smile came over with a menu. She stared at Daniel for longer than was necessary and fumbled her words when she spoke. She scuttled away, and Catherine could see her blurting out something to the barman.

'Famous, you lucky bugger,' Toby said. He winked. 'Pity you're not able to take advantage.'

'It's not funny, Toby,' Daniel said. He looked round the pub. 'I mean, we're in the middle of bloody nowhere and I still can't escape. I'm well over my allotted fifteen minutes of fame and I've had enough.'

'It's *because* we're in the middle of nowhere. The yokels are so bored out of their minds that when any Z-lister comes in, it's major news.'

'Thanks, a Z-lister now, am I?'

'You can't have it both ways, mate, but don't worry; the next time I visit, you'll be in the presence of the one and only Mr Toby Paget, a household name and an A-rated celebrity. You won't even be noticed.'

When the waitress returned with a tray of drinks, she served them with another smile, but her hand trembled as she placed a pint of lager in front of Daniel.

The conversation over dinner skirted round the incident in London. Even Toby wasn't so tactless to dwell on it. Later though, when they'd reconvened to the armchairs round the fire, his concern appeared heartfelt.

'It's helped, right?' he said, his voice beginning to sound a little slurred. 'Moving away from the city and out here? You've been able to work things through in your mind and balance the books. You've — how can I put it? — resolved your issues?'

'Not yet, but I'm getting there.'

Catherine sat back in her chair and listened, not quite believing what she was hearing. Daniel was opening up, talking to Toby like he hardly ever talked to her. Perhaps it was the alcohol or the tiredness from a day out biking across the moor, perhaps it was just that they were old friends. Whatever, Daniel was leaning forwards, eager to share the misery he'd been living with.

'So, it's like you've got some hideous disease. You saw the way the waitress reacted? I'm a psychopathic nutter who batters innocent people to death.'

'You're not a psychopath, sweetheart,' Catherine said. 'And the burglar wasn't innocent.'

'But that's what everyone believes. If I can snap once, I can snap again. Bam, bam, bam, and the waitress is lying in pool of blood on the floor.'

Toby leaned in too. 'And will you snap again?'

'To be honest, I don't know. Given the same set of circumstances, the same amount of stress, I guess I might.'

'That's enough.' Catherine put her hand out and touched Daniel's knee. 'You've been over this dozens of times and it doesn't help.'

'It's helping me.' Toby grinned. 'Helping me to decide if my old mate might beat me over the head and eat my brains for breakfast.'

Toby laughed at his own joke, but Daniel appeared uneasy. Catherine could see the conversation had unsettled him.

'Perhaps it would be better if we moved onto another topic,' Daniel said. 'But thanks, Toby. For listening.'

'That's what friends are for, right?' Toby shrugged and brightened. 'Hey, someone told me this neat thing the other day. Want to hear it?'

'Sure, Toby,' Catherine said, hoping to move the conversation on.

'It's the definition of a true friend.' He was animated now, putting on a show. The old Toby. 'I'm sure we can all agree a true friend will help whatever the circumstances, yes? They won't judge or lecture, they'll just listen and support you. They'll be there for you no matter what sort of trouble you're in. I guess that's the way I feel about Dan, and I hope the feeling's reciprocated.'

'Nothing controversial about that,' Daniel said.

'No, not at all, but here's the rub: a true friend would help you bury a corpse without asking questions. Say I turn up at your place in the middle of the night with a stiff in the boot of my car, would you help me?' Toby nodded to Daniel. 'No questions asked?'

'Well, it depends on—'

'No, Dan!' Toby reached across the table and held Daniel's wrist. He was drunk now, Catherine could tell, but his eyes were alert. 'No questions asked. That's the point. You either help or you don't.'

'But say it was a kid in the boot. Say you were a paedophile or a rapist. I wouldn't want to help you then.'

'Hopefully you wouldn't be friends with a paedophile. See where we're going with this?'

'Shall we order a coffee?' Catherine asked. She'd been hoping for a discussion about politics or a piece of literary gossip that Toby had picked up from Barry Henderson at the agency. Perhaps him droning on about his book deal. Not this. 'I'll get them.'

Daniel ignored her and instead hunched towards Toby. 'You're saying if I'm your friend, I should trust you'd have a good reason for having a corpse in the boot of the car?'

'Exactly. A bloody good reason.' Toby smiled. 'There's even a name for a friend like that, you know? A dead body buddy. I like to think you're my dead body buddy, Dan.'

'Jesus,' Daniel said. 'I might be, but don't risk it. Anyway, you'd struggle to fit anything in the boot of *your* car.'

'I'd cut them up.' Toby winked at Catherine. 'With a chainsaw.'

'Let's have those coffees,' Lisa said, meeting Catherine's gaze and scraping back her chair and rising. 'How do you want them?'

'I don't.' Toby pushed himself up too. 'Get me a whisky, I'm going for a slash.'

With both Lisa and Toby gone, Catherine perched on the edge of her armchair and reached out for her husband.

'We should go after this,' she said. 'You've had too much to drink and you're tired.'

'For fuck's sake, Cathy, I'm not a kid.' Daniel brushed her hand away. 'If I want to talk about what happened I will. Toby's from way back and he understands me at least as well as you do.'

'I know and it's good to talk, but perhaps we should move onto another subject.'

'What do you suggest? The state of the criminal justice system? Home security? Head injuries?'

'Dan, all I—'

She was interrupted by a clash of breaking glass. She turned to look for the source of the sound. Over by the bar area, the waitress knelt and began to pick up the pieces of a wine bottle from the floor. Toby stood nearby, hands raised. A man in a shirt and tie — the manager Catherine guessed — appeared and remonstrated with the girl.

'It wasn't my fault,' she said to the manager. She glared at Toby. 'He fucking groped me. What do you expect me to do, just stand there and let him put his hands in my knickers?'

'Shush, let's keep this down.' The manager waved his hands and turned to Toby. 'Sir, would you mind coming into the office with me?'

'I'm good, thank you,' Toby said. He started to walk away. He spoke over his shoulder. 'It was a simple misunderstanding.'

'No it wasn't,' the waitress shouted after him. 'He can't be allowed to get away with it.'

The manager wafted his arms again and followed Toby over. Toby dropped into his armchair and reached for a half-empty wine glass. He necked the contents as the manager placed a hand on his shoulder.

'I'm going to have to ask you to leave. I'll have your bill made up and brought over.'

'What about her?' Toby turned his head to where the waitress was having a heated conversation with the barman.

'I'm going to add a hundred-pound tip. I assume you're OK with that? If you're not, then I'm afraid I'll have to call the police.'

'That's fucking outrageous.' Toby put his wine glass down. He gave Catherine a wink. 'Still, I assume for that amount of money I'll get her phone number?'

'Toby!' Daniel grabbed Toby by the arm. 'Let's just shut up, pay the bill, and get out of here.'

'You're with him, are you?' The manager looked at Daniel and froze. It was as if he'd seen a ghost. 'Do I know you from somewhere?'

Daniel sighed. 'You've probably seen me on TV.'

'On TV...?' The manager paused as if he was mentally ticking off names from a list of celebrities. He shook his head. 'No, that's not it.'

'Come on.' Toby took a wad of notes from his wallet. He pressed them into the manager's hand. 'This will more than cover it. And tell the tart she wasn't worth ten let alone a hundred.'

Catherine was already out of her seat. She saw Lisa returning from the toilets, so she moved to intercept her and led her towards the door. A chair tipped and fell to the floor as Toby and the manager scuffled.

'What's going on?' Lisa said, looking back.

'Your husband's going on, I'm afraid.' Catherine took Lisa's arm and guided her outside, and they headed up the street to where they'd parked. 'Let's just get to the car.'

They walked down the road and got in the Jag. A minute later Daniel and Toby appeared. They both slipped into the rear seats.

'Fucking hey, that was brilliant, right?' Toby said. 'Thought the local boys were going to lynch us for a moment.'

Catherine turned to the back as Lisa started the car. 'You piece of shit. I don't want you ever visiting us again, understand? How a grown man can behave the way you do I just don't know.'

'I wos 'aving a laff, darlin', alwight?'

'You call sexually assaulting a young girl a laugh?'

'I touched her leg and she was as up for it as I was until she dropped the wine bottle. Then she had to cover up her mistake by crying wolf.'

'Toby, you are one of the most despicable human beings I've ever had the misfortune to meet.'

'Bit harsh. What do you reckon, Daniel?'

'I reckon we've both drunk too much,' Daniel answered. 'We should probably just shut up.'

'Shut up. Yes. Bloody good idea.'

The journey back from the pub took place in near silence. Lisa drove and Toby and Daniel lay slumped in the back. Catherine sat in the front passenger seat and followed the beams of the car's headlights as they painted the twisting lanes. Every now and then she gave directions to Lisa, but nobody else said a word.

'We're here,' she said as Lisa swung off the lane and rolled the car down the track.

'Nightcap would be nice.' Toby's plaintive voice came from the rear. 'Cup of tea, even.'

He sounded like a little child who'd been told off, Catherine thought, not a grown man who was a sex pest. She ignored him as they climbed out of the car.

'Are you planning on working late?' Toby again. He looked at Catherine before gesturing over towards the barn. 'Only I'm not sure I could rustle up much for you if you want me nude.'

She resisted the urge to snap and instead followed Toby's gaze. The door to the barn stood open and light blazed from inside.

'Cath?' Daniel was beside her. 'Did you leave the door open?'

Earlier, Catherine had shown Lisa round the workshop, but she was sure she'd locked up.

'No, I didn't,' she said. 'Somebody's been here.'

'Daniel will sort it.' Toby pushed Daniel in the back. 'Best man to have beside you when you're in a spot of bother.'

'Shut the fuck up, Toby.' Daniel shrugged off his friend and walked over to the barn. Catherine followed.

'Shouldn't we call the police?' Catherine said. She could see the glass panel in the door had been smashed and was counting the cost in hundreds of hours of work lost should any of her pieces be missing.

Daniel glanced at her. He pointed into the workshop and his hand went to his mouth almost theatrically. 'This is appalling.'

At first, Catherine couldn't see what the problem was. In the centre of the workshop stood a figure she'd just finished. The statue was three-quarters life size, a woman, naked aside from a modest robe which covered her lower half. But it wasn't the statue which had shocked Daniel, it was what was hanging above. A thick rope, looped in a noose and rising to the beam overhead.

'What is it?' Toby stood at the entrance. He'd sobered somewhat but could only gawk in astonishment at what he saw. 'Bloody hell.'

'I think you *should* phone the police.' Lisa's voice came from behind Toby. 'Now.'

Inside the house, Lisa took control. Daniel and Toby were too pissed to be useful, so she shooed them to the living room and made a pot of strong coffee. She gave Catherine a hug and stood beside her.

'I've got Constable Jencks' number,' Catherine said. 'He's a local bobby who came round the previous time.'

'This has happened before?'

'Yes.' Catherine explained about the guts on the doorstep and the rats in the kitchen.

'And the police did nothing?'

'They visited, but that was it.'

'Did you tell them it was a hate crime?'

'Hardly that, Lisa,' Toby said. 'I mean Daniel's not black, Catherine's not a rug muncher and, as far as I know, neither of them own a fucking prayer mat.'

'For God's sake, Toby, grow up.' Lisa. Uncharacteristically angry, a scowl on her face. 'Can't you see how distressing this is for Daniel and Catherine?'

'Sorry.' Toby hung his head. 'Well and truly pissed. Thought a little humour might help. Obviously wrong about that.'

'What do you mean by, "a hate crime", Lisa?' Catherine said.

'I don't know.' Lisa shrugged. 'Perhaps I'm wrong. It just feels as if this is prejudice.'

'We're an oppressed minority group, are we?' Daniel said. 'Londoners?'

'Not Londoners in particular: incomers, immigrants, foreigners. It doesn't look like the locals care much for outsiders.'

'The thing is,' Toby said. 'Is it outsiders in general, or one person in particular?' He put his arm round Daniel. 'By which, Danny boy, I mean you.'

Chapter Nineteen

Foster rose early and fed the livestock. He was back in the house and enjoying a fry up when the door knocker rapped out a triple beat. Jess barked and scampered to the back door.

'Who the blazes is that?' Foster scraped back his chair and considered the untouched fried egg. He was saving it for last and now it would spoil. The knocker clattered again. 'Alright, alright. What's the bloody rush?'

The back door opened to reveal a uniformed police officer. The man's nose hooked over thin lips and there was a blotch of pale skin on the cheek near the left ear. A stain or a mark.

'Sergeant Jencks?' Foster blinked and rubbed his eyes. It couldn't be. The man must have retired years ago. Retired or died if fortune was favouring good folk.

'It's Constable *Brian* Jencks, Mr Foster,' the officer said. 'Every time I come here you make the same mistake, confusing me with my father. I do look a little like him.'

'Right,' Foster said. Jencks was a bloody doppelganger, a chip off the old block, the poor fuck. The elder Jencks had been a right pain, always poking his nose in where it wasn't wanted. 'I remember now. Your father.'

'Yes.' Jencks flattened his lips together. 'I've got some questions for you about World's End Farm. What happened down there.'

'What happened down there was for the best. The Murrins had what was coming to them and those boys deserved to—'

'I don't mean back then, I mean now.'

'*Now?*' Foster crossed his arms and folded them. 'I don't know what you're talking about.'

'Do you deny you've been down there?'

'Of course I've been down there. I went to be neighbourly, didn't I?'

'You went to try and scare them away, just like you've done with everyone who's moved in there in the past thirty years.'

'Nonsense.'

'It's not nonsense, Foster. There's been a break-in at World's End. An intruder managed to get into the barn. They smashed the glass on the door to gain access.'

'You mean the workshop?'

'The barn's where it happened, Foster, and you bloody know it.' Jencks' right eye twitched.

'The barn then. Did they take anything?'

'I'm not talking about the break-in, I'm talking about the Murrin boys.'

'You're getting in a muddle, Jencks. Which crime are you trying to pin on me? One that happened recently or an event from way back when you were a nipper? Make your mind up.'

'You were fucking involved. My father knew you were and now so do I.' Jencks' voice was raised and there was the eye again. Blinking as if a speck had wedged itself beneath the eyelid.

'It's done. Over. Those boys are buried six feet under. Your father investigated and found nothing.'

'He was met by a wall of silence. Nobody from round here would open their bloody mouths.'

'Not surprising. Most of the village celebrated.' Foster sighed. 'Anyway, t'was half my lifetime ago. There's no point going over it all again.'

'Everyone still talks about it down at the station. The case was never closed. I take the files out a couple of times a year, just to keep familiar.'

More like every week, Foster thought. Take them out and jerk off over them probably. 'Maybe you should let it lie. Might be better for your constitution.'

'The break-in.' Jencks wiped his forehead and flicked his hand.

Even though it was a cool morning, there were droplets of sweat on his fingers. 'Let's get back to that. What do you know about it?'

'Like I said, I ain't been down there since they moved in.'

'You're lying, Foster, just as you lied all those years ago. That's what my father told me. You knew stuff, but you didn't tell. That's right, isn't it?'

'Have it your way. I don't see how any of that is related to your break-in.'

'There was a rope.' Jencks shuffled closer, his face just inches from Foster's. 'A piece of rope had been tied in a noose and led up over the beam. *The very beam*, do you hear me?'

'So?' Foster tried to appear calm, but inside he was burning up. Jencks had understood the message too.

'Don't mess with me, Foster. Did you do that as a joke?'

'I didn't do anything.' Foster crossed his heart. 'On my mother's grave.'

'You're a lying fucker!' Jencks reached out and held the front of Foster's shirt. He clenched his fists and shook Foster back and forth. Then all of a sudden he let go, realising he'd gone too far. He turned and marched away and stopped in the middle of the yard. 'If I catch you within half a mile of that place, I'll have you, understand?'

'Sure.' Foster shut the door and went back into the kitchen. The egg was stone-cold and slimy, so he picked up the plate and held it down low. Jess came across and gobbled the egg down in one go and gave the plate a lick. 'There you go, girl.'

Foster put the plate on the drainer and went and sat in the armchair next to the range. He tilted his head back so he could see out the window. Jencks was driving off, the police car passing the sheep shed and heading up the lane. As the car disappeared, Foster had an overwhelming sense of foreboding. A wet sensation brushed his hand and he looked down to see the dog snuffling his fingers.

'You know something's wrong, old girl.' Foster shook his head. 'Me too, but I'm buggered if I can fathom out what the heck's going on.'

The mystery was the rope of course. Hanging there with a noose tied at one end. There was he, breaking in to cause mischief, and somebody had switched it round. Given him the scare of his life. But the door to the barn had been locked so whoever put the rope up there must have had a key. Not only that, but they must have known all about what happened at World's End half a lifetime ago.

Chapter Twenty

The weekend with Toby and Lisa was soured by the break-in and the couple left soon after breakfast on Sunday. Catherine had all but forgotten what a complete wanker Toby was, and as for Lisa, well, she'd been a trooper. There was an inner strength to the woman which had revealed itself in the way she'd reacted after they'd found the noose. She'd even managed to rein in the worst of Toby's excesses, and Catherine wondered if she'd misjudged the state of the couple's relationship. As they'd left, she'd taken Lisa to one side and embraced her.

'Here, I want you to have this.' Catherine handed Lisa a heavy bubble-wrapped package. 'It's not the piece you had your eye on but perhaps it will do for now.'

'Oh, Cath,' Lisa said. 'That's amazing.'

'And if there's ever anything I can do.' Catherine looked over to where Daniel and Toby were loading the luggage into the Jag. 'You know…'

'Thanks. Toby's Toby. I'll cope.'

As the Jag cruised up the track away from World's End, Catherine hoped she would.

After they'd gone she went out to buy some groceries, and when she returned she found Daniel working on the broken pane in the workshop door.

'Your policeman called round,' he said. 'Not that he reassured me much. Never met such an odd fellow in my life. He took all of three minutes to check the workshop and then buggered off.'

'Perhaps he recognised you,' Catherine said. 'Decided to go for back up.'

'No, he didn't have a clue.' Daniel chipped at a piece of glass in the frame and looked up. 'To be honest, we might have overreacted. Being drunk and all. I guess it was just vandalism, nothing more.'

'Dan, what the heck's got into you?' Catherine stood by the door, not believing what she was hearing. 'There was a noose. It was a warning of some kind. Get out or you die!'

'You're being melodramatic, Cath.'

'Melodramatic? What about the other stuff? The intestines and the rats?'

'This will be the end of it. There won't be any other incidents. I can promise you that.'

'What are you talking about? Jencks told me every new occupant was hassled until they moved out.'

'We're different, you'll see.' Daniel went back to chipping at the glass. The conversation was over.

In the days that followed they argued several times. She wanted to move away, back to London, whereas he didn't. She thought they'd given country living a fair shot, he disagreed. She felt the strain was affecting their relationship, he couldn't see it.

One morning, she stood at the kitchen window as the rain slatted down over the dank and colourless moor. When Daniel shuffled into the kitchen for breakfast, she tried to explain herself yet again.

'Look at the place,' she said. 'It's always pouring or blowing a gale or both. There's something wrong here. Remember what the policeman told me about the others? They were all made to leave.'

'Nonsense. The other day there was an article in the paper explaining that people move house on average every six years. It's just a coincidence. Jencks has got a chip on his shoulder and won't let it go. I guess there's so little crime round here he needs to invent a story to keep busy.'

'This type of place is supposed to be a forever home. You don't just get up and leave unless there's a reason. Well now we've got one.'

'Love, wait until the spring. This will seem like our forever home by then, I promise. You'll change your mind, you'll see.'

'I will have *lost* my mind by then, Dan. I'm going crazy here, especially when you're away. I thought the whole point of moving was to be able to spend more time together?'

'It's always like this at the end of a project, you know that.'

'I'm frightened when I'm alone.'

'Then we should get a dog.'

'Be serious. The guts, the rats, and the noose. Someone out there wants to do us harm.'

Daniel was silent for a beat. 'Look, in January I need to go away for a few days, after which I'll be here for several months. I won't have to go to London aside from the occasional meeting, and I can do that without staying overnight.'

'Promise?'

'Yes, I promise.' Daniel touched Catherine on the cheek. 'And when the spring arrives, if you're still not happy, then we'll have to see about moving again.'

'Honestly?'

'Yes, but it won't come to that, not once the days start getting longer. Spring comes early down this part of the world. Before you know it, the trees will be budding and the sun will be warming our backs.' Daniel shrugged. 'Now, I'm going to go down to the village to post a letter and pop into town to get some printer paper. Do you want to come?'

'No.' Catherine said. 'I need to press on with my new piece.'

Daniel nodded and left the room. Five minutes later the front door clicked shut and she heard Daniel's car start and head up the track to the lane.

She made herself a cup of coffee and took it to the living room. As she drank the coffee she looked across to the bookshelf where there was a photograph of her and Daniel on holiday. Bodrum, wasn't it? Somewhere in Turkey anyway. Happy days before the burglar had broken into their house, before a piece of Daniel had broken. She wasn't sure the damage could be completely repaired, but if it could, perhaps she was being unreasonable about wanting to return to

London. Could it be that World's End might restore his sanity?

This will seem like our forever home...

Daniel had told her his heart was here and yet, as she scanned the room, she wasn't sure he was telling the truth. Either side of the inglenook hung a picture. Watercolours of Dartmoor which she'd purchased. In one corner there was a designer lamp which had come from an upmarket Scandinavian store. Her choice, her credit card. The sofa and armchairs they'd brought from London, but she'd selected the material for the curtains, and the occasional table over by the window she'd found in an antique shop in Exeter. The bookshelf the same. She took another sip of coffee and put the cup down on the table.

She strolled to the window. In the open-fronted garage there was a space beside the 4x4 where Daniel's car was usually parked. But the car and Daniel were gone. Absent.

She went into the hallway where her shoes tapped the blue slate floor which she'd sourced. In the kitchen, the units had been down to her, the layout too. She thought about the soft furnishings in their bedroom and the design and styling of the bathroom, the ensuite, and the under-the-stairs shower room. They'd had the garden remodelled to her specifications. The garage and workshop plans had been drawn up by an architect, but it had taken him three tries before Catherine had been satisfied with the elevations he produced.

She felt a draught blow across her. Daniel was strong-willed, dominant even, and yet here she was listing all the choices she'd made and he'd gone along with. Despite his claims of how much he loved the house, his emotional investment appeared to be minimal.

She left the kitchen and went upstairs. She stood on the landing and let out a long breath before opening the door to Daniel's studio. The place was a mess. Post-It notes on the edge of the monitor screens. Scraps of paper jotted with chord sequences and rhythm patterns. Coloured markers strewn across the desk. Daniel's guitar was on a stand, but a set of discarded strings had been thrown on the floor.

She nodded to herself. Daniel had chosen the computer desk and the ergonomic chair. They'd brought the shelving from their house in London. He'd been particular about the way the room was set up and quite obsessed with a Venetian blind which hung at one of the windows. He always kept the slats closed, arguing that the barn, with the Dartmoor landscape beyond, was too distracting. However, there was a second window without a blind. He hadn't seemed bothered about the view through that.

When it came to his own room, Daniel had made the decisions, but for the rest of the house he'd left it up to her. At the time she thought he was just being magnanimous or disinterested or lazy. Now she doubted such a simple explanation. There was some other reason he'd been unwilling to touch the blank canvas the house had been.

She went across to the computer chair and sat. The chair was almost like a rocker in the way you could move back and forth. You could swivel too. Never mind the view, she thought, the chair could be distracting for hours. She put her foot on the floor and rocked. She bit her lip.

She leaned back and gazed at the vaulted ceiling. Two rough oak beams bisected the room. Hundreds of little woodworm holes dotted the surface of the beams. Before they'd moved in, all the beams had been stripped of paint and the woodwork treated. Despite her misgivings about World's End, she loved the way the interior looked now. Especially upstairs where you could see the structure of the house exposed. She stared up to where a tie piece ran between the two beams. It always fascinated her how the huge pieces of wood were secured with tiny pegs. She rocked and closed her eyes. Was that the way her relationship with Daniel worked? The whole damn edifice held together with tiny pegs?

Her earlier thoughts about Daniel's lack of input and passion to do with the house made her wonder about his attachment to the place. To her as well. Perhaps moving was simply a ploy to get her away from London, and his words assuring her Gemma was history hadn't been true. She pictured the girl with her legs spread, Daniel between them, a smile on Gemma's face directed not at Daniel, but at Catherine.

She opened her eyes and was about to swing her legs from the desk when a flash of metal near the roof apex caught her attention. A small security box sat wedged in the angle at one end of the tie beam. She recognised the box as one they'd bought years ago but never used. She hadn't seen it when they moved and assumed it had been thrown away.

She peered at the box, trying to imagine what Daniel might want to keep inside and why he'd hidden it up on the beam. She moved her legs from the desk, rocked upright, and stood. She stretched up. The crossbeam was at least an arm's length beyond her fingertips. She looked round. The computer desk was too far away, while the chair had a mesh covering so she couldn't stand on that. She went out onto the landing, trotted downstairs, and returned with a broom.

She stood beneath the crossbeam and lifted the broom handle into the air. She tapped the metal box. It slid sideways and fell from the beam, and as it fell she dropped the broom and held out her hands to catch the box.

Part of her didn't want to look. If Daniel had hidden the box, he obviously didn't want her to see what was inside. She tried to imagine the contents. The box wasn't big, about the size of a hardback book and a couple of inches deep. It could contain photographs. Perhaps old snaps of past lovers. She felt a tinge of jealousy, but if that was the sum of the contents she wouldn't mind. It was other types of photographs she was worried about. Photographs of children for instance. She shuddered. Of course, there could be other items in there. Memorabilia. Jewellery. Items that weren't precious but meant a lot to Daniel.

No use worrying, she told herself, just get on with it.

She sat in the chair with the box on her lap. She clicked the little clasp, surprised to find it wasn't locked, and flipped the lid up. Photographs. Just as she suspected. Then she smiled. Realised Daniel didn't want to keep this from her. Least ways not forever. This was some sort of surprise. The top photograph was an old black-and-white image of World's End Farm. She flipped the picture over, looking for some sort of date. The back was blank apart from a scrawl of pencil in the top right corner: *46/C*.

She put the picture to one side and took out the next one. It was another image of the farm but taken from a slightly different angle. She turned this one over too: *43/E*. She moved on. There were several more pictures. Some of the house, some of the land, some of the track leading from the lane. She frowned. Where had Daniel found these? She had no idea.

More pictures. The house. A wooden stable which no longer existed. The open-fronted barn...

The last picture fell from her hand and fluttered to the floor and she found herself gasping for air. She swallowed and lowered her head to look down at her feet. The picture had fallen face down. She could see the writing on the back: *2/B*. She bent and picked up the picture. She placed it flat on the desk and stared open-mouthed.

The photograph had been taken square on to the front of the barn. Two lengths of rope hung from the huge crossbeam. A man dangled at the end of each rope, their hands tied behind their backs, their feet touching nothing but air.

Chapter Twenty-one

Catherine picked the photo off the desk, slipped off the chair, and sat on the floor. She put the picture at her feet and looked at the image for several minutes. She turned her head to take in the blind that Daniel had insisted remained closed at all times. She understood why now: the view through the window was of the barn.

She returned her attention to the photograph. It had been taken from quite a distance so as to get the whole of the barn in the picture, but there was no doubt the men were dead. The ropes were secured round their necks and their bodies hung limp. There was a look about their faces she couldn't put her finger on. They were young, for sure. Not much older than boys. Late teens or early twenties. She wanted to believe all the photographs had been taken a long, long while ago, but in one shot there'd been a car like the one her dad had owned when she was a child. A round light at either side of a rectangular grill. A slanting hatch at the rear. An Austin Maxi. The picture wasn't recent, but it had been taken within living memory.

She pulled out her phone and snapped a shot. Then she sighed. The shock had gone, replaced by a feeling of inevitability. Now they'd *have* to move. There could be no arguing with it. She couldn't stay knowing two men had died within a stone's throw of where she slept, knowing too that somebody had hung a rope in her workshop as a warning to leave World's End or face the consequences.

She blinked and cocked her head on one side. There'd been a bang from downstairs. Was it the front door? She stuffed the photographs back into the metal box and clicked the lid shut. She peered at the crossbeam. There was no way she could replace the box without a stepladder, so she slid it under the desk. She tiptoed out onto the landing. Crockery chinked in the kitchen. Catherine eased down the stairs. Now she could hear water running into a glass. Whoever was in the kitchen moved to a chair and sat down. She felt a shiver as she thought of Constable Jencks and Joe Foster. Had Jencks returned or was it Foster with a dead animal in his hands?

She paused at the kitchen door. Daniel sat with his back to her. Then he swung round. Blue eyes and lips widening into a smile.

'Catherine,' Daniel said. He clunked the glass down on the table and stood. 'What's wrong, sweetheart? You look like you've seen a ghost.'

'Oh, Dan!' Catherine said. 'Am I glad to see you.'

She ran across the room and flung her arms round her husband. She buried her face in Daniel's chest and held him tight.

'Whatever's the matter? The way you're behaving it's as if I've been gone for weeks, not just an hour or so.'

'You bastard.' Catherine relaxed her grip and pushed herself away. 'Where the hell have you been? Why didn't you call?'

'Call? I was at the Post Office and the supermarket. Why would I need to call?'

'I just—'

'How about lunch? I'm famished.'

'Sure, but...'

Daniel was gone. She heard him hang his coat up in the hallway and then climb the stairs.

She was on autopilot as she filled a pan with water and set it to boil. Found some pasta sauce. Grated some cheese. Took a bundle of dried spaghetti and placed it in the pan. There was a beer in the fridge and she cracked it open. She took a glass from a cupboard and turned to take the beer upstairs. Daniel was standing in the kitchen doorway.

'Have you been in my room?' He held the metal box in one hand. 'Because I found this on the floor.'

'I was...' Catherine poured the beer into the glass and handed the glass to Daniel. 'I was cleaning. Anything to distract myself from getting down to work. I was dusting up round the beams and knocked that down. Sorry, I just left it where it fell. Forgot to pick it up.'

Daniel's voice dropped to a whisper. 'You didn't open it?'

'No, love.' The denial came without a thought as to the consequences. 'I did wonder why it was up on the beam. Is it important?'

'Are you sure you didn't open it?'

'Yes.' Catherine glanced at the hob. Steam was rising from the pan. 'The water.'

'It's just some stuff I had lying around.' Daniel came over to the table and placed the box in the centre. 'I should have thrown it all away.'

'Pictures of old girl friends?' Catherine used a wooden spoon to stir the pasta. 'Love letters?'

'Yes. As I said, it's not important.' Daniel took a swig of his beer and looked her up and down. His gaze met hers. 'Not now I have you.'

Catherine tried to force a smile, but all she could think about was the lie Daniel had just told about the contents of the box.

Chapter Twenty-two

She hardly slept that night. She lay awake listening to the sound of Daniel breathing, wondering how he could sleep so soundly knowing what had happened in the barn. Every time she closed her eyes she saw the men hanging there. Every time she opened her eyes she saw the exposed beams above her head and thought about the rope someone had left in her workshop. Why wasn't Daniel concerned? Why was he hiding the horrors of the barn from her? She determined that if he wasn't going to tell her then she would have to find out for herself. Whatever it took.

In the morning, she realised her opportunity for investigating further was limited. Daniel was head down and working like crazy to finish his movie score. For the next few days he barely left his room except for meals and sleep. Finally, after an all-night stint fuelled by half a dozen cups of coffee, he'd had enough.

'I'm going to take a shower and then go into Exeter to do some mindless shopping,' he said over breakfast. 'I'm almost finished but I need some downtime. Want to come?'

'Not sure.' Catherine tried to sound non-committal as her heart jumped. She made a humming noise and said: 'Actually, not. I want to start sketching out some ideas for a new commission. Is that OK?'

'It's fine.' Daniel yawned. 'I'll be lousy company anyway.'

He took an age to get himself ready and finally leave the house. Catherine stood on the doorstep and waved him off, and as soon as his car reached the lane she dashed back inside. She went upstairs but hesitated outside his room. Did she want to do this? Yes, she thought.

Daniel had lied about the contents of the box. He was the one being distrustful.

She opened the door. The office was neat — a sure sign that Daniel *was* nearly finished since he always tidied up at the end of a project. She stepped in and looked up to the crossbeam. She tilted her head, puzzled. The box wasn't there. She must be mistaken, she thought, or Daniel must have placed it in a slightly different position. She moved sideways to change the angle but couldn't see any better.

She went downstairs and out to the barn to get a stepladder. She brought the ladder inside, placed it beneath the beam, and climbed up. Definitely no box. She climbed down and began to search the room. There were two drawers in the desk. The top contained the usual office fare of paperclips, Sellotape, a couple of writing pads. The bottom drawer was locked. She hunted round for the key, first in the office and then through the rest of the house. After half an hour she'd found several odd keys, but none of them fitted the drawer lock.

That was that. If the box was in the desk, short of breaking the drawer open, she couldn't get to it. Time for plan B. She put on a coat and went outside to the garage. Daniel had gone in the BMW, so she had to take the pickup. The 4x4 started up with a belch of black smoke and a rattle, and it took three attempts to get the gear stick into first, but then she was away, powering up the track.

The village was as dead as one might expect on a winter midweek day. The Post Office was closed and there was nobody about. Catherine parked down the far end and made her way to the church. In the porch she looked at the noticeboard and took out her phone to note down the details of the local history society. Surely they'd know about what had happened at World's End Farm? She was scanning down the poster, searching for some contact details, when she heard a polite cough behind her. She jumped sideways, dropping the phone.

'That's me,' a voice said. 'The name you're looking for.'

Catherine jumped. Peter Carmichael, the vicar, stood next to the church door. It was almost as if he'd magically appeared or passed through the door without opening it.

'Oh!' Catherine put a hand to her chest. 'You gave me a fright.'

'Sorry,' Carmichael said as he bent to pick up the phone. 'But there's no need to be scared.'

'No, of course not.' She took the phone and gestured at the noticeboard. 'You run the history society?'

'Yes. There's a group of us who get together once a month. I think being rooted in the past gives one a sense of community, as well as helping us realise we are but mortal beings here on earth for a short time and all subject to the grace of God.' Carmichael smiled but then put on a straight face. 'However, believing is not a prerequisite for being a member, far from it. Are you considering joining?'

'Not as such.' Catherine held up her phone and thumbed until she'd brought up the picture she'd taken of the photograph in the metal box. She angled the phone towards Carmichael. 'But I would like to know more about this. What happened, who did it, and whether these boys were subject to the grace of God.'

'Shit,' Carmichael said. He swayed slightly, and he reached out for the stone wall as if he needed to touch a solid surface. 'Apologies. That's not the sort of language I normally use, but I haven't seen a picture of it before.'

'But you know about... *it*?' Catherine put her phone away. 'You're aware of what happened at World's End?'

'Yes.' Carmichael stood upright, his composure back with him. 'Shall we go to the vicarage? We can have a cup of tea. Lord knows I need one now.'

'If the tea comes with an explanation, then yes.'

Carmichael led the way. There was a large stone house adjoining the churchyard, but he dismissed the building with a wave.

'That used to be the vicarage until the church sold the place off. I live in a little cottage now, but it suits me fine.'

The cottage in question was at one end of the thatched terrace. A low front door led to a room with bookshelves on three of the four walls. Catherine sank into an armchair while Carmichael chinked crockery in a kitchen out the back.

'Here we go,' he said when he returned a few minutes later carrying a tray with a teapot and cups and saucers. A plate held a selection of biscuits: Jammy Dodgers, Bourbons, and Chocolate Hobnobs. He smiled. 'Economising on the housing means I can go a bit mad with the catering budget.'

Right, Catherine thought. She'd just brought up the brutal hanging of two young men and Carmichael was wittering on about his elevenses.

'Now, where were we?' The vicar gave her a blank stare, as if he didn't have a clue what she was doing there.

'The murders that took place at World's End Farm.'

'Murders, yes.' Carmichael eyed a Jammy Dodger but had second thoughts. 'A dreadful business. Before my time of course. Way before.'

'When exactly?'

'1982. The bad winter. I only know about what happened from what I've heard, but most anyone local over the age of fifty can remember. Not that they'll be able to tell you the truth, the whole truth, and nothing but the truth. You see, time clouds the memory, and gossip and rumour serve to obfuscate the historical facts. I don't suppose anyone knows the full story.'

'But there *are* facts, right?'

'Oh yes.' Carmichael stood and went to a bookshelf where his fingers hovered near an array of box files. He retrieved one and sat back in his chair. He opened the file, withdrew a folded newspaper page, and passed it across. 'Take a look at this.'

The page was the cover of the local paper and the headline read *Double Murder on the Moor*. Below the headline there was a picture of World's End Farm. Catherine read the article. The two dead men had been brothers. The Murrin brothers. They lived at the farm with their parents, but at the time of the murders the parents had been away on a short break. While they were gone, it snowed heavily, and nobody came down to the property for several days. When the parents returned, they found their sons hanging from a beam in one of the barns. Police were investigating but had ruled out a suicide pact. So far, no motive for the killings had been established. Catherine glanced at the date at the top of the page. March 2nd, 1982.

She drew in a deep breath and remembered not to swear. 'Were any of the previous owners aware of this?'

'I guess some were and some weren't.'

'But everyone round here knows?'

'Those of the right age, yes.'

She shook her head. She was surprised the murders hadn't come to light when they'd bought the place. The estate agency hadn't mentioned anything. But then they wouldn't. She remembered a court case where a house buyer had taken a vendor to court because the vendor hadn't been honest about the fact a murderer had dismembered a victim in the bath. The judge ruled that the vendor was under no obligation to inform the buyer about the history of the house and thus the case was lost. In their own situation back in London, Daniel's notoriety had meant it had been impossible to conceal the fact that a violent death had occurred in their house and they'd had to take a reduced offer. However, in a few years' time, the current owners could sell without mentioning the fact and be entirely within the law.

'You weren't being honest with us before,' Catherine said. 'You said there'd been a number of minor incidents at World's End. I wouldn't call this minor.'

'I wasn't referring to the murders.' Carmichael seemed taken aback. 'I'm sorry if I misled you. I meant events such as the offal on your doorstep.'

'But they must be related?'

'One would think so.' Carmichael accepted the article back, and he folded the page and replaced it in the box file. 'Although I can't understand why anyone would do such things.'

There was silence and Catherine took the opportunity to take a mouthful of tea.

'Who were the Murrins?' she said.

'They were landowners. The family name goes back centuries and they have a number of plots in the graveyard.' Carmichael took a sip of tea himself. 'But they weren't liked. Their way of managing local affairs was a little heavy-handed. Of course, that could just be to do with class. The Murrins held themselves up to be the Lords of the Manor and I don't suppose their self-designated position sat easily with everybody.'

'And you discovered all this through the history group?'

'Through the group and from hearing local gossip. I arrived in the parish a mere seventeen years ago, so I'm afraid all my information is second-hand.'

'Could you put me in touch with anyone who knows more?'

'Are you sure that's wise?' Carmichael cocked his head. 'Digging up the past isn't necessarily the best way of securing the future.'

'I can't possibly sleep easily until I know why those boys died. Perhaps not even then.'

'Nobody was caught or charged, and the case remains open. I doubt you'll have any greater success than the police in solving it.'

'What about the parents? Are they alive?'

'Mr Murrin is a resident in the graveyard. He died of cancer a year or so ago. I officiated at the funeral, but myself and the sexton were the only people present. Oh, and the local policeman, Constable Jencks. A sad state of affairs for a man to go into the ground unloved and unremembered.'

'And his wife?'

'I believe Murrin split from his wife soon after the murders, and she moved away. She's probably dead too by now, otherwise I'd have thought she might have come to the funeral.'

'So who should I speak to?'

'I need to ask the individuals concerned first, but have you thought of your neighbour, Joe Foster? He's lived at Steddings Farm all his life. I'm sure the police have talked to him, but he's a funny fellow and I can well believe he might be a little distrustful of the authorities. I'm sure he'll be able to tell you all about World's End from way before the murders.'

Catherine nodded. Foster certainly was odd, and she wasn't sure she'd be comfortable alone with him. On the other hand, distrusting the police was a feeling she could identify with, and if Carmichael wasn't going to play ball with his history group buddies, Foster might be her only option.

The conversation changed to lighter matters. The weather, the state of the local economy, whether Catherine and Daniel would agree to giving the lecture he'd suggested. When Catherine had finished her tea, she thanked Carmichael for his help and promised to talk to Daniel about the lecture. Carmichael showed her to the door. As she was leaving he touched her arm.

'Was there anything else?' Catherine said.

'I...' Carmichael paused. 'No, nothing.'

'Bye then.' She went out into the street.

'Look, I doubt there's any real danger, but be careful up there nevertheless, OK?'

Carmichael shut the door before she had the chance to speak. As she walked away from the row of cottages, she had the uncomfortable sensation that she was being spied on by multiple pairs of eyes.

Chapter Twenty-three

Them Murrin boys ran wild for years. From when they could walk, almost. But it was when they reached their teens that they began to go bad. When they started to change from boys to men.

Old man Murrin owned several farms, including the one I was born and raised on. He had a string of houses in the village too. Some tied to jobs, some just rented out. Back in the nineteenth century, the family had thousands of acres, but by the nineteen eighties that had dwindled. Never mind that the estate was a poor reflection of what it had been, with all the big houses sold off long ago, Murrin behaved as if he was the Lord of the Manor, and if anyone was to blame beyond the boys themselves, you'd have to say it was their old man.

The problem was he'd let them do as they pleased for years, and if there was any discipline, well I never set my eyes on it. 'Spare the rod, spoil the child,' was a phrase my pa often used, and I'm not sure if he knocked the sense into me or knocked the stupidity out, but these days, when I read all the stuff in the papers, I can see where he was coming from. I'm not saying if Murrin had beat his kids they'd have turned out different, but to my mind it would have been worth a try.

As the boys matured, their hormones started to kick in, and they began to yearn for what nearly all young men want: girls. When I was their age I was the same. I thought nothing of taking a lass to a haybarn for a little horseplay and a grope. We all gotta learn and that's the way we did it back then. Least out here in the country. Today a kid which did that would be labelled a sex offender, go on some register. Shit, we were doing what came naturally and the girls were as up for it as the boys. I don't suppose much has changed evolution wise. Not below the waist. It's in the head area where things have gone wrong. Politicians and the like. Meddling.

Still, what the Murrin boys got up to wasn't just the overexuberance of adolescence. It was far, far worse. You see, when I was a teenager and I went in a little forceful, I'd get a kick in the nuts or a slap round the face, and I soon learned there were better ways of wooing.

The Murrins had a way of avoiding that hassle. They chose young girls who were the daughters of tenants or employees. If a lass refused to go with one of them, the boys had a word with their father. Repairs didn't get done or the rent went up or the family got evicted. Other times people found their wages docked for some petty reason or they were threatened with unemployment. Mostly the girls complied and the Murrins went about their business and nobody complained.

Well, it wasn't fine nor dandy, but life carried on. Nobody said nowt, or if they did it was to Sergeant Jencks and he didn't pay much heed to anyone but the Murrins. As time went by the boys grew older and, as is the way, bolder. There were whispers in the village about doing something, but nobody wanted to be the first to act. And I dare say the Murrins would have gone on unopposed for years had it not been for Helena Hodgson and her brave but unfortunate dad.

Chapter Twenty-four

The visit from Constable Jencks unsettled Foster. He wondered if the policeman was serious about not going within half a mile of World's End. Foster's bottom fields were closer to the farm than that. He wouldn't put it past Jencks to hide behind a hedge and spring out and arrest him. He thought about the heroes in the paperbacks on his shelf. Men from a different age. They wouldn't have been unsettled. They'd have confronted Jencks face to face and had it out with the man. What they'd have made of the rope dangling from the beam though, was another matter. Perhaps they'd have been clever enough to decode the puzzle, but Foster was buggered if he could. He decided he'd better heed Jencks' warning and stay away from the bottom of the valley.

Two weeks before Christmas, Barney Weston invited Foster over for an early festive dinner. Barney had lived at the top of the valley for as long as Foster had lived at his place and, like Foster, Barney's family had bought their farm off Mr Murrin. Like Foster, Barney was widowed. Unlike Foster, he had three children — two sons and a daughter — and they had young families of their own.

'They're all be visiting on the day itself,' Barney said. 'It'll be hell and I'll have to be on my best behaviour.'

'That'll be difficult,' Foster said.

'Which is why I thought we should have this little gettogether now.'

'Appreciate that.'

'Refined company, right?' Barney carved into a plump pheasant. Arranged beside the pheasant were two partridges. Steam rose from a tray of roast potatoes and roast parsnips, alongside sat a bowl of sprouts, some carrots, red cabbage the colour of Barney's face, and enough Yorkshire puddings to feed an army. It was a fine spread. 'Just thee and me and these three gorgeous birds.'

'You should be a comedian.'

'Except there ain't much to laugh at. I mean look at us, a pair of old codgers all on our lonesomes. The only wenches we can pull are these ones.'

Foster eyed the pheasant. 'If I could find a woman as juicy as that, I could die happy.'

'Have you seen the one in the bakery in town? She's a big lass. Plenty of loving to spare. I could see her bent over the counter while I pop a French stick in her oven.'

'She's not a day over forty. She won't be interested in an old bloke like you.'

'I'm working on it, Joe, working on it.' Barney cut a slice from the pheasant and slid the steaming meat onto Foster's plate. 'Talking of working, how's that little project of yours going?'

'What project?'

'Scaring the hell out of the new people at World's End Farm.'

'I never.'

'Not what I heard on the grapevine.'

'I don't know what you're talking about.'

'That's what you always say.'

'To tell the truth, Barney, I have been down there a few times. Only...'

'Only what?'

'The last time I went, somebody had beaten me too it. They'd rigged a bloody great hank of rope up over a beam in the barn and tied a noose in the end of it.'

'You're joking me?'

'Do I look like I'm joking?' Foster began to tuck into his food. Gravy ran down his chin and he picked up a paper napkin. 'Nearly gave me a heart attack. The next thing was Constable Jencks coming up to my place and accusing me of setting the rope.'

'What do you expect if you go sneaking around down there?'

'But I didn't do it. That's the point. I left a pile of sheep's entrails on their front step. Released a load of rats into their kitchen. I never went in the barn with no rope.'

'So who did?' Barney eyed their glasses. They were well down. He poured some more wine. 'You're the one nutter round here crazy enough to do such a thing, aren't you?'

'You'd think so.' Foster picked up his glass and moved his hand to swirl the wine. 'But I've got this feeling. It's like somebody's come to teach me a lesson. To pay me back.'

'But it was years ago and anyway, who knows what happened that day?'

'Nobody but you and me, Barney.'

'There you go then.'

'And the Murrins.'

'Now you're acting plain stupid. The brothers are dead and the old man is too.'

'Exactly.' Foster shifted his gaze. Barney had laid out some crackers on the table in an attempt to be festive. 'The ghost of Christmas Past.'

Chapter Twenty-five

Catherine didn't mention her meeting with Father Carmichael to Daniel. To do so would mean she'd have to reveal she knew what was inside the box, and before she did that she wanted more answers. It wasn't until the week before Christmas she got another chance to play amateur sleuth. Daniel had arranged to meet a friend for lunch in Exeter and would be gone for several hours. More than enough time to pop up to Joe Foster's place and find out some more about the Murrin family.

She decided a gift of some kind would soften Foster's hard exterior, so as soon as Daniel had left she set about baking a cake. The cake would also give her an excuse to call round.

She was nervous as she drove the 4x4 to the top of the track and swung onto the lane. As she climbed the side of the valley, a glance over her shoulder gave her a view of World's End Farm sunk in the dip. The face-like façade squinted at her through a blur of rain, almost as if it was giving a wink and throwing out a taunt.

My secret to know, yours to find out.

Foster's place lay off to the right. A lane dived down in a deep cutting before emerging to cross several boggy fields. Huge potholes dotted the lane and the 4x4 rumbled over them, the suspension bouncing like a pogo stick. At the end of the lane, several buildings clustered round a farmyard. To one side sat the house, an overgrown and unloved garden to the front. Narrow windows with peeling paint, the glass in need of a clean, curtains drawn closed in the upstairs rooms. Smoke tumbled from a chimney, snatched down the valley by the wind.

Catherine pulled into the farmyard and got out. She walked up to the front door, stepping over a pile of beer bottles. A letter slot had a piece of wood tacked across and a message had been hand painted on the surface of the door.

No cold callers, no salesmen.

Welcoming Joe Foster was not, and Catherine thought about forgetting the whole thing and getting back in the 4x4. She could flip the locks down and be gone. But before she could turn around, metal scraped on the back of the door and Foster was opening up, his dog rushing out past Catherine and into the yard.

'Mr Foster?' She was aware of a quiver in her voice. She cleared her throat. 'It's Catherine, remember? From World's End?'

'Aye,' Foster said. 'What d'ya want?'

'I brought you a cake.' She held out the Tupperware box containing a Victoria Sponge. 'I never thanked you for the pheasants. This is to return the favour.'

'I see.' The dog ran back up the path, sat at Catherine's feet, and gazed up, expectant. Foster looked at the dog, as if he relied on the animal as a judge of character. 'That'll be kindly, I guess.'

'Yes, well.' She struggled for words. Foster stood in the doorway, making no effort to be friendly. The dog lifted a paw and Catherine crouched. 'What's her name?'

'Jess,' Foster said.

'She's so sweet.' Catherine balanced the cake container on her knee and stroked the dog.

'Hmmm.' Foster stamped a foot. 'Was there anything else you'd be wanting?'

Now or never, Catherine thought. She stood and smiled. 'I'd love a slice of that cake, perhaps a cup of tea to go with it?'

Foster's face creased and he averted his gaze, but then he nodded.

'Alright.' He opened the door. 'This way.'

She stooped into the dark hallway and squeezed past. Foster called the dog in and shut the door. Catherine smiled again, trying to conceal her nervousness.

'You've lived here all your life?'

'Born in the living room.'

'Well, it beats the USA.' Catherine laughed at her joke, but the humour was lost on Foster. He waved at an opening and she made her way through to a cramped kitchen. An old range stood on one side, the fire door open, the glow of hot coals within. An armchair sat next to the range and crammed in a corner was a circular table. 'Cosy,' she said.

'It suits me.' Foster stood at the range and dragged a blackened kettle across to the hotplate. 'But it was crowded when Ma and Pa were alive.'

This was a stroke of luck, Catherine thought. Foster had started talking about the past with no prompting. 'Do you have siblings?'

'Two brothers and a sister, but my sister died when she was a baby. My brothers are dead too, but that was later.'

'I'm sorry.'

'No need to be, it was nothing to do with you.'

There was an awkward silence until the kettle began to hiss. Foster retrieved a china teapot from a shelf and added several teaspoons of leaf tea from an old tin that bore a picture of the Queen. Catherine opened the Tupperware container and placed it on the table. Foster was busy delving into cupboards and pulling out plates and cups and a sharp knife. He gestured at the table and Catherine took a seat.

'It must be nice growing up in one place and staying there all your life,' she said. 'I guess it provides you with a sense of security.'

'Wasn't much security back in them days,' Foster said as he used a teaspoon to stir the leaves in the pot. 'My parents were tenants. The Murrins could've booted them out whenever they wanted.'

'The Murrins? They lived at our place, right?' Catherine pretended to be only mildly interested. She took the sharp knife and sliced the cake. 'I'd like to know more about them, more about the village and the local area as it was back then.'

'To be honest, I try to avoid too much thinking about what's been and gone. It can't change anything and only causes worry.' Foster poured the tea. He added milk without asking if she wanted any and pushed a cup across the table.

'Thank you.' Catherine reached for the cup and sipped. Foster peered at the floor. The silence wasn't simply uncomfortable, it was painful. Damn it, she thought, the chance had gone. She could hardly jump straight into a conversation about the murders.

'That's the real reason you've come here, isn't it?' Foster continued to stare at the floor. 'World's End. You want to know the history and all.'

Catherine almost spluttered a mouthful of tea. She carefully put the cup and saucer down. 'There was the cake as well, but yes. That was astute of you.'

'Not really.' Foster raised his head and for the first time he smiled. 'Father Carmichael phoned me a couple of days ago. Said you might be paying a visit. Anyone else and I'd have told 'em to fuck off mind you, but Father Carmichael helped me with my wife when she was ill. He was good with her whereas I wasn't. I owe him.'

'That's very—'

'I'll tell you what I know and what I reckon you need to know and that's it. Can't say whether you'll like it or not though.' Foster lifted his cup and took a huge slurp. 'Where do you want to start?'

'I found a picture taken at the farm. It shows two young men hanged from a beam in the barn. I understand from Father Carmichael those men were the Murrin brothers and they were murdered.'

'They were that. Will and Red Murrin. Will was twenty and Red was eighteen.'

'And the police had no idea who did it?'

'I guess if they had they'd have nabbed 'em by now.' Foster put his hands palms up. 'The problem was they had a long list of suspects. Virtually anyone from round here with an ounce of sense, a grain of decency, and an eye for justice.'

'They weren't liked then?'

'*Liked?* No, they weren't liked. They were despised. Not only the brothers, the whole family.' Foster scratched his head. 'You gotta see it like this. For generations this country has been set up so the ruling classes get what they want. They've stolen land, raped people's daughters, enslaved men and women.'

'You're talking about feudal times.'

'Feudal times and not so feudal times. Even as recently as when those boys died. You see, old man Murrin owned half the village and a whole sweep of land bordering the eastern edge of the moor. If you knew what was good for you, you doffed your cap and didn't question too much what the family got up to.'

'So they treated people badly. It doesn't sound like an excuse for a lynch mob.'

'It wasn't simply treating people badly. Things went way beyond that. And there weren't no lynch mob, neither.'

'But what did the Murrins do which justified killing them?'

'All the things I said.'

'Theft, rape and slavery?'

'Just so.'

'In the seventies and eighties?'

'Yup.'

'What about the police?'

'Sergeant Jencks was the local copper.'

'Jencks?' Catherine didn't understand. 'But he's way too young.'

Foster smiled. 'Oh, you've met *Constable* Jencks, have you? His old man was Sergeant Jencks — like father like son, unfortunately — and Jencks' wife was a cousin of the Murrins. Somehow the misdemeanours got overlooked.'

'But we're not talking about misdemeanours. You said rape.'

'Rape, murder.'

'*Murder?* Surely not?'

'Some folk say so and I have no reason to doubt them.'

'How did they get away with it?'

'Jencks bent the rules. The area was his little fiefdom. Plus, you have to remember the position of some of the victims. If you lived in a tenanted farm owned by the Murrins and your daughter comes home and tells you the brothers have messed about with her, what do you do? Jencks was master of the law hereabouts, and if you complained to Mr Murrin he'd either deny what happened or say the boys got a bit frisky. Pursue the matter further, and you'd lose your farm. Same applies if you lived in a tied cottage. Your house and job depended on staying loyal to the Murrins.'

'It sounds terrible.'

'It was, but I dare say the Murrins aren't unique. Been happening for centuries all over.'

'And they just carried on unopposed?'

'Right up until somebody put a stop to it on March 2nd, 1982. The killing of them boys marked the end of the Murrins. The old man and his wife divorced and moved away. The estate was broken up and sold off. I tell you the day after those boys went into the ground, the valley smelled a sweeter place.'

'So who killed the brothers?'

'After all these years, what does it matter?'

'But it was probably a local, which means there's a killer in the area. Doesn't that make you worried?'

'No, but there's not much worries me these days.'

'I can't feel the same about the place now. The thought of those bodies hanging in the barn.'

'Does your husband know about this?'

Catherine hesitated. In her mind she pictured the metal box with the photographs inside. Daniel's secret. 'Yes, he does.'

'And he's not bothered?'

She didn't know how to answer that. She thought of Daniel's strange behaviour as regards the house. The way he insisted on the blind overlooking the barn being down. That had to be contrasted with his adamant statement that World's End was their forever place.

'I don't think so,' was the best she could manage, but Foster appeared satisfied. She took a mouthful of cake and sipped at her tea. All of a sudden she felt uncomfortable. She looked to the window. The sky outside had darkened to a bruised purple, the light draining away. 'I'd best be going.'

'You haven't finished your tea.'

'I want to get back while it's daytime.'

Catherine rose and as she did, Foster's hand shot out. He gripped her wrist with a strength that belied his age. 'There'll not be anything else you want to be telling me? About something more recent that's been happening down at World's End?'

'Ow, you're hurting me.' Catherine wrestled her arm, but the old man's grip was clamped fast. A teacup clinked and toppled and the table cloth slid sideways. 'Please.'

'I was asking you a question and you haven't answered.'

'I don't know what you're talking about.'

'Someone put a rope up in your barn. Tied a noose. It might have been a joke, but if it was, it was a bad one.'

'We don't know who did it, but they also put guts on our front doorstep and scared me to death with a load of rats.'

'That was me, girl.' Foster grinned at her. His teeth were white and perfect. The gums a bright pink. She realised the teeth were false. 'But I didn't do anything with a rope.'

'You?' Catherine jerked her arm again and this time Foster's hand loosened. She stepped back towards the door. 'Why?'

'Because by rights nobody should be living at World's End Farm. The house is cursed, a place where evil reigns. Believe me, I was doing you a favour.'

'Oh God.' Catherine felt dizzy. She staggered into the hallway. 'You're crazy. I'm going to report you.'

'To Jencks?' Foster laughed. 'There's nothing you can prove and nothing he can do. Best you get on back to London where you belong.'

Catherine picked up her wellingtons and her coat and wrenched the door open. She ran across the yard, feeling the mud soak through her socks. She was climbing into the pickup when Foster emerged from the house. He stood under the porch.

'Secrets come back to haunt you, understand?' he shouted. 'Same way as lies do. No good ever comes of them, believe me. You make sure to tell your husband that, d'you hear?'

Catherine slammed the door shut and put the key in the ignition. Foster made no move to come after her. She shoved the pickup into gear, dropped the clutch, and roared away into the growing darkness.

Chapter Twenty-six

Catherine was too shocked by what had happened to tell Daniel. She was embarrassed and frightened, and not only of Foster; Daniel would go mad if he found out what she'd been up to, and she didn't want another argument.

Now the list of things she was keeping from him was lengthening: Finding the box, speaking to Peter Carmichael, Foster's admission that he'd left the intestines and dumped the rats, his assertion that he hadn't been the one to set the noose in the barn. Easy to see how a partial truth became an untruth, she thought. Two days later she casually fashioned another outright lie.

'Just have to go out to the shops,' she said to Daniel. 'I need some more sketching paper.'

'Fine,' Daniel said. 'Don't mind if I skip it, do you? I want to crack on and finalise as much as possible before we go away.'

With Christmas approaching, the town was busy and the car park rammed, and Catherine had to wait twenty minutes to find a space. Once she'd parked up, she hurried along the High Street to the estate agency that had handled the sale of World's End.

Boscombe and Lever were an upmarket outfit dealing in country and waterside properties, and the furnishing inside reflected the kind of clientele they hoped to attract. The carpet was plush and the lighting subtle. To one side of the office a sofa and two armchairs circled a fireplace where real logs crackled with yellow flames. An expensive coffee machine stood nearby, along with a mini glass-fronted chiller containing water and juices. There was also a Christmas tree adorned with tasteful decorations. At the other side of the office, two agents sat on high-backed leather chairs behind antique desks.

'Ms Ross.' The agent they'd dealt with, Frank Lever, rose from his seat. As Catherine approached, Lever extended his hand. 'A pleasure to see you again. How's life at the beautiful World's End Farm?'

Lever was sixtyish. A bald patch on the top of his head was fringed with tufty grey hair. He had a circular face and round glasses to match and wore a tweed suit with a striped tie. The image he intended to portray was completed with a set of magazines arranged in a neat line on the desk in front of him: *Country Life*, *Shooting Times*, and *Horse and Hound*.

'We're thinking of selling.' Stuff the niceties and get straight to the point, Catherine thought. Lever's bonhomie was an act. He'd worked his charm on them six months ago, but she wasn't going to be taken in twice. 'Moving back to London.'

'Oh, I'm sorry to hear that.' Lever's face fell as he sat down, but she could see percentage symbols lighting up in his eyes. 'Is that a definite decision?'

By which he meant did Daniel know or was this just some silly idea she'd got into her head.

'Yes,' Catherine said. 'Pretty much.'

'Country living not for you then?' Lever held his hands up in apology. 'It happens quite often, don't worry. The other way around too. I've had clients who've sold up and moved to the South East. A year later they're back complaining about the traffic and the noise and the crime. The money you can earn in the city is a compensation for some, but you can't buy paradise.'

'I thought that's what you were selling. *Dream homes for Special People* is your firm's motto.'

'Ah, yes.' Lever conceded the point. 'But one person's paradise can be another's hell. I'm guessing you miss the hustle and bustle of the city, the shops and restaurants and theatres. If I moved to London I'd miss the solitude, the wide-open spaces, the moorland animals.'

For a split second, Catherine saw the rats tumbling through the cat flap. She gave an involuntary shiver. 'Something like that.'

'So.' Lever placed his hands flat on the desk, signalling the philosophising was over and it was time to get down to business. 'You'd like us to handle the sale. Well, we'd be happy to. As you know, the market is tight at this juncture and properties like yours are always at a premium and—'

'How many times have you sold World's End in the last thirty-five years, Mr Lever?'

'Pardon?'

'I understand the house has changed hands many times since the Murrins lived there. I assume you handled most of those sales. I'd just like to know how many owners there have been since 1982.'

'1982.' Lever repeated the year. 'I would have been in my mid-twenties and a junior. My father or Mr Boscombe Senior would have dealt with any sale which took place.'

'But you were working here, and you'd have known what happened up at World's End.'

'1982. Let me see...'

'Mr Lever, please don't try to pretend you don't know what I'm talking about. Two of the Murrin family were murdered at the farm. They were hanged in the very barn which is now my workshop.'

Lever swallowed. He flinched and leaned back as if Catherine had a bad case of halitosis. 'Would you excuse me?'

He stood and walked over to the chiller cabinet. He removed a couple of bottles of carbonated water and a carton of fruit juice and took two plastic glasses from the dispenser on top. Back behind the desk, he unscrewed the lid from one of the bottles and poured water into a glass. He took a sip, before offering Catherine a choice of the remaining water bottle or the fruit juice. She held up a hand to decline both drinks.

'An unpleasant business,' Lever said. 'Shocking.'

'I can tell you it was pretty shocking to find a picture showing the young men hanged in the barn. *My* barn.'

'Yes, I can imagine.' A flat smile. A sigh. Resignation. Lever took another sip of his water. 'I can only apologise.'

'How many sales, Mr Lever?'

'Six or seven, perhaps. Possibly a couple more.'

'Doesn't that strike you as odd? An average of a little over four or five years between sales for a property, which as my husband keeps telling me, is a forever home?'

'Your husband. Yes.' Lever was staring at the bubbles fizzing in his glass. 'I take it he doesn't want to move?'

'No.' Catherine decided to have a drink after all. She opened the carton of juice and poured it into the glass. Some globules of orange spilled onto the desk and crept towards the magazines. There was an awkward pause as Lever fumbled in a drawer and found a box of tissues. He passed one across and Catherine mopped up the juice. 'But that doesn't make any difference, I still want out.'

Lever sighed. 'Once again, I'm sorry. I'd hate to feel a Boscombe and Lever customer was unhappy with our service. That's not what we're about.'

'No, not in your brochure, Mr Lever.' Catherine waved across to the entrance where a display rack held several glossy leaflets. 'Hunky, sporty-type man with an attractive wife posing in a gleaming new kitchen. Kids round their ankles. No worries. But that's not reality. Reality is two men brutally murdered not thirty feet from where I sleep. Or rather, from where I *try* to sleep.'

'OK, let's get this sorted.' Lever had done apologising. A customer hovered at a board near the entrance and Lever wanted to move to safer ground. 'I assume both your names are on the deeds, so I'll need your husband to sign the instruction too. However, we can get started by making an appointment for an agent to visit and carry out a valuation. I believe you've made some significant improvements to the property. The way the market is, you'll get a good price and make a substantial profit.'

Hands on the desk again. A smile. As if the bottom line was all that mattered.

'You misled us, Mr Lever. Don't you feel bad about that?'

'Misled you, how?'

'By not informing us about the murders. Legally, I'm sure you're under no obligation, but morally?' Catherine laughed. 'No wonder estate agents are down there with politicians and used car salesmen.'

Lever's smile became a sneer. 'So you'd like me to mention the murders in the particulars I draw up for you? Up near the top or would a brief mention in the footnotes do? Perhaps I could put a line in the introduction like, "has an interesting recent history" or, "of great interest to amateur detectives".' The sneer became naked aggression. 'Boscombe and Lever have no liability at all in this matter, now or in the past. At no time did I mislead you or was anything other than completely honest. Perhaps it might be better if I dealt with your husband over this matter.'

'Whatever, you deceived us both.'

'That's where you're wrong, Ms Ross.' Lever leaned forwards. Any attempt at friendliness had vanished. 'Quite wrong.'

'How so?'

'Your husband was the one who called and made an offer, right?' Lever waited for an answer. Catherine nodded. 'Well, as you know, the offer was way below the asking price, and I asked him how he could justify such a low opening bid. He told me he was aware of what had happened at the property.'

'*What?*'

'Your husband knew about the hangings, Ms Ross. He, at least, bought World's End Farm knowing full well the two Murrin boys had been murdered there. The fact he chose not to share the information with you is, I'm afraid, not the fault of Boscombe and Lever.' Lever gave a little snigger. 'After all, we're not relationship counsellors.'

Catherine's throat was dry and the words wouldn't come. She started to reach for the orange juice but thought better of it. Lever was nodding, smug written all over his face. She staggered to her feet and ran from the office.

Chapter Twenty-seven

I can't say no more or less about World's End than the place is cursed. Quite how, I don't know. I'm not sure if I believe in ghosts or demons any more than I do God or the Devil, but there could still be something down there which can influence events or muddle people's heads. Perhaps there's radiation in the soil or the water is bad. Maybe an ancient ley line runs under the house or the rocks are generating a magnetic field which can manipulate atoms and such. I guess a scientist could come with a meter and take readings, but no amount of measurements could explain it fully because the one thing you can't account for is the human element. By which I mean the Murrin family.

Must have been three weeks into the snow when the trouble happened and the cause of it all was a white pony the Hodgsons owned. They'd named the pony Mischief and he was a tough little Welsh Mountain, as happy pulling a load of logs for Mr Hodgson as he was carrying Helena or her siblings across the moor. He was a fine animal but — as his name suggested — was prone to escaping, and often took advantage of a loosely-tied gate or a rickety fence to make a dash for freedom. Many a time I'd caught the cheeky gelding trotting up the lane and had to take him home. Truth is I didn't mind. It gave me an excuse to see Helena. However, the Hodgson's place bordered World's End Farm and the Murrins weren't quite so obliging or nearly as friendly. Old man Murrin threatened that the next time the pony strayed, he'd slaughter the animal and use it for dog food.

So, there I was, riding back up the lane on my mare, having been to the village to check for post. As I passed the grey stone pillars at the entrance to World's End, I saw Helena standing a little way down the track, the two Murrin boys, Will and Red, beside her. I pulled up my horse and dismounted. The boys squared up to me. Will was twenty and tall and lanky, with black hair and bushy eyebrows. He was fit and strong, but I was sure I could take him. Red, as his name suggested, had orange-brown hair. Freckles dotted his cheeks beneath narrow eyes. He was eighteen, not full-grown, but heavy and thick-set. I'd heard from others he fought dirty. It figured. Red wasn't quite right in the head. There was a spark of madness which could flare up and lash out, and you could tell from the way he fidgeted that he was always on edge. You'd expect Will, being the eldest, to be the leader, but for some reason he deferred to Red. Perhaps he was as scared of his brother as everyone else.

'You alright?' I said to Helena.

'She's fine,' Red said. He bobbed his head at Helena. 'Ain't you, sweetheart?'

'Yes.' Helena said. Her eyes were brim full with tears. She wasn't fine. Far from it.

'She's looking for her pony and we've found him.' Will pointed back down the track towards World's End. 'The animal's down in the barn. Dad put him there. Says he's going to cut him up for the dogs.'

'Yeah.' Red grinned. 'Chop, chop, chop. Woof, woof, woof.'

'You don't have to let that happen,' I said. 'You could just give the pony back.'

'That's right!' Red smacked himself on the forehead. 'Stupid me. Why didn't I think of that? We could just give the pony back. How about it, Will?'

'But Dad wouldn't be happy,' Will said. 'In fact he'd be hopping mad. We'd get into trouble.'

'Yeah, we would. Big trouble.' Red tutted. 'Still...'

'What?'

'I guess we could help Helena out if she paid us.'

'But she ain't rich, Red.'

'No.' Red stepped over to Helena. He touched her on the cheek. 'There's other things she is though.'

I raised a hand and moved forwards. 'Now look—'

'Fuck off, Foster!' Red spat the words out as he marched over to me. 'We're going to discuss the situation with Helena and work out some kind of deal, right? That's none of your business, so why don't you get back on your horse and head on home. Otherwise I'll be telling my old man about the hassle you gave us. How you hit me.'

'I never did.'

'You did, Foster.' Will, puffing himself up like a cockerel defending his territory. 'And who's my father going to believe? His own son or some thirty-something stay-at-home? One word from me and your family will be kicked off your farm before the month is over. Now run along up the hill to mummy and daddy.'

I looked at Helena, but she averted her eyes. 'If I hear about anything bad happening, I'll—'

'You'll what?'

'You'll see.' I walked back to my horse and mounted, my face flushed with anger. Took the reins and urged the mare onwards. Regretted doing so every single day of my life since.

Chapter Twenty-eight

A few days before Christmas, Foster was on his regular Thursday jaunt into town. Shopping. Pint of Guinness. Single malt. Packet of plain crisps. The pretty barmaid wasn't serving, and he had to make do with a young spotty male who poured the Guinness like he was running water for brushing teeth. No pattern in the head either. Plus the whiskey was acrid and the crisps stale and tasteless. Foster tutted to himself and left the pub.

He was hunched over and making for his Land Rover when he heard someone call his name.

'Joe! Hang about!'

Foster turned. A fat fellow with a slicked back wisp of hair and a face the colour of beetroot was barrelling along the pavement. Barney.

'You good?' Barney said as he approached. 'Only I've not had payback for that dinner. You'll be inviting me down for Sunday lunch in the New Year, yes?'

'Could be.'

'Will be, my lad. Especially with the little surprise I've got to show you.'

'I don't like surprises, Barney. You know that.'

'You'll like this one, but we'll need to be quick because she might not be in there for long.'

'Who? And in where?'

'You'll find out.' Barney winked. 'And afterwards we'll have a drink.'

'I've just had one.'

'You're going to want another.' Barney tugged at Foster's arm.

'Come on.'

'I...' Foster resisted the tug of his arm, but then gave in. It wasn't as if he had much else to do. 'Alright.'

'Grand.' Barney led him back down the street, chattering ten to the dozen about the unseasonal warm weather and how at this rate they'd be cutting the hay in April. He wheeled in front of a shop window. 'Here. Take a gander.'

Foster looked. Dozens of photographs of houses stuck in columns on display boards. Beyond the pictures, a plush office with two desks.

'What's this?'

'It's an estate agent, Joe. They sell houses.'

'I know that, you daft bugger. Why the heck are you showing me? I'm not selling up, if that's your game. It'll be over my dead body before you get the top meadow.'

'No, you fool.' Barney pointed. 'Look who's in there.'

Foster squinted at the window. At one desk a woman agent sat staring at a computer screen, while at the other an elderly man was talking to a female client. Mid-thirties. Long black hair. Attractive.

'Bloody hell.'

'Mrs World's End, Joe.' Barney slapped Foster on the back. 'That Ross woman. She must be in there to put the place on the market.'

'Shit.' Foster stood open mouthed. He didn't know what to feel. Not elation, for sure. Perhaps, surprisingly, a tinge of sadness. Yet he couldn't explain the reason for the way he felt, certainly not to Barney.

'I have to hand it to you, you've done it again! Can't be much more than six months since the last *For Sale* board came down. Got to be a record, right? Let's go and have a drink to celebrate.'

'Yes.' Foster said. 'Celebrate.'

Chapter Twenty-nine

The day after her visit to the estate agency, Catherine and Daniel left for Norfolk to spend Christmas with Catherine's parents. She sat in the car and brooded as they sped east, itching to bring up her discussion with Frank Lever. Daniel chatted away, oblivious to her mood. It was good to have a break from both work and Devon, he said. She opened her mouth to agree but he'd already begun to tell her that, despite looking forward to the holiday, he was going to miss the house and their little piece of heaven. Never mind. It was just for a few days and returning home was always the best part of any journey. Leaving the motorway and cresting the hill at Exeter Racecourse. The moor spread out in the distance. World's End Farm nestled in an invisible valley somewhere ahead. Pure magic, yes?

The hours went by and she pretended to sleep, all the time trying to fathom why he'd kept the information about the murders secret. Was he so in love with the house that it made no difference? Perhaps it was the very fact that violent death had visited World's End as it had visited them in London. Perhaps once you'd bludgeoned a man's life away you looked on killing in a different, dispassionate, light. Was Daniel so devoid of emotion, so cold? She didn't want to believe so and it didn't fit with the Daniel she loved.

She mulled over the ongoing deception. She could understand, if not forgive, why he'd neglected to tell her if he'd discovered the pictures *after* they'd moved, but the knowledge he'd known about the murders *before* they'd bought World's End was distressing. It suggested continued duplicity, and if he was prepared to lie about the house, what else might he be hiding from her and why?

Despite her worries, Christmas in Norfolk turned out to be a real treat. Big open skies, endless beaches with a crisp wind blowing in from the North Sea, a traditional dinner, presents under the tree, sherry, mince pies, the whole works. For a time, Catherine forgot about their problems back in Devon. It helped that Daniel hardly mentioned World's End and appeared to enjoy the visit as much as she did. He took part in her father's tedious party games, played Scrabble with her mother, and helped Catherine's nephews and nieces run riot. She realised her extended family was something of a substitute for Daniel as his father had died some years back, his mother was in a care home and suffered from Alzheimer's, and he had no siblings. Seeing him with her own brother's and sister's kids made her consider mentioning children to him once more, but she checked herself. The way their relationship was heading, he wouldn't be responsive.

They broke the long journey back from Norfolk to Devon with a stop-off in London, and on the morning of New Year's Eve they found themselves wandering through Camden Market. It felt like old times, but when Catherine suggested to Daniel that perhaps they'd been a bit too hasty in moving, he snapped at her.

'Are you mad?' He scowled. 'Moving is the best thing we've ever done.'

'But...' Catherine looked past Daniel at the stalls, at the throng of people. She thought of how isolated they were out in the wilds. 'Don't you miss all this?'

'We're here aren't we? Enjoying it now. The converse isn't true though.' He let go of her arm and waved at the crowds. 'None of these people can experience what we have on the moor. They can visit, but they can't live like we do. You can't imagine the inspiration I get from looking out the window at the clouds floating by, or hearing the wind whistling down the valley. I thought you'd feel the same.'

'I do, only...'

Catherine never finished the sentence. Daniel drifted away to a stall selling bagels and the next minute her mouth was full of doughy bread and cream cheese. The conversation was over.

Later that evening, they celebrated the arrival of the New Year on the banks of the Thames with thousands of other people. As the rockets exploded above, she saw World's End Farm sitting lonely in the valley beneath a spread of icy stars, mad Joe Foster stalking the bounds, a heaving sack full of rats slung over his shoulder and a string of intestines slippery in his hands.

On New Year's Day they lunched with Toby and Lisa. Catherine had protested, but Daniel wouldn't listen.

'Is there nothing about me you like?' he said. 'You don't like the house I love, you disparage my friends. You don't appreciate how hard I work or the quality of my music. In fact I wonder if you think much of me at all.'

Where the hell did that come from? Catherine was mystified, but instead of having another shouting match, she agreed to the lunch. It turned out not to be as bad as she'd expected. Toby was in an odd mood, quieter than usual, and his lewd comments were minimal. Catherine even found herself prompting him for conversation.

'How's the writing coming on?' she asked.

'Slowly,' Toby said. 'Like pulling your own teeth.'

'Toby's finding it hard to concentrate,' Lisa said. She put her hand on her husband's arm. 'And with a deadline looming, that's not good.'

'It's the pressure.' Toby looked at Daniel and Catherine. 'I guess you two know about that with your own work.'

'Yes,' Catherine said. 'You have to remove the distractions from your life and reduce the areas causing you stress, so you can focus on just the one thing. Works for me.'

"Remove the distractions… yes.' Toby looked over at Daniel. 'Dan, is that your advice too?'

'Um, yeah.' Daniel was non-committal. He took a sip of wine and broke eye contact. 'I guess.'

There was an underlying tone to Toby's question and Daniel's answer, Catherine realised. A subplot she wasn't aware of.

'Here's to Catherine.' Toby raised his wine glass. His mood had brightened. 'May she continue to solve all our problems throughout this year and beyond.'

Daniel winced. He too raised his glass. 'Catherine.'

Within a few minutes, Toby's downbeat mood returned, and it was left to Catherine to make conversation with Lisa, while the men kept an uncomfortable silence broken by a few mumbled words about the latest football scores.

After the lunch, she asked Daniel what was up with his friend. Had Toby come to the realisation his sexist and overbearing persona wasn't going to be an asset now he was going to be in the spotlight?

'No,' Daniel said. 'It's his publishing deal. Barry Henderson hasn't been able to get as much as he first thought.'

'Right.' Catherine wasn't surprised. Henderson spoke a lot of bluff. 'And the movie?'

'There was no movie, not down on paper anyway. It was just an idea Barry floated as a possibility.'

'But Toby's car?'

'Bought on the never-never. Put down two grand and you can drive a fifty K Jaguar out of the showroom and look like you're a high roller.'

'He's still being published though, isn't he?'

'Yes, but there's something else affecting him, something personal.'

'Lisa? She hasn't seen the light and threatened to ditch him?' Catherine laughed, but realised her guess didn't make sense bearing in mind they'd just had lunch together. 'He's not ill, is he?'

'I can't tell you. Sorry, I promised.'

Another secret, she thought. Silly little Catherine can't be trusted with anything important. But perhaps it wasn't so much a secret as continuing deceit. No longer silly Catherine, but stupid Catherine for letting the wool get pulled over her eyes yet again.

Once more she tried to get her head around what Daniel was up to but try as she might she could only return to his infidelity. Still, the fact he might be cheating on her again was incidental when considering the lie about the pictures in the box, aside from the possibility that he'd wanted to ensure the move went smoothly. He'd found the perfect little house, in the middle of nowhere, and he didn't want the pictures of the dead Murrin boys to spoil that. With Catherine removed to the country, he could continue his philandering up in London without her knowledge.

After spending one more day in London exploring old haunts, they returned to Devon. They drove down the track to World's End in the afternoon gloom, fine rain misting the horizon. As Daniel stopped the car, Catherine shivered. The interior of the car was a warm cocoon, the lights on the dashboard displays somehow comforting, the plush upholstery soft and yielding. Outside, the house stood grey and cold, the stone walls fortress-like and oppressive. She let Daniel open up and carry the luggage into the house while she just sat in the car. After a while, she clambered out and made her way inside.

Daniel was in the kitchen, whistling a theme from one of his scores while he rustled up some food, so she went into the living room and slumped on the sofa, aware she was wallowing in self-pity. This couldn't go on. They had to come to some sort of agreement over the house or else their relationship would be at an end. This place or me, she pictured herself asking, finding it scary that she didn't know how Daniel would answer.

The next day Daniel rose early, and by the time she'd showered and breakfasted, he was already in his room working on some last-minute revisions to his score. The following week he was due to return to London to meet the director and run through all the music once more. He'd be gone for several days and the thought of being alone in the house almost overcame her.

On the Sunday before he left she tried to articulate her feelings, but once more he went on about how life would change once the weather improved. There'd be lambs in the fields and the woods would be filled with daffodils, snowdrops and bluebells. The sun would warm the moorland, and the brown tinge would be banished with a spread of green. They'd be living in the garden. Didn't that sound appealing? Catherine wanted to yell, *it's not the bloody weather, it's the double murder which took place in the barn*, but she kept her mouth shut.

Early Sunday evening, she was alone in the kitchen when the phone rang. She answered in a daze, surprised by who the caller was.

'Peter Carmichael,' the voice said. 'The vicar, remember?'

'Yes,' Catherine said, wishing she hadn't picked up. The last thing she wanted to think about right now was having to give a talk to a bunch of locals.

'I tried ringing over the holidays, but you must have been out or away.'

'Yes, we were away.'

Silence. As if Carmichael was preparing himself.

'Look, Peter, about the talk you wanted us to—'

'Oh, don't worry about that, I'm calling about something completely different.' More silence. Carmichael clearing his throat. Catherine could almost imagine him hopping from one foot to the other. Finally he spoke. 'It's about the Murrins.'

She froze for a second and glanced at the ceiling. Daniel was working up there. She moved from the kitchen to the living room and closed the door.

'OK. Do you have some more information for me?'

'Yes, but not about what happened. This concerns something which took place recently.'

'Connected with World's End?'

'No, but it's to do with Mr Murrin.'

'I thought he was dead?'

'Yes.' Carmichael paused. 'Look, I'm not even sure I should be telling you this, but I've been struggling with it and I've concluded I should.'

Catherine inwardly groaned. Talk about going round the houses. 'Anything I can find out is useful.'

'OK.' More silence until Carmichael cleared his throat. 'Murrin moved away from the parish and to the other side of the moor decades ago. He wasn't one of my flock and I hadn't personally met him, but about a year ago — February I think — I heard he had advanced cancer and had tried to take his own life. He'd ended up in hospital down in Exeter and I decided to pay him a visit.'

'To give him absolution?'

'No, no. The Murrins have a plot in the graveyard and I guessed he would want to be buried there alongside his sons. To be truthful, it was a practical matter, but I can't say I wasn't interested in seeing if the man matched up to the image which I'd heard so much about.'

'And did he?'

'I'm afraid what passed between myself and Mr Murrin on that day will remain confidential. That's not the reason I called you.'

'So why did you?'

'Please, if you just listen, all will become clear.' There was another pause. 'Now, as it happens, two days later I had to visit a parishioner on the same ward as Murrin. He too had terminal cancer. I went and sat with him for half an hour, but as I got up to leave, I saw a man at Murrin's bedside. At the time I thought nothing of it and it wasn't until I met you and your husband in the churchyard, and later when I talked to you alone, that I realised it might be of some importance. I was going to tell you back then, but I didn't feel it was my place to. Gossip and rumour lead to bitterness and distrust I find, especially within a marriage.'

'So what made you change your mind?'

'Just that, I'm afraid. Gossip and rumour.'

'Sorry?'

'The news on the grapevine is you're selling up, is that correct?'

'It's not finalised yet, but yes. Anyway, I don't see what bearing that has.'

'I thought you should be in full possession of the facts before you make your decision.'

'I don't understand?'

'You need to know who I saw that day at Murrin's bedside. Now, I can't be one hundred per cent certain but I'm pretty sure all the same.'

'And?' Catherine's hand was clenched round the phone. 'Who was it?'

'Someone you know very well, Ms Ross.' Silence. Then Carmichael's voice, lower and softer and with just a hint of compassion. 'Your husband. Daniel.'

Chapter Thirty

After her phone conversation with Peter Carmichael, Catherine went upstairs. She stood on the landing outside Daniel's room. A cacophony echoed from within. Cymbals clashing, the blare of a brass section, the rumble of timpani. A quieter passage followed. A piano trickling down the scale, the deepening notes interwoven with a haunting melody from a flute. Next came a discordant section which finally resolved into a wash of bold major chords piling atop one another in a triumphant finale.

She had no idea about the structure of the movie or its story, but as the last chord died she found herself crying. Daniel was a genius. Complicated, confused, sometimes angry and frightening, but a genius nonetheless. She loved him so much and yet the secrets between them were eating away at the bond they had. As she wiped away her tears, the door to the room opened and Daniel emerged. He looked drained, as if the music had sapped all his energy, but he smiled as he came across and put his arms round her.

'Love you,' he whispered in her ear.

'You too,' Catherine said.

As they held each other, she fought to control herself. Half of her wanted to tell him about what Carmichael had revealed, about Frank Lever and Joe Foster, about Murrin and the boys who'd died in the barn, about — perhaps — Gemma and the mistrust she felt over Daniel's trips away. Her other half urged her to keep quiet, to let the moment go on and on, to wait until Daniel returned from London before she ripped up the foundations they were standing on.

The cautious Catherine won, and she allowed Daniel to lead her to the bedroom.

Later they ate and went to bed early so he could be fresh for his trip the following day. They made love again and she fell into a deep sleep. The cold woke her, and in the dark she reached out for Daniel, only to find he'd already left for London.

Monday and Tuesday passed uneventfully. Catherine tried to focus on her work but found herself increasingly distracted by Carmichael's revelation that Daniel had gone to see Mr Murrin as he lay dying in a hospital in Exeter. Carmichael had said that had been a year ago, way before they'd come down to Devon to view World's End Farm. Try as she might, she couldn't think of a reason Daniel would be visiting Murrin. Murrin hadn't lived at World's End for over thirty-five years, and she wasn't even sure if the house had been on the market back the previous February, but she supposed it was possible. She recalled Daniel had been away for a week around that time, supposedly on a movie set somewhere near Bristol. It was when he'd returned that they'd had their massive argument and Daniel had suggested moving away from London.

Had he already lined up World's End as a potential buy back then? Perhaps he had and had got wind of the murders and wanted to get the story of what happened from Murrin. But that didn't make sense. Would he, a total stranger to Murrin, go so far as to pester a dying man for answers to an event which happened several decades before?

She resolved to discuss it with Daniel. One way or another the whole sordid business had to come out in the open. She'd tell him what she'd been up to and what she'd discovered and demand an explanation. He'd be angry and hurt she hadn't confided in him, but she could counter with the fact he'd been keeping secrets from her. She didn't relish the coming argument but, weirdly, knowing it was inevitable allowed her to relax a little, and by Wednesday morning she was back in her workshop, chipping away at a block of marble, her mind for a while free of worry.

When she came out of the barn to return to the house at lunch time, she stopped midway across the yard, aware there was a heavy feel to the air. Clouds were building in the west and the sky above the farm bore an ethereal layer of haze, the underside of which was tinged with burnt ochre. She recalled Daniel's words about the spring and went inside and flipped the radio on to hear that the Met Office had issued a severe weather warning for the South West. High winds and rain would bring widespread disruption, and later the rain would turn to snow; substantial accumulations were forecast. The local news station advised moorland residents to stock up on food and make sure their cars were equipped with shovels, snow chains and emergency supplies. The consensus on the lunch-time phone-in seemed to be to stay at home, hunker down, and prepare for the worst.

From the sound of the weather report she could well be snowed in at World's End, and she tried not to let a feeling of claustrophobia overcome her as she watched the dark rain clouds tumble over the ridge. By five o'clock the day was gone, and a black gloom surrounded the house. She closed the blinds in the kitchen and went into the living room and drew the curtains. She double checked the locks on the doors front and back and went to the kitchen and cooked herself an elaborate meal.

After eating the food and clearing away, she curled up on the sofa, switched the TV on, and found a decent movie. As the film began to play, a shriek could be heard above the title music. It was the wind spilling down the valley and howling as the air was forced between the house and the barn. Catherine shivered. She longed to be able to look outside and see a streetlight or a passing car. To feel that just a few steps away others were also watching television or eating their evening meal. She blipped the volume on the TV up a notch and tried to concentrate on the programme.

Sometime later the trill from her phone jerked her awake. The movie had ended, and the late-night news was reporting the storm. She picked up her mobile and answered.

'Hello?'

'Help. Please, Catherine, I need your help.'

PART THREE

The Body

Now...

Chapter Thirty-one

If only she hadn't answered the phone, Catherine thought. She wouldn't have heard Lisa's voice asking for help, and she wouldn't have driven across the moor to rescue her and bring her back to World's End. She wouldn't have given her a bed for the night. She wouldn't have stepped out into the snow that very morning and found a nasty surprise in the back of Lisa's car.

If only.

She sat on the floor in the bathroom trying to recover from the shock. She thought about the way lightning had struck one, twice, three times: Daniel bludgeoning the burglar with the statue, Will and Red Murrin hanged in the barn, the body in the car.

'Daniel, where are you?' She whispered the words to herself, feeling pathetic and weak and lost. 'Please come home.'

She pulled out her mobile. There was no reply to the text she'd sent last night. She composed a new one, this time stressing the urgency. Whatever he was up to in London, she needed him to call. Right now.

She pressed 'send' and waited. When they'd first got together they'd texted each other dozens of times each day, Daniel's clever quips arriving mere seconds after she'd sent him a message. Now there was nothing. It was as if he was somehow part of this, his very absence a piece of the conspiracy.

She glanced at the screen, aware a couple of minutes had passed. There was still no answer from Daniel. Since she'd set out to find Lisa last night, time had flown by in a blur. She cast her mind back to the phone call and the drive onto the moor in the bad weather. The state

Lisa was in and her insistence they rescue her car. Her extreme tiredness when they got home and, this morning, the horrific revelation of the reason Lisa had braved the storm to get here:

You understand now why I had to come. I'm in trouble and you're the only person I can turn to. We need to get rid of the body, bury it somewhere it will never be found. It's why I came here. I knew you'd be able to find a solution. I knew you'd help a friend in need.

Catherine stood and went to the window. Snow was falling, swirling in the air on the strong wind, and the landscape was sheathed with a thick layer of white. The red Audi stood out front, and she shivered at the thought of what was lying in the back under the parcel shelf. Whose body was it in there, wrapped in carpet and plastic and contorted to fit in the tight space?

'Cath?' A knock on the bathroom door. Lisa must have let herself in through the kitchen entrance. 'Are you OK in there?'

There was a pause and the door handle moved down. Catherine went across and flushed the toilet and ran the tap on the basin.

'Because I need your help. I really do.' Lisa's voice whispered from behind the door, like smoke in the way the words finessed their way into the room. '*Please...*'

'Christ, Lisa,' Catherine said, turning the tap off. 'I'm having trouble dealing with this. With why the fuck you've come here with a body in the boot of your car.'

'I've come because I had no one else to turn to, because I knew you'd understand. This was the only option I had left. And remember what you said to me after the break-in? You said you owed me. You said if I needed help, I was to call you.'

'I didn't mean I would help you dispose of a body. You're asking me to be complicit in a crime.'

'Catherine, I'm the victim here.' The handle on the door moved again. 'Look, you stay in there for a bit and think about it.'

The handle popped back up and a floorboard creaked as Lisa went downstairs.

Catherine splashed more water on her face. This couldn't be happening, could it? Not again. One horrid mess after another. Murder and death. Some sort of predestination. No escape from what was written.

She unlocked the bathroom door and a chill brushed her face as she walked across the landing. She peered over the banisters. The front door stood open, flakes of snow blowing into the hallway. She went downstairs and looked out. Lisa stood over by the rear of her car, staring into the open boot.

'It's Toby, isn't it?' Catherine said. The notion came to her out of the blue as the obvious explanation. Toby the sex pest. Toby the harasser. Toby the wife beater and abuser. The signs had been there all along. The way Lisa followed meekly in her husband's footsteps, deferring to him on every subject and letting him take the limelight. How he was able to get away with sleeping with his students and yet keep a faithful wife at home. His general attitude towards women.

She thought of the irony: it had been Toby who'd told the dead body buddy story in the pub and here was his wife putting his words into practice. Catherine rebuked herself for being so blind. 'I'm sorry, I should have realised.'

Lisa gripped the lip of the boot. She was silent for a while, as if she was considering whether to answer or what to say. Then she turned.

'I loved him, you know,' she said. 'Once, a long time ago. Maybe even now.'

'Come inside,' Catherine said, the emotion from earlier replaced by a strange calmness, almost as if somebody else was controlling her actions. 'We need to work out what to do.'

'OK.' Lisa made a thin smile of acknowledgement and reached up and slammed the rear hatch shut.

In the kitchen, Catherine busied herself with making coffee and a plate of toast. Lisa sat at the table, almost as if she was a neighbour who'd just popped round for a chat. Not someone who was barely more than an acquaintance who'd arrived uninvited with the body of her husband stuffed in the back of her car. Catherine half expected Lisa to begin a conversation about clothes or the weather or the latest movie release.

She put the toast on the table and poured the coffees. She sat down as Lisa took a piece of toast.

'I'm sorry,' Catherine said. 'About what's happened.'

'Not your fault.' Lisa munched on the toast. 'Nobody's fault but Toby's. Perhaps mine for being such a fool.'

'This has been going on for years, right?'

Lisa nodded. 'Ever since we were married. He was violent from the start, but I thought I could change him. He never seriously hurt me, not bruises and stuff, but he'd force me to do things I didn't want, and if I protested he'd hit me.'

'You should have left.'

'That's easy to say, less easy to do.'

'Yes, a stupid statement, I apologise. I can't imagine what it must be like. Daniel wouldn't hurt a... well, he'd do anything to protect me.'

Lisa didn't respond. She took another piece of toast. Catherine stood and went to the kitchen window. She lingered, taking in the moorland sheathed with white. Snow continued to fall in fat flakes, and a fence post at the side of the garden wore a cap several inches high.

'What are we going to do?' Lisa said.

'Can't you call the police and explain what happened? Tell them he's been abusing you all these years? If you killed him in self-defence, it might not even go to trial.'

'But I didn't kill him in self-defence. He'd had a bit too much to drink and he forced me to have sex. Afterwards, he passed out on the sofa. I stood there and thought of all the times I'd been scared of him. Then I bashed him over the head.'

'You bashed him...?' Catherine heard herself gasp. She had a sudden flashback. The burglar in the house in London. Blood on the stripped-pine floorboards. Daniel with one of her statues in his hands.

'Catherine? Are you OK?' Lisa stood and joined Catherine at the window. She looked out at the snow. 'We're safe for now, aren't we? No one's coming in this.'

No, Catherine thought. No one was coming, not even Daniel.

She went across to the sink and ran water from the tap. Filled a glass. She was conscious Lisa was watching her. Waiting. She tried to weigh her options. The sensible one seemed to be to call the police.

However, the police would almost certainly be interested that Daniel was her husband, a friend of Toby's, and somebody who had killed before, albeit in different circumstances.

Setting that aside, there was the moral argument. If Lisa had suffered at the hands of Toby, didn't she need to be helped? The police would take her away in handcuffs and there'd be a trial. There was no guarantee she wouldn't be convicted of murder and handed a life sentence. Catherine thought of how close Daniel had come to being prosecuted, of how stressful it had been. And there was no doubt Toby was a monster. She'd seen it with her own eyes when he'd assaulted the girl in the pub.

'Catherine?' The whisper came from just behind her, Lisa's voice silky smooth. 'I can't do this without you.'

'Give me some space, Lisa.' She moved away and stood by the door to the hall. 'A few minutes alone, OK?'

'Sure.' The fear and emotion in Lisa's voice had gone, replaced by a tone which was harder and more determined. 'But don't take too long about it.'

Catherine went upstairs and lay on her bed. In her heart she wanted to help Lisa, but she needed to get things straight in her head. For instance, what would the consequences be if she got caught and had to stand trial? The defence argument would go that she had simply helped a friend who'd suffered years of rape and abuse. She'd broken the law, but who wouldn't do the same in similar circumstances? She tried to imagine serving on a jury herself and having to weigh up the evidence.

Not guilty.

It was more complicated than the two words suggested of course, but she was pretty sure most right-minded people would come to the same conclusion. That being the case, the second part of the problem was where to dispose of the body? If she could solve the second part, the first issue — the consequences of a trial — would never arise.

She got off the bed and went to the window and looked out across the moor. She let her mind wander, as if she'd just emerged from her workshop after several hours of intricate work with a chisel. If she was to help Lisa, she had to find a location to hide the body which was one hundred per cent secure. If anyone spotted them on the way there, they were fucked. If a dog walker found the body in a month's time, they were fucked. If erosion revealed the body in a year, they were fucked. She thought about the walks she and Daniel had been on since they'd moved, trying to recall somewhere suitable. Then she remembered a walk they'd taken which circuited old mine workings.

She returned to the kitchen to find Lisa pouring coffee from a fresh pot into two cups.

'I'll help you,' Catherine said. 'It's not the rational thing to do, but I guess it's the moral thing.'

'Oh, Catherine!' Lisa put the coffee pot down and both hands went to her face. She sobbed, her whole body shaking. 'Thank you!'

Catherine went over and gave Lisa a hug. 'But we must do this right, OK? You need to get your story straight, so you don't slip up when questioned.'

'OK.' Lisa wiped tears from her eyes. 'I've already thought of that. I came to visit you and when I got back to London, Toby had gone. I'll report him missing a day later.'

'They'll want to come and interview me, so we need to work out what we were up to. Luckily, with all this snow, we can say we stayed in the whole time.' Catherine paused. 'That just leaves us with the small matter of the body. We've got to find the perfect hiding place because this is forever. We take this secret to our deathbeds.'

'I understand, but I thought it would be easy to find a spot up here on the moor?'

'There are loads of remote places, but how will we get the body to one of them? We'll have to carry it and realistically that means a few hundred metres tops from a road or a track. Now, you're lucky, we have the 4x4, but it can't go cross country. Imagine if we got stuck in the middle of nowhere with the body in the back? There's the weather, too. More heavy snow is forecast, so we've got to get this done quickly.'

'Shit, I didn't realise it would be so difficult. What are we going to do?'

'There are two options. One, go far away. The advantage is we considerably lessen the chance of a connection to here and thus back to you. The problem is the snow. The roads are already several inches deep and if we have an accident or get stuck, we're in big trouble. There's also the issue that the farther we go, the less I know about the area, and the less likely we can find a decent hiding spot.'

'And the second option?'

'We find somewhere close by. It just so happens I know a place where the body will almost certainly escape discovery.'

'That sounds perfect.'

'Fingers crossed, it might be.' Catherine pointed to the table. 'We can't hang about, so drink your coffee and we'll go.'

Chapter Thirty-two

After they'd fortified themselves with fresh toast, Catherine sorted out some winter clothing for Lisa — a hat and scarf, a pair of woollen gloves, a coat — and they went outside. The snow showed no sign of stopping and the wind had strengthened. She started the pickup and backed towards the rear of Lisa's car.

'We'll put the body in and cover it with a tarpaulin,' Catherine said, opening the tailgate and pointing to a sheet of blue plastic. 'It's the best we can do.'

As they bent to lift the package from the back of the car, she swallowed and tried to fight the fresh bout of nausea which swept up from the pit of her stomach.

'Are you OK?' Lisa said.

'Let's do it.' Catherine swallowed. 'Before I'm sick.'

The two of them struggled to lift the body from the car and across to the bed of the pickup. The plastic wrapping made the whole package slippery and the snow-covered ground didn't help. Once it was in, Catherine threw the tarpaulin across.

'There's this too.' Lisa stood with a smaller bundle in her arms. A black bin bag with layers of tape wrapped round and round. 'Clothes and other stuff he was wearing. Best get rid of it all, I thought.'

'Put it in.' Catherine closed the tailgate of the 4x4 and went over to the garden shed and retrieved two spades.

'Hopefully we won't need these,' she said as she placed them in the back of the pickup. 'But better safe than sorry.'

They both got in and Catherine drove away from the house. She stopped at the junction with the lane. A single set of tracks in the snow marked the passing of a vehicle some minutes before. Catherine pulled out onto the lane, turned right, and headed up the valley.

Snow tumbled from the sky, and as they climbed the hillside and drove past the turning for Joe Foster's place, the valley below was lost in a maelstrom of white.

'Where are we going?' Lisa said. She peered ahead. Snow was now plastered on the windscreen round a semi-circular pattern cleared by the wipers. 'Not far, I hope?'

'A mile, no more.'

Catherine concentrated on driving. In four-wheel drive, the pickup made light work of the hill, the wet snow yielding as the chunky tyres bit the road surface. The tracks of the other vehicle had all but disappeared as they carried on up the valley and passed a huge column of granite that stood like a weird bedecked statue, its top layered with snow, the sides black in contrast.

'We're here,' Catherine said. She gestured at a tumbled-down building. A rough gravel track led away from the building and curved down the hillside. She indicated and took the track.

'What is this place?' Lisa said. She looked at the building and beyond to where the track rounded a deep quarry with an azure lake. 'Some sort of reservoir? It appears deep enough to dump a body in.'

'That's not a good idea. I'd worry about it rising to the surface.'

'Where then?'

'This is an old mine. Most of the workings have long since been filled in, but half a mile down this track is an open shaft. I walked there with Daniel a few weeks ago. The shaft seemed pretty deep, so we'll dump the body there.'

'I'm glad you're on my side,' Lisa said. 'Otherwise I'd be stuffed, right?'

Catherine didn't answer. This was all too easy. Too easy in a practical sense, but too easy psychologically as well. She should be feeling more than she was. Guilt or anger. Fear, perhaps. Instead the emotion which rose to the surface was impatience. She wanted this over and done with, Lisa gone, and Daniel home. Already she realised she wouldn't be able to confide in him. He'd never accept Toby was the monster Lisa had described and, despite misgivings, he'd want to go to the police.

'Here,' Catherine said, pulling the 4x4 off the track. A glance back the way they'd come showed only the cliff with the lake below. They were no longer visible from the road. 'We need to walk to the shaft. There's a footpath, but it'll be a struggle.'

She opened the door. The snow was getting heavier now, great wet flakes sweeping across the moor on an ever-strengthening wind. Lisa climbed out the other side and came round. Catherine put the hood on her coat up and gestured to Lisa to do the same

'It's turning into a blizzard, isn't it?' Lisa pointed back the way they'd come. The track was a sheet of white. 'Will we be able to get out?'

'I hope so.' Catherine went to the rear of the vehicle. 'Come on, let's get on with it.'

She opened the tailgate and drew the tarpaulin to one side. Lisa moved to help her. Catherine shifted the roll of carpet and plastic so Lisa was able to grab hold of one end. She backed away but as the bundle came out, Lisa let go. The body thumped down onto the ground.

'Fuck, Lisa! What are you doing?'

'Sorry, I'm freezing.' Lisa stood there shivering, her arms crossed over the front of her chest. 'I'm not sure I'll be able to carry the body.'

'Shit.' Catherine hadn't thought the roll of carpet was so heavy, nor Lisa so weak. If anyone came across them now they were in all sorts of trouble. Luckily the snow was showing no sign of stopping. In fact, with the wind building, drifts would soon be forming on the road. Nobody in their right minds would be out on the moor in this weather. She chuckled to herself. Madness.

'What are you laughing at?' Lisa said.

'The irony. We might get stuck on the way home, but this snow could be working to our advantage.' Catherine reached into the back of the pickup and found the tow rope. 'Look, we can tie this round one end and haul the body across to the mineshaft. The plastic will slide over the fresh snow. It will be much easier than carrying it.'

She tied a large loop at each end of the rope so they had two handles they could pull with. She doubled the middle of the rope and made a slipknot. She placed the slipknot round the bundle and tightened it. She handed a loop to Lisa and showed her how to hook it over her shoulder. Then she pointed out onto the moor and they took up the slack on the rope and started to walk.

The plastic slid across the snow-covered heather, and where there was no heather the going was even easier. The only difficulty came when they encountered a patch of broken stone, but in ten minutes they'd managed to drag the body a quarter of a mile.

'I'm knackered,' Lisa said, standing with her hands on her hips. 'How much farther?'

'There.' Catherine pointed to a low hummock off to the right. A rickety fence circled the hummock. Barbed wire atop broken sheep netting. Several of the supporting posts leaned over and as a barrier the fence was ineffectual. 'That's the entrance to the mineshaft. We'll flatten the fence and push the body over and into the shaft.'

'How deep is it?'

'I don't know, but Daniel dropped a stone down and we didn't hear it hit the bottom.'

They tugged the body the last few steps and Catherine bashed the fence down and told Lisa to stand on the wire. She bent and rolled the bundle across the fence.

'Are we good to go?' Lisa pointed at the gaping hole.

'Wait,' Catherine said. She knelt by the roll of plastic-covered carpet. 'Shouldn't we remove this? We could take it back to the farm and burn it. If the body was ever found, then the fewer clues discovered with it the better.' Catherine began to tear at the plastic.

'No!' Lisa snatched at Catherine's arm. 'Please don't!'

'Lisa, what the hell's got into you? I'm trying to help.'

'Please!' Lisa lurched back, edging dangerously close to the mineshaft. She put her hands to her face. 'I can't bear to see him again. To see what I did. It just reminds me of what happened, of how he—'

'Be careful!' Catherine stood and pulled Lisa away from the hole. 'You head back to the track. I'll take care of this.'

'Oh!' Lisa retched. 'I feel faint. I think I'm going to be sick. Can you help me?'

Catherine grabbed Lisa by the waist and together they staggered beyond the fence to where a granite boulder poked above the snow. 'Sit here.'

'You won't...?' Lisa peered through her fingers at the polythene wrapped bundle. 'You know, you won't...?'

'No,' Catherine said. Lisa had lost it. The sooner they got out of here and home, the better. Give her the rest of the day and night to recover and then send her on her way. 'I'll tip the body over the edge and we'll have to hope the shaft is deep enough.'

'OK.' Lisa's voice croaked and she fought to swallow. 'Just get it over with.'

Catherine moved to the body. She rotated it so one end pointed towards the hole and lifted the other end and shoved. The plastic package slid on the snow and the body inched closer to the edge of the shaft. She paused to remove the tow rope and gave a final heft. The bundle tumbled over the edge, one end rising before it fell away. There was the sound of some pebbles hitting the sides of the shaft, but that was it. No great splash or thud. Perhaps the body was still falling, and the mine was way deeper than she'd thought.

'Come on.' She went back and helped Lisa to her feet. As they headed off, she had to hold a hand to her eyes. The wind was howling towards them and the snowflakes stung her skin as they struck her face. She could just about make out the trail they'd forged across the heather and the 4x4 parked up by the track, but the moor beyond was invisible behind the whiteout, a billion flakes churning in the air.

The return journey to the pickup took almost as long as the outward one because Lisa was a virtual deadweight. She rambled a succession of monosyllables and Catherine wondered if she might be verging on hypothermic. Back at the vehicle, she propelled Lisa up and into the passenger seat. Once she was seated herself, she turned the ignition key and set the heater to max.

'Are you awake?' Catherine touched Lisa on the arm.

'Uh huh.' Lisa sniffed and lay back. 'Sorry.'
'Not to worry. Let's get you back, OK?'
This time there was no answer. Lisa was asleep.

Chapter Thirty-three

The first I heard of what happened at World's End Farm was from Barney's mother. She'd talked to Sergeant Jencks' wife and then run over to our place to tell my ma the news. She arrived hot and breathless, and after she'd stripped off her winter gear, she was hustled into the kitchen where she recounted the story.

Mr Hodgson, it appeared, had dropped dead while visiting the Murrin's farm. He'd had a turn or similar. Will Murrin was sent down to the village to fetch Jencks. Will rode down but Jencks came back with him on foot and by all accounts the policeman was close to dropping dead himself by the time he got up to World's End. Mrs Murrin gave him a glass of water and he sat in the parlour until he'd recovered. After that he took a gander at Mr Hodgson. The poor bloke lay at the foot of the stairs. He'd been trying to get up to see Red and Will, but Mr Murrin had intervened. There'd been a bit of shoving and a lot of shouting and Hodgson had just collapsed.

'Went down like a bullock hit with a cow punch,' Mr Murrin said to Jencks. 'Couldn't do nothing for him 'cept lay him out for Hargreave to deal with.'

Hargreave was the local undertaker and, even as Jencks was struggling up the hill on foot, Hargreave was preparing to drive up to the farm across the fields on a borrowed tractor and trailer, a wooden coffin strapped in place.

'And you never touched him?' Jencks asked.

'Never laid as much as a finger on him.'

'What was he here about? Why was he so angry?'

'*Something about a pony of his going missing.*'

'*He accused you of taking it?*'

'*Aye, but I told him I didn't know what the hell he was talking about.*'

'*And that was it?*'

'*No. For some reason he'd also got it into his head that my boys had interfered with his eldest daughter, Helena. He told me he was going to kill 'em both. Well, I couldn't let him up the stairs after he'd threatened them.*'

'*Had your boys touched Helena?*'

'*They say they didn't and I believe them. If you want my advice, you'll check on them gypsies camped down Ashburton way. Been plenty of trouble, I hear. One young lass raped, but you'll know all about that. To be honest, I wouldn't be surprised if they've stolen the pony as well.*'

Jencks nodded. He appeared satisfied with the explanation. '*If you didn't touch Mr Hodgson, and your lads don't know anything about some funny business with Helena, you needn't worry.*'

And that was the end of it. Jencks stumbled back through the snow drifts down to the village and went to the pub where he drank three pints of bitter, the beer paid for with a crisp twenty-pound note which most people reckon came straight from Mr Murrin's wallet.

Now I ain't saying where the money came from, but it was telling that Helena was never visited by Jencks, and there was no further investigation into Mr Hodgson's death. Doctor Davies got hustled away from his warm fireside to examine Hodgson, and after he'd done so, he pronounced him dead from a heart attack. Would have been funny if he wasn't dead because by the time Davies got up to World's End, Hargreave had Hodgson laid out in the coffin on the trailer, ready to take him back down the valley.

Of course, I knew what had happened, but I kept it to myself. I said nothing to Jencks and nothing to my ma or pa. The only person I told was Barney. He was a tenant of the Murrins too, but he had a wife to keep happy and three children to clothe and feed. He understood my dilemma.

Mr Hodgson's funeral took place a week later, but none of us locals were invited. I watched from across the field at the back of the church as the coffin went down into the frozen ground and a small group of mourners trudged away. Helena and her sisters and their mother, all in black in stark contrast to the white snow, a chill in my heart which had little to do with the weather.

Chapter Thirty-four

Foster woke having dreamed of the house again. He lay staring at the ceiling, his breath clouding the frigid air in much the same way as his worries had clouded his mind as he'd fallen asleep the night before. He shook himself awake, tugged off the blankets, and rose from his bed, hoping the memories would fade. A glance at the window told him that might be difficult as the sky was dotted with white flakes wafting to the ground. A thick covering of snow lay folded across the moorland close to, while in the distance a crag stood in dark contrast. Above the rocks heavy grey clouds were segueing in from the west. Nothing else moved save the water in the stream, a narrow strip of dark turbulence snaking down the valley.

He went to the window and loosened the catch. Fresh air breezed in along with a gurgle from the stream. Foster echoed a cough in response, a throaty cough full of phlegm and badness. He worked up the phlegm in his mouth and took a well-aimed spit through the window. He eyeballed the bank of cloud.

'Sod it,' he said, before turning to the old armchair where his clothes lay in a pile. 'That's all we bloody need.'

Downstairs, Jess was up and scratching at the door before he was halfway along the hall. He let the dog out, watching as she scampered across the yard leaving a line of pawprints behind her.

Foster closed the door and went to cook breakfast. Three chops and some bread fried up with a couple of tomatoes, a load of mushrooms, and some halves of potato he had left over. After a cup of tea, he went to feed the stock and do his chores.

In the barn, the sheep shifted in their pen, restless. He checked the water pipes to their drinking troughs hadn't frozen and poured the corn mix into the feeders. The ewes forged past him, save for one solitary animal that stood over in a corner.

'What's wrong, you bugger?' Foster said.

He walked across and caught the ewe, deftly swinging the animal round and standing astride her. He bent her head to the side and lifted her lip and examined her teeth and gums. He checked both her eyes. He changed position to face the animal's rear and raised her tail. Her fanny was pink and her arse clean. Well, he thought, if she didn't want to eat there wasn't a lot he could do. He'd never been much for vets and besides, in this weather no one would be doing outcalls.

By the time he'd finished his rounds, the snow had become much heavier. He stomped back to the house, his boots leaving deep prints in the yard. The dog whirled round him in ever widening circles. As he got to the back door she began to bark.

'Shut it,' he shouted, and kicked a boot into the snow. White flurries arced in the air, but the dog made no effort to chase them. She yapped and ran towards the yard gate.

'What's up, gal?' he said, wondering why she was so excited. It couldn't be the stock because, aside from four rams in a little walled paddock behind the house, all the sheep and the bullocks were in one of the barns. 'You found something? You want me to come and look?'

The dog barked in response and slipped through the gate and ran into the adjoining field. Foster plodded after her, guessing she might have sniffed out a ewe which had strayed over from Barney's place. The dog raised her nose in the air and barked again.

Foster squinted into the distance where the swirling snow was an almost impenetrable fuzz. Like a TV switched on with no signal. Great wet flakes stuck to his face and drifts were beginning to form against the stone walls to either side of the gate. He looked over at the dog. She stood like a pointer, one foot off the ground, head outstretched. Whatever she was interested in was out there, beyond the pasture, up on the moor.

Five minutes later, Foster was trundling along on his tractor. The cab was rudimentary, a solid glass windscreen with a surrounding frame of metal. The frame supported a canvas and PVC cover, but the once clear PVC was now barely translucent. The dog sat in the transport box at the rear, yapping a continual encouragement to Foster. They climbed the rough moorland track, pitching, rolling and yawing as if the tractor was a sailing dinghy on a stormy lake, but the big tyres front and rear had no trouble gripping the ground, even as the hill became steeper. Foster sat relaxed, with his fingers hardly gracing the steering wheel, making the occasional adjustment to the throttle lever.

Halfway up the hill, he stopped the tractor. He jerked on the handbrake and clambered down from the cab. Now, with the wind at his back, he was able to scan the fields below him. The snow blanketed everything. His farm lay way down the valley, the grey stone house surrounded by virgin white.

'You having me on, girl?' Foster said. 'Pulling a fast one just to make the day a bit more interesting? You little devil.'

The dog slunk away, no longer as excited as before. Foster turned to the tractor, but as he heaved himself up into the cab, a light flashed yellow on the ridge by the old mine workings. There. And again. Then a sweep of headlights as a vehicle drove out onto the road. What sort of idiot would be out on the moor on a day like this?

His first thought was fly tippers. A load of tyres had been dumped at the workings a few months ago. A pair of fridges and a washing machine had followed. Still, he doubted anyone would bother in this weather. The other possibility was plain old-fashioned thievery. The track from the road led down to the edge of his land where there was an ancient linhay. Years back, there'd been cows there in the winter. Now Foster used the barn to store some odds and sods. Fencing wire, posts, a couple of pieces of machinery. And it was most likely the machinery they were after. There was a hay tedder and a mole drainer, both of which could be attached to the back of the tractor. Neither were hi-tech or worth much, but thieves were thieves. He tutted to himself. He'd come this far, he might as well go and see what the buggers had been up to.

The snow was even worse by the time he drove the tractor into the little yard in front of the linhay. He got out and went across to the open-fronted barn. The tedder and drainer were parked in the left-hand bay. The fence posts wore a frosted icing of snow, and the ground around the barn was white and untouched, the only disturbance being Foster's boot prints and the tyre marks from his tractor.

He walked across the yard to the gate which allowed access to the open moor. A track led from the gate up to the old mine workings and back to the road. Beside him Jess whined and gave a sharp yap.

He hummed and hawed for a few moments. The area of moor beyond the gate was Duchy land and of no concern to him. There was no need to investigate further. On the other hand, what else did he have to do? He could head out onto the track, see what was what, and take the easier route home along the road. If he found anything suspicious he might report it to the authorities. Or he might not.

He'd driven a short way along the track when he came across a set of tyre marks. The snow was heavier than ever, but even so the ruts hadn't been covered so much he couldn't tell what had happened. A vehicle had come down the track, reversed round, and gone back the way it had come. Someone had got lost and taken a wrong turn. No fly-tipping, no thievery, nothing to get excited about.

'That's it then,' he said. 'Home.'

A bark came from the transport box at the back of the tractor. Jess leapt down from the box and ran across the heather. Foster ignored her and instead grabbed the gear stick and rammed the tractor into reverse. He backed round and opened the door to shout to the dog. Which was when he saw the strange furrow in the snow leading away from the track. The dog sniffed at the furrow and barked up at him, as if to say, 'I told you so.'

'What's this?' Foster shifted the stick into neutral and clambered down from the cab. A U-shaped depression headed towards a low mound with a fence round it. One of the many mineshafts on this part of the moor. An object had been dragged over the heather, Foster thought. An object heavy enough to leave a smooth, snow-lined channel.

He scratched his chin. The wind buffeted him and a gust caught the door of the tractor, slamming it shut. The air was a swarm of snowflakes and the blizzard was showing signs of getting even worse. He'd barely be able to see well enough to stay on the road, and in these conditions he didn't fancy the alternative route back over the fields.

'It'll wait,' he said to the dog. She lifted her head and sniffed in the direction of the mineshaft. 'Whatever's down there won't be moving far. We'll check it when this has blown over, right?'

With that, Foster went back to the tractor, opened the door and climbed back in. The dog took one last sniff and bounded towards him. She jumped up into the transport box as he put the tractor into gear and headed off.

Chapter Thirty-five

By the time they made it back to World's End, the snow had begun to drift. Within an hour all moorland roads would be impassable. Catherine thought about her texts to Daniel. Was he on his way home? If so, he'd struggle to make it up the valley.

She woke Lisa, hustled her inside, and made sure she was warm and dry. Next, she set a pan of pasta to boil and found a jar of pesto. When the pasta was done, she tossed a good dollop of pesto in and served the food in a couple of bowls. They ate in silence, partly because they were both tired and partly because Catherine couldn't think of a meaningful topic of conversation. When they'd finished, she cleared away and went upstairs. She lay on her side on the bed so she could see out the window. Snow continued to fall, the blizzard grey against the sky like a plague of locusts swarming in the air.

She tried calling Daniel, but once again she reached his voicemail. She sent another text, but her message went unanswered. Finally, she composed an email, praying somehow it would get to him.

A minute later, the phone still in her hand, she felt a buzzing. She looked down at the number, but it wasn't one she recognised.

'Hello?'

'Catherine.'

'Daniel!' Catherine said, her heart going into overdrive. 'Where the hell have you been?'

'I lost my phone or it was stolen or something. Sorry, darling.'

'Why the hell didn't you call before?'

'I was caught up in meetings and then this snow. London's ground to a halt, you know? I meant to call last night, but I was out with Toby and we both had way too much—'

'*Toby?*' She hadn't heard right, had she?

'Yes. I know, I know, but it was just a drink.'

'Did you say *Toby?*'

'Now don't get angry, love. He's very apologetic about what happened back in the autumn and—'

'Last night?' Catherine was having trouble comprehending. Facts, she thought. Get the facts. 'Do you mean you were out with Toby Paget yesterday evening?'

'Yes, of course Toby Paget. How many other Tobys do we know? Look, it was just a few jars and a curry. Cath, come on, he's a friend. I can't just dump him.'

'Daniel, I...' She didn't know what to say. The world had stopped spinning and flipped. She closed her eyes, visualising Lisa downstairs sprawled on the sofa, recalling the way she'd stood at the rear of her car a few hours before.

I loved him, you know. Once, a long time ago. Maybe even now.

'Are you OK, love? You sound ill.'

'No, I'm not OK.' Catherine said. 'You need to come home, Dan. Right now.'

'What's the matter? The electric's not off, is it? I've heard the weather is pretty bad down there, but if you sit tight I'm sure everything will be alright.'

'It's not the power, Daniel, but I'm scared.'

'Something's happened.' Daniel's voice was flat. He sounded cross. As if Catherine was behaving like a silly little girl again. 'Something like the rats or the guts. Well I've told you not to worry. Nobody is going to hurt us. It's just—'

'Please, Daniel.'

'Shit, Cath. I'm still going through the score with Wes and won't be finished until tomorrow. Anyway, half the motorways are closed and they're saying not to travel unless absolutely necessary.'

'Daniel...' She realised she sounded pathetic, but what else could she say? That Lisa had arrived with Toby's body in the back of her car and they'd buried it up on the moor only it wasn't Toby's body any longer because how could it be when Daniel had had dinner with him the previous night and—

'If Heathrow is open, Wes will be flying to LA on Saturday. That's the deadline for finalising the score. So, weather permitting, I'll set off first thing Saturday.'

'Right.' She could hear in his voice that he'd planned it all out.

'If there's a serious issue with the snow then you need to phone the emergency services, OK, Cath?'

'Yes, Daniel.' She was on autopilot now. Parroting out words.

'I've got to rush. Any problems send me a text. You've got the new number. Love you.'

He was gone. She kept the phone pressed to her ear in case he changed his mind or miraculously reconnected, but there was nothing but dead air.

She dropped the phone on the bed and stood and went to the window. The snow was swirling in a myriad of vortexes as if a powerful conjuror was manipulating the air. Far up the valley, beyond her vision and lost in the whiteout, lay the mine workings. The ruined buildings and the tumbled-down chimney. The quarry with the azure lake. The mineshaft with a body lying at the bottom. A body Lisa had said was Toby but now, it appeared, must be someone completely different.

Chapter Thirty-six

The next morning, Foster woke to the sound of silence. He pushed back the blankets on the bed, staggered to the window, and looked out. The world lay tranquil beneath a deep blue sky, a frozen landscape of white, devoid of movement.

'Ho hum,' Foster said, reaching for his clothes. He didn't bother removing his pyjamas but pulled his trousers and shirt over the top. The extra layers would keep him warm.

Downstairs, he fed the dog a plate of scraps and fixed himself some breakfast. After he'd eaten he went out into the glare of the day. In the yard the snow crunched beneath his feet, the crisp surface frozen hard, but underneath the flakes light and fluffy. Like a meringue, he thought. He fed the sheep and the bullocks and tossed some hay to the rams in the little paddock out the back. The sick ewe he'd spotted the day before didn't look any better, so he corralled her in a pen away from the others and gave her some extra feed.

After he'd finished with the stock, he went to the big barn he used as a workshop. Propped up one end were three wooden ladders. They weren't part of a set and didn't fit together, but Foster reckoned they'd do. One by one he carried them outside and loaded them onto the flatbed trailer. He backed the tractor to the trailer, hitched it up, and set off up the hill, the dog scampering after him and barking until he whacked on the anchors and let her jump up into the cab.

The tractor half ploughed and half rode the deep snow, but he arrived at the linhay without incident. All signs of his visit the previous day had been erased by a thick covering of white. He swung onto the track and followed it until he could see the mineshaft off to the left. He nudged the tractor round and bumped across the snow-covered heather, stopping well outside the fence. He climbed down from the tractor, his shepherd's crook in his hand, and headed for the shaft.

As he approached the fence, he stopped and looked round. The blue sky and the sun and a complete absence of wind were just the sort of conditions which might encourage people onto the moor. Still, they'd struggle to get up here because the lane from World's End down to the village would be blocked. Unless the snowplough came, the only way onto this part of the moor was on a tractor or by foot.

'Careful, Jess,' he said to the dog as she bounded through the snow. 'Stay away from the edge.'

He cursed. The dog didn't have a clue what he was talking about. He delved in his overcoat pocket and found a piece of baler twine. He fashioned a loop, called the dog to him, and put the loop over her head. At the fence he bent and tied the other end of the twine to a post.

Now, with the dog safe, he clambered over the fence, careful not to catch himself. The shaft was ringed with a cornice of snow; step too close to the edge and he'd be down the hole in an instant. Not that the shaft was deep. Thirty feet or so. He'd climbed down with his brothers when he was a kid. Slid down a rope to the bottom, disappointed to find the hole was an exploratory working which led nowhere. If he slipped and fell the worst thing would be that the fall wouldn't kill him. Unless someone came along, he'd lie down there until he starved to death.

With the vision of a prolonged and lonely end in mind, he stayed well clear of the edge as he worked round the hole. He took his crook and bashed at the snow, knocking away the cornice. The shaft was larger than he remembered, and he was glad he'd been cautious. He tied a bowline round his waist and led the other end of the rope to the trailer where he secured it to the rear axle. He retrieved his big spotlight from the cab and returned to the shaft. The rope snapped taut just as he got to the edge of the hole, so he was able to lean out and peer down. He switched the spotlight on and shone the beam into the blackness. Way down below, propped up in one corner of the shaft, was a bundle of plastic. Six feet long, a foot or so wide.

'There you go, Jess,' he said. 'I was right. Fly tipping of sorts.'

The dog whined in response, but the whine carried a hint of distress, as if she'd detected the change in mood of her owner. Foster moved away from the edge and went over to her. He caressed her under the chin before untying the rope from round his waist and walking to the trailer.

Each ladder was ten feet long. Tied together they'd just about reach to the bottom of the shaft. When he'd gone down there before, with his brothers, he'd been young. They'd used a knotted rope. No way at his age could he do that again.

He slid the ladders from the trailer and one by one took them over to the hole. Using a length of rope, he secured the first ladder and lowered it into the shaft. When it had almost disappeared, he took his flick knife and a bundle of twine from his pocket, cut several short lengths, and used them to tie the bottom rung of the next ladder to the top one of the first. He did the same with the final ladder. The whole contraption was a bit rickety, but it would be a lot easier than trying to descend using a rope. Despite that, he pulled a fresh coil from the trailer, tied it on, and dropped that down too. If the ladders broke or fell down, he wanted a backup plan.

With the rope and ladders prepared, he checked Jess was secure and moved across to the shaft. As he put his feet on the top rungs of the ladder, the rope strained, and the ladder creaked. He glanced across at the dog.

'Excitement, Jess,' he said. 'Beats digging holes any day of the week.'

He eased himself down the first ladder until he reached the top of the next one. Transferring between the two was tricky, but once he was safely on the second ladder, he began to descend again. At the third ladder he repeated the little dance with his feet and easily moved on to it. This distance from the surface most of the natural light had gone, and as he got to the bottom of the final ladder he flicked the torch on. He chuckled to himself as he realised he'd estimated the depth of the shaft perfectly. The ladder hung just a foot from the bottom. A pool of water glinted in the beam from the torch and at the edge of the pool lay the bundle of polythene.

Foster took a minute to get his wind back before stepping off the ladder. He gasped as the icy water came up to his knees. He grasped for the rope which hung down the side of the shaft and, using the rope for support, waded across the pool to the package. Part of the polythene sheet had ripped away from one side exposing a fold of carpet. The carpet had a large crimson stain at one end.

'Well bugger me,' Foster said. 'Too big for a dog and too small for a horse.'

He stood in the water and thought about what to do. There didn't seem much doubt that there was a body wrapped in the plastic and carpet, and most people faced with such a thing would call the police. But Foster wasn't most people. He imagined Jencks sniffing round the hole and then heading down to Foster's place to see what he could unearth. No, better forget about phoning the coppers. He could leave the body where it lay, but if he did that he'd be tossing and turning when he tried to get to sleep later.

'Only one thing for it.'

Foster bent and tied the rope round the roll, tightening the knot until he was sure it wouldn't slip. He scanned the bottom of the shaft, shining the torch into every corner. Rock, earth, water, a trio of beer cans, the skull of a long-dead sheep. Time to get out.

Like a diver pausing to decompress on an ascent to the surface, Foster had to stop halfway up. He was tired and his limbs ached from all the activity. He looped his arm over a rung and hung there for several minutes. How different from when he'd played down here all those years ago. He'd shimmied up and down the rope numerous times. Jostled round the edge of the shaft with his brothers. They were dead now, both of them. Martin had died young, crushed under a tractor. Jimmy had made seventy, but not a day longer, wheezing out a last breath as Joe had sat by his hospital bedside and pondered the birthday card he'd written him in the car park a few minutes earlier.

Foster shook himself from his melancholy and began to climb again. At the top, Jess barked a welcome as he hauled himself up over the edge and fell in the snow, exhausted. He crawled over to the dog and let her lick his face. After he'd recovered, he dragged himself to his feet and climbed up onto the tractor. He inched along in creep gear and the rope tightened. He continued to drive forwards until he saw the plastic crest the edge of the hole. He rolled the tractor another six feet and applied the handbrake.

He got down from the cab and went back to the shaft. Some more of the plastic had come away revealing a beige carpet wrapped snugly with reams of tape.

'Now then,' Foster said. 'Let's get you somewhere safe so we can see what we've got, shall we?'

With some difficulty he manoeuvred the roll of carpet over to the trailer and hefted it up and in. Next, he dragged the ladders from the mineshaft, loaded them on and tidied up all the ropes, and set off for the linhay.

He parked the tractor alongside the stone barn and got out. At the rear of the trailer he bent and lifted the roll of carpet onto his right shoulder.

'Bloody hell!' He groaned under the weight and staggered across to the steps which led up to the hayloft. At the top he barged the door open, managing a few paces before he dropped the bundle down on the floor and collapsed alongside. The dog ran into the room and licked his face again. 'Hell, Jess, I swear this'll be the death of me.'

Foster lay back and gazed at the rafters while the dog sniffed round. The air was dry and musty but carried another odour as well. He wrinkled his nose and rolled away from the carpet. He got to his feet, shooed the dog out, and knelt. He took his knife and cut through the plastic and the tape. He pulled the plastic to one side and peeled back the carpet.

Blonde hair stained dark with dried blood. A smart jacket, now crumpled. Short skirt and stockings. A touch of thigh where the skirt had ridden up the girl's legs.

'Fuck.' Foster sat back on his haunches and rocked to and fro. 'Where the hell did you come from, lass?'

Chapter Thirty-seven

Catherine rose late. As she dressed she looked out of the bedroom window. Pristine white spread into the distance, softening stone walls, thickening the top bar of a nearby gate, and narrowing the stream so only a thin strip of water slid between a succession of mini icebergs. The sun hugged the horizon, a golden light bleeding upwards into a patch of blue.

There'd been an uncomfortable silence the previous evening as she'd sat in the living room with Lisa. At some point she'd blipped the TV on and they'd watched news reports of the severe weather. The death toll across the country was up to ten and there were continuing warnings about not making journeys unless they were essential.

Later, Lisa had fallen asleep on the sofa, and Catherine had gone to bed. She'd stayed awake for a long time going over Lisa's story. Lisa had painted a picture of Toby as violent and abusive, herself as the battered wife whose one recourse was to kill her husband so she could escape the hell of domestic misery. The best way to tell a lie was to embellish a partial truth and Lisa had done that in spades.

Downstairs, Catherine made herself breakfast. As the kettle rumbled to a boil, Lisa sidled in.

'Morning,' she said, pulling a mug from the drainer. 'Coffee would be great.'

'I've been thinking. You need to get back soon, otherwise it will seem suspicious.' Catherine spooned coffee into the pot, looking sideways at Lisa. 'For one thing, you need to report Toby missing and you can't do that from here.'

'You're right,' Lisa said. 'When the snow clears, I guess I'll be gone. As soon as I get home, I'll phone a few friends and ask them if they've seen him. I'll wait one night and call the police the next day.'

Catherine took a carton of milk from the fridge and put it on the table. Glanced at Lisa. She was fiddling with the coffee pot. Nervous. Lying. Repeating the fiction about Toby being dead. To what end Catherine couldn't imagine. Lisa had to realise that at some point after she'd gone, Catherine would hear Toby was very much alive. The game would be up.

While Lisa drank her coffee and ate some toast, Catherine went back upstairs. If the body wasn't Toby's, then who was it they'd dumped in the mine? She tried to conceive of a situation where Lisa could've killed someone who *wasn't* Toby, but none came to mind. She should call the police, she realised. Better to admit her part now than to do so later when her inaction could be construed as guilt. She pulled out her phone, but her fingers hovered over the screen, reticent to press the digits. From out of nowhere a phrase her father was fond of repeating came to her:

Get your ducks in a row...

Yes, she thought, it wouldn't do any harm to return to the mine. There could be some clues up near the shaft or perhaps the roll of plastic and carpet was lying on a ledge a few feet down and she might, by some miracle, be able to retrieve it.

Her mind made up, she put on some extra clothing and snuck downstairs. The TV blared out from the living room. She peered round the door. Lisa sat on the sofa staring at yet another weather report where a cluster of snow symbols appeared on a map as a forecaster waved a hand over Scotland.

Catherine crept over to the front door and put on her coat. She slid her feet into her wellington boots and opened the door. Her breath made a fine mist in the air as she walked to the garage. She checked the pickup over and got in and started up. As she left the garage, Lisa opened the front door.

'Where are you going?' she shouted, her face scrunched up in anger.

Catherine lowered the window. She tried to appear calm. To double bluff the bluffer. 'To get some supplies. With the roads the way they are, I'll be a while, but I'll be back as soon as I can.'

'Wait! I'll come with you.'

'Better not, hey?' Catherine let the clutch up and the car inched along. 'The fewer people who know you're here, the less chance of anyone asking difficult questions.'

Before Lisa had a chance to answer or move, Catherine hit the accelerator and headed up the track away from the house. She glanced in the mirror and shuddered. Lisa was standing there, staring.

At the top of the track, Catherine stopped and looked left to where the lane dipped between high banks. The snow had blown in and half-filled the cutting. The way to the village was blocked. Good. That was her excuse for turning right. Lisa wouldn't have a clue about alternate routes and Catherine's plan was to say she'd tried several ways, but all were blocked.

She grasped the wheel, shoved the pickup into gear, and swung to the right. In places, the snow on the road up to the mine was several inches deep, but the wind had scoured much of it away and she arrived at the turning without trouble. She coasted onto the track and down to the derelict mine buildings where she hit the brakes and skidded to a stop, shocked at what she saw. An ocean of snow rolled into the distance, unblemished white aside from a set of vehicle tracks leading to and from the mineshaft.

Somebody had been here.

She drove on until she got to the spot where she'd parked the previous day. She got out and followed the tracks across the snow. The tyres which had made the tracks were chunky and wide, deep indentations marking the tread pattern. They'd been left by a large vehicle such as a tractor. When she arrived at the mineshaft, she could see the fence surrounding the hole was even more broken than the day before and numerous footprints crisscrossed the little enclosure. Scattered near the edge of the hole lay several pieces of silver gaffer tape, and an area of snow had been flattened smooth as if an object had been dragged from the shaft and left to lie on the ground for a while.

'Shit,' she said to herself. The game had changed. If the situation was serious before, it had now become desperate.

She bent and picked up the pieces of tape and shoved them in her pocket. A quick skirt round the shaft yielded nothing else of interest so she hurried back to the pickup, intent on getting home as quickly as possible. As she approached the 4x4, she paused. The way she'd come — up the lane and down the track — was the way anyone would have approached the mineshaft. And yet there were no tracks but her own in the fresh overnight snow. In fact the chunky tyre marks ran away from the lane and led towards Joe Foster's farm.

Her mouth dropped open as she considered the implications. Had *Joe Foster* retrieved the body from the shaft? It didn't make sense. If he had discovered the body he'd have called the police. He wouldn't have moved it, and he wouldn't have taken it back down to his place. Catherine stared at the tracks once more. The evidence said otherwise.

She swore again. She never should have gone along with Lisa's plan. Never should have helped her. She got into the pickup and started up, but instead of turning round and heading for the lane, she steered down the track, following the marks in the snow. The track edged round the curve of a hill and along the side of a field to a gate. A stone barn stood next to the gate, a small corral to the front. The tyre tracks led through the gate and round the barn.

She parked the pickup at the gate, climbed out, and went through. More tracks in the snow. She peered down the hill, her eyes following the tyre marks as they weaved across several fields to where a farmhouse and a collection of outbuildings sat in the valley. Smoke curled up from the farmhouse chimney. It had to be Foster. He *had* taken the body.

She turned her attention to the barn. He'd stopped here, but why? At the far end of the barn, a set of stone steps led up to a second level. A hayloft perhaps. Catherine went across. Pieces of snow lay on the steps, diagonal lines which had fallen from the sole of a boot. She tilted her head and climbed the steps to the upper storey where a door stood open. As she entered the loft area there was a rich smell of hay, and dust motes glided in a shaft of light which shone through a cracked slate in the roof. She moved in and blinked, her eyes growing accustomed to the gloom. Several bales of straw lay to one side and nearby a piece of plastic sacking contoured over a bulky object. A triangle of carpet poked out from under the sacking.

Catherine walked forwards and bent. She placed her hands on the plastic sack, about to throw it back. She paused. Did she really want to see what was underneath? Yes. She tugged the plastic a little.

'Oh God!' Her heart jumped as the plastic slid away to reveal a hand with long, red fingernails. A silver bracelet round the wrist.

She tugged the covering some more before pulling it away completely. She winced at the sight of the corpse lying on the piece of carpet. A young woman. Once smart clothes now dirty and stained. The head was twisted to one side, the blonde hair matted with blood and, where the hair parted, jagged pieces of white bone pierced the scalp. The skin on part of the neck was blotchy with dark bruising and blood had crusted round the left ear. The girl's top lip lay curled up, a tooth hanging by a thread of gum.

Catherine shifted her position so she could glance at the face. She put her hand to her mouth as she gagged, and a chill crept along her arms and across her chest. This was impossible. Stupid, crazy, fucked-up. There was no sense to any of it. She remembered the snaps on the phone, the shaky video, the laughing girl she'd seen behind the rain-streaked glass of the restaurant. The corpse looked so different but there was no doubt this was her: Gemma. The young intern from the agency. The girl Daniel had been screwing up in London.

Chapter Thirty-eight

She drove back to World's End in a daze. At one point her concentration went and she skidded off the lane and grazed the front wing of the pickup on a snow-topped grassy bank.

As she reversed back onto the road she felt a wash of despair. Reality didn't compute. It didn't make sense. Lisa had well and truly duped her. She thought again about the act Lisa had put on, remembering when they'd been about to drop the body down the mineshaft. Catherine had wanted to remove the plastic and carpet, but Lisa had pretended she couldn't face seeing her abuser again, couldn't face seeing Toby again. Now, of course, it was obvious why Lisa hadn't wanted to unwrap the body, but at the time Catherine had fallen for the story because it was so believable.

However, knowing the story was false didn't explain why Lisa had turned up with Gemma's body in the back of her car. Catherine hadn't even realised Lisa knew Gemma, although Gemma worked at the rights agency used by both Toby and Daniel, so Lisa could have met her there. Catherine gripped the steering wheel, her whole body tensing as another possibility came to mind. Had Daniel brought Gemma round to Toby and Lisa's place one evening? Had Lisa acted as hostess, serving dinner, pouring wine, laughing along with everybody at how stupid Catherine was?

Even if that was the case — which was bad enough — Catherine couldn't see how it could lead to Gemma being bludgeoned to death, wrapped in a roll of carpet and bundled into Lisa's car.

Bludgeoned to death...

Christ.

She began to drive off, but tears blurred her vision. She wiped the moisture from her eyes. Was *Daniel* mixed up in all this? Daniel, Toby and Lisa? Or was it Daniel and Lisa alone? Could they be involved with each other somehow?

Angry now, she rammed the gearstick forwards and hit the accelerator. The Toyota slewed in the road and she powered off. At the turnoff to World's End she stopped again. The house loomed in the distance, Lisa's red Audi out front. Catherine lowered the window. A chattering sound like a helicopter drifted up the valley, and she could just make out a plume of snow jetting out over a hedge about half a mile away. The snowplough. The yellow vehicle was chomping through the drifts and before long it would reach World's End and the lane to the village would be passable. Lisa would be able to leave.

Catherine drove down to the house and pulled alongside Lisa's car. Snow had slipped from the roof, melted by the morning sun, but the front windscreen remained a solid slab of white. She climbed out of the pickup and went over and tried the rear hatch. It was locked. She wanted to check inside the car, but if Lisa caught her doing so it would look suspicious. In the distance, the mechanical rhythm grew louder as the wind changed direction. The snowplough, she thought. It gave her an excuse to move the car.

She went over to the front door and eased it open. She edged into the house. The keys to the car lay on a shelf in the hallway. The TV blared from the living room and she peered in. Lisa lay slumped on the sofa. Either she was absorbed in the programme or she was asleep.

Catherine picked up the keys and crept back outside. At the car she blipped the locks and went to the rear and popped open the hatch. Aside from a long thread of beige carpet, it was bare. She closed the boot, clicking it shut rather than slamming it down, and went and sat in the driver's seat. The car smelt clean and fresh, a hint of leather and plastic. She realised the Audi was brand new, like Toby's Jaguar. Daniel had said the book advance had been less than Toby expected, that the Jag had been bought on credit, but if that was true it didn't make much sense that Toby and Lisa would take on even more debt by buying a second new car.

She leaned over and opened the glovebox. There was an ice scraper and some car-related documents — a manual and some warranty information. She didn't know what she'd been expecting to find but there was nothing here. She took out the scraper. It was hardly adequate, but she only needed to move the car a short distance into the garage to cover up what she'd been doing. A minute later she'd cleaned a patch of windscreen and driven the car into the garage. She'd left the scraper lying in the snow, so she retrieved it, tapped it to knock off the ice, and went to replace it in the car. Because the scraper was damp and might drip on the documents in the glovebox, she decided to drop it in the door side pocket.

Which was when she froze.

An item made from leather lay in the bottom of the pocket. A phone case. A *familiar* phone case. She reached for the case, her hand almost disembodied and moving in slow motion. No, she thought, please don't let this be happening. The fact the case could be here was confirmation of her worst fears. She touched the leather, knowing exactly the make and model of phone that would be inside. As she opened the flap, she saw the black bumper round the phone, the little pocket for business cards, the plastic sleeve which contained a picture of her standing on a beach in Turkey.

'Where have you been?' Lisa's whine came from the living room as Catherine opened the front door. 'You've been gone hours. I was worried.'

Catherine looked at her watch. 'Less than two hours.'

'What took you so long?' Lisa emerged into the hallway and glanced down at Catherine's empty hands. 'And where's the shopping? I thought you said you were going for supplies?'

'I couldn't get down to the village. I got stuck in a drift and had to go for help. A neighbour towed me out with his tractor.'

'I see.' Lisa's eyes narrowed. 'And that took you two hours?'

'Jesus, Lisa, drop it will you? I'm tired and cross and I just want to get a bite to eat and have a rest.'

'Uh huh.' Lisa wasn't listening. She tried to peer outside as Catherine closed the door. There was a frown on her face. 'You moved my car.'

'Yes. The snowplough's on the way here. I thought it would be better to get the car under cover and out of sight.'

'I see.' Lisa stood blocking the hallway, her right hand outstretched palm up as if she was a school teacher demanding a piece of gum from a naughty pupil. 'My car keys.'

'Your keys?' Catherine stuttered, even as she was pulling the fob from her pocket. 'Oh, yes. Here.'

'Thanks.' Lisa took the keys and her mood changed. 'I suppose if the road is clear I should be off.'

'I guess.' Catherine tried to sound a little downbeat. 'The sooner you leave, the less chance there is of something happening to complicate the situation.'

'I'd better gather my stuff together then.' Lisa smiled and made for the stairs. 'But a coffee before I go would be great.'

'Yes, sure.' Catherine scampered down the hallway. In the kitchen she busied herself making the drinks, but as soon as she heard a creak on the ceiling she took Daniel's phone from her pocket. She had no idea what Daniel's lock screen code might be, so she tried the obvious numbers: his birthday, her birthday, a combination of the two, their birth years. None of them worked and the phone remained locked. After several attempts a message flashed up saying she couldn't try again for ten minutes. Damn it! She went over to a cupboard and placed the phone at the back behind some tins of food. As she pulled her hand from the cupboard, she realised she was shaking.

'Catherine?' Lisa seemed to materialise in the middle of the kitchen. 'What are you doing?'

'Soup.' Catherine removed two of the tins and put them on the work surface. She closed the cupboard door. 'Carrot and coriander or tomato and basil?'

'But it's not even twelve?'

'Yes, but wouldn't it be good to get some warm food inside you for the journey?' Catherine took a saucepan from a shelf and put the tins in, unopened. She went to another cupboard and began to rummage inside. 'I've got some part-baked bread somewhere.'

'Are you alright?' Lisa slid across to the hob and looked at the two tins sitting in the pan. 'You seem nervous.'

'I guess I am.' Catherine retrieved a packet of rolls, grasping hard to prevent her hands from shaking. 'Perhaps more worried than nervous.'

'About the body?'

'Yes, but about being here on my own too.'

'I could stay if you want me to?'

'No,' Catherine said. 'We need to stick to the plan. You should get back to London as soon as possible so you can report Toby missing.'

'Yes.' Lisa flicked one of the tins with a finger nail and canted her head over on one side. 'I'd best do that, hadn't I? Report Toby missing?'

Catherine wondered if Lisa knew where she'd been. Knew she'd discovered the truth about the body, knew she'd found Daniel's phone in the car. She glanced at the knife block near the hob. She needed a pair of scissors to open the packet of bread, but next to the slot holding the scissors sat a large carving knife. She could walk across with the intention of getting the scissors and instead grab the knife and defend herself. She could yell at Lisa to get out and lock herself inside the house and phone the police. Lisa's gaze followed Catherine's to the block.

'Perhaps I'll skip the soup and the coffee,' Lisa said. That weird tilt of her head again. Like a demented marionette with a painted smile and unblinking eyes. 'Now, why don't you go and get my bag from upstairs and carry it out to the car? I'll just have a drink of water and then I'll join you, OK?'

Catherine nodded. She tried not to run as she left the kitchen and went up to the guest room and found Lisa's bag. There was a momentary temptation to look inside, but she remembered Lisa's expression and thought better of it. She hurried back down to the hall.

The front door was open and Lisa was standing over by the garage. At the end of the track, a big yellow tractor was turning round and heading back down to the village. A glint came from the orange flashing light on its roof and at the rear a hopper spun salt out onto the road. When it had disappeared, Lisa went into the garage and reversed her car out into the yard. She opened the door but remained sitting in the car.

'So,' Lisa said. 'Looks like I'm good to go.'

'Yes.' Catherine crunched across the frozen slush and handed Lisa her bag.

'I'm not sure we'll cross paths again, Catherine, but thanks for your help. You've done more than you can imagine.'

'Daniel.' Catherine couldn't contain herself any longer. 'Something's going on between you isn't it?'

'I'll give you a piece of advice, Cath.' Lisa wound the window down and closed the door. There was a smile on her face as she started the engine. 'You need to keep an eye on that man of yours. You see, he just can't seem to keep it in his trousers.'

Lisa floored the accelerator and the rear wheels spun before they gripped and the car sped away up the track. Catherine stumbled and went down on her knees. She watched as the car's brake lights came on when Lisa reached the lane, reminded of the day she and Daniel had arrived at World's End. She remembered the removal van, its indicator blinking a goodbye as it left them in the suffocating quiet of the countryside. Now, as Lisa's car disappeared, the same quiet descended once more, and Catherine collapsed in the snow, wetness on her arms and her legs and her face.

Chapter Thirty-nine

I never spoke to Helena about what happened. I tried, but she didn't want to see me. A few days after Mr Hodgson's funeral, the family upped sticks and left. No trace. No forwarding address. The mother and the three daughters. Gone. Back east was what people said, but I don't even know if that's the truth. All I know is I never saw her again.

A week after she'd gone, I received a letter from her. The postmark wasn't clear and offered no clue as to where it had been sent from. The letter explained what had happened. The parts I knew and the parts I didn't. I still have the letter and even though I haven't taken it from its envelope for years I can remember the words she wrote. Every last one. Her description of the boys leading her round to the barn. Taking her to the hayloft. The way they held her down while they took turns. Warning her that they could do what they liked because their word was as good as the law. And afterwards laughing as they'd showed her the carcass of the pony, dead all along.

The worse of it hadn't been the violation, she said. Nor seeing Mischief skinned and lying there waiting to be chopped up for dog food. What had shocked her more than anything had been what she'd learned about human nature. The Murrin boys had been cruel and heartless, possessing the most awful kind of viciousness and depraved in mind and body. Jencks had been pliant and toadying, willing to look the other way to feather his own nest. And I, Joe Foster, she said, had committed the worst offence.

There came a tirade directed at me, but I don't like to recall that part of the letter too often, even though the words are imprinted in my mind. She called me a coward. Said I had betrayed my own heart. She blamed me for the death of her father, a man she said was the polar opposite of me. A brave man, prepared to stand up to the Murrins, to stand up for what was right.

I'd shed tears before, on the day Helena had left, but now I cried properly. The tears weren't for her suffering though. Not for her dad either. They were for myself. What a piteous creature I was. I'd lost the girl I loved. I'd lost my self-respect. I'd lost my very soul.

These days the letter stays hidden in a tin. Sometimes I open the tin, but I never remove the letter from the envelope. It is enough for me to look at the handwritten address and imagine her writing my name in anger. And even after all these decades, the envelope retains Helena's scent, and if I breathe in I can smell her perfume. A hint of musk. A trace of lavender. A dusting of magic.

Chapter Forty

He dreamed of her that night. Somehow they were together. He hadn't been a coward, but a hero. He'd saved the day and she was grateful. It was the Murrins who'd upped and left and the snow had melted and spring had arrived. Blossom on the trees, the smell of the earth warming, the sight of swallows weaving over the moorland heather. In the dream he was with Helena up near the mine workings. They were lying in soft grass, her legs wrapped around him, the sweet taste of her on his tongue, the rising passion as she called out his name. Joe! Joe! Joe! Her pleasure ended with a scream of terror, and Foster looked up from between Helena's thighs and felt a different kind of heat on his face. Fire! A crackle as flames ripped through a patch of dead bracken. Columns of choking black smoke and then Foster was wide awake, hacking into his pillow, the sweet taste of Helena gone, replaced by the foul badness of bloodied spit.

He rolled out of bed and crouched on the floor bent double. He retched mucus and snatched the sheet from the bed and coughed into it.

'Bloody hell,' he said.

He took a gulp of air. And another. There was a smoky aftertaste, and for one horrid second he feared that he'd forgotten to tamp down the fire and put the spark guard in place. In the dark, he stumbled to the bedroom door, opened it, and peered down the stairway. Silence but for the tick of the clock in the hall below. He went to the window, already open half an inch, and pushed the glass. Fresh air wafted in, carrying with it a trace of melting rubber. Foster blinked. Far up the valley light brushed the horizon, red and yellow tendrils reaching into the starry sky.

He scrabbled for his clothes and pulled them on, tripping as he struggled with his trousers. Downstairs, Jess rose from her basket with a look which said, *what's up?* but Foster waved her away.

'You stay here, old girl. Safer for you.'

He put on his jacket, yanked his boots on, and went out into the night. He lumbered across to the tractor and started up. The vehicle's lights cut across the snow in a swathe of brilliance as he powered away from the farm and up the hill. A few minutes later he was approaching the linhay. The barn stood grey in the falling snow and there was no sign of any fire.

Foster puffed out a sigh of relief and turned onto the track. Up ahead, a glow of red *did* mark a fire of some kind. He drove up the track and stopped near the smouldering wreck of a vehicle. The car had been alight for some time. The glass had popped out and the tyres were gone, the rims resting on the track. Snow had melted in a circle round the fire and the area beyond had been blackened by debris.

Foster climbed down from the tractor and approached. The flames had died down, but even so he couldn't approach closer than ten steps. The heat was intense and thick black smoke billowed into his face. Every now and then a piece of the car crackled or snapped and there was a hissing as fluid boiled away under the bonnet. He looked across the moorland. In the gloom he could just make out the low hump of the mineshaft rising from the snow. No coincidence, he thought.

Back at the linhay he climbed the stairs. He plopped his big torch on its side and pointed the beam at the body on the floor. He folded the carpet and plastic back round the body as best he could and secured it with baler twine. He dragged the bundle to the stairs, slid it down, and hefted it across to the transport box on the tractor. Ten minutes later he had the body in the barn back at the farm.

Inside the house he stripped off his jacket and hung it up. He put his boots in the shoe rack. Snowmelt dripped from the boots and formed a puddle on the floor. Each droplet of water made a little sound. *Plip, plip, plip.* Time passing. The world moving on. Foster went through to the parlour. He stoked the fire and chucked on a couple of pine logs. The wood crackled and glowing embers darted up the chimney. Foster sat in his armchair and dozed fitfully until he was woken by Jess barking. He rubbed the sleep from his eyes and rose. He opened the back door to find Jencks standing there. A narrow smile graced the policeman's lips.

'About bloody time.' Jencks stamped his feet in the compacted snow. He stared at Foster's face and down at his hands. 'You know about the fire, I see.'

'What?' Foster turned his hands over. Black grime on the fingertips and the side of his first finger where he'd wiped his face. 'Well, yes. Reckon I might do.'

'So why the hell didn't you call 999?'

'It was the middle of the night. Couldn't see you bothering and the fire engine wouldn't have made it up to the mine workings. Besides, the car was well burnt out by the time I got there. The flames were dying down and with snow on the ground there was no danger of it spreading.'

'And this morning?'

'I was going to call as soon as I got up.'

'The fuck you were.' Jencks raised a fist, almost as if he was going to strike out, but his hand morphed into an accusing finger which he jabbed at Foster. 'Did you recognise the car?'

'Nope.'

'Did you see or hear anything suspicious?'

'Other than the car burning, no.'

'You haven't noticed anything odd recently?'

'No.'

Jencks swung his head. The tractor stood outside the barn where Foster had left it in the small hours.

'You know, I've been reviewing the file again? The Murrin murders.'

'Please yourself, but like I told you before, you're wasting your time.'

'I'd give my right arm to know what happened. To solve the mystery.'

Bet you would, Foster thought. Bet you'd like to succeed where your father and the others failed. You'd be quite the hero among your police colleagues. Not that many local folk would thank you.

'Have you any ideas, Mr Foster? I'm pretty sure you've got a good notion of what went on down at World's End.'

'Yes, I have.' Foster tapped his head. 'I've kept the secret for all these years, but I'm getting on now and I guess it's about time I told the truth.'

'Really?' Jencks' mouth hung half open and Foster could see saliva building within. 'So, what happened?'

'The best I can say is for that one day I believed in God. Not before, not since, but right about then.'

'Sorry, I don't understand?'

'Divine intervention, Constable Jencks. God flew over this part of the moor and touched the ground. When he flew off, the Murrin boys were left swaying in the wind, and a great many people offered up a silent prayer in thanks. To be frank, your father was lucky God didn't choose to send him a little message too because he was on the wrong side of good and evil.' Foster tutted and gave a wink. 'Then again, maybe God did leave a mark, huh?'

Jencks swallowed, all the skin on his face reddening except for the patch on his cheek. 'I could arrest you for that, Foster. Verbal abuse. Discrimination.' He stomped his feet again. 'If I find you're mixed up in burning that car, I'll have you.'

Jencks marched away across the yard and got into his 4x4. As he started up, Foster could see the red face and the patch of skin as white as snow on one side.

'You can fucking try,' he said to himself.

Chapter Forty-one

Catherine woke as the sun struggled to emerge from the bottom of the valley. A harsh winter ball of yellow refusing to climb much above the southern horizon. She tensed and blinked. She let out a sigh. Lisa had gone. There was nothing to worry about.

Except Daniel.

He'd texted saying he'd leave London early in the morning and, weather permitting, he'd try to be back by early afternoon. Catherine felt the tension rise again. She tried to figure out what she should tell him. What questions she should ask. How he might reply.

The previous evening she'd nearly had a breakdown thinking about what had happened. Lisa and Toby and Daniel and Gemma. Poor Gemma. She'd hated the girl when she'd been alive, but she'd never wished her dead.

Catherine tried to work through the possibilities, but hardly anything made sense, and what did make sense wouldn't add up. Why, for instance, was Daniel's phone in Lisa's car? The phone itself had refused to give up its evidence — Catherine had tried several times to gain access but failed — and the only explanation Catherine could come up with was that Lisa had given Daniel a lift somewhere. Had the two of them bumped into each other in a chance meeting or had Daniel left the phone after a prearranged rendezvous? The latter suggested he'd been seeing Lisa up in London.

Seeing Lisa...

If *seeing* her was all he'd been doing, fine, but as much as Catherine tried to imagine a scenario which didn't put Daniel in bed with Lisa, the facts pointed to her husband cheating once again.

She got out of bed and went to the ensuite to take a shower. When she emerged she caught sight of herself in the full-length mirror. Steam had clouded the surface and her reflection was indistinct. Was that how Daniel now saw her? Blurred and watery? No longer attractive? Lisa was a Plain Jane compared to Catherine, yet the frisson of sexual allure didn't work on looks alone. Was it possible Daniel had somehow fallen in love with Lisa? Perhaps he'd been a sympathetic shoulder to cry on and one thing had led to another. Then again, the Daniel Catherine knew wouldn't have stolen his best mate's partner. But that was the Daniel *she* knew. There was another Daniel. One who kept secrets — like the contents of the metal box. One who took advantage of his trips away to have as much fun as possible. While she thought *her* Daniel was in a studio working late at night, the other Daniel could be out at a bar picking up women for casual sex. How many trips had he made in the time they'd been together? How many nights away?

By the time she'd finished drying her hair, the sun had erased the shadows and the snow glared with a brilliant white. The sky was a deep blue but for a pall of black hanging in the calm air at the top of the valley. A column of smoke smudged upwards in overlapping circles, spreading to form the shape of a triangle, the tip of which pointed down at the mine workings.

Catherine dressed, went downstairs, and made herself breakfast. She put on some warm clothing and headed outside. The mist sat languid on the horizon, taunting her, and she hesitated by the pickup before getting in. She started the engine and drove up the valley. Several vehicles had compacted the snow on the road and as she turned off and rounded the derelict buildings, she spotted a police 4x4 and a Dartmoor Park Authority Land Rover parked at the side of the track. Fifty metres from the vehicles, smoke spiralled upwards from the wreck of a car. A police officer in uniform and a park ranger stood nearby. She was about to put the pickup in reverse when the policeman waved. It was Constable Jencks.

Shit.

Catherine rolled the vehicle forwards and stopped a little way short of the police car. She got out and walked over.

'Hi,' she said, trying to appear casual. 'I saw the smoke from down the valley.'

'Mrs Ross.' Jencks said, the words coming as if in accusation, as if she had no right to be there.

'Catherine Ross.' She gestured down the valley. 'World's End Farm, remember?'

'Yes, of course.' Jencks flinched as if someone had tugged a hair from his head. He pointed at the car. 'Joyriders. No need to get excited.'

'I told you, I don't buy that,' the other man said. Mid-forties with fair hair and a soft accent. He wore a Berghaus jacket with a DPA logo on the chest. 'Not in this weather.'

Jencks shrugged. 'So if it wasn't youth, then who?'

The ranger didn't answer so Jencks turned back to Catherine. 'You didn't see or hear anything last night, did you?'

'No. I saw the smoke this morning. I don't quite know why I came up here, it just seemed unusual.'

'Unusual.' Jencks said the word slowly, so it came out elongated.

'Yes. We didn't get burning cars on our doorstep in London.'

'London.' Jencks tilted his head to one side and spat. He stared down as the globule of liquid sank into the snow. 'And you haven't noticed anything odd round here in the last few days? Perhaps before?'

'No.' Catherine swallowed. 'Not since... you know...?'

'The rope.' Jencks shook his head. 'Never got any further with that.'

'You were going to come and take fingerprints.'

'Resources, Mrs Ross, resources.' Jencks gestured towards the smouldering car. 'Maybe you'll take a look? It's quite safe now, been alight for hours, not much left to burn.'

Jencks didn't wait for an answer. He began to trudge towards the vehicle. Catherine followed. The car was a skeleton of metal gone white in the intense heat, the interior blackened from melted fittings. Smoke rolled out and drifted skyward. There was a smell of burning plastic. The rear hatch had sprung open and the bonnet warped.

'Do you recognise it?' Jencks asked.

'No, but I'm not good with cars.'

'It's an Audi TT Coupe.' Jencks crouched near the rear where some plastic from a bumper had puddled and hardened. 'Red.'

Catherine felt a rising panic. Now Jencks had mentioned the make, the shape did seem familiar. All too familiar. She remembered the curve of the bonnet as she'd bent to attach the towing hook. The way the rear hatch angled as it opened when Lisa had first shown her the body.

'Shit!' She let out the expletive without thinking.

'Mrs Ross?' Jencks said. 'Are you OK?'

'No. I mean yes. It's a right mess.' Catherine waved her hand absently. 'A mess to clear up.'

'There's more to tell though, isn't there?'

'Yes.' Catherine swallowed and tried to stall. 'I was up here a couple of days ago. Out on a walk. What if the joyriders had come along then?'

'You were out for a walk in that bad weather?'

'Yes.' Catherine bit her lip. She was heading for trouble. 'Only they wouldn't have come along. Not with all the snow.'

'No.' Jencks cocked his head at her. 'Anyway, we'll be able to identify the owner because the number plates are still there. It'll be a shock though, I'm sure. Fires always are and a car like this is worth a penny or two. Not many round here can afford such an expensive vehicle. Tends to be incomers who go for the fancy cars.'

'Incomers?'

'Yes, incomers.' Jencks tutted. 'More money than sense.'

'I'd better be going,' Catherine said. She turned her head, unable to stop herself from glancing down the track to the stone barn. The body was in there. All Jencks had to do was climb the stairs to the upper floor and peer in. There'd be prints and fibres everywhere. 'See you later.'

'World's End Farm.' Jencks said.

'Sorry?'

'Never mind.' Jencks was staring across to the barn too. He nodded to himself. 'Goodbye, Mrs Ross.'

'Bye.'

Catherine strolled away, forcing herself not to look back. She smiled as she passed the ranger and then got into the pickup. By the time she'd reversed round, Jencks was already halfway between the burnt-out car and the barn, head down, striding purposefully.

Chapter Forty-two

After Jencks had gone, Foster double locked the back door and went to the tall metal cupboard in the hallway. Inside, a shotgun stood in a rack and a box of cartridges sat on a shelf. He took the gun out and cracked it open. Made a play of staring down both barrels before loading the gun with two cartridges. He took the gun and the box and placed them by the back door. He'd done nothing wrong in this instance, but even angels got punished sometimes. And, to be fair, he didn't come close to being an angel.

He usually drank tea at breakfast, but today he dug out a jar of instant coffee from the back of the pantry. The coffee was black as coal, with a strong and bitter taste. When it was cool enough he drank the whole lot down in one, leaving just the dregs. He stoked up the fire and sat in his armchair and felt the warmth from the flames.

'Bugger,' he said. 'Ain't nowt so bad as a job that needs doing when you don't want to do it.'

He stood and went into the kitchen. Made himself breakfast. Two rashers of bacon, a plate full of eggs, and enough fried bread to make him feel dizzy. Next he went out and saw to the stock. The ill ewe was no better, but he fed the rest of the sheep and the bullocks and then went over to the barn.

The girl lay atop an oak door Foster had placed on an old pig sticking bench. Back in the day the bench had witnessed its fair share of bloody murder. He and his brothers had been tasked with getting the pigs to the bench and holding them down while his father stabbed them in the chest. Even now he could remember the shrieks made by the animals as they struggled to escape. Foster wasn't squeamish, but the slaughter had left a mark on him. It wasn't the act itself, it was the way the pigs *knew* what was going to happen to them.

He lifted the plastic sheet from the body. The girl was done knowing much about anything. He took a pair of dagging shears and sharpened them up with an oil stone. He began to cut away the woman's clothing, snipping up the arm of the jacket. He sliced across the shoulders on both sides and down the other arm. He lifted the front of the jacket off and chucked it in a bucket. As he started to unbutton the white blouse beneath, he found himself looking at the woman's eyes. They were wide open, and Foster had a strange sense that the last seconds of her life had been profoundly shocking. He squinted to avoid the eyes, but he could feel the woman staring all the same.

'You crazy fuck,' he said, turning back. 'You're dead, aren't you? You can't come back, can't hurt me.'

Even as he spoke he realised he was the crazy one. And not simply crazy, plain damn wrong as well. The girl *was* dead, *wasn't* coming back. On the other hand, he was pretty sure she was going to be the cause of a whole lot of trouble.

'Strewth.' Foster put the shears down and stomped off to his workshop at the back of the barn. He found a pair of welding goggles. They had opaque black-green glass and you couldn't see through either way. He took the goggles and placed them over the woman's eyes. He lifted her head and worked the elastic strap round the back. 'Better. Much better.'

The rest of the clothes came off easily. The blouse with a fancy label. The skirt and the sheer stockings. The underwear, black and lacey. Items a woman might wear if she wanted to surprise her husband. Foster cut the knickers off, tossed the underwear on top of the rest of the clothing, and moved to examine the body.

He started with the head. The girl was blonde, the hair soft and shiny where it wasn't thick with congealed blood. There was a large gash in the scalp at the rear of the skull and he put a finger into the gash and felt the sharp edge of bone. She'd been hit with a heavy object. A hammer or a rock, he reckoned. Her face was a mess too, her mouth full of broken teeth, her top lip torn and ragged. Likely she'd been struck more than once.

Foster began to work his way down the torso, tipping the body onto one side so he could check the back as well. There was a graze on one arm and a purple speckled bruise on the left side of the stomach, some bruising on the breasts as well. He gaped at the crotch where the pubic hair was as short as a ewe's fleece after shearing. A piece of metal glittered between the woman's lips and Foster shuddered and reached out a finger to touch the silver object. A ring. Right through…

He blew out a breath and hummed to himself. He'd seen girls with studs in their noses, once some runt of a lad with a ring piercing an eyebrow; never thought a lass would do this though. He wiped his hands on a rag and thought about what folks got up to these days. Their habits. People running round and doing just what the hell they liked. He stood. It was what it was and just because he didn't like it didn't make the facts any different. And it didn't mean the girl deserved to die just because she wanted to go and shave off her bush and pierce herself silly.

He left the woman lying naked and uncovered and headed to the house. As he went in he glanced at the thermometer fixed to the outside wall. Minus two. As long as a thaw didn't set in, the body could lie out there for a while.

Inside, Foster chucked a log on the fire. He felt light headed and considered making himself a bite to eat. Instead he sat in his chair, hypnotised by the flames flickering up the chimney.

At some point the dog barked a warning. Foster rose from his chair and went out into the yard. He opened the barn door and went in. The dog wanted to follow, but he told her to wait outside. He went across to the table to check on the girl. She was still there. Still dead. He felt a pang of guilt that he'd left her naked and uncovered, so he picked up the plastic sheet from the floor and draped it over the body.

'Bugger,' he said when he came back inside. 'Bloody bugger.'

Once the snow had done falling and all the roads were clear, people would be searching for the girl. Not just Constable Jencks but other policemen. Detectives, those forensic guys in white coveralls, a team of officers working their way across the moor. A pretty lass like her would attract plenty of news coverage too. He'd been stupid to retrieve the body from the mineshaft. Even dumber to bring the girl back to the farm.

He went to the kitchen where he peeled three large potatoes, quartered them, and put them in a pan of water on the stove. As the water came to the boil, the phone rang.

Foster shifted the pan to the side and picked up the phone.

'Hello?' he said.

'Joe, it's Barney. You alright down there? Still alive?'

'I'm speaking ain't I?' Foster crooked the phone under his neck and patted his pockets for his tobacco. Barney could talk like a hungry chicken, but right now Foster wasn't in the mood for a chat. 'What do you want?'

'Just being neighbourly, Joe. Enquiring, like.'

'Enquiring as to what?'

'You're health. Old man like you needs someone to look out for him. Especially since Edith's gone.'

'I'm two years younger than you and it's not as if you're shacked up with anyone, is it?'

'Working on it, working on it.'

'Ain't we all.' Foster flattened a cigarette paper in his palm and pinched some tobacco onto it.

'So, you're keeping OK, are you?'

'You do want something. It's not like you to be calling otherwise.' Foster rolled the paper and licked the edge. Stuck the cigarette in his mouth and looked around for his lighter.

'You been up near the mine, Joe? Yesterday?'

'Might have.'

'You either have or you haven't.'

'Yeah, I was up there. One of my rams went down that shaft with the busted fence. Had a hell of a time getting him out.'

'I thought I saw you pottering about from over at my place. OK, is he?'

'Broken leg. Got him in the barn. Might have to shoot him.'

'And you've no idea how he got down there?'

'You know what sheep are like.' Foster spotted his lighter on the table. He stretched across for it. 'Your stock doing OK?'

'The fact is, Joe, I was up by the mine too. I went over the back way to get to those bullocks I've got wintered in that tin shack. This was Thursday in all the bad weather, so I took the dray, you know that tractor of mine with the four big wheels? It was snowing like a shitstorm, but the beast got me through.'

'This going anywhere, Barney? Only I'm cooking my tuck.'

'Patience.' Barney cleared his throat. 'I was driving up to the crossroads at the top when I saw a vehicle at the mine. Not yours, this was Thursday, not Friday when the weather had cleared. A Toyota pickup it was. One of them Land Cruisers. And there was a lass driving it.'

'Fancy that. They've only just got the vote an' all.'

'Yes. Anyway, it was down the track a way and drove up to the road and skidded off down the hill. I didn't bother much because I was keen to get to the bullocks, but when I saw you there the next day I got to thinking.'

'Got to thinking what?'

'I got to thinking who'd be up there in a blizzard?'

'An idiot.'

'An idiot, yes, and there's only one set of fools round here with a Land Cruiser, right?'

'I wouldn't know.'

'I thought them lot down at World's End Farm had one?'

'Can't say I've ever noticed.'

'Don't be daft, you must remember what type of vehicle they own? You've been stalking around down there enough.'

'Getaway with you.' Foster finally lit the rollup. He took a deep drag. 'Anyway, what would they be doing up there?'

'That's what was bothering me, but I wouldn't have been half as interested if I hadn't spotted you at the very spot a day later. And there's the fire this morning, too. I could see the smoke from my place, so I rang the ranger. He put me straight. A car he says. Right up by the mine where I saw the pickup and your tractor. A very odd set of coincidences.'

'I told you, I was fetching the ram.'

'I know what you told me, Joe, but I'm not sure I believe you. I guess I might come by tomorrow to see that ram. I could look at its leg if you like. I'd want to take a gander at the others, too. Just in case I fancy a loan of one or two come the tupping season. Last time I was there you had them in the little field round the back, correct? I remember the animals. Fine beasts. All four of them. That's right, isn't it?' There was a pause and then Barney said the next words all spaced out. *'Four... of... them?'*

'Sure.' Foster cast an eye at the stove where the potatoes were on a rolling boil. 'Dinner's spoiling, Barney. Thanks for calling, got to go.'

There was a stifled cry from the phone before he managed to slam it back on the cradle. Barney. Should've been a detective or a journalist. Perhaps a truffle-hunting pig the way he could sniff out a tasty morsel. Foster bit his lip.

The rams were the problem. Barney had the numbers spot on. Four. If the git sauntered over tomorrow and saw four healthy rams in the field, he'd want to know what had happened. Had there been a miracle? A laying on of hands which had healed the tup's leg? Foster thought about going out into the field and breaking the leg of one of the rams. Or he could shoot one and bury it. Perhaps he could just hide one somewhere, like upstairs in his bedroom, and *say* he'd had to shoot it because the leg wouldn't heal. Only, months later, Barney might be amazed at how the animal had come back to life.

More interesting and more pressing was the information about the mysterious pickup. Except there wasn't anything mysterious about it. Barney was right, there was only one place nearabouts the vehicle could have come from. The mystery was what the fuck it was doing up near the mine in the middle of a blizzard. And Foster reckoned he pretty much had that worked out too.

He took a fork and prodded a spud. They were done. Well done.

Chapter Forty-three

Back home, Catherine changed the sheets on the bed in the spare room and stuffed the bedding into the washing machine. She vacuumed the room and burned the cleaner bag on the rubbish pile outside. She stood and looked up the track and went inside to the kitchen. She pulled a knife from the wooden block and cut up an apple and nicked her finger as she did so. A pinprick of blood appeared so she took some kitchen roll and dabbed the blood away. The red inked out in a radial pattern and she peered at the stain, trying to discern some hidden meaning in the blotches and lines, the answer to a multitude of questions. Why had Lisa set fire to her own car and dumped it near the mineshaft? More than that, where the hell was she now and what was she up to? And what about Toby and Daniel, where did they fit into Lisa's mad scheme to dispose of Gemma's body?

The stain offered no answers, so she chucked the tissue in the bin. As the lid on the bin clanged shut, she heard a car.

Daniel!

She glanced at her reflection in the hallway mirror, ostensibly to see if she appeared presentable, in reality to check for signs of guilt.

As she opened the door, he stood with his back to her, leaning into the rear of the car to retrieve a bag. He turned. His blue eyes danced beneath his jet-black hair and he smiled.

'Cath, sweetheart!' He dropped the bag in the snow and ran across and embraced her. His face nuzzled in at her neck. 'I've missed you so much.'

Catherine went rigid, arms by her side.

'What's wrong?' Daniel said. He leaned back. 'Not pleased to see me?'

Catherine came to her senses. She had to act normal, if possible. 'Yes. I missed you too, but I was scared and when you didn't call, I was angry.'

'I explained about that. I lost my phone.'

'So you say.'

'Catherine? Is there anything I should know?'

'With the storm and the snow, I was so worried.'

'You shouldn't have been. I was fine. I told you I'd be back today and here I am.'

'I didn't mean you, I meant me. Weren't you concerned? I was alone in this godforsaken place. Snowed in. Desperate.'

'Godforsaken? Desperate? Whatever's got into you, Catherine?' Daniel went to the car to pick up his bag. 'Now, any chance of something to eat? It's been a long drive and I'm famished.'

'There's been trouble round here.'

'Oh?' Daniel cocked his head on one side. 'What sort of trouble?'

For an instant she thought about telling him about Lisa and the body which was supposed to be Toby's but instead turned out to be Gemma's. Then she remembered the phone in the car and Lisa's parting words.

He just can't seem to keep it in his trousers.

'A car fire up the road,' she said. 'It happened last night at the top of the valley. The police say it was probably joyriders.'

'There you go then. Now, what about that food and maybe a beer?'

Catherine nodded. Daniel had always been hard to read, now more than ever. Was Lisa lying about Daniel? She could have been making it up, but that didn't explain his phone in her car.

Inside, she fixed some lunch. They ate in near silence.

'Sorry,' Daniel said. He appeared to think the lack of conversation was his fault. 'I'm tired from the drive. That and being away. Nothing like a strange bed to give you restless nights.'

Catherine stayed quiet. Was Daniel being plain stupid or was this an attempt to goad her? She realised that at some point she'd have to have it out with him but had no idea where to begin. Should she tell him about Lisa and Gemma's body? Of course, if he was somehow involved, he already knew all about it. And if so, he knew that she knew. Perhaps he was playing a game, waiting for her to make the first move.

She stood and cleared away the lunch, expecting Daniel to speak at some point, but he didn't. He left the kitchen and she heard him climb the stairs, take a shower, and go to his work room.

At a little after four in the afternoon, as the sun nudged the ridge on the western horizon, there was a rapping at the front door. Daniel came down the stairs and opened up.

'Cathy,' he shouted back to the kitchen. 'It's Constable Jencks. He wants to ask you some questions.'

Catherine heard Daniel exchanging pleasantries with Jencks as he showed him through.

'Mrs Ross,' Jencks said. 'Just following up on the car.'

'It's Ms Ross,' she said. 'And as I told you before, I didn't know about it until this morning.'

'So you say.' Jencks took out a pad and pencil. 'The issue is that I have a witness who saw a red Audi TT turning out from your track yesterday. Did anyone visit you recently? Either in an Audi or any other vehicle?'

'No.' Beside her, Daniel made an almost imperceptible movement of his head, as if Jencks' words had piqued his interest.

'How do you explain the car?'

'I don't know. Perhaps somebody took a wrong turn.'

'Mr Ross?'

'It's Daniel Young. We're married but have our own names.'

'I see.' Jencks' face contorted in discomfort. 'And what do you know about the car?'

'Nothing. I was away, officer. I arrived back at lunch time today.'

'Right.' Jencks tapped his pencil on the pad. 'Well, we've managed to identify the owner of the vehicle.'

Catherine tried to stop herself shuddering. If the police knew the car belonged to Lisa, it wouldn't take them long to connect her, via Toby, to Daniel and Catherine. Catherine opened her mouth, but Jencks spoke first.

'Do either of you know a Gemma Hicksmith?'

'Oh...' Catherine clasped her hands together. Daniel's lips parted but he smacked them closed before Jencks looked up. The next couple of moments ticked past at a pace that suggested time was stopping, and it seemed to her as if Jencks was frozen like a waxwork. In the space between the seconds she wanted to be able to turn to Daniel and ask him what they should do or say, because she had a sense that what she said next, what *either* of them said next, would determine the rest of their lives. But time wasn't stopping and she found herself speaking without focusing on what she was saying. 'It's *Gemma's* car?'

'You *do* know a Gemma?'

'No,' Daniel said abruptly. 'We don't know a Gemma, *do we, darling*?'

'No.' Catherine's denial came out flat, almost as a whisper. 'No, sorry, we don't.'

'Are you sure? It sounded like you did just now.'

'Gemma...? What was her surname again?'

'Hicksmith. She's from London.' Jencks ambled over to the window and looked out at the barn. 'You're from London, aren't you?'

'There are ten million people in London.' Daniel's voice was at the edge of a whisper too. 'We know fifty or a hundred, tops.'

'And no Gemma?'

'No.'

'Where is she, this Gemma?' Catherine glanced at Daniel. 'Does she know how her car got up on the moor?'

'Let's just say we haven't been able to contact Miss Hicksmith yet. When we do I'm sure she'll be able to explain.' Jencks put his pad away. 'If you remember anything else useful, please give me a call.'

He wheeled about and disappeared into the hallway. Daniel followed and let him out.

Catherine sat at the kitchen table staring at the cupboard where she'd hidden Daniel's phone. She thought about what to say to him. She had to choose her words with care. His phone had been in what she'd thought was Lisa's car, but the fact that it was Gemma's car cast a different light on the situation. Perhaps Daniel wasn't involved with Lisa at all. When she'd believed the car had been Lisa's it had seemed obvious he was tied up in some way with both Lisa and the body, whether it had been Gemma's or Toby's. Now she wasn't sure.

After a minute, Daniel returned.

'He's gone. I waited until he got to the end of the track.'

'What the fuck is going on?' Catherine lashed out at a kitchen chair, pushing it so hard it toppled over and crashed to the floor.

Daniel flipped his hands palms up. 'I don't know.'

'Gemma's car, only—' Catherine censored herself mid-sentence. She couldn't tell Daniel that Lisa was driving Gemma's car since she hadn't told him about Lisa's visit. And she hadn't told him about Lisa's visit because of the phone in the car which suggested Lisa and Daniel were somehow involved with each other. But, of course, that was irrelevant now. Jesus! She clenched her fists and stared at her husband. She sensed emotion boiling away below his flat expression.

'Only what?' Daniel said.

'You and Gemma. I thought it was over.'

'It is. You know that.'

'Please don't lie to me, Dan. I know you've been seeing her.'

'I haven't.'

'You have.'

'OK.' Daniel sighed. 'I did meet her up in London on Tuesday.'

'I knew it!'

'We had a drink, that's all. I wanted to check she was OK.'

'So you have been fucking her. You bastard. You promised.'

'An hour together, that's all it was. She needed support. She'd run into a spot of trouble and I wanted to help.'

'Help yourself, no doubt.' Catherine shook her head. She no longer knew what to think. Daniel had admitted meeting Gemma on the Tuesday and the next evening the poor girl was dead and trussed up in the back of her own car and on her way down the motorway. How could Daniel *not* be involved? Despair swept over her. She lowered her voice to a whisper. 'Just leave me alone, would you?'

'Catherine, look at me.' Daniel walked across. He held out a hand

and lifted Catherine's chin so she was forced to meet his gaze. 'We'll find out why Gemma's car is down here, but you have to believe the last time I saw her was in a Starbucks in Hampstead.'

'Hampstead?'

'Wes is renting a house near the heath. It has a full editing suite in the basement. I could only spare an hour, so I said to Gemma we'd have to meet locally. Check my wallet. I still have the receipt for the drinks. One latte and one hot chocolate.'

'Hot chocolate.' Catherine looked into Daniel's eyes. 'That was yours?'

'Of course.'

'And that was the last time you saw her?'

'Yes.' Daniel stepped back, his hand dropping from her chin. 'We talked for an hour and then I had to go back to work.'

'And what did you talk about?'

'This and that.'

'You said she was in trouble. What exactly?'

'I don't know, but it was personal to her. It didn't concern me and it's nothing for you to be worried about.'

'Are you sure about that?'

'Yes.' Daniel held her gaze before moving to pick up the chair Catherine had knocked over. He set it back in place and turned and left the room.

Chapter Forty-four

After Mr Hodgson was buried and the rest of the family had left, the rumours about what had happened multiplied. However, Sergeant Jencks made it clear the matter was closed. Hodgson had died of a heart attack, and if anybody knew of any other reason the family had moved away, they should come forward. Needless to say, nobody dared to. I don't know whether it was from fear or some misguided idea that the power the Murrins held was God-given. I never was one for God though. My pa told me human hands wrenched me from my mother's womb and human hands would hold the spade that would dig the hole I'd be buried in. Not much Godly in either.

Whether the Murrin's power came from a divine right or not, with each new piece of gossip and with every fresh rumour, the clamour for justice grew. It ended, of course, with the murder of the boys not more than a month after the death of Mr Hodgson. Who carried out the killings, well, nobody knew, or if they did they wouldn't say, but you could tell folks weren't sad to see them gone. That much was apparent at the funeral. A scattering of mourners stood in the graveyard to see the brothers buried alongside each other, but there was a large crowd watching from the lane. Some people had brought food and drink, intent on a party. I wasn't sure on that, but I wasn't going to argue, and I didn't refuse when someone offered me a bottle of beer.

Sergeant Jencks wasn't best pleased. He went back and forth berating folk, trying to get them to move along. He was put up to it by old man Murrin I guess. The family's influence was waning though, and if anything illustrated the fact it was what happened when Murrin left the churchyard. Somebody lobbed a bottle of pop, the liquid frothing out as it spun over and over, the sticky mess raining down on him and the wife. Murrin shifted his head from left to right, scanning the crowd as if searching for the perpetrator, before walking to the car. A murmur from the crowd grew and faded, and in the silence that followed, a pitiful sob from Mrs Murrin lingered in the air.

Not long after the funeral, Murrin split from his wife. She moved up country while he retreated to a cottage on the far side of the moor, a broken man. The estate was sold off and my family was able to buy our farm. Can't say many people were sorry to see the Murrins go, and if there were any, I never heard of them.

Chapter Forty-five

Foster dozed through the afternoon until the clock in the hall chimed four. It was time for action, he thought. The girl in the barn had to be connected in some way to the couple down at World's End. They'd done her in, driven up to the mine, and tossed her body in the shaft, believing they could get away with murder. Who she was, Foster had no idea, but he figured the answer wouldn't come from another nap by the fire. At his feet, the dog stirred, rising and staring at him with bright eyes.

'Not this time, Jess,' Foster said as he pushed himself up from the armchair. 'You've got to stay here and guard our friend in the barn.'

He went out into the hall and opened the big pine box that sat under the stairs. The rubberised dairy suit was stuffed down under a pile of footwear. Foster hadn't worn it since the day the couple at World's End had moved in. He dragged out the suit and gave it a shake, loosing dust and a cluster of mouse droppings. He dumped the suit on the floor and went upstairs. He found an old fisherman's jumper and two pairs of thick woollen socks. He pulled the jumper on over his existing clothing and slipped both pairs of socks on his feet. In a drawer under the bed he found a white pillow case.

Down in the hall, he struggled into the parlour suit. He lumbered into the living room and the dog barked at him until he reassured her.

'It's me, Jess, you daft bugger.'

He took his shotgun from where it was leaning against the wall in the hallway and scooped up a handful of cartridges. He took the rucksack, the pillow case, and the gun, and went out into the yard. A light flutter of snow drifted across the sky. Foster nodded appreciatively, folded the pillow case over the gun, and began to lumber down the valley, the dairy suit creaking with each step. The dog waited at the gate to the yard, whining until the ghostly figure disappeared into the whiteness.

Foster trudged along the drovers' track, at one point having to wade through the deep snow which had drifted into the cutting. He huffed and puffed and by the time he'd arrived at the gate where the track broke out onto the fields above the farm, he was hot and sweaty.

He stood and leaned on the gate. The house lay in the distance, fields of pristine white between him and the boundary wall. In contrast to the unmarked snow lying in the fields, the yard in front of the house was messy with slush and mud. The silver pickup truck stood in the garage.

Foster stared back up the track. He'd struggled down so he could struggle back again. In half an hour he could be sitting in the parlour watching the sparks fly up the chimney. A big mug of tea. Bit of a doze.

'Fuck it.'

He rearranged the pillow case around the shotgun so that nothing dark was showing except an inch of the barrel. He tightened the hood on the dairy suit. Then he clambered over the gate and into the deep snow. He edged round the first field and dropped to his hands and knees and crawled along the wall of the second field. On all fours the snow was up to his shoulders. His limbs ached and his face was numb. The chill seeped into his brain and at one point he began to get delirious. He thought about his wife lying dead in the grey morning light. The girl back at his place. The Murrin boys hanging lifeless in the barn at World's End.

'Not going to happen,' he said.

He reached the boundary wall as the day faded to dusk. He crawled to the gateway and peered through. Light poured from a window in the gable end of the house, and two figures moved behind the glass.

Foster realised he'd wasted his time with all the creeping about. Catherine Ross and her husband were having a right old ding-dong and were oblivious to anything. She was raising her finger, jabbing at her husband. He was shaking his head and shouting, before he stormed from the room. A few seconds later a flare of light came from an upstairs window. Foster sat and waited. In fifteen minutes the glow in the west was no more than a glimmer. The couple were hunkered down in there and they'd not be coming out again tonight.

To be on the safe side, he waited another quarter of an hour. Now, night had fallen. A light wind caressed his face, but overhead a bank of cloud hung unmoving. He rose, crossed the driveway, and made for the garage. He'd brought a small torch with him and now he flicked it on and began to examine the pickup.

Clods of snow sat frozen under the wheel arches, and when he went to the front of the vehicle he spotted a spray of heather caught in the front bumper. At the back, he bent and ran his fingers over the rear lights. There was no way he could tell if this was the vehicle he'd seen in the blizzard the other day. He stood and peered into the bed of the truck. A blue tarp lay at the far end. He heaved himself up, crawled across, and pulled it aside. There. A bin liner plastered round with silver tape. The same kind of tape he'd seen on the carpet. Barney had been right. The truck *had* been up at the mine.

Foster shoved the bin liner to the rear of the truck and clambered down. Whatever was inside felt heavy, like half a sack of spuds, but had been wrapped in a soft and yielding covering. He cradled the bundle in his arms and trudged away from the house and across the fields. He ploughed his way back up the drovers' track and found Jess waiting for him in the farmyard. Her coat was thick with frozen snow and Foster bent and brushed it from her back. The dog whined and rushed over to the house. She scratched at the door.

'Alright, girl,' Foster said. He lumbered over to the barn, dumped the bin liner in a corner, and headed back inside. Jess barked at him. 'You and me both. Hungry like half a horse wouldn't be enough.'

Foster propped the gun up in the hall and peeled off the dairy suit. He stepped into the parlour and went to the hearth where he placed kindling on the dying embers of the fire. Next, he rustled up some dinner for the dog, raiding the fridge for some eggs and a piece of raw steak he'd rather fancied himself.

The dog guzzled down the food, swallowing the steak without even chewing. Foster watched her until she'd cleaned her bowl and then went back to the fridge. There was a plastic Tupperware box with the remains of a three-day-old stew. He sniffed the contents, poured it into a pan on the stove, and picked up the phone. He cradled the phone under his chin and took out his tobacco and began to roll a cigarette.

'Hello?' Barney's voice came down the line.

'It's Joe,' Foster said. 'Did you come by today about that ram?'

'No, I never. I was just winding you up. I don't care what you're up to up at the mine or down at World's End. You could be shagging the woman, and if you were I'd be pleased for you. You do what you like and I'll do what I like. At our ages that's the only way to play it.'

'I ain't shagging her and, to be honest, I wouldn't wish myself on her or anyone.'

'Liar.'

'The ram. Do you want to know about the ram?'

'There wasn't a ram, what do you take me for, Joe? I ain't no idiot.'

'I don't know about that, but you're right about the ram.' By now Foster had finished rolling the cigarette. He fished out his lighter and lit up. He took a deep drag. 'There wasn't no ram down the mineshaft, but there was something else. Come over to my place and I'll show you. Could be I might need a bit of friendly advice.'

'Are you talking now? Because it's getting late.'

'It'll keep until first thing tomorrow, but it won't keep much longer. Get here by eight. I'll have the kettle on.'

'I'll be there.'

Foster placed the phone back in its cradle and took another drag on his cigarette. He didn't want to believe the couple at World's End were involved with the death of the girl, but there didn't seem much doubt about it. They'd assaulted her and dumped the body in the mine. The poor lass couldn't have been more than twenty-five at the most. The fact she was a similar age to Helena Hodgson wasn't lost on Foster. History repeating itself. Rape and murder and misery. He wondered where the hell it would all end.

Chapter Forty-six

They'd argued again the previous night, but the morning brought an uneasy truce. They orbited each other like boxers in a ring, neither wanting to be the first to throw a punch and leave their guard open for a counterattack. They breakfasted separately and Catherine returned to the bedroom. A little later she heard a rapping on the front door. A commotion came from the hallway, voices raised.

Downstairs, she found Constable Jencks and two other police officers standing in the kitchen. Daniel sat at the table, his head in his hands.

'What's going on?' Catherine said.

'We're taking your husband in for questioning, Mrs Ross,' Jencks said. 'It appears he hasn't been honest with us.'

'Daniel?'

'They found out about Gemma, sweetheart. About the affair. They also know what happened up in London with the burglar.'

'You lied, Mrs Ross. You said you didn't know Gemma Hicksmith and yet you do know her. You know her very well.'

'It was my fault.' Daniel looked up and raised his head. 'I asked Catherine to lie for me. Don't blame her.'

'Take him outside, Ken.' Jencks gestured to the door. 'I want a word with Mrs Ross.'

Daniel got to his feet and the two officers escorted him from the room. At least they hadn't put handcuffs on him, Catherine thought.

'I don't understand,' she said. 'This was ages ago and Daniel was never charged with the death in London. It was self-defence. You're just jumping to conclusions.'

'Ages ago, you say?' Jencks smirked. 'I don't think so. We know your husband met with Gemma a few days ago.'

'He told me about that. They just had a coffee together. Gemma had some sort of problem and Daniel was going to help her out. He hadn't seen her beforehand.'

'Really?' Jencks didn't disguise the snort. 'And you believe that?'

'Yes. He promised me the affair is over.'

'Promises are cheap and lies are the currency used to buy them.' Jencks tapped the end of his nose. He lowered his voice. 'But the truth always comes out in the end.'

'I don't know why you imagine Daniel has anything to do with Gemma's disappearance. What could he possibly gain from it?'

Jencks reached into his pocket and extracted a folded piece of paper. 'We were sent this by officers in London. It's the missing person's report for Gemma Hicksmith. Look at the photographs, Mrs Ross. Tell me what you see.'

Jencks passed the paper over and she unfolded it. There were several lines of text below two pictures. The first image was of Gemma dressed in clubbing gear, smiling, laughing. Catherine thought of the night when she'd spied on Gemma and Daniel in the pizza restaurant. Below the first picture there was a second one, also of Gemma, only she was holding—

'Joshua Hicksmith, Mrs Ross.' Jencks' finger came in over the top of the paper and jabbed at the photograph. 'Gemma's three-month-old baby. Bonny, isn't he?'

'*What?*' Catherine lurched forwards. She steadied herself by grabbing the edge of the table and then slumped into a chair. 'I don't understand?'

'Of course you don't, love. Few women do when their husband turns out to be a love rat.'

'Are you saying...?'

'We believe the baby is Daniel's child.'

'No!' She continued to stare at the photo until Jencks snatched it back. 'It can't be.'

'My theory is blackmail. The affair continued and Gemma got pregnant. That was when she decided to extort money from your husband. I guess he tried to argue with her and persuade her to relent, but she wouldn't have it. Now we find Gemma and the baby are missing, which leads to the obvious conclusion she pushed your husband too far and he cracked. Face it, Mrs Ross, he murdered the pair of them.'

'You're crazy, Daniel would never use violence like that.'

'Never?' Jencks tutted. 'You've a short memory, Mrs Ross. He brutally attacked a man and killed him.'

'That was completely different. He feared for his life and acted in self-defence.'

'There was talk about unnecessary force being involved.'

'It was just that: talk. The case was dropped.'

'Perhaps that was a mistake.' Jencks folded the piece of paper and popped it into a pocket. 'I'm sure we'll have some more questions for you, so please don't go anywhere.'

'Where are you taking him?'

'Exeter Heavitree. He'll be booked in and interviewed.'

'But there's no evidence anything's happened to Gemma, no body.'

'We've recovered the car. Forensic officers are checking it over.'

'This...' Catherine struggled to speak, saliva catching at the back of her throat. 'This can't be happening.'

'Would you like me to send a family liaison officer out here or I could call back myself later if you'd like?'

'No.' Catherine tried to clear her head. No body in the car. Of course there was no body in the car. And while there was no body it was going to be difficult for the police to charge Daniel with murder. 'I'll be OK. I'd prefer to be alone for a while.'

'Don't worry, if your husband is innocent, there's nothing to be concerned about.' Jencks smirked. Plainly he thought Daniel was guilty as hell. 'I'll see myself out.'

Catherine didn't move. She waited until the front door clicked shut and inhaled deeply. In, out, in, out. Although she'd tried to defend Daniel, everything Jencks had told her made sense. She didn't want to believe his accusations, but when she factored in Lisa, the chain of events seemed obvious: Despite Daniel's denials, he'd continued the affair with Gemma, sleeping with her whenever he got the chance. However, at some point he'd also begun screwing Lisa. Eventually, the complications of deceiving three women became too much, and he decided to dump Gemma. By that time though she was pregnant, and once she'd had the baby she threatened to expose the affair to Catherine. Daniel had flipped and the same anger which had resulted in the death of the burglar had led to him killing Gemma.

Catherine felt her body tense. Had she really been living with someone so violent all this time? A man capable of cold-blooded murder? She thought about his passion and anger, the way he sometimes appeared so distant and mysterious. It had all been part of the appeal, but now those same qualities made her fearful. If Daniel really was guilty, this was for the best, she thought. The police would discover the truth, including her own role in the disposal of the body, and Daniel would go to prison for life. If she came clean now, perhaps she'd be able to plead mitigating circumstances. A good defence lawyer could argue she'd suffered a kind of abuse, she could even embellish the truth a little. A jury trying a man who'd killed twice using extreme violence in both cases, would believe whatever she said.

The tears came then, in a flood, the thought of losing Daniel almost too painful to contemplate. And yet lose him she must. She had to shut him out of her mind and concentrate on looking after herself. There was hell to come: the arrest and trial, the media intrusion, whatever sentence she might receive for her part in disposing of the body. But at the end there was the thought that she could sell World's End and rebuild her life. She'd go to her parents' house. They had plenty of room and they'd gladly put her up for a few months. She could even take her old place in her dad's workshop.

She sniffed through the tears and tried to pull herself together. She needed to pack some clothes, and tomorrow she'd head off. She wiped her face, feeling better at the thought of Norfolk and her parents and home.

Chapter Forty-seven

Foster was having a shave when the parp of an airhorn caused him to jump and nick himself. He dabbed his cheek with cold water and went to the window. A bloody great tractor sat plumb centre in the yard. Barney's dray. Four huge wheels, all the same size, made the vehicle a monstrosity, but it could cover any terrain. Barney hung out of a door. Foster cracked the bathroom window open and waved. He finished shaving and went downstairs.

'Where the heck's my tea?' Barney said, as he came into the kitchen. 'You said to be here at eight.'

'Put the kettle on,' Foster said. 'I'll cook us some breakfast.'

'Your sheep aren't settled. You've not fed them.'

'No.' Foster bent to the fridge and flinched as a spasm went up his back. He retrieved a pack of bacon and some lard. 'Be my guest if you fancy it.'

'I fancy some food.' Barney looked concerned as Foster straightened up. 'But I'll give you a hand after breakfast if that's what you be needing.'

'Thanks, but it's not why I got you down here.' Foster found a frying pan and placed it on the stove. He used a knife to curl a lump of lard into the pan. Added the bacon. 'This is more serious.'

'The ram which wasn't a ram?'

'Just so.' The bacon rashers spat and Foster flipped them with a wooden slice. 'There wasn't a ram and I didn't meet the woman from World's End Farm.'

'But she was up there at the mine. I saw her.'

'You saw her, but did you see what she was doing?'

'No, just the pickup driving away.' Barney scratched his head. 'Can't say she was there for fun though. Not on the worst day of the winter.'

'Was she alone?'

'Couldn't tell. The snow was coming down so thick I could only make out who was sitting on the driver's side.' Barney paused. 'You going to tell me what this is about?'

Foster pointed to the kettle. Steam was jetting from the spout.

'Make the tea,' he said.

A little later, tea drunk and bacon sandwiches eaten, Foster took Barney out to the barn. They stood by the double doors in the strong sunlight. Barney stamped his feet in the snow.

'Well?' he said.

'You'll be keeping this secret.' Foster gestured at the barn. 'About what's inside. You'll not say a word to anyone.'

'You asking or telling?'

'Both.' Foster heaved open the door and a shaft of sunlit air canted in. There was a smell of hay and animal feed layered over an odour of decay. He beckoned Barney over to the old door where the tarpaulin lay over the body. 'You might be wanting to step back so you don't get too much of a shock.'

Barney didn't move so Foster yanked the tarp off in one sweep.

'Fuck.' Barney's mouth dropped open. 'Oh, fuck.'

The body had changed colour and any hint of life had gone. Whites and pinks had been replaced by greys and purples. The woman's lips had curled back revealing blackened gums. The welding goggles sat over the eyes.

'I found her in the mineshaft,' Foster said. 'I reckon the World's End couple dumped her there. Must have been when you spotted their pickup.'

'They killed her?'

'Either she did or he did.'

'What the hell are those?' Barney had noticed the goggles. 'Sex? Kinky sex?'

'No,' Foster leaned across and lifted the goggles off. 'I put them on because I couldn't stand her dead stare.'

'You crazy idiot.'

'But talking of sex, she's not right down there.' Foster gestured at the woman's crotch. 'There's a ring.'

'How do you know?'

'I had a look. I did a sort of autopsy. Like on those cop shows.'

'I'm worried about you, Joe. This your new hobby or summat?'

'I wanted to find out how she died.'

Barney cast a glance up and down the length of the body, flinching when he came to the head wound. 'Bloody hell, obvious, wasn't it?'

'Yes, she was given a right clonk or two.' Foster pointed at the blonde hair dark with blood. 'The best you can say about her death is it was quick.'

'What sort of sicko would get off on this?'

'Don't know, but there's more.'

'There had to be.' Barney groaned. 'Go on.'

'Yesterday evening, right after you told me you'd seen the pickup near the mine, I went down to World's End. While I was there I saw the couple arguing, but I examined the pickup on the off-chance I might find something.'

'I'm guessing you did.' Barney looked up and Foster nodded. 'Are we talking money, Joe?'

'No idea.' Foster gestured to a corner of the barn. 'But I brought it back here.'

'Now I know you're crazy. Haven't you seen those movies where somebody accidentally gets hold of a bag full of drugs or stolen cash? Hell, those stories never end in a good way.'

Foster went and stood by the doorway and looked at the sky. The sun seemed brighter than ever. He pointed at the eastern horizon. A line of grey cloud stained the lower edge of the blue.

'More snow. A lot more snow.'

'I heard the forecast.' Barney came across, his gaze following Foster's gesture. 'They said a good twelve inches.'

'Wind, too.' Once more, Foster jabbed a finger at the sky, this time at the wispy mares' tails overhead. 'Going to blow hard.'

'Excuse me for asking, but don't we have more important things to talk about than the weather?'

'We do and we don't, Barney.' Foster bent and shifted the barn door, scraping it closed over the frozen snow. He straightened, putting a hand to his back as he did so. 'We do and we don't. Let's have another cup of tea and afterwards we'll check the money. See where we're at.'

Foster made a pot of tea and dug out some biscuits from the back of a cupboard.

'Why not call the old bill?' Barney said.

'We don't want the police sniffing round here, do we? Not again.'

'It's been over thirty-five years, Joe. They're not going to connect the two events.'

'Jencks is already trying to connect what's going on now with World's End Farm. You see, Barney, the police like coincidences. They're not clever and it makes it easier for them. They look for patterns and lightning striking twice is a pattern, even if decades have passed. I haven't got a huge number of days left on this earth, but I don't want to spend those I have in prison. Do you?'

'I guess not.' Barney scratched the back of his neck. 'Better for me if I'd been out when you called.'

'That it might have been.' Foster dunked a biscuit in his tea. 'But you weren't, old pal.'

They were back in the barn. Foster had retrieved the bin liner and placed it next to the body.

'We should look through these first,' Foster said. He pulled out the bucket containing the woman's clothes and used his feet to clear an area of concrete, kicking the loose straw to one side. He tipped the clothes onto the concrete. 'See if we can find a clue as to who she is.'

'D'you suppose we're safe?' Barney prodded the black underwear with a stick. 'To touch this lot? I mean she smells a bit rich, doesn't she?'

'Whatever.' Foster lowered himself to his knees and picked up the jacket. 'I've touched more than those fancy knickers and I'm not dead yet. Plus, I gave you breakfast and I forgot to wash my hands before I started cooking.'

'You're kidding me?'

'Straight up, no.'

'Shite.'

Foster began to examine the jacket, his fingers delving into each pocket. When he'd finished he handed it to Barney.

'Here, you double check I've not missed anything.'

'I'm not doing them knickers.'

'If they'd been on the woman at the bakery, you'd have been keen to get your hands on them.'

'You're right about that.' Barney craned his head round to stare at the body. 'But she's alive, isn't she?'

Foster continued searching the clothing. He checked the cuffs and the collar on the shirt. He examined the sheer stockings. Finally, he picked up the black underwear and ran the silk material over his fingers.

'What the heck are you looking for?' Barney said.

'I don't know until I find it.' Foster tossed the underwear on the pile of clothing. 'But there's nothing here.'

'They must have disposed of her ID somewhere else. Unless it's in that sack.'

'Could be.' Foster glanced at the bin liner but moved across to the body. 'But why?'

'They kept it separate so she can't be identified, you sheep's dick.'

'I mean, why did they kill her?'

'She not they. It was the World's End woman I saw up at the mine.'

'Her husband's involved, I'm sure of it.'

'You said so before, but how do you know?'

'His eyes. They're too blue. There's something about him that's not quite right.'

'Prejudice, Joe. We don't do it these days, remember? Everyone's got to have a fair shot. Loons, nancy boys, foreigners. Them religious people with tea-towels on their heads. Even folks with dark blue eyes.

You'll have one of those anti-discrimination officials round your place taking away your subsidies if you're not careful.'

'They can bloody try.' Foster ran a hand across the woman's belly. The stomach had swollen as if air had been pumped in, and there was a neat scar below the belly button, just above the close-shaved triangle of pubic hair.

'What are you doing?'

'Just checking a hunch.'

'She's got some weight on her,' Barney said. 'If she's from London then it must be good eating up there.'

'It's crap. I once went to a posh restaurant in the West End when I was on that NFU panel. Looked fancy, true, but the food wasn't much more than a mouthful. I'm surprised they're not all skin and bone.'

'Perhaps she stops in or does a Big Mac and fries every night.'

'Perhaps. Now let me think, damn it.' Foster slid his hand up to the woman's breasts. 'I've got a hunch, Barney.'

'About what?' Barney's gaze followed Foster's hand as it touched the left nipple. 'You one of those patholowotsits now, are you? Or perhaps you're just a pervert.'

'Let's look in that bag.'

'You know, this is all fucked up, but one thing I'm sure of.'

'What's that?'

'I don't want to be coming over here again, Joe. Not for this kind of job. I'll keep you company with a cup of tea and a cake or come round to help with a difficult lambing, sure. Not this.'

'You great big wuss.' Foster cleared straw from another section of the concrete floor and placed the bin liner in the centre. 'Now help me with this.'

The bag was wrapped in silver tape, so Foster took his knife and flicked out the blade. He sliced open the top of the bag and a colourful fleece blanket pushed through the slit. He tore the plastic apart. Beneath the plastic, the blanket folded round and round.

'Bloody hell,' Barney said, 'We could be rich if that in there's money.'

'I don't reckon it's money, Barney.'

'What then?'

'Not sure.' Foster began to unroll the blanket. There was a smell now. Rotting and bad. Shit and piss. Decay. The blanket opened out.

'Christ Almighty!' Barney said. 'This is...'

'Yes.'

It was as he'd guessed after he'd spotted the scar on the woman's stomach. Nestled in amongst the fleece blanket, pink and fleshy like a young piglet, was the corpse of a baby. That such a tiny creature could ever grow and walk and speak and live and love, seemed amazing to Foster. He found himself wanting to say a few words to Barney. Not a eulogy or a prayer, but words which might help the two of them make sense of the situation, except there was no sense to any of it, so he decided he'd be better off saying nothing at all.

Chapter Forty-eight

Catherine slept uneasily. She rose several times in the night and checked the locks downstairs. At one point she noticed the security light had come on outside but could see nothing beyond the glare. In the morning, she thrust aside the curtains to flurries of snow, and as she ate breakfast the radio was talking of more bad weather. Sub-zero temperatures across the country were refreezing the melt and heavy snow was forecast to arrive the next day. Travellers making non-essential journeys should change their plans.

She quickly finished her toast and went to the bedroom and stuffed some clothes and toiletries into a bag. She looked round the house and realised she'd have to come back and pick up the rest of her possessions. She found a packet of biscuits, made herself a flask of coffee, and filled a plastic bottle with water. A blanket seemed a good idea, so she got one from upstairs. She piled everything in the hallway and went outside.

The pickup and Daniel's BMW sat side by side in the garage. She considered taking the pickup, but the thought of driving the beast three hundred miles to Norfolk was too much, so instead she started the BMW and brought it round to the front door. She took her bag and the other stuff and shoved the whole lot on the rear seat. Then she went back inside for a final check.

As when she'd left the house in London, there was no real need, but an invisible force seemed to pull her in. She stood in the hallway and glanced up the crooked stairs. She went into the living room with its low ceiling and exposed beams. She crossed the room to the woodburner and touched the black metal. She'd let the fire go out last night and her fingertips sensed only a residual heat. She stood there agonising over where it had all gone wrong. Her gaze wandered to the big window and the view across the valley, the moorland sheathed in white. It was both beautiful and bleak.

As she turned to go, a glint caught her eye. The sun reflecting on the windscreen of a taxi as it turned in the lane. Closer, in the foreground, a figure trudged towards the house, head hung low, body swaying from side to side.

Daniel.

Catherine ran into the hallway, intending to slam the front door and lock herself inside the house, but for some reason she found herself hesitating, almost as if the act of closing the door would be to admit defeat.

'Cathy,' Daniel said as he crossed the driveway. 'Thank God.'

'They let you go.' Catherine stood beside the door.

'Eventually. You don't sound ecstatic about it.' Daniel passed the car and took in the luggage on the back seat. 'Going somewhere?'

'Leaving.'

'Leaving?'

'Yes.' She paused and studied Daniel's face for a reaction. There was none. 'It's for the best. I can't take this any longer.'

'I didn't have anything to do with Gemma going missing. You have to believe me.'

'And the police, do they believe you?'

'Self-evidently or else they wouldn't have released me.' Daniel reached the door. 'But I don't care about them, it's you I'm worried about.'

'Me?'

'You and me. Us.'

'There is no *us*, Dan. Not now.' Catherine gestured at the car. 'I'm leaving, right?'

'Please, Cathy, let's go inside and talk this through. You're being irrational.'

'Yes, that's me.' She made a pat smile. 'Silly little Catherine and her stupid little worries.'

'I didn't mean that, I simply want you to believe me about Gemma. The last time I saw her was in Hampstead. She gave me a lift back to the edit suite in her car. A technician saw her drop me off.'

'Is that what you told the police?'

'Yes and they've checked my story out. They're satisfied.' Daniel came inside the house and closed the door. 'For now.'

The sound of the latch closing echoed in the hallway. Neither of them moved. Catherine realised Daniel was waiting for her to speak, to make some gesture of reconciliation, but she couldn't bring herself to do so. She hadn't been able to go, but nor could she make up with Daniel. She was stuck in a liminal space between the two choices, frozen like the landscape outside.

After a minute, Daniel clicked one foot on the floor. A double tap signalling her time was up. He went to the kitchen and there was the suck of the fridge opening, the chink of a glass, the glug of milk being poured. Catherine walked down the hall and stood at the kitchen door. Daniel was drinking the milk from a pint glass, his back to her.

'Gemma hasn't gone missing, Dan,' Catherine whispered. 'She's dead.'

Her husband took perhaps a fraction longer to react than she might have expected had the news come as a complete surprise. There was a moment when he ceased drinking, but the glass remained at his lips for a couple of seconds, as if he was weighing his next move.

The glass came away from his mouth and he clunked it down onto the work surface and pivoted round.

'*What?*' He wore a white milk moustache which would have been comical in any other circumstance. Now, as he spoke, it was like a marker reminding Catherine of the way he'd reacted. 'What the hell are you talking about?'

'She's lying in a barn not a mile away from here.'

'Catherine, you're crazy and — yes — irrational.'

'She's fucking dead, understand? She's in a barn up near the burnt-out car. I've seen her with my own eyes. Hell, I've touched her. She's been bludgeoned over the head. *Bludgeoned*, understand?'

'Did Jencks put you up to this? I bet he did.' Daniel nodded to himself, but all Catherine could focus on was the white line of milk. 'There is no body, Cath, come on, admit it. This is a clever attempt at entrapment. Now I get why they released me so soon. Well, it can only work if I'm guilty, and I'm not guilty of anything.'

'You're guilty of lying to me about Gemma and her baby.'

'The baby.' Daniel dropped his gaze. 'You know about the baby?'

'Of course I know about *your* baby.'

'No, that's not true. I'm not the father.'

'Can't you just stop lying for once? It all makes sense to me now. How stupid I was. You said it was over, but you were still fucking her. She got pregnant and that's when you got scared. You decided to move well away from London, so she couldn't suddenly turn up on our doorstep.' Catherine laughed but the sound was a cackle. Like she *was* crazy. 'Only she has turned up on our doorstep.'

'If Gemma *is* dead, I didn't kill her.' Daniel held up his hands in a gesture that said not guilty, not me. 'The police let me go, right?'

'Is that all you can say? You dismiss her death as if she never mattered, and I guess to you she didn't, not once you'd dumped her and started fucking the next one.'

'Catherine...' Daniel inched towards her.

'Did you imagine you could go off to London and screw around with no consequences? You continue your relationship with Gemma and she gets pregnant. Next you bed Lisa, your best friend's wife. Gemma starts to cause problems, so you and Lisa decide to kill her.' Catherine stopped. Her husband was standing in the middle of the kitchen, his face blank. Then she had it. Realised the whole of his plan. She moved into the hallway. 'Shit, I've just worked it out. I'm next, aren't I?'

'Cathy.' Daniel was across the kitchen now. 'You're getting it all wrong. There's an explanation if you're prepared to listen.'

'Listen?' Catherine backed up along the hall as Daniel closed on her. 'I'm not going to listen to more of your lies.'

'No lies, just the truth.' Daniel smiled, but his boyish charisma was absent. 'Honestly.'

'Honestly? Being honest is beyond you, Daniel.' Catherine darted for the stairs. She bounded up them two at a time.

'Wait!' Daniel stood at the bottom. He made no attempt to come up. 'Just hear me out, OK? You up there, me down here.'

'You lied, Dan. From the day we first came here.'

'Specifically, Catherine?'

'The secrets inside that metal box.'

'For God's sake, I told you, it contains personal photographs—'

'They're not personal photographs, Daniel. Tell the fucking truth for once. There's a picture inside the box and it's of two young men. They're dead. They've been hanged from a beam in our barn.'

'You looked.' Daniel appeared wounded. As if Catherine had wronged him in some way. The tone of his voice lowered. 'You went through my private things.'

'I find a strange box hidden in my husband's room — my husband who I'd recently caught cheating on me — of course I bloody looked!'

'Right.' Daniel appeared wounded, as if she'd sliced him with a knife. 'I came across the pictures when I was doing research on this place. It was after we'd had our offer accepted. I didn't want to put you off, so I kept quiet.'

'Liar. The estate agent told me you knew about the killings when you made the offer.'

'OK, so what if I did? I figured once the barn was converted the slate would be wiped clean, and if you never found out there'd be no harm in it.'

'History can't be wiped, Daniel. That was the problem in London.' Catherine paused. 'Those photographs are connected to what's going on now, aren't they?'

'Don't be stupid, what happened in the barn was decades ago. It's completely irrelevant.'

'Irrelevant? So explain why you visited Mr Murrin, the father of those two dead men, at the start of last year before we'd even set eyes on this place, before we'd even considered moving?'

'I can't.'

'Why, Daniel? Why?'

'Forget Murrin, forget the photographs, we've got to focus on the present. If the police don't find Gemma soon they're going to assume the worst.'

'And they'd be right. I told you, she's dead.'

Daniel stared up at her. She wondered if she'd have time to lock herself in the bedroom if he decided to rush her. Whether the door would be strong enough to hold him back.

'Dead,' he said. The word came out with no emphasis. It could have been a question or a statement. Perhaps the ambiguity was deliberate, Catherine thought. He knew/he didn't know. He'd killed her/he hadn't killed her. Daniel took a deep breath. 'Tell me. From the start.'

'Lisa arrived here on Wednesday night with Gemma in the back of her car. She duped me into helping her dispose of the body. We dumped it in the old mineshaft at the top of the valley, only Joe Foster found the body and took it to one of his barns.'

'Slow down, Cath. None of this is making any sense. Joe Foster the farmer?'

'Yes. I've no idea why he took her or what he's doing with her.'

'But the police? Why didn't you tell them? And why the hell did you help Lisa?'

'She told me the body was Toby's. She said he'd abused her and she'd killed him. I never would have helped her if I'd realised the truth.'

'Bloody hell, Catherine, you don't believe I could be involved in any of this?' Daniel looked up at her, his eyes unblinking, the deep blue unreadable, but a pained expression on his face. 'I cared for... I mean...'

'You loved Gemma.'

'No, not like I love you.' Daniel put his right foot on the bottom stair. 'But I never would have wanted anything bad to happen to her.'

'We need to go to the police and explain what's happened.'

'No,' Daniel said. He'd come up three stairs now. 'We can't. Don't you see how it would look? They already suspect me.'

'But if you're innocent you don't have to worry. There'll be forensic evidence on the body and a murder weapon somewhere too.'

'You still don't believe me, do you?' Five steps. His left hand gripping the banister. 'You think I killed Gemma.'

'I don't know, Dan. You've lied to me too many times.'

She thought about the box again. It should have been the least of her worries, but she couldn't get the photograph of the hangings out of her mind. The way the men had dangled at the end of the bar taut rope, their arms and legs limp. This hadn't been a killing in the heat of the moment, this had been planned. A cold-blooded murder. An execution. A lynching, perhaps. The image faded from her thoughts to be replaced with a picture of the dead burglar which Daniel's lawyer had shown her. He lay in a tangle of limbs, his face disfigured by violence.

'Here,' the lawyer had said, pointing to the burglar's right arm. 'This is our problem. There are bruises on the wrist and hand from the statue, but there are some pressure marks too.'

'So?'

'I'm afraid the police are claiming your husband pulled the man's arm away so he could hit him. There are three strikes on the arm and another four to the unguarded head. Daniel went a long way past simple self-defence.'

'Shit.' She blinked, back in the present.

'Catherine,' Daniel said. Halfway up the stairs now. 'There's nothing to worry about, love, I promise.'

'Stop!' Catherine said. Her hand went to her back pocket and she snatched out her phone. In half a second she'd dialled nine, nine. 'Any closer and I'll call the police.'

'No need to do that, Mrs Ross.' A voice floated up from downstairs. Daniel turned and Catherine peered over the banisters. Constable Jencks stood in the hallway, another uniformed officer behind him. 'We're already here.'

Chapter Forty-nine

Daniel descended the stairs and Catherine followed. Jencks stood in the hall.

'We came in the back way.' He tilted his head towards the kitchen. 'But we had our reasons for entering uninvited.'

'Thank God you did!' Catherine said. 'I need to tell you something.'

Jencks blanked her and marched forwards. 'Catherine Ross—'

'You know who I am,' Catherine said. 'What is this?'

'Catherine Ross.' Jencks held up his hand and repeated her name. 'I'm arresting you on suspicion of the murders of Gemma Hicksmith and her child. You do not have to say anything, but anything you do say may be given in evidence.'

'*What*? Are you crazy?'

'We've found a marble statue in the mineshaft up near the burnt-out car. There's no sign of the body but blood on the statue matches Gemma's blood type. This morning your husband confirmed the statue is one of yours.'

'Daniel?' Catherine realised she'd been duped. 'Why?'

'It's for the best, sweetheart.' Daniel kept his voice low. He gave a resigned smile. 'Just tell them the truth.'

'I told you it was Lisa!' Catherine said. 'Lisa killed Gemma. I didn't have anything to do with it.'

'Please, Mrs Ross,' Jencks waved at the door. The other officer stood there. He held a pair of handcuffs in his hands. 'Let's discuss this at the station.'

'NO! Don't you see? He's setting me up. Him and Lisa.'

'Mrs Ross—'

'It's not Mrs Ross, it's Ms Ross. That's *my* name. Why on earth would I take the name of my lying, cheating husband?'

'Catherine.' Daniel. Calm and steady. 'It will be easier if you go with Constable Jencks. Please don't make a scene.'

'A scene? You expect me to roll over and take this?'

The officer moved behind her and seized one of her wrists. She struggled, but Jencks stepped closer, his face up against hers.

'Easy now,' he said. 'We wouldn't want this to get violent.'

Catherine let her arms fall limp. Resisting was pointless. Cold metal closed round her right wrist and her arm was pulled behind her. Jencks took her left hand and wrenched it backwards. The other cuff clicked shut.

'There, all done.' Jencks smiled like a dentist after an extraction. 'Let's go.'

He whirled her about face and guided her from the house. Catherine craned her head round as she went. Daniel stood on the threshold staring at her, his blue eyes devoid of emotion.

They took her to Heavitree police station in Exeter. The booking in process was tedious and demeaning. She was made to remove all her clothing and undergo an intimate examination, after which she was given a Tyvek paper suit to wear. She spent half an hour with a young duty solicitor who didn't look long out of short trousers. She recounted the events since Lisa's arrival in the storm, leaving out her visit to Joe Foster's barn.

'If that's what happened, then tell the truth,' was his only comment. His lack of legal nous wasn't reassuring.

With the help of the solicitor, she prepared a written statement and was then left in a room with a female custody officer for company. An hour went by. And another. Catherine's questions as to what was causing the delay were met with a shrug and the offer of a cup of tea. After another wait, the solicitor returned, and she was taken to an interview room where Jencks sat next to an intimidating female officer he introduced as DC Ann Taylor. DC Taylor set up some recording equipment and pointed to a camera high on one wall where a red light blinked. She stated the date and time and Jencks leaned across the table.

'Mrs Ross,' he said. 'You understand the seriousness of this offence?'

'I didn't do it.'

'We've read your account, but you might want to reconsider your answer in a moment or two. Ann?'

DC Taylor had thick, dry lips and a thin tongue. When she smiled the effect was akin to an anaemic burger sandwiched in a lightly-floured bap.

'We've found fingerprints on the statue, Catherine. They're yours.'

'Of course they're mine, the statue came from my workshop. I gave it to Lisa as a present when she visited in December. She must have used it to kill Gemma and then thrown it in the mineshaft at the same time as she dumped the car.'

'Your fingerprints and Gemma Hicksmith's blood, Catherine. I'm sure you can see why you are now the prime suspect in her disappearance.'

'You've charged me with murder.'

'No, you haven't been charged. You've been arrested on suspicion of involvement in the murders of Gemma and her baby.'

'There's no body.'

'In your statement you told us there was.'

'Jesus! You can't have it both ways. Are you saying you now believe me about the body, but not Lisa?'

Jencks held out his hand in front of DC Taylor. She seemed put out and her lips parted, the ham-like tongue sliding from one side to the other.

'As you can imagine,' Jencks said. 'Our colleagues in London are all over this and locating Gemma and her baby is a high priority. As soon as we had your statement we got straight onto them. They were very interested in your story about Gemma.'

'There you go,' Catherine said. The boy lawyer gave her an encouraging look. 'I told you it was Lisa.'

'You did.' Jencks tapped the table. 'However, there's a problem with Lisa. She's in London with her husband, Toby. Police officers visited her to check your story and she says she didn't come to visit you, a fact her husband confirms. I'm afraid your account is pure fiction.'

'She's lying. She turned up with Gemma's body in her car. She was in my house, slept in the spare room, and the next day we put the body in the mineshaft.'

'So your statement says.' Jencks peered at a pad on the table in front of him. 'No mention of Gemma's baby though.'

'There was no baby. Lisa must have disposed of it elsewhere.'

'Lisa wasn't involved, Catherine. This is all down to you.'

'No, that's not true!'

'Ann?'

DC Taylor gave another one of her smiles as she reached for a computer tablet. 'Catherine, do you recognise this?' The DC touched the screen and a sound file began to play.

If I ever hear anything about Gemma again, I swear I'll kill the slut, understand? You go within a mile of her and you'll regret it...

Catherine gave an involuntary shake. That was *her* voice.

Jencks waved his arm again and DC Taylor ended the playback. 'This was a message you left on your husband's voicemail on the 12th January last year. You said, "I swear I'll kill that slut". Yes or no?'

Next to her, the boy lawyer squirmed in his seat. He looked as if he was about to wet himself. 'My client—'

'Your client is here to answer questions. This is a simple one. Catherine, did you say you'd kill her?'

'No.' Catherine shook her head. 'I mean yes, that's what I said in the message, but it was just an expression. I was making an idle threat.'

'Your husband has been seeing Gemma. In fact, worse than that, she's had his baby.'

'No, he told me it's not his.'

'In his statement to us he said he isn't sure, but whatever, he's been seeing Miss Hicksmith and you threatened to kill her if he went within a mile.'

'I didn't know about the baby until yesterday.'

'So you say.' Jencks looked down at the pad again. 'Your husband says you have a violent temper. Apparently you threw a glass at him a couple of years ago. His arm required several stiches.'

'That was an accident. The glass hit a wall and a piece broke off and cut him. We laughed about it afterwards. I can't even remember what the argument was about. Something silly like the colour of a new sofa.'

'Something silly and yet you resorted to violence to make your point?'

'No!' Catherine said in despair. Why were they twisting her words? 'I was angry, yes, but the glass hitting him was just unlucky.'

'That's not how he remembers it.' Jencks resumed his examination of his pad. He looked up. 'Is there anything else you wish to tell us at this point, Mrs Ross?'

'I didn't kill Gemma. I don't know where she is if she isn't in the mine. For some reason Daniel's lying. I found his phone in Lisa's car and that leads me to believe he's having an affair with her. Either she's trying to frame me or they both are.'

'Lisa's car?' Taylor jumped in, quick to spot Catherine's mistake.

'I mean Gemma's car.'

'Your husband has already explained to us that he must have left his phone in the car when she gave him a lift last Tuesday.' Taylor paused. 'Did you kill Gemma up in London or down here, Catherine? Did you drive the car to Devon or did Gemma turn up on your doorstep? I can see it would have been a shock, especially if she had the baby with her. Some kind of reaction from you would have been quite understandable.'

'This is madness,' Catherine said. She glanced at her solicitor. He was staring blankly, plainly way out of his depth. 'Look, I didn't kill Gemma, OK?'

'And aside from your denial?' Jencks parted his lips. 'Anything you want to add to your statement?'

'No.' Catherine said, her voice low and quiet. She sat back and crossed her arms. Why didn't they believe her?

'You killed Gemma Hicksmith and her baby.' Jencks thumped his fist on the table. 'You concealed the body and burned the car. Come on, admit it!'

'No I didn't!' Catherine screamed the denial and hung her head in her hands. This couldn't be happening to her. This was a nightmare she would soon wake up from. Daniel would be there at her side and he'd be the old Daniel. Mysterious but loving. Exciting but faithful. Strong but never violent.

'Catherine?' DC Taylor. Her words slipping out soft and gentle. 'You need to tell us where the body is. If your story about Lisa is true, then there'll be forensic evidence which might prove your innocence. Finding Gemma and her baby is vitally important. There's her parents to consider too. As you can imagine, they're going through a very tough time. Their daughter and grandson are missing and they need answers.'

'I didn't do it.' Catherine kept her head low and sobbed. 'I didn't kill Gemma.'

'You've said that, but did you hide her? Did you bury her or conceal her? Is she on your land or farther away? Please, Catherine, we need to know where the body is.'

'We dumped it in the mine, honestly.' Catherine told the truth and hoped the lie that followed would be missed. 'I don't know where it is now.'

'The body isn't an *it*, Catherine, the body is Gemma. She didn't go walkabout, you moved her, didn't you? The car fire attracted our attention, so you went back to the mine and retrieved the body. You took Gemma and hid her. We know the location must be close because the snow would have prevented you from going farther afield.'

'There's no sense to it.' Catherine looked up and fixed the police officer with a stare. 'Why would I set light to the car and attract attention to the mine?'

'Sometimes people know they've done wrong.' DC Taylor slid her hand across the desk and turned it palm up. It's OK, the gesture said. You can trust me. 'Sometimes they deliberately leave evidence behind as a cry for help.'

'I didn't kill her and I didn't move her!' Catherine shouted. That was the truth of it so what more could she say? She thought about telling them she'd seen the body in the little barn near the mine, but she didn't see how it would help her situation. Once they had the body they'd have fingerprints on the plastic wrapping, fibres from her clothing, just the evidence they needed to press charges. Of course Lisa had touched the package too, but she'd been wearing Catherine's clothes and a pair of borrowed gloves. There could be other evidence wrapped up with Gemma, but if Lisa had planned carefully, there might not be. Catherine had taken great pains to clean up back at World's End too. She'd washed the clothes she'd lent Lisa and vacuumed the house. She'd burned the dust bag and wiped down any surfaces and door handles Lisa might have touched. There was no evidence to prove her story about Lisa visiting. There was Gemma's son to consider as well. Where was he? She was pretty sure he hadn't been in the roll of carpet. Perhaps the poor baby was alive somewhere. Perhaps he was even with Lisa and Toby.

'Come on now, Catherine,' Taylor said. 'You can tell us and this will all be over. We'll find her eventually, but it will look much better if you help us with our enquiries.'

'For God's sake I didn't kill Gemma! How many more times do I have to say it?'

'The body, Mrs Ross.' Jencks. His voice was sharp compared to DC Taylor's. 'Because the body can answer all our questions. Your refusal to disclose where it is must be read as evidence of your guilt.'

'But...' Catherine pushed herself upright and turned to her lawyer.

'If you know, you'd best tell them,' the young man said.

Catherine bowed her head.

After a minute of silence, Jencks tapped on the table with his pencil. 'We'll wrap now and continue tomorrow.'

'Tomorrow?' Catherine sucked in a gulp of air. She could feel panic rising within. 'You mean—'

'You'll be staying in overnight, Mrs Ross.' Jencks switched the recording equipment off. 'It will give you a chance to ponder your future life in prison.'

***

The cell had white tiles and a grey floor. A thin blue PVC mattress on a raised platform matched a blue stripe which ran round the walls at waist level. A stainless-steel toilet sat in one corner and there was a sink set into the wall. The room reeked of disinfectant and the sterile nature was reinforced by the bright lighting.

Catherine stumbled into the room in a daze and slumped on the bed. The custody officer asked her if she wanted a meal. She looked up and nodded blankly. When the officer had gone, she lay back on the bed and gazed at the ceiling. Would this be what she woke to for the next twenty-five years?

A while later the custody officer appeared with a plastic meal tray, a plastic cup, and plastic cutlery. The food was no better or worse than the fare you might expect at a motorway service station: lumpy mashed potatoes, overcooked carrots, thick sausages, and watery baked beans. The tea was lukewarm and too strong. When the officer returned to take away the tray, he brought her a couple of magazines. *Devon Life* and an old *Cosmopolitan*. Catherine caught a glimpse of the *Cosmo* cover and almost laughed at the irony. Nest to a headline that promised, 'Mind blowing sex in minutes', was another which proclaimed, 'What to do when your ex turns nasty'. She put the magazines to one side and lay back on the bed. The ceiling offered no more inspiration than before, so she rolled on her side, curled herself up, and tried to sleep.

With her eyes closed, all she could see was Daniel's face. His blue eyes. His smile. Once, the hidden depths of his psyche had been mysterious to her, a part of him she'd never been able to discern. Now the mask had fallen away, and she realised the mysteriousness had a sinister element to it. He hadn't backed her up when he'd been interviewed. In fact he'd done the exact opposite by telling the police about the voicemail and the incident with the glass. He'd betrayed her and there could only be two reasons for it: One, he believed Catherine had killed Gemma. Two, he'd killed Gemma and wanted to shift the blame onto her. Both reasons made her shiver. Daniel's electric touch, this time not an exciting tingle, but a painful shock.

At some point she must have drifted off because raised voices woke her. Shouting and swearing. The muffled sounds of people in the corridor outside. A scuffle. Violence. The noise faded away, but she didn't fall asleep again until much later.

The rattle of the door locks jerked her awake. Daylight showed behind the thick glass blocks in one wall, and she barely had time to register she'd been asleep for hours, before a custody officer came in and stood by the sleeping platform. Hovering behind was DC Taylor.

'You're free to go,' the custody officer said. 'We'll get you booked out and a car will take you home.'

'Huh?' Catherine eased herself up onto one arm. 'I don't understand?'

'You remain a suspect,' Taylor said. 'But we're exploring several lines of enquiry. You'll be interviewed again in due course.'

Catherine swung her legs round and sat on the bed.

'Ten minutes.' The custody officer dropped a bag containing her clothes on the floor and jabbed at the toilet. 'Freshen yourself up and all that, OK?'

She nodded, vaguely aware of the door closing. Could Daniel be behind this? Had he had a change of heart and decided to back her in the way she'd stood behind him up in London? It seemed unlikely.

A few minutes later she stood at a counter as the custody officer booked her out, and a little while after that she was sitting in the back of a police car, heading for Dartmoor and World's End Farm.

Chapter Fifty

I've never done much praying and I guess I won't know if that was a mistake until I pass myself. By then it will be too late because I ain't been to church in years and I've got no intention of changing my ways now. I couldn't say if old Murrin had faith or not, but if he did, he must have been baffled at what the Good Lord was up to. Murrin was in his early fifties when his two eldest sons were murdered. A while later he split from his wife and spent the next thirty-five years on his own. His health gradually deteriorated and, a year or so ago, a cancer began to consume him. He was the wrong end of his eighties and I guess the end was all too apparent.

One sunny winter's day, Murrin went to Haytor for a picnic. How he climbed the huge granite outcrop in his condition no one knew, but somehow he struggled up there carrying a picnic hamper. He spread a blanket on top of the rock and laid out a selection of fine meats and cheeses, fresh bread and fruit. He poured a decent red wine into a crystal glass. Cut the cheese and meat with a silver knife. Served the food on a china plate. It was as if he was trying to recreate a happier and more prosperous time.

Later that day he was found at the foot of Haytor in a sorry state. He'd smashed his skull on a boulder and broken numerous bones, but lingered in the hospital for a week, his mind just the wrong side of gone. All that time I guess he thought about what had happened. How his boys had turned out. How his life was fading away.

I visited him the day before he died. Flowers sat in a vase by the bed, but Murrin didn't look so fresh. A greyness had overwhelmed *him, an affliction which was more than the sum of his injuries. I stood at the foot of the bed and as he met my eyes, I smiled. He closed his own eyes as if to banish me. Perhaps he thought I was an apparition or demon, but when, a few minutes later, he opened his eyes again, I was still there. I smiled once more and even though I didn't speak, I think he realised. I'm pleased about that. If he'd gone to his grave without the truth, there would have been something missing. I'd have felt differently too. Not better or worse. Just different.*

Chapter Fifty-one

After they discovered the baby, Foster discussed with Barney what to do.

'The police, Joe,' Barney said. 'That's the only option now.'

'I'll phone them,' Foster said. 'But I'll leave you out of it, right?'

Barney climbed up into his big tractor and drove off and Foster berated himself for lying to his friend. No way was he going to call Jencks. The officer would arrest him and, once he was banged up in a police cell, Jencks would be able to search the house and come up with whatever he needed to put Foster away for the Murrin murders.

Fat chance, Foster thought to himself.

The issue was the girl and who was guilty of killing her and the baby. But he had a pretty good idea about that.

He slept on it, and in the morning everything seemed a whole lot clearer. When he went to feed the stock though, his mood darkened. The sick ewe he'd separated from the flock was lying on her side, legs stiff, eyes open and unblinking. He looked across the barn to where the other sheep were eating. They seemed fine. He guessed the ewe's lamb had died inside her and she'd got sepsis. There wasn't much he could have done to save her. Sad, but that was farming.

After finishing the rest of his chores, he clambered up into the loft space above his bedroom. There was crap up here going back to when he was a child. Stuff his ma and pa had never thrown away and Foster and his wife had never bothered with. Boxes of old business documents associated with the farm. Crates full of his parents' clothes. Toys he remembered from when he was a kid. An old fiddle of his, it's neck broken by his brother Jimmy during a heated argument. A roll of cream carpet, one end of which looked as if it had been a nest for a colony of mice. Electrical equipment he'd been meaning to repair but was now decades past being useful.

Foster sat on his haunches, careful not to step off the joists and put a foot through the plaster-covered lathes below. By rights he should have cleared the mess years ago; now he'd never bother. Somebody else would do it after he'd died. Perhaps sorting through everything with care and marvelling at the rich slice of history; more likely simply throwing the whole lot into a skip and ferrying it to the local tip.

Never mind that, he thought. Focus. He hadn't come up here to reminisce.

He crept across the joists to the rear of the loft space. A rough stone chimney breast ran up to the pitched roof. The mortar had dried and shrunk and in places black tar oozed between cracks. He reached for a stone in the face of the chimney, his fingers closing round the edges. He worked the stone free and drew it out. Behind the stone lay a tobacco tin encrusted with soot. He extracted the tin.

Down in the kitchen, he wiped off the soot and tar with a rag and washed his hands clean. As he dried his hands, he realised they were shaking slightly.

'Daft idiot,' he said. 'Scared of what you might find, yeah?'

His fingers caressed the tin, further delaying the moment of truth, and then he was opening the lid. As a lad he'd used the tin to store all manner of knickknacks. Later, he'd thrown away the rifle bullet, the trio of polished stones, the dried rabbit's foot on a silver chain, and all the other items in there which were precious to a boy but meaningless to a man. He'd replaced them with the letter from Helena and a bunch of photographs. The tin's purpose had changed. It had transformed from a safe deposit box into a time machine. Lift the lid and travel back. Try to remember, try to forget.

Foster stared down into the tin. He took the letter out and placed it to one side. He sorted the photographs, picked out three images, and put the remainder with the letter. He turned his attention to the three pictures.

The first photograph showed a young woman standing next to an apple tree. White blossom, flowers in the meadow behind and on the girl's patterned dress. She had bright eyes and dark hair. A smile which suggested she had much more going for her than looks alone. Foster found himself breathing heavily, his eyes starting to water. Why, he pondered, was love unrequited so powerful, while love fulfilled ebbed away until, as with his wife, you had separate bedrooms and nothing to say to each other?

He placed the picture of Helena on the table and retrieved the next image.

This photograph showed two graves side by side in the churchyard. The Murrin boys. You could make out their names and ages: Will Murrin, 20. Red Murrin, 18. Mr Murrin had wanted more on the stones than their names and dates, but Hargreave, the undertaker, had advised against it. Later, in The Crown, he'd explained to an attentive audience why.

'Forever in our hearts? God Bless? Rest in Peace?' Hargreave swept his arms round. 'None of you lot would have stood for it because it would have been complete bollocks, right?'

Everyone nodded as one and there was silence and contemplation until somebody said an appropriate epitaph would have been, 'Rot in Hell.' At that point the conversation disintegrated into a free-for-all with everybody shouting out their own ideas.

'Scum of the Earth.'

'Good Riddance.'

'Piss Here.'

Foster put the photograph down a little way from the image of Helena and considered the third and final picture.

The colours had polarised over time. The vivid green of a lush meadow. An impossible deep blue for the sky. In the foreground of the picture a handsome man wearing a yellow T-shirt stood with the leading rein of a carthorse in his hands. Behind him a woman held a toddler on the animal's back.

Foster smiled. The man in the yellow T-shirt was him. Good-looking back in his thirties. Younger of course, but happier too. The woman holding the young child was Ellen Murrin. The *new* Mrs Murrin. Murrin's previous wife had died when Will and Red were approaching their teenage years and he'd remarried, presumably in a vain attempt to provide his sons with a stable family background. Ellen was in her late-thirties. She had a fine figure and a nice face. How she'd ever ended up with Mr Murrin, Foster had no idea.

He concentrated on the final person in the picture, the boy. The lad wore a smile of pure delight, and Foster was transported back to the day the picture had been taken. It had been the summer before the incident with Helena and the brothers. Mrs Murrin had been walking with the child in a carrier, but she'd felt faint as she'd passed the Foster's farm. Foster's mother had given her some water and the kid some cool milk. As Mrs Murrin was leaving, the horse trotted over to the gate. The boy looked so entranced that Foster suggested he sit on the animal's back, and Foster's mother snapped the photo. The animosity with the Murrins was forgotten. The woman and the boy were innocents. A new wife and a half-brother.

'They were blameless,' Foster said aloud as he looked down at the picture.

After the hangings, Ellen Murrin had split from old man Murrin and gone up country, taking the nipper with her. Nobody knew what had happened to the pair of them. When Murrin had died a year ago, not a single relative had come to the funeral. In fact there'd been nobody by the grave except Father Carmichael, the sexton, and Constable Jencks. Foster had stood outside the churchyard and peeked through the trees as Murrin had gone into the ground, unloved and unmourned.

'You thought he'd come back from the dead?' Barney had ribbed when he discovered Foster had watched the internment.

'No,' Foster said. 'I think they call it closure.'

Foster tilted the picture. He'd woken in the middle of the night and been convinced, but now he wasn't so sure. Perhaps his memory of the photograph had been as faded as his memory of the actual event.

He stood and went over to the mantelpiece. There was a pot with pencils sticking out and, amongst the pencils, a small circular magnifier with a brass surround and a wooden handle. He sat back down and took the magnifying glass and waved it above the picture. The colours blurred and flared at the edges of the glass, while at the centre the image enlarged with a bulbous distortion. He positioned the magnifier over the boy's face and lifted it a little to adjust the focus.

'Fuck,' he said as he leaned back in the chair. The photograph and magnifying glass dropped into his lap. 'I was right.'

He hadn't wanted to believe it and ever since the notion had arisen he'd tried to put it from his mind, hoping the truth might work its way round to a resolution he'd be happy with. The trouble was, he thought, the world went on whether you liked the way it was going or not. You couldn't change it, you couldn't fight it, and you couldn't stop it. His mother had said to him that everything connected to everything else, that everything you did had consequences. The photograph proved she was right.

He'd got the first inkling when they'd moved in. He'd known in his head, but his heart had tried to deny it. The noose hanging from the beam in the woman's workshop had provided a further clue: whoever had hung the rope up had known about the death of the Murrin boys and had left it as a message.

Foster picked up the magnifier and hovered the glass above the picture once more. The young boy's face swelled and shrunk. Dark black hair, snow white skin, and the eyes, the eyes were the same colour as the endless summer sky.

Chapter Fifty-two

She was given a lift back to World's End in a police 4x4, arriving as snow began to fall from dull clouds. After the police officers drove off, Catherine didn't go inside. Instead she went over to the garage. The bay alongside the pickup was empty. Daniel had gone.

She hesitated before going into the house. He'd gone, but when would he be back? And when he came back would she be safe? She glanced up the track, but the police car was nowhere to be seen. A chill slid over the back of her neck as she realised she was on her own. She needed to get in and out fast. She unlocked the front door and entered. A note sat propped up on the table in the hallway.

I'm going to London to sort this out. Love Daniel.

The word *love* momentarily confused her, but of course that was Daniel. He'd want to have his cake and eat it. Catherine almost laughed at his audacity. He'd gone to London to see Lisa and plot their next move, and yet he thought he could do so guilt-free by pretending he still cared. How cold and calculating. How very... *Daniel*.

She shuddered at the notion that this was all planned. Had he told the police more than they'd revealed? Was the *love* meant to placate her, to lull her into a false sense of security? She realised he must have worked it all out. Or rather *they* must have worked it all out. Daniel and Lisa.

Catherine tried to imagine how the murder had happened. In the heat of an argument, for sure. Gemma had confronted Daniel about Lisa, and Daniel had cracked. The next second the poor girl was lying with her brains bashed in and he was already working out what to do as she died in front of him.

That didn't seem right, though. The pieces of the puzzle didn't quite fit together. For instance, where had Daniel killed Gemma and when? He'd been working long hours and staying in a hotel, which suggested Gemma had been killed at her flat. But that didn't make much sense because the police would have been there and examined every inch for clues. He had to have killed her elsewhere. His hotel room? No, impossible. The house he'd been working at in Hampstead? Again, impossible. Lisa and Toby's place? That didn't seem a credible explanation either.

She picked up the note and went to the kitchen. She dished herself a bowl of cereal and sat at the table for a long time. She made a coffee and let it steam and cool. Outside, the day remained grey as if refusing to dawn. From where she sat, she could see the barn. She remembered the way Jencks had reacted when he'd first visited, as if what had happened there years ago had some bearing on events taking place in the present.

When the coffee was tepid, Catherine took the cup to the sink and poured it away. She watched as the brown liquid ran down the plughole. When she looked up at the window, she was startled to see Joe Foster standing near the barn, staring at the very spot that Jencks had been interested in. He was hunched inside a heavy overcoat, the surface of which was dusted with snow. He turned and his eyes met hers.

Catherine remained at the sink and held Foster's gaze. She shivered. This was the man who'd tried to scare her from the house using a sheep's innards and a box full of rats. He'd assaulted her and if she hadn't run away, who knows what he would have done to her. He'd taken Gemma's lifeless body from the mine and put her in a barn. He wasn't sane, he wasn't normal.

She went to the back door and opened it.

'Mrs Ross,' Foster said. 'Got a couple of things I need to show you.'

'Right.' Catherine said. The old man's face was pale and his eyes weary. She realised she was no longer scared of him. Not after all that had happened. 'Do you want to come in?'

'No. You need to come out here.'

She nodded and put on her wellingtons and followed Foster as he crunched across the snow and went round the house. His Land Rover stood over near the barn, the rear door open, and when Foster got to the vehicle, he delved inside, scraping a wooden box onto the tailgate.

'Here,' Foster said. It was an old fruit container, two feet by eighteen inches. Faded yellow bananas printed on the outside. A fleece blanket inside. 'You'll be telling me what you know about this.'

Catherine leaned in as Foster flicked one edge of the blanket away. A large baby doll in a little sleepsuit. A distorted face with blotches of black. Catherine was perplexed as to why anyone would want such an ugly looking object as a toy. Then she realised it wasn't a doll at all.

'Oh God!' She screamed and staggered back, her hand over her mouth. Her legs went from under her and she collapsed to the ground. She stared up at the barn and saw a creature launch itself from a beam inside, wings spreading as it swooped down and glided out. She blinked and craned her head towards the sky, dizzy and confused. 'An angel,' she said.

'No.' Foster's face was inches from hers, a waft of foulness like smelling salts in the way the stench brought her to her senses. He leaned back, giving her space. 'A pigeon. You should shoot them by rights or they'll have your vegetables.'

'The baby.' Catherine felt a void open within her. She wanted to go across and take the child from the box. Cradle it in her arms and give the poor thing love and warmth. She sat up and mussed her hair. 'Gemma's baby.'

'If Gemma's the lass you chucked down the mine, then I reckon you're right.' Foster lowered his face again and he grabbed her. Bony fingers clasped her shoulders and pressed hard into her flesh. 'The question is, why did you fucking kill her?'

They were in the kitchen. Catherine sat slumped in a chair at the table, while Foster struggled with the continental style tap as he tried to fill the kettle. After he'd grabbed her, Foster had dropped Catherine down in the snow and slid the box back into the Land Rover. He closed the tailgate and suggested they go inside. She'd agreed meekly, unsure what else she could do.

'You going to tell me?' Foster said as the kettle began to boil. 'Why you had to kill that young woman and her child?'

Catherine looked down at her hands. Her fingers were turning red as her circulation returned.

'I didn't kill her or the baby,' she said.

'You dumped the girl in the mine with no more thought than if you were taking rubbish to the tip, and I found the baby in a bin liner in the back of your pickup. If Jencks had the evidence, you wouldn't be sitting here now.'

'And if he realised you'd taken the body from the mine, you wouldn't be here either.'

'You know about that? Well, that's the truth of it, but I didn't do no killing.'

Catherine looked up. 'And neither did I.'

'You tell me what happened then. From the start. From the day you moved in.' Foster had found two cups and the teabags. He poured the hot water into the cups and dunked the bags in. 'No, scratch that. Tell me from before you came here. Tell me everything.'

So she did. She started with how she'd met Daniel and recounted the incident with the burglar and Daniel's affair with Gemma. She told Foster about the decision to relocate from London and how World's End Farm had been the one place they'd viewed, how Daniel had been insistent the house was their forever home. She explained how she'd become worried after finding the pictures of the Murrin boys and had sought answers from Peter Carmichael and the estate agent. She described the phone call from Carmichael, how he'd said he'd seen Daniel on the hospital ward where Murrin lay dying. Finally, she told Foster about Lisa and Toby and how Lisa had turned up a few days ago with a body in the back of her car.

The teas had been drunk and a large puddle of snow melt surrounded Foster by the time she'd finished.

'I helped Lisa dispose of the body,' Catherine said. 'But I had no idea it was Gemma Hicksmith, and I didn't even know about the baby. I do remember there was a bin liner, but Lisa told me it contained clothes. I completely forgot about it and never could have imagined Gemma's child was inside. You have to believe me.'

Foster didn't speak for a while. He appeared to be weighing the evidence. 'I reckon I do,' he said finally. 'Your reaction to seeing the corpse of the little one convinced me.'

'So, are you going to tell the police?'

'If I was going to tell them, I'd already have done so, and I wouldn't have bothered moving the body from the mine to the linhay and from there to the barn at my place.'

'But you're not involved with any of this, why did you risk implicating yourself?'

'I've got my reasons. Just like I had my reasons for wanting you out of World's End.' Foster tapped the side of his nose. 'But if I tell the police, it's over. Not just the thing with the girl, but the whole story. Best find the truth of it before turning the final page.'

'And what is the truth?'

'Well, this might be able to help us with that.'

Foster reached into the pocket of his overcoat and took out a tobacco tin. Catherine thought about saying she'd prefer he didn't smoke but changed her mind. It seemed petty and insignificant and if a cigarette was going to help Foster concentrate, then fine.

The old man's fingers clutched at the tin and prised off the lid. Catherine saw she was wrong. The tin was empty except for several pieces of paper. No, not paper, photographs.

'Helena Hodgson.' Foster was jabbing at a picture which showed an attractive young woman standing next to an apple tree in blossom. His hand shook slightly as he laid the photograph on the table. His eyes were blank, a hint of moisture as he blinked.

'She's beautiful,' Catherine said. 'She has an inner light, a presence.'

'I wouldn't know anything about that.' Foster coughed and cleared his throat. 'She lived at the next farm down the valley from here, nearer the village. More of a smallholding to be honest. Incomers, her family were. From London.'

'London?' Catherine cocked her head. 'We're not all bad then?'

'Life was different in those days and one or two foreigners didn't matter. It's when you lot started buying all the little cottages and turning them into holiday homes that local folk got mad.'

Catherine moved the conversation on. 'What happened to Helena?'

'The Murrin boys happened to her.'

'You mean…?'

'Yes. They had their way with her just like they'd done with other girls, but this time they didn't get away with it and Helena's father came up here to sort them out.'

'He was the one who hanged them?'

'No, when he arrived at World's End, Mr Murrin intervened. There was a scuffle and when it was over, Mr Hodgson lay dead at the foot of the stairs. He'd had a heart attack apparently. At least that's what went on the death certificate.'

'Oh no,' Catherine said, unable to believe what she was hearing. More death, more tragedy.

'Plain murder, most people thought, though none would say so to Murrin's face.' Foster slid another photograph across the table. Two gravestones. 'Will and Red Murrin. They were found hanged in the barn a few weeks later.'

'Father Carmichael showed me a press cutting. The police never found out who did it.'

'No, they didn't.'

'You said this place was cursed, and I believe you now. That's why you were trying to get us out with the guts and the rats and the noose.'

'I'm sorry about the guts and the rats,' Foster said. 'But like I told you before, I didn't set the noose.'

'So who did?'

'When I broke in the noose was already there, which means it was someone who had a key to your workshop.'

'There's only one key,' Catherine said.

'You've found the answer then. If it wasn't you, it must have been your husband. He did it to scare me off.'

'Daniel? But why would he do that?'

Foster appeared not to have heard her and was fingering another photograph. He pushed it across the table. This time the image showed a man holding a huge carthorse. Atop the horse sat a young child, perhaps two or three years old. A woman held the child, her hands reaching up to grasp round the waist.

'That's you,' Catherine said, pointing at the man holding the horse. 'But who are the woman and the toddler? She looks familiar, but I can't place her.'

'That's Mrs Murrin and John Murrin Junior. This was taken about thirty-five years ago. Before the trouble.'

'Junior? You mean there was a younger brother?'

'Much younger. He was a half-brother. Will and Red's mother died when they were in their early teens and Murrin remarried. This is the new Mrs Murrin. I don't reckon she realised what the hell she was getting into.'

'You don't worry about the future when you're in love.'

'Love? I'd be surprised if anyone could have loved old Murrin. There's something else though. About the hangings.' Foster's voice lowered in volume to no more than a whisper. 'About the boy.'

'Go on.'

'He was at World's End when it happened, and he must have seen his brothers hanged. Watched them as they were hoisted up and struggled for their last breaths.'

Catherine thought about how awful such an event would be for a young child. What sort of effect it would have on him. 'So he knew who did it?'

'He couldn't say. He was two years old, perhaps a bit more. The coppers couldn't get anything out of him that made any sense.'

'Where were the parents? Shouldn't Mrs Murrin have been looking after him?'

'You'd think so, but Mr and Mrs Murrin were away. London of all places.' Foster half smiled. 'They were gone for a week, leaving Junior to be looked after by Will and Red. There'd been heavy snow and the lane was blocked with drifts. Nobody came down to the house and it was left to Mr and Mrs Murrin to discover the bodies when they returned from their break.'

Catherine put her hand to her mouth. Foster and Peter Carmichael had painted an awful picture of the elder Murrin boys, but no parents deserved to see their children murdered like this. Another thought struck her. 'The young Murrin must have been alone in the house?'

'Yes. The police said he was stuck in there for the best part of four days. But here's the thing: somebody had been into the house and made sure he was OK. He'd been given meals and the range had been kept stocked with fuel to keep the place warm. The house was tidy and the boy was clean.'

'How do you know all this?'

'Common knowledge. You've only got to ask in the village.'

'It's terrible he was left alone.' Foster's story, if true, was shocking. As shocking as the dead baby and Gemma with her head bashed in. 'But I don't see how it's relevant to what's going on today.'

Foster stretched across and touched the picture, but his gaze flicked across to the image of the Murrin brothers' graves.

'Do you believe people are born bad?' he said. 'Or are they made that way by circumstances?'

'Sorry?'

'Will and Red. Were they evil from the start?'

'Do you mean the concept of original sin?'

'Original sin? Sounds like my ma might have been interested in that.' Foster shook his head. 'But no, I was thinking of genetics or the way those boys were brought up by their father.' He raised a hand and gestured at the room. 'Or even something to do with this house. With World's End Farm itself.'

'I don't know.' Catherine was surprised Foster was interested in having a philosophical argument. 'In the end, does it matter?'

'It might.' Foster took a magnifying glass out from his coat pocket. He passed it across. 'Here, take a look through this.'

'Is there a secret message?' Catherine took the magnifier.

'A message, yes.' Foster folded his arms and sat back. 'Hidden in plain sight. Check out the kid.'

Catherine held the glass over the picture. The magnifier wasn't a good one and the image distended at the edges. She raised and lowered the glass until the boy snapped into focus and she could see the detail clearly. Foster was talking, but she hardly heard his voice as she realised what she was seeing. *Who* she was seeing. The picture blurred as her hand shook and she had the sense that the world had become a black void, and she was but a speck of dust spinning amongst billions of atoms. It was as if her life was dissolving before her and not one certainty remained. She lowered the glass again, concentrating on the boy's eyes. An endless depth of blue sucked her in until she had to drop the glass to the table and look away to stop the nausea.

'Daniel,' she said. 'My husband.'

PART FOUR

The Killing

Chapter Fifty-three

When I discovered Helena and her family had gone, I felt bereft. For a week I sulked. I fed the stock, made sure there was enough wood to keep our place warm, and ate the food my ma put in front of me; I did nothing else but brood.

One evening, after Ma had told me to pull myself together, I ambled down to the village to have a beer or two in The Crown. While I was there, I overheard a conversation from a nearby table.

'Suzy, it was.'

'The woman who lives on her own up at Spring Head?'

'So I heard.'

'They never?'

'Apparently they did. Invited themselves in to conduct a property inspection. Took them two hours and I don't suppose they were in there checking the fixtures and fittings.'

'Fucking Murrins. You'd think with what's happened, they'd quit their messing.'

'Only one way they're ever going to quit, and you know it.'

Whether what I'd heard was gossip or the truth, I didn't much care. My mind was made up. I downed my beer and left the pub. The long walk home gave me an hour or so to reflect, and by the time I passed the gate to World's End, I'd figured out what I was going to do.

My chance to act came at the beginning of March. There'd been a partial thaw and Mr Murrin had taken the opportunity to go away for a few days to a landowners' conference up near London. He'd taken the Mrs with him, leaving Will and Red at the farm. You'd have to be a fool to let those two take care of anything other than chaos and trouble, but it suited me well enough.

Barney had given me a bottle of Laphroaig for Christmas and the whisky stood, unopened, in its fancy cardboard tube in the glass-fronted drinks cabinet in our parlour. Upstairs, on the nightstand beside my ma's bed, sat a bottle of sleeping pills. I took the whisky and the pills to a dark corner of the barn. I fetched a pestle and mortar and a funnel. I ground two dozen of the pills to powder and carefully opened the cardboard tube and the bottle and poured the powder into the whisky. I replaced the cap and upended the bottle several times until the powder had dissolved. I sealed the bottle back in the tube.

Nobody saw me leave our farm and head down the drovers' track to World's End. I left a trail of footprints in the snow but wasn't much bothered. A big fall was forecast for that afternoon. Six to twelve inches on the moors. An avenging army could have marched down the track and back again and by evening all trace of it would have vanished.

I rapped on the door and Red opened up. He couldn't have been more surprised had I been Elvis.

'What the fuck do you want?' he said before shouting back over his shoulder. 'It's that bloody Joe Foster, Will. Come to sort us out while dad's away, I reckon.'

'Are you fucking joking?' Will's voice came down the hallway before he did, his lanky form stooping under the low ceiling. He raised his head as he came to the door. 'You're not fucking joking. What are you playing at, Foster?'

I held up the tube of whisky. Even though I had fifteen years on the brothers, they'd always treated me like a kid. The whisky acted like a spell on them though, and two pairs of eyes widened.

'Big boys' juice,' Red said, smiling. His face twisted. 'What's the catch?'

'No catch,' I said. 'Thought we could bury the hatchet. Move on. I mean, I've not said anything about what happened with Helena and I don't intend to. We're neighbours after all.'

'Your family are nothing but tenants and don't you forget it.'

'You're right, neighbours and tenants. Tenants most of all. Hence the present.' I held up the whisky again and tried to put on a swagger. 'Now, are we going to do this or what?'

'Rock and fucking roll,' Red said. He nodded to Will who was looking sceptical. 'What do you say?'

'Sure.' Will snatched the bottle. 'But he can piss off.'

Will disappeared down the hallway and Red grinned.

'You heard my big brother, Foster,' he said. 'Fuck off, right?'

I didn't have time to answer as Red slammed the door in my face. I allowed myself a smile before I turned and walked over to the grassy bank surrounding the house. I hopped over and into the snow and settled down to wait.

Chapter Fifty-four

Snow was falling as Foster drove away from World's End. Big flakes of white spinning down from a grey sky. He grasped the steering wheel and tried not to look back. The past few days had marked the beginning of the end, he thought. Wheels turning full circle. Winter would soon turn to spring just as summer always faded to autumn. The Murrin boy — John or Daniel — had come back, drawn by Foster knew not what. Did he want to avenge the deaths of his brothers? Perhaps he was here to seek atonement for their heinous crimes. Whatever, Foster was in no doubt his arrival had somehow caused the current situation, a situation which was fast coming to a head.

Catherine Ross played no part in the murders of the girl and the baby, he was sure of that now. Daniel had to be the one responsible. Had seeing his brothers hanged made him bad or was it the fact he shared half of their genes? Whatever it was, Foster had advised Catherine to get out. He'd even offered her a bed for the night but wasn't surprised when she declined.

'I need to see him,' she'd said. There'd been anger in her voice, but a steely determination too. 'I need to hear him explain in his own words about his brothers and the farm. About Gemma and the baby and why he killed them. I need to try and understand how he could do such a thing, not for his benefit, but for mine.'

Foster had shrugged. She could do as she pleased, he said. Privately, he thought she was mad to stay, but crazy situations demanded crazy responses. He understood that from personal experience.

Back home, Foster fixed himself some food before collapsing in the armchair in the parlour. He was tired. All this thinking. It had never suited him and recently he'd done plenty. Almost enough for a lifetime.

A bang snatched Foster from his thoughts. A shadow phased on the ceiling and he dragged himself from the chair and went to the window. Ghostly white figures slid wraith-like towards the house and the barn, and blue light flashed across the snow. The scene was like a science fiction film, and an absurd notion that this was a visitation from friendly aliens come to solve all his problems flashed through his mind. The bang came again.

'Open the door, Mr Foster. Open it now or we'll break it down.'

Foster shook his head. Aliens, yes. Friendly, no. It was Constable Jencks.

He went into the hall. His shotgun leant against the wall and he put out a hand to pick it up but then changed his mind.

'Fuck it,' he said to himself and opened the door.

'Got a warrant,' Jencks said as Foster stood aside. 'To search this shithole.'

'Why?' Foster said.

'I don't have to give a reason.' Jencks was in the hallway. He peered into the kitchen and sniffed. 'But, just so you know, it's because you've got that girl in here. You kidnapped her and brought her home for some nefarious purpose.'

'Nefarious?'

'Yes.' Jencks came closer. He leered at Foster, their noses almost touching. 'It means you're a fucking pervert.'

'I'm not,' Foster said.

'You might believe you're clever.' Jencks gave Foster a push in the chest. 'But you're so thick you didn't think your plan through.'

'I don't know what you're talking about.'

'Tracks, Foster. Made by a tractor. Going hither and thither up on the moor. Some of them even go out to the mineshaft. Now why would they do that?'

'One of my sheep fell down there. I went to get the animal out. You can ask...' Foster's voice trailed off. He wasn't going to bring Barney into this.

'Ask who?' Jencks gave another push and this time Foster staggered back. 'No one, right? Because it's all down to you. The girl came down here from London intending to visit Mrs Ross, but she took a wrong turning and got lost in the snow. You came along and offered to give her a hand. What happened next I can only guess, but one thing led to another and you raped and murdered her.'

'You've got it wrong.' Foster shifted to the side as two uniformed officers barged past and made for the upstairs rooms. 'There's no girl here, but search all you like if it makes you happy.'

'We will.' Jencks yanked Foster's arm. 'Now get out of our way.'

'Fine.' Foster stepped into the yard. Jess rushed by and made for a man who stood holding a police dog on a leash. She barked twice and ran back to Foster.

'S'alright, old girl.' Foster bent down and patted her, pulled a piece of twine from his pocket, and slipped it round her neck. 'But best you stay with me for now.'

The barn doors stood wide open and officers headed inside. The dog handler followed and shouts echoed from within. Jencks came running from the house.

'Something up, huh?' he said. 'Best go and see.'

Foster tied his makeshift dog lead to a hook by the door and followed Jencks across the yard. In the barn, torchlight swept about as the searchers penetrated the darkest recesses. Over to one side, a forensic officer crouched by a rolled-up carpet. The dog handler was pulling his animal away.

'It was hidden beneath some hay bales,' the forensic officer said. 'Looks like we might have hit the jackpot.'

'Blimey,' Jencks said. 'At this rate, we'll be back at the station for supper. Do you like sausage and mash, Mr Foster? Or perhaps a nice steak and kidney pie? I'm sure we'll be able to find a square meal for you once you've answered our questions.'

'I ain't going anywhere,' Foster said. 'Got my stock to feed. Besides, I've done nothing wrong.'

'We'll fucking see about that.' Jencks stood back as another forensic officer knelt beside the carpet. 'Looks to me as if the chickens might be coming home to roost.'

'Ain't got no chickens,' Foster mumbled. Jencks was dancing about like an excited chicken himself. 'Fox had the last of 'em a couple of years ago. Buy my eggs from the supermarket now.'

Jencks wasn't listening. He dismissed Foster with a wave and craned forwards. One of the officers was using a knife to cut away some string and tape. He motioned for Jencks and Foster to step aside.

'Anything you want to tell me before we open this up?' Jencks' eyes darted from the carpet to Foster. 'You know, a confession? It would save a whole lot of hassle.'

'She was a lovely lass, but it's better this way. She'll not suffer any longer.'

'You pervert.' Jencks raised a fist. 'Back in the day, my father would've clouted you one and nobody would have raised an eyebrow. I'll just have to satisfy myself with the knowledge that you'll die in prison.'

'Here we go.' The white-suited officer began to unroll the carpet. The inner surface was slick with blood and there was a strong smell of urine. 'Fuck, boss, this is a bad one. Lord knows what he's been up to with her.'

'I knew you were odd, Foster,' Jencks said. 'But I never suspected you were a regular psycho.'

Now both forensic officers worked the carpet. They unrolled another section and exposed a mass of translucent plastic. Red liquid sluiced behind the thin film, viscera slopping around, body parts pressing up against the surface.

'Bloody hell, looks like he's gone to work with a knife. She's been hacked about and sliced to ribbons.'

'She was sick,' Foster said, beginning to enjoy himself immensely. 'I tried my best, but I couldn't save her. I was going to burn her but for the weather. Thought I'd wrap her up to keep her safe until I could get some dry wood under the carcass.'

'Carcass?' Jencks' face torsioned into a scowl. 'That's a young woman you're talking about, not a piece of meat.'

'Well, I was going to cook her up, but she didn't look that tender.

Perhaps she would've done for the dog.'

'You bloody nutter.' Jencks pushed at Foster and gestured outside. 'Come on. I've about seen and heard enough from you.'

As Foster tramped towards the barn door, Jencks took hold of his right arm and twisted it behind his back, shoving the hand upwards. Foster flinched and Jencks reacted by striking him in the head. He went down to his knees.

'Resisted arrest,' Jencks said. He turned to the forensic officers. 'You saw that, didn't you?'

Neither answered. They'd peeled back the plastic and now they gaped at the corpse. Part of the skull had been crushed and the intestines slithered from a gash in the belly.

'It's not her, it's not Gemma Hicksmith.' One of the officers pointed down to a mass of blood-soaked wool. 'In fact this isn't even human.'

'Huh?' Jencks let go of Foster and rushed back. 'What the fuck do you mean?'

'It's a dead sheep, boss. Baa baa, lamb chops, and knitted jumpers.'

'Told you,' Foster said, still on his knees. 'She'd been ill for a while, but it wasn't worth calling the vet out. Anyway, never trusted those so-called experts much.'

Jencks stared down at the dead ewe before whirling round. He ran towards Foster and aimed a kick at him. Foster took the blow in his midriff and rolled away.

'You bastard.' Jencks kicked out again, this time his boot hitting Foster on the cheek. 'Reckon you can get one over on me, do you? Well, I'll teach you a lesson you won't forget.'

Foster brought his arms up to shield his face, but before the next strike came, an officer arrived and wrestled with Jencks. Jencks brushed off the man's grip and bent over Foster. 'I don't know what kind of game you're playing, but I'll have you, d'you hear me?'

Foster looked up from the mass of straw he'd fallen in. He opened his mouth to make a pithy comment, but before he could get the words out, Jencks stomped off into the yard.

***

By four o'clock the police had gone. Foster nursed his bruised ribs, debating whether to take up the forensic officer's offer.

'If you want someone to back up your complaint,' the officer had said as he cast a glance at his fellow CSI. 'Then that's me. I saw it all and you didn't resist arrest or put up any kind of struggle. Plus you're seventy, aren't you? An old man. Jencks is a bloody disgrace.'

Foster had nodded, feeling every year of seventy, as the man went onto explain that Jencks wasn't well liked. He appeared to have inherited his father's obsessive nature, and once he'd got an inkling in his mind he wouldn't let it drop. He wasn't, according to the officer, much of a people person.

Foster stood in the bathroom and looked at himself in the mirror. There was a bruise on the left side of his face and his ribs ached like crazy.

'No,' Foster said to himself. 'Not much of a people person.'

He smeared some antiseptic cream on the bruise, wincing as it stung, and then went downstairs and made himself some dinner. The house was a mess, drawers open, clothing strewn about, rugs and carpets rolled back. They'd tried to take his shotgun too, even though Foster had a licence. Jencks didn't seem to care, but another officer took him to one side and whispered a few words about overstepping the mark. Foster was given a verbal warning about keeping the gun under lock and key in the metal cabinet, and that was that.

He set to work putting the house straight and, as the afternoon faded into evening, he went outside into the darkness. He drove the tractor up to the mine workings and headed out on the road. A short journey along the compacted snow took him to an old sheep fold. Tumbled down walls surrounded a small paddock and over in one corner stood a concrete water tank. The tank, little more than a glorified trough, had been there for decades. The concrete had cracked and it no longer held water.

Foster climbed down from the tractor and shone a torch into the trough. They were still there. The girl and the baby. He'd wrapped them up in a fresh piece of plastic and secured the package with twine. Now, he hefted the package out and put it in the transport box. He drove back to the mine workings and round to the quarry with the lake. He dragged the body from the tractor to the diving board, a flat rock which jutted out above the lake. He and Barney had jumped from the rock as kids, plunging into the icy water on hot summer days, daring each other to do somersaults, once even riding off the platform on two old push bikes.

Foster slid the package out to the end of the rock and took a length of chain and coiled it round the body. Just before he rolled it over the edge, he paused. He thought of the girl and her baby, thought of his wife and how they'd had no children of their own. Thought of Helena. He peered at the water where a million stars blazed on the mirrored surface and gave the package a gentle push. It plummeted down and there was a great splash and a series of waves rippled out from the impact point. The body floated for a few seconds and then sank into the blackness and Foster watched long after it had been swallowed by the void. Watched until he shivered as a full moon rose and his bones and heart grew cold.

'What did you do with her?' were the first words Foster heard when he answered the phone later. 'By the number of vehicles heading down to your place, they must have searched every square inch.'

'Barney,' Foster said. Even though Barney was on the other end of the line and couldn't see him, he tapped the side of his nose out of habit. 'That's for me to know and you to find out.'

'Don't be stupid, you idiot. I ain't going to tell anyone. And what happens if you drop dead? Nobody will ever know where their final resting place is. The parents will never have — what did you call it? — closure? I saw them on the telly making an appeal and they're in a right state.'

'Well they ain't going to be feeling any better when they find out she's dead. This way they've got a bit of hope.'

'You've lost it, mate. The only thing they're hoping is that she's not fallen into the hands of some nutter.' Barney paused. 'Not that I'm saying you're one, of course.'

'She's in the quarry lake.'

'You put her in there?'

'I just said. I dropped her off the diving board. You remember it?'

'Can hardly forget. We used to jump from there when we were kids. A house and a half to the water and then the bottomless depths.'

'It's not bottomless.'

'It's deep though. I once took a fifty-yard length of rope and tied an iron bar to the end. When I lowered it in, it never touched the bottom.'

'However deep the lake is, she's down there. They'll not find her unless they go diving and I don't suppose they've got the resources for that.'

'And the little one?'

'Aye, he's there too. Resting with his ma.'

'Not exactly cosy down in the icy depths.'

'It's as good as anywhere.'

'I guess.'

There was silence, as if Barney was imagining the girl and the baby floating in the blue water. Foster had tried to banish the memory of the bundle sinking into the blackness, but now a sudden vision came to him. The girl alive, clawing a hole in the plastic, swimming to the surface, screaming at him.

'Joe?' Barney said, his voice lower and softer. 'Are you alright?'

'No,' Foster said. 'Not really.'

Chapter Fifty-five

After Foster had gone, Catherine drifted through the house, moving from room to room. She touched the exposed stonework and ran her fingers over the rough beams. She looked at the furniture and the items they'd brought from London, looked at the changes they'd made, the interior decoration, the colour schemes. As she'd noted before, Daniel hadn't made any of the choices. It was as he'd been afraid to touch the house, and now she worried that the decisions she'd made had pained him. After all, it was self-evidently Daniel's house, Daniel's childhood home.

Much later, after she'd eaten her evening meal, she stood at the kitchen window. The moon washed the barn with a pale light, the stones luminescent and ghostly. Daniel had witnessed his brothers' execution. What would that do to a little boy? And why come back to a place with such awful memories? She had so many questions, but there was no one to answer them.

She made herself a coffee and sat in the front room and every now and then took a sip. At ten o'clock she heard a vehicle outside.

Daniel?

She leapt up and ran and unlocked the front door. Threw it wide. There was a pink Jaguar parked on the drive. The car door opened.

'Toby!' Catherine jumped backwards. 'What the hell are you doing here?'

'Catherine,' Toby climbed out of the car, his head hung to one side, a black and purple bruise round his left eye. 'We need to talk.'

'Stop!' Catherine eased the door closed until there was just a crack.

'I don't want you in the house.'

'For fuck's sake, look at me!' Toby raised a hand to his head. 'Your husband did that. Daniel, my supposed mate!'

'*What?*'

'Daniel and Lisa are having an affair.'

'They can't be. I mean... Daniel told me...'

'Whatever he told you, it's a lie. They're in cahoots. Crazy. They killed Gemma and decided to try and frame you. How do you think the statue got in the mine?'

Catherine relaxed her grip on the door and let it open. 'How do you know all this?'

'They told me some of it and I guessed the rest. Now they want me out the way. Lisa intends to collect the book money and Daniel wants this place.'

'It doesn't make any sense.'

'They're lovers, Catherine. You need to accept that. And you need to wake up to the fact your husband is a killer.'

'No.' Catherine blinked. Saw Toby getting nearer. His face blurred in her tears. 'I... I...'

'Here.' Toby supported her as she staggered back into the hallway. 'Let's get you sat down.'

He guided her to the living room and then he was gone. She heard the tap run in the kitchen and a minute later he was back with a glass of water.

'Thanks,' she said, taking a sip. 'I nearly fainted.'

'I'm not surprised. It's a lot to take in. Believe me, I never suspected they were having an affair until I saw Gemma on the news. Then I started to put two and two together.'

'You worked it out?'

'I guessed and then I confronted them.' Toby half shut the eye with the blackness round it. He winced. 'Which is when Daniel attacked me.'

'In London?'

'Yes, at home. If I hadn't run they'd have killed me. They're probably on their way here now, but I drove like crazy.' Toby tipped his head towards the window. 'They won't be here for a bit though.'

'We have to phone the police before they get here.'

'No, not yet.' Toby grimaced. 'The body. We need to find out where it is and get rid of it. Otherwise it will be their word against ours. From what Daniel said, your fingerprints are on the statue which was used to kill Gemma. They would be of course — it's your statue — but your prints are all over the plastic the body is wrapped in too. Then there's the carpet fibres. There could be microscopic traces on your clothes. That's why we need to make sure the police never find any of it.'

'I can't believe this is happening.'

'It'll be OK.' Toby edged closer. He looped an arm round Catherine and gave her a hug. 'Once we've sorted out the problem with the body, we can go to the police. Without the body they can't touch you.'

'The body.' Catherine stared down into her lap. 'Yes.'

'So?' Toby cocked his head. 'Where is she? She's not in the mineshaft because the police would have found her if she had been.'

'No, she's not there. Our neighbour, Joe Foster, took the body. She's in his barn.'

'Why the fuck did he do that?'

'I've no idea, Toby.' Catherine tilted her head back and half laughed. 'But then I don't have much idea about any of this.'

'Not to worry.' Toby stood. 'We need to go there now, OK?'

'Sure. It's up the way, but we can take the 4x4.'

'Good girl.'

Catherine put out a hand and Toby steadied her as she rose from the sofa. She retrieved the keys to the Toyota and put on a coat.

Outside, a light snow had begun to fall, and Toby's car already bore a feathery coating of white.

'I always loved the snow,' Catherine said. 'Not now.'

'Come on,' Toby said. 'We need to get moving.'

'Yes.' Catherine trembled as she stood in the snow, half in a daze. A flake landed on her nose and she brushed it away. The frosty touch brought her to her senses. 'Let's go.'

They jumped into the Land Cruiser and Catherine started it up and drove out of the garage. The snow was coming down faster now and she fretted that she should have fetched a shovel and checked the tow rope was in the back. No time for that, she thought, no time for anything.

The vehicle slipped and slid as they climbed the hill and then took the narrow lane down to Foster's place. The lane dove down between high banks and the headlights picked out jagged rock and withered trees. She'd driven this way before, but that had been in daylight. Now it was like descending into a canyon. They came out at the bottom and followed the lane as it twisted towards the farmhouse. A solitary lamp shone from the corner of an outbuilding and a yellow glow came from an upstairs window.

'Coast it,' Toby said, indicating the gear stick. 'We don't want him to know we're here.'

Catherine knocked the Toyota into neutral and rolled into the farmyard.

'Gemma must be in there.' Catherine indicated the barn. 'That's what he told me.'

'And did he say why he'd taken her?'

'No.'

'It doesn't matter, I guess. Let's go and get her.' Toby opened the door and got out. Catherine did the same. They padded through the snow to the barn. The door stood ajar and Toby reached for a light switch just inside. A couple of weak bulbs came on above their heads. 'Where is she?'

'I don't know.' Catherine gazed round. Straw bales, some farm machinery, a tool bench. The place seemed a mess, but there was no sign of Gemma. No sign of the carpet and the plastic either. Toby was turning to the door, but she hesitated, a nagging thought at the back of her mind. *No sign of the carpet and the plastic...* the plastic? A chill washed across her chest as she recalled the words Toby had used back at World's End when he'd insisted they needed to find the body: *Your prints are all over the plastic the body is wrapped in. Then there's the carpet fibres.* How the hell did he know Gemma was wrapped in plastic and carpet? 'Toby? How did you know the body was in the mine?'

'*What?*' Toby snapped back at her.

'How did you know Gemma was in the mine?'

There was a moment of tension before Toby spoke. 'The TV. Or haven't you been watching?'

'The TV. Yes.' That could explain how he knew about the mine, but it didn't explain his knowledge of the plastic and the carpet.

'Come on.' Toby was leaving the barn. He didn't seem to have picked up on Catherine's unease. 'The farmer must have moved her.'

Before she could stop him, Toby had crossed the yard. He rapped on the back door and a dog barked from inside. A light went on in a downstairs window, the latch on the back door clattered, and the door cracked open. Foster stood at the threshold with a shotgun pointed out into the night.

'Who's there?' Foster squinted and waved the gun.

'It's Catherine, Mr Foster,' Catherine said as she came across and stood a little way behind Toby out of his line of vision. She raised a hand and waved at Foster and then pointed at Toby and made a chopping motion at her throat.

'And who the fuck are you?' Foster lifted the gun, the barrel just inches from Toby's chest.

'I'm me.' Toby smiled. 'You might call me a friend.'

'Friend or no friend, I don't take kindly to being roused from my bed at this unholy hour.'

'Sorry about that, old man.' Toby jerked his left arm and knocked the gun to one side. His right arm twisted upwards and punched Foster in the face.

'Toby!' Catherine screamed and ducked as the gun went off. She fell to the floor and when she looked up, Foster was lying in the hallway with Toby standing over him holding the shotgun. 'What the hell are you doing?'

'Leave this to me.' Toby thrust the shotgun at Foster. 'Now, don't get any ideas that I don't know how to use this, because I do. Corporate team building days with my wanker city friends to thank for that.'

'This is crazy, Toby.' Catherine pushed herself up from the snow and stood. 'Joe will tell us where Gemma is without all this.'

'Safer this way. Now, you heard the lady, what did you do with Gemma's body?'

'I don't know what the hell you're talking about.' Foster winced and sat up. 'Gun or no gun.'

'You idiot, don't make this difficult.' Toby lowered the gun and thrust it sideways, bringing the stock round to smack Foster in the chest. 'Tell us where the bloody girl is.'

Foster groaned and let out a puff of air. 'She's gone and no fucker's ever going to know where.'

'Leave him alone!' Catherine grabbed Toby by the shoulder, but he shoved her away. She skidded on the snow and went down to her knees.

'One last time. Where's the girl?' Toby raised the shotgun again and then stepped back into the farmyard. 'Five. Four. Three.'

'OK.' Foster raised a hand. 'She's in the lake at the quarry. Must be a hundred feet down. More. The police will never find her.'

'Great.' Toby smiled. 'And since you're the cause of all this hassle, why don't you just fuck off? Two. One.'

Catherine closed her eyes a second before the bang and then she was scrabbling away on her hands and knees across the yard. Toby went back in the house for a few seconds.

'Kind of him,' he said, waving a small cardboard box at Catherine as he came out. 'Left a load of cartridges by the back door.'

'No, Toby.' Catherine tried to stand. 'Please!'

'Shut up, bitch.' Toby cracked the gun and reloaded. He pointed the gun at her. 'You're coming with me.' He yanked her up and shoved her over to the pickup's passenger door. 'Get in and shuffle across. You're driving.'

Catherine climbed up, Toby's hand pushing her from behind. 'For God's sake why are you doing this?'

'Why?' Toby waved the gun as he got in. 'Because, just like that thick farmer, your stupid husband had to meddle. Now shut up and get us out of here.'

She drove the pickup out of the farmyard and back up the narrow lane. Snow was falling heavily now, sweeping across the headlight beams as the wind corkscrewed down the valley.

'Daniel didn't kill Gemma,' Catherine said as she gunned the 4x4 onwards into the whiteout. 'You did.'

'She tried to blackmail me. What was I supposed to do? Roll over and take it?'

'So the baby was yours, not Daniel's?'

'Yeah, it was mine and I'd have paid my dues, but that wasn't enough for young Gemma. Not by a long shot.' In the darkness, Catherine saw Toby's teeth flash white. 'Thought she was clever, didn't she? Thought she could extract every last penny from me. She said if I refused to pay it would be the end of my writing career.'

'I don't understand? How could Gemma having your baby do that?' Beside her, Toby made a sound, half a laugh, half a snort of derision. She glanced across at him. Those teeth again as he grinned in the darkness. She had it then, recalling the same expression on his face when he'd tried to explain away the incident in the pub. The causal manner he'd dismissed the waitress' complaint.

She was as up for it as I was.

'Bloody hell, I get it now. You raped her, didn't you?'

'No I fucking didn't. I gave her a lift home one night. She was drunk, I was drunk, we were both adults. End of story.'

'In that case, what were you worried about?'

'Let's just say her memory let her down and her account of our entanglement differed somewhat from mine. Unfortunately, these days the police will believe anything a little cow like her says. If the case had gone to trial, even if I'd been found not guilty, I'd have been ruined. I'd have been dropped by my publisher and the chance of me ever getting another teaching job would have been remote.'

'So you murdered her?'

'Look, Henderson had already given her a bundle of cash to quit her job and stay shtum. How else do you think a young intern like her managed to afford to make a down payment on a brand-new Audi? If she'd left it at that and kept quiet like a good little girl she'd be alive, but no, she had to get greedy, didn't she? She wanted more, more, more. Now, just shut up and drive.'

Barry Henderson. Daniel and Toby's agent. Her opinion of Henderson was already low, but Toby's admission the agent had tried to pay off Gemma bumped it several notches lower.

Catherine concentrated as they crossed a patch of ice. The back of the pickup slid out, but she eased the steering wheel round and coasted into the skid. The road was becoming more treacherous by the minute and so was her position. The way Toby had justified his actions showed how little empathy he had. He'd murdered Gemma and her baby and shot Joe Foster. He was capable of anything.

Ahead, the blizzard raged. The windscreen wipers were just about keeping pace, but every time they swished from side to side they left a line of compacted snow. Soon she'd have to stop to clear the screen.

The lane narrowed as it cut through a dip and rocks came in from either side, snow plastered to the black granite. The road was a band of solid white and the tracks they'd made on the way out had vanished. She should reduce speed, she thought. Take it steady in case the vehicle slid to one side or the other and hit the rocks. Instead she rammed her foot hard down on the accelerator.

'What the—' Toby jerked back in his seat and the gun flailed in an arc. 'Slow down!'

Catherine twisted the wheel to the right and the 4x4 slewed round as a wall of rock filled the windscreen. She reached for the door handle and threw the door open as they smashed into the rock face. There was a *bang* as her airbag exploded, and she lurched forwards, the softness of the bag on her face tempered by the wrenching of her seatbelt as it locked. In an instant she'd unbuckled the belt and jumped out the door. The passenger door of the 4x4 was hard against the rock face and Toby was for a moment trapped. Catherine made for the side of the road and dived onto the snow-covered heather, rolling over and falling away down the slope.

'Catherine!' Toby's voice shouted out in the wind. 'What the hell are you playing at?'

She picked herself up and stumbled away, edging down the hill. The lights from the Toyota shone out into the night, and she spotted Toby move in front of them. He stood in the road, shielding his eyes from the snow, the gun crocked in one arm. For an instant he remained still, but then he was after her, bounding off the road in a great leap.

Catherine didn't wait to see where he landed. She turned and ran as best she could. In the darkness, the snow was a grey blanket concealing the rough ground beneath; one stride and her feet met solid rock, while the next they plunged into a mass of heather. She fell once more, scrambling to pull herself up. Toby was a lumbering figure in the background, a shadow in the swirling flakes of snow. A yeti made real. In the gloom, she wasn't sure where she was going, just downwards. Down to the valley bottom, down to World's End.

And at World's End?

She didn't know, but there was nowhere else to go.

The moorland ended at a snow-capped stone wall, but there was a break a little way to the right. A wooden gate and beyond a smooth field of white sloping down to the line of trees which marked the drovers' track. She arrived at the wall and ran beside it to the gate. Foot on the lowest bar, leg up and—

'Got you!'

Toby was right there. As she lifted herself over the gate, his hand wrapped round her ankle. She fell face down with Toby holding onto her foot. She kicked out with her other leg and caught him in the face, but his grip was vice-like.

'Let go of me!' She hung upside down from the gate with her face and shoulders rammed into the snowy ground. Toby's fingers pressed harder, but her right foot slipped out of her sock and came free from her boot. She fell to the ground.

'Stay there!' Toby yelled and began to climb the gate.

Catherine ignored him and jumped to her feet. She ran away from the gate and headed down the field, one foot bare, the other with the remaining boot on. As she ploughed through the deep snow, she realised she'd never be able to outrun him. He powered across the field, shoulders down. She put her hands out as he drove into her, but he was too powerful. The force of the impact knocked her to the ground, a hard lump in the soft snow smashing against her head.

She was aware of Toby's weight on top of her, of her right foot searing like a burn, of snowflakes brushing her face. Then her vision dimmed to grey, then black and then — blissfully — nothing.

Chapter Fifty-six

Foster came round in a daze. He touched his chest, moving his fingers over his skin, first to where the man had smacked him with the butt of the gun, second to where the wadding from the cartridge had hit him.

'Hell.' He wheezed in a puff of air, flinching as he did so. A rib was bruised if not broken, but at least he was alive. 'One good turn deserves another. That'll be it.'

A couple of days ago he'd taken two cartridges and opened them up. Removed the lead pellets, resealed the cartridges, and loaded them into the gun. If Jencks came calling again he wanted to scare him, not kill him. Of course in the end Jencks *had* come calling and Foster had done bugger all, but the fact the cartridges were primed with only powder and wadding had saved his life.

Bloody Nora.' He pushed himself up and bit down on his tongue. Nausea overcame him and he felt as if he was going to be sick. After a minute, he straightened and staggered across the hallway to the phone. Picked it up and punched in a number.

'Joe?' Barney answered after three rings. 'That you?'

'How d'you know?' Foster said.

'Who else would be calling me at midnight?'

Midnight?' Foster looked at the grandfather clock. Both hands pointed heavenwards. 'I've been out for over an hour, Barney.'

'Out where and why do I need to know about it?'

'Out cold. Unconscious.'

'You had a turn, mate?'

'Not a turn, a fright.'

'To do with the girl?'

'Yes, her. I could do with a hand.'

'Now?'

'Yes, now.'

'I'm on my way, Joe. Be ten minutes.'

'Good. And one more thing, bring your rifle. The one you were supposed to turn in years ago, only you told the police it got stolen.'

'You got a vermin problem down there, Joe?'

'Yes, you could say that.'

Chapter Fifty-seven

'Sorry,' she heard Daniel say.

It was summer. A warm sun beating down. The splash of water every few seconds. A feeling she was floating. Catherine opened her eyes. She was in a rowing boat and Daniel was sitting opposite her pulling on the oars. They were floating on a wide river and as the blades of the oars dipped and rose, they glided along. In the fields bordering the river there were cows and sheep. A large horse with a small child on its back. Blue eyes and a wide smile.

'Sorry about what?'

'This.' Daniel let go of both oars and gestured with his arms. 'The mess is entirely my doing. I was selfish and secretive and I should have been neither.'

'I don't understand.' The meadows were beautiful, full of flowers, and in the distance an old house stood on a low hill. The house seemed familiar. 'There's nothing wrong, is there?'

'No, my love.' Daniel hadn't picked up the oars, but the boat continued to move. Perhaps the current or the wind was pushing it along.

'Well then.' She closed her eyes, feeling the sun again. She lifted one foot and dangled her leg over the side of the boat. Icy water brushed her skin. 'You don't have to be sorry, do you?'

'I should have told you the truth before we moved here.'

Catherine opened her eyes and looked at the house again. Those little windows, the crooked chimney pot at one end, the slate cowl at the other. The border wall of stone. The brook to one side, the pond at the back. The barn. Oddly, snow began to flutter down in the summer heat. 'Where are we?'

'Where do you think?' Daniel said. Somehow his arms were round her now, cradling her, protecting her. 'World's End.'

The surroundings flickered and the sky morphed into a white ceiling, the river to a blue patterned duvet, the fields to thick carpet. She was in their bedroom at the house.

For an instant she panicked, but then she remembered. 'Toby.'

'He's downstairs with Lisa. They've locked us in our room. He said if we try to escape he'll shoot us.'

'He's got Joe Foster's gun?'

'Yes.'

Catherine tried to sit up, but dizziness overcame her. Daniel fluffed a pillow and helped her raise her head a little. 'What happened?'

'You were knocked out. You banged your head on a rock and had mild hypothermia. Toby brought you back here.'

She tentatively placed a hand on the back of her skull where it throbbed. The room blurred as she fought a sudden wash of nausea. After a minute, she felt better. She blinked and glanced at the window. It was dark outside. 'What time is it?'

'One or two in the morning. I don't know exactly because they've taken my phone, but you must have been unconscious for an hour. I was so worried.' Daniel hesitated. 'Toby and Lisa killed Gemma, the poor girl. She tried to blackmail Toby.'

'I know. He told me about it, about Henderson and the payoff, about how that wasn't enough for her.'

'When I met Gemma last week in London that was the first time I'd seen her since... well, you know? Anyway, she had the baby with her. I hadn't even known she was pregnant and for one awful moment I thought it might have been mine. The dates were wrong though. She was worried about something but wouldn't tell me what. She made me promise if anything happened to her I would make sure Joshua was OK.' Daniel paused, reflective. 'I was so taken up with work, that I dismissed her concerns as paranoia.'

'But if she wouldn't tell you, how did you find all this out?'

'Henderson. At least the part about the initial payment he made to hush Gemma up. After you were arrested, I drove to London on Monday evening. I checked into my usual hotel and yesterday morning I went straight to the agency. Henderson was out, so I had to wait until he returned. As soon as he did I asked him about Gemma. Getting the facts was like drawing blood from a stone, but eventually I managed to get him to tell me the truth, which was that he'd paid Gemma off to keep her quiet over a sexual harassment charge she'd made against Toby.'

'But surely the police must know all about that?'

'That's just it, they don't. Henderson told me the agency would have to close if the payment to Gemma became public knowledge. He said if it did turn out foul play had taken place he'd go to the police, but if he'd done so at the outset and Gemma turned up safe and sound, he'd have put ten people out of work for no reason.'

'Idiot.'

'Yes. After he'd told me, I figured the rest of it out. Remember on New Year's Day how Toby's ebullient mood had changed from when we saw him before Christmas? He confided in me that he was being blackmailed. It was when I spoke to Henderson I realised who the person was.'

'Gemma.'

'Yes. Then I remembered the way Toby had acted the week before, when I called round unexpectedly. He wasn't at all pleased to see me and he didn't invite me in. He said Lisa wasn't feeling well and, as he didn't want to disturb her, he suggested we should go out for a curry.'

'It's not surprising he wasn't pleased to see you. That was the night Lisa was driving here with Gemma's body. He was probably trying to make sure there wasn't any evidence at their home.' Catherine flinched. 'Perhaps he was even cleaning up the mess.'

'Yes, that's possible. Anyway, this time, armed with the info from Henderson, I went to see Toby again. I confronted him, but he denied being involved in Gemma's disappearance. We had a blazing row about trust and friendship, the result of which was a scuffle.' Daniel looked smug. 'I hit him with a right hook and left him lying on the floor.'

'And as soon as you did, he and Lisa must have driven down here. I guess when he arrived Lisa must have got out at the top of the track or stayed hidden in the back of the car, so he could spin his story to me.'

'Yup. I'd taken a taxi to the agency and to Toby's place, so I had to find another one to give me a ride back to my hotel and the car. I was a couple of hours behind him and he drives like a nutter.' Daniel smiled. 'Goes without saying, I guess.'

'And when you got here?'

'He was standing in the hall with that shotgun. Game over.'

'Why didn't you call to warn me or ring the police?' Even as Catherine asked the question, the answer came to her. 'You still had suspicions about me, didn't you?'

'Yes. The whole story about Lisa turning up with the body could have been a lie. Especially if you were involved with Toby in some way.'

'With Toby?' She laughed, wincing again as her head throbbed. 'You must be joking.'

'I guess it does sound a little far-fetched.' Daniel grinned.

'And you and Lisa?' She felt Daniel's arm round her tense as she spoke. 'She told me she'd slept with you. Is that far-fetched?'

'She came onto me once.' Daniel looked her square in the face. 'But I resisted her advances. She wasn't happy about being rejected though.'

'Right.' Catherine was surprised to find she didn't care if Daniel was lying or not. When she thought of Gemma and the baby, who he'd slept with was inconsequential.

'There's another thing I haven't told you.' Daniel paused and he squeezed her again. 'About this place. About me.'

'I know about the Murrin boys, Dan. I know they're your brothers.' She reached out and touched Daniel's cheek. 'What I can't understand is why you wanted to come back here to live?'

Daniel opened his mouth to speak, but as he did the bedroom door opened.

'It's called facing your demons, Cath.' Toby stood in the doorway with the shotgun cradled in his arms. 'Daniel confided in me and, to be honest, I advised him against the move. But hey ho, the old boy ignored me. Luckily it's all worked out for the best.'

'I thought I was your friend,' Daniel said.

'You don't have any friends, Dan. Not real ones. You're like an ice block. Anyone touches you and you melt away.'

'That's not true,' Catherine said.

Toby shrugged. 'True or not, it was fortunate that I knew Daniel. I mean, Gemma was lying dead in our house with a gaping head wound, so it didn't take a genius to work out what to do. Sure, we could have dumped her body near London, but when Lisa reminded me about the dead body buddy story I'd told in the pub, it made more sense to bring Gemma down here. Then, when Lisa arrived, Catherine seemed to believe it was *my* body in the boot of the car. To be honest, we hadn't even thought of that, but Lisa went along with Catherine's misconception and it was a fantastic move.'

'I wish it had been you.'

'Now that's not very nice.' Toby glared at her. 'Anyway, the burnt-out car was supposed to lead the police to the mine where they'd find poor Gemma with her skull smashed in. A moderate amount of detective work and they'd discover an ex-lover, who'd killed before, living not a mile from her body. It would have been case closed if that bloody farmer hadn't messed it up.'

'You're despicable,' Catherine said. 'You were willing to see Daniel go down for a crime he didn't commit.'

'Harsh.' Toby made a comedy face as if he was in pain. 'I'd have visited him in prison.'

'It never would have worked,' Daniel said. 'Never will work. You've lost your mind.'

'Perhaps. But Gemma was out to ruin me. I've spent years chasing this dream and I wasn't about to let her get in my way.' Toby briefly let go of the shotgun barrel and made a grasping motion with his left hand. 'Fame and recognition were so tantalisingly close, the thought of having them snatched away was unbearable. This was the best way.'

'Let us go.' Daniel unwound himself from Catherine. He stood. 'For old times' sake. We'll help you get out of this. We can think of a way to play it. At least let me take the blame so Catherine can go free.'

Catherine turned to Daniel. She realised with a shock that this was far more serious than her or Daniel going to prison. For Toby to be sure of his plan working, neither of them could be left alive.

'Dan's right.' She sat up, ignoring the groggy feeling and the pain in her head. 'Gemma's dead. There's no way we can bring her back, but you can stop the killing now. You can publish your books, collect your royalties, and leave us in peace. The police are never going to find the body and the investigation will flounder.'

'You're forgetting about the farmer.' Toby patted the gun. 'I shot him. That was a mistake, but now somebody's got to take the rap for killing him.'

Shit. Catherine had been so wound up with her own predicament that the incident with Foster had receded in her mind. She thought of him lying dead in his hallway with the dog whining over him. He was an odd fellow and she'd been scared of him for a while, but nobody should have to die like that.

'They'll catch up with you, Toby.' Daniel was trying again. 'You know they will. Why make it worse for yourself?'

'Shut up.' Toby waved the gun. 'It's time for action, not talking. I want both of you downstairs. Now.'

Chapter Fifty-eight

By three in the afternoon, the two brothers were blottoed. I peered in the parlour window and could see Red lying on the sofa, while Will had slumped to the floor. Both were unconscious. I went round the house and let myself in through the kitchen. I heaved them out, one at a time, and dragged them to the barn. I took the two hanks of rope I'd brought with me from my rucksack and slung 'em up over the beam. I tied the brothers' hands behind their backs with some twine and fashioned a noose at the end of each rope. I laid the boys beneath the beam and slipped the nooses over their heads and round their necks. After that, I led the other ends of the ropes across the yard and made them fast to a gate post. Finally, I got Red's horse from the barn, put the cart harness on her, and took her over to the gate. I sat against the gate post and waited for the brothers to wake up.

Will was the first to come round. He leapt to his feet and as soon as he did so I tightened up the rope so he had to remain standing. His shouts soon brought Red to his senses and I tightened his rope too. Then I walked over. They were cursing at me and spitting like rats caught in a cage trap, but I took no note.

I chose Will to go first, because Red was the worst of them and I wanted him to watch his brother die. I hitched the rope to the horse and led the beast on. Will tippy-toed and then he was swinging. Red tried to get over to him, but there was nothing he could do. I halted the horse and tied the rope off to the fence post. Will dangled, his face turning purple. He twitched and jerked and after a minute I didn't know whether he was dead or not, but he sure stopped moving quicker than I'd have liked.

Next I did Red. The horse made light work of pulling his heavy frame up, but all credit to Red for trying to make a fight of it. He clamped his legs round a wooden stanchion, hanging on like some demented monkey, but I just let the horse pull the rope until his legs broke free and he swung in a great circle, bashing into his brother. I tied the rope off and watched as he struggled. Like Will, his legs flailed about and his body contorted this way and that, but he lasted longer. A lot longer. Must have been six or seven minutes, maybe ten, before he was still. I just stood there, transfixed, until whatever it was that made him human had gone and he was no more than flesh and bone.

I took the horse back to the stable. I mixed up some food in a bucket. Barley and oats. Put some extra hay in the haynet. I found a brush, and while the horse ate, I groomed her. I used a comb on the mane and tail. Picked out the feet. I've always liked horses. Their power and grace. Their smell. The trust you can see in their eyes. I've never known a horse born bad. They get turned that way by mistreatment. You can usually work with them though. An apple or a carrot. Patience. Calm words and soft hands.

I returned to the barn and stared up at Will and Red. Then I went to the gate post and sat in the snow, sat for a long time as the bodies hung in the fading light. I closed my eyes and listened to sounds that were just off silence. The wind caressing the bare trees. A bell chiming from way off down in the valley. The distant hoot of an owl. Snowflakes gliding to the ground. The creak of the ropes as the two brothers swung in the breeze.

Chapter Fifty-nine

Wedding bells. Peeling across the valley from the village church. A white dress and a veil which, when lifted, revealed not his late wife but Helena. He leaned in to kiss her and the bells sounded again as she dissolved into a grey mist.

Foster blinked in the darkness and listened to the ringing. Tried to remember. A stiffness had spread through his chest and down his arms. He blinked again and now the room came into focus. The range. The sink with a pile of washing up. Jess sitting beside the chair, gazing up at him, her eyes black in the gloom.

The phone gave another *ring-ring*.

'Shit.' He'd passed out again, but the call had woken him, slicing the silence like a cat wailing on a still night. He rose from the chair and answered the phone. 'Yes?'

'Joe? It's Barney. Why didn't you pick up the first two times, you daft clown?'

'I was unconscious again.' Foster put an arm out to steady himself. It was like the house had been in an earthquake, the floor slanted at forty-five degrees. 'What is it?'

'The road to your place is blocked. That Ross woman's Land Cruiser. The bloody thing is stuck fast at the top.'

'You can't get down here?'

'No.'

'They haven't gone far if they're on foot. Must be headed for World's End.'

'Who, Joe? You're not making any sense.'

'Never mind sense, Barney, there's a fucker at World's End and he's got my shotgun and Catherine Ross. He came up here and took a potshot at me. I wouldn't be surprised if he's the one who killed the girl and her little one.'

'Got you.' There was a pause. 'I think.'

'You get down there but stay at the top of the track. Don't try to be a hero. I'll give a flash on my torch once I'm at World's End, right?'

'Joe, shouldn't we call the police?'

'They ain't coming. Not in this snow. It's you and me, old pal.'

'But we don't owe them anything. Stupid to risk our lives for incomers.'

'The husband ain't an incomer. He's born and bred just the same as you and me. And I do owe him.'

Foster replaced the phone in its cradle and went into the hallway where the clock ticked and tocked in the same way it had done for decades. He remembered his father winding the weights every week to keep the pendulum going.

'If you didn't know about this you could never fathom it.' His father had crouched down next to the young Foster and held the winding key up. 'And if you lose it, the clock is useless, and time will stop.'

Foster had studied his father as he'd replaced the key behind a little panel on the inside of the door and winked. A secret given from father to son. The key to how the world worked. The answer to life's mysteries. Only now Foster was beyond the age his father had lived to, he realised the key wasn't such a big deal after all. It flashed gold but was made of brass. The secret was no secret, merely an illusion. However much you wished it, the passage of time could never be stopped.

He glared at the clock before going to the parlour and sitting at his mahogany roll-top bureau. The bureau contained all his farm and personal documents, and inside a sprawl of papers lay scattered across the leather writing surface. He took a pad of paper and a pen and began to write.

A few minutes later, he rose from the desk and returned to the hallway. He found a torch and put on his coat. He took one last look at the clock and then opened the back door and stepped out into the night.

Chapter Sixty

In the living room, Toby told Catherine to sit on the sofa. He motioned Daniel over to the desk where Lisa stood with a pad and a pen.

'You're going to do exactly what I say.' Toby jabbed the shotgun towards Catherine. 'Or else I'm going to shoot your wife in the hand. It won't kill her, but I guess she'll be screaming quite a lot. Better to cooperate.'

'Don't listen to him,' Catherine said. She wasn't sure where her bravado was coming from, but she saw with absolute clarity what was going to happen. 'They're going to kill us whatever we do.'

'Possibly.' Toby sneered. 'But there's quick and easy or slow and painful.'

'Lisa?' Catherine looked across the room. 'Surely you can see sense? Do you want to spend the rest of your life in prison?'

'No.' Lisa smiled. 'I don't want to spend *any* of my life in prison.'

'Get on with it.' Toby prodded Catherine's arm with the gun. 'I'll give you ten seconds.'

'OK, what do I do?' Daniel had taken the paper and pen. 'Write some exoneration or a confession? Like it was all my fault?'

'Not quite.' Toby grinned. 'I want you to write a suicide note.'

'No!' Catherine stood up, brushing the barrel of the gun away. 'Daniel, don't!'

'Sit the fuck down!' Toby took the gun in one hand and thrust the other at Catherine. His fist caught her full in the face and she slumped back on the sofa. Blood trickled down her chin from a split lip. 'Next time you move, I'll shoot you.'

'This isn't the way, Toby.' Daniel. His voice quiet. 'You'd be better off just getting out of here.'

'Wrong. This *is* the way. The *only* way.' Toby chuckled. 'Don't you see how perfect it all is? You, scarred by your memories as a child, decide to return to World's End Farm to confront the nightmares that are haunting you. Sadly, it doesn't work. The ghosts take over. You kill Gemma and the baby and then you go and kill Joe Foster.' Toby patted the gun. 'If we get your fingerprints on this the police will believe you shot him.'

'Why would he do that?' Catherine mumbled through her swollen lip. 'Foster hasn't done anything.'

'Oh, Cathy. Dan's been keeping secrets from you. Foster was the one who killed the Murrin boys. He hanged Daniel's brothers from a beam in the barn while poor little Danny watched it all from the house. They danced on air in front of his eyes. Died as he stood there helpless.'

'Dan?' Catherine looked over to the desk. Daniel was head down, fighting his emotions. 'Is this true?'

'I don't know for certain,' he said. 'But it's possible. Foster had good reason. To be honest though, many people round here had good reason.'

'Exactly.' Toby nodded. 'Just as you had good reason to shoot Foster, blood being thicker than water. You see, Catherine, underneath it all, your Dan is truly a Murrin. I mean, face the facts: Killing that burglar, assaulting and killing Gemma, getting revenge for the deaths of his brothers, killing you in a fit of rage, and even attacking Lisa and I as we tried to prevent his mad spree.' Toby touched the bruise round his eye. 'I'll be hailed as a hero and Dan, guess what? Our agent will be delighted. Sure, he'll lose the pittance your soundtracks bring in, but the publicity will do wonders for my book. To be honest, I can't see much of a downside.'

'You bastard.' Daniel stood. He raised his arms and came towards Toby. 'I'm not—'

Toby swung the gun round and fired. The floor at Daniel's feet exploded in a mass of carpet and floorboards and he fell back, colliding with the desk.

'Sit back in the chair and write!' Toby yelled through the cloud of debris. Daniel appeared dazed. He was on his hands and knees, struggling to rise from the floor. 'Lisa's written it down so all you have to do is copy her words out.'

Daniel pushed himself into a sitting position. He rubbed his eyes. 'Give me moment. You don't want my handwriting all shaky, do you?'

'That's more like it.' Toby smiled at Daniel. 'You're considering my welfare. Helpful. If only you'd been as obliging earlier.' Toby turned to Catherine. 'Now, while Dan's recovering, let's get you sorted.'

Catherine flinched as Lisa came over. She had a roll of green cord in her hand. Catherine recognised it as having come from the garden shed.

'Best be a good girl,' Lisa said. 'Toby will get angry if you don't behave.'

'Too right,' Toby said. 'Lisa's going to take you upstairs while I remain here. I've got the gun trained on Daniel and if Lisa isn't back in five minutes, I'll shoot Dan and come looking for you, understand?'

Catherine glanced at Daniel. He got up off the floor and sat at the desk, but he caught her eye and nodded.

Lisa shoved Catherine out into the hallway and she made for the stairs.

'Wait there.' Lisa went into the kitchen and over to the knife block. She pulled out a carving knife and held it up. 'Just in case you get any funny ideas.'

'You don't have to do this,' Catherine said as they went upstairs. 'I know Toby's abused you. You're his pawn. You're under his control. The police will realise that and you'll get a reduced sentence.'

'The little woman,' Lisa said. 'That's what you believe I am?'

'I don't mean it in a demeaning way.' As Catherine said the words she knew she was lying. She *did* mean it in a demeaning way. Lisa was beholden to Toby, somehow beguiled by him. It was as if she had no identity. She was an add-on. The hugely entertaining Toby and his wife... sorry, I've forgotten your name? Catherine could empathise because in some small way her relationship with Daniel was similar. Men like Toby and Daniel hogged the limelight. Their stars burned brightly, and it was easy to be blinded. 'I was the same with Daniel. I felt as if I was nobody compared to him. Insignificant. But I learned to step out of his shadow and take control of my own life. You can do that too.'

Catherine stopped. The words appeared to be wasted on Lisa because she raised the knife once more.

'You're talking nonsense,' Lisa said. 'The sort of tosh you might find in the Sunday Supplements. I was the one who killed Gemma. The tart came round looking to steal our money. She sat in our living room making demands until I snuck up behind her and smashed her head in with your statue. Save the pity for yourself, you silly cow. Now get in Daniel's room.'

Catherine lowered her head. She'd misjudged Lisa again. Perhaps underneath the surface Lisa was the strong one and Toby was subservient in the relationship.

'The baby,' she heard herself say as she walked across the landing. 'Who killed the baby?'

'Toby did. You know how he can't abide children. Well, when Gemma went down, the baby started to make a right racket. Toby didn't like the noise, so he held a pillow over its face. Simple. They should put that in those parenting books. A permanent solution to sleepless nights.'

Catherine stumbled as she entered Daniel's room. The vision of Gemma lying on the floor and the baby screaming for his mother was too much. She pondered the awfulness of the world. How people like Toby and Lisa could exist. How circumstances had conspired to bring them together, and why their psychopathic tendencies had emerged when Gemma had come along.

'Sit on the chair,' Lisa said as she followed Catherine in. She pointed to Daniel's computer chair. 'Arms behind your back.'

'Ow!' The cord cut into Catherine's wrists as Lisa made a pair of loops and tugged them tight. 'You're hurting me!'

Lisa ignored her and continued to unravel the cord, taking it round Catherine's waist and down to her feet. She tied her ankles together and cut the cord with the knife.

'We're done,' Lisa said. 'I'd better get back downstairs before Toby decides I've been gone too long.'

'Please.' Catherine's eyes filled with tears. She sensed this would be her last chance to get through to Lisa, to appeal to whatever humanity lay hidden deep inside. 'This is so senseless. You can let us live and still escape.'

'It's not senseless.' Lisa stood in the doorway. 'Toby told you why it has to be this way. Weren't you listening?'

'I was listening, but I wasn't convinced. You know how the police always get to the bottom of these cases eventually. Forensics and all that sort of stuff. Toby's got it wrong. His stupid plan means you *will* get caught and you *will* go to prison.'

'You bitch.' Lisa shot across to Catherine and slapped her in the face. 'Don't you ever call my husband stupid.'

The cut on Catherine's lip started to bleed again and she twisted her head away, prepared for another blow. It didn't come, and when she looked up, Lisa had gone.

Chapter Sixty-one

Snow was falling. Heavy snow. Great chunks of the stuff. As if some weather demon was throwing handfuls down at a time. And the wind was building too, swirling the snow in circles as if the motion might confuse Foster and prevent him from getting to World's End Farm.

'Funny,' Foster said aloud as he struggled along the drovers' track. 'But the joke's wearing thin, right?'

He raised a fist to the sky and tilted his head back, willing whatever supernatural being was up there to answer him, but there was no response save for a howl as the wind swept down the valley.

Barney must be there by now, he thought. He'd be at the end of the track waiting for Foster's signal. But then what? He didn't have a plan, no idea what they might do. All he knew was some oaf of a man had his shotgun. That was a point against. On the other hand, the man was from London. He didn't know the terrain and he didn't know they were coming.

They...

They weren't exactly the 7th Cavalry, nor a pair of those superheroes with special powers. Just him and Barney. One of them seventy, with a dodgy ticker; the other seventy-two, with a gammy leg. On the other hand, they'd have Barney's rifle and the element of surprise. They could sneak up to the farm and Barney could take a potshot at the fellow. It wasn't noble or honourable, but to be honest he didn't give a fuck.

Foster forged through the last drift and emerged onto the fields above World's End. In the distance, the house glowed like some awful plug-in Christmas decoration, light blazing from every window. He tramped across the top field until he got to a gate. There was one more field and then the house. Foster peered to the right. Somewhere out there in the darkness, Barney was waiting.

He took out his torch and carefully shielded one side of it. He pointed the torch away from the house and flashed it on and off. Once. Twice. Three times. He repeated the sequence. Where the heck was— there! A flash of headlights from the dray, dimming from a harsh glare, to a warm glow, to off.

Foster moved to the gate to the last field and opened it. He made for the corner where the field bordered the track and waited by the stone wall, half smiling to himself. Barney *sounded* like the 7th Cavalry at least.

'Pssst,' Foster said as the clomping footsteps got closer. 'Over here.'

'Joe?' The voice came from the darkness and then there was Barney. 'Bloody hell. You took your time.'

'Never mind that, let's get down there. First sign of the fucker who came round my place and you take him, OK? Don't worry about legality and self-defence and all that crap, just line him up in the sights and shoot the bastard.'

'Shoot the bastard. Yes.' Barney stood in the gloom. Hands in pockets. 'Might be a teensy-weensy problem with that.'

'What?' Foster glowered at Barney. Hands in pockets. *Hands in pockets*? 'Where the bloody hell's your rifle?'

'I couldn't find it. I thought the gun was hidden in the loft, but when I went up there it wasn't. So I wondered about the cellar, but nope, no sign. Then I figured it must be—'

'You pillock,' Foster said. 'That's all we need. Two old blokes with mobility problems and now we add dementia to the mix.'

'I ain't got dementia.'

'And we ain't got no rifle either.'

'We could drive to the village.' Barney gestured towards the track. 'Get some help.'

'No.' Foster followed Barney's gaze. The snow was much heavier. 'We might get stuck, even if we went down in the dray. Plus there's the time. Not enough of it.'

'So?'

'We'll improvise.'

'What's that supposed to mean?'

'You know, like when you use a length of baler twine to bodge a fence together?'

'Now you're the one who's got dementia. You told me the man down there has your shotgun. Baler twine isn't going to help much.'

'Let's see.' Foster turned to the house. 'One thing's for sure, standing here nattering won't do us much good. Come on.'

Foster beckoned Barney into the field and they made their way along the wall, keeping stooped over so as to stay out of sight.

'Flaming hell, my leg won't stand for this,' Barney said. 'I could do with one of them all-terrain mobility scooters.'

'Stop moaning and keep quiet,' Foster hissed.

The field dropped away and they followed the wall down to the stone and grass bank which marked the boundary to the house.

'See anything?' whispered Barney as they reached the gate.

'In the front room.' Foster gestured to the house. 'That's Daniel — the husband — at the desk. Can't see the guy who nobbled me. Toby, Catherine called him.'

'Perhaps he's not here.'

'We can but hope.'

They watched Daniel sitting at the desk, hunched over. He had a pen in one hand.

'He doesn't seem distressed,' Barney said. 'He'd hardly be writing a letter if there was anything amiss in there.'

'Where's the wife though?' Foster scanned the other windows. 'And that pink car out front. It doesn't belong to them.'

'How do you know?'

'I've seen it before. They're not alone in there.'

Barney touched Foster on the shoulder. 'You're right.'

'It's him.' Foster peered through the falling snow. A figure crossed in front of the living room window. It was Toby, the man who'd turned up at The Steddings with Catherine. He held Foster's shotgun and was pointing it at Daniel. 'They're moving.'

Toby was waving the gun at Daniel, but the latter seemed reluctant to move. Eventually, he stood and left the room and Toby followed. A minute later, the pair emerged from behind the house and headed for the barn, Toby jabbing the shotgun in Daniel's back. A woman was walking behind them. Mousy brown hair. Thin face.

'That's not Catherine, is it?' Barney said. 'I remember her as a bit of a stunner.'

'I don't know who she is.' Foster said. The woman was carrying something looped over her right arm. 'What the heck are they up to?'

'Changing a lightbulb by the looks of it.'

'Hey?' Foster saw what Barney meant. Daniel had retrieved a stepladder from the depths of the barn. He opened it out. 'I don't understand.'

Toby waved the shotgun at Daniel and as the woman approached, Foster realised what she was carrying. Rope. A coil of rope.

'Christ Almighty.' He got it now. He blinked as the nausea grew, bile forcing its way up his throat. There was a tightness across his chest and his vision was gone, the scene a blur of white as his eyes filled with moisture. 'I can't see, Barney. What's happening?'

'The poor bugger.' Barney gulped. 'The woman's tied a noose in the end of the rope. They're telling Daniel to climb the ladder and fix the rope over the beam. They're going to hang him.'

'It's my fault,' Foster said. 'I was trying to do what was right, but I should've left it alone.'

'What happened back then can have no bearing on this, Joe. And those boys deserved to die.'

'Daniel doesn't though. He was just a toddler. As innocent as that baby I tipped into the quarry.' Foster blinked again. Wiped the back of his hand across his face. There was white and grey now. The outline of the barn. Matchstick figures in the snow. A blob of pink marking the location of the vagina car. Foster staggered to his feet. 'We can't just watch.'

'Don't be stupid.' Barney stood and grabbed Foster by the shoulders. 'He's got a gun.'

'I can't just stand here.' Foster put a hand on the gate.

'It's too late, Joe. Daniel's up the ladder and they've got the noose round his neck.'

'No, Barney,' Foster said as he opened the gate. 'It's never too late.'

Chapter Sixty-two

Catherine sat on the chair in the middle of the room. She didn't know why they'd put her up here, but there was no rationale to any of their actions. They'd gone beyond any reasonable behaviour and it was as if they were driven by an insanity which possessed the pair of them.

She wriggled her hands, trying to see if she could get free, but Lisa had wrapped the twine round and round so Catherine's arms were bound together from her wrists to her elbows. She scanned the room, searching for anything that could help her escape.

Daniel's workspace wasn't a traditional office. There were several monitor screens and a mixing desk. A computer cabinet nestled under one end of the desk and Daniel's laptop sat on top. The lid was down, but the blue power light flashed on and off. The machine was on standby.

She leaned over in the chair and used her feet to scrabble forwards. The chair glided across the carpet, moving closer and closer. At the desk she bent double, her nose down next to the laptop's lid. She pushed under the lid and the laptop slid backwards, but then it snagged the mixing desk and she was able to lever the lid open. She manoeuvred her head in the gap until the screen was vertical. There was a whirring and the screen flashed into life, a password box appearing in the centre.

No problem, unlike with Daniel's phone, she knew his computer password: *worldsend*. She'd told him to use a more secure one, but he'd been insistent. She bent to the keyboard and with some difficulty used the tip of her nose to tap the letters. She hit *return*, the screen blinked, and she was in.

She looked at the icons on the screen. What to do? She could open a web browser and use one of Daniel's social media accounts to send a message. She could write an email. She could use Skype to call a phone number. Yes, Skype, she thought. She'd ring her parents. As she bent to the mousepad she saw a flash on the screen. A notification: *Plug in mains power now or the computer will hibernate.*

She sat up. Daniel's laptop bag lay on the floor near the desk. When he'd arrived home, he must have taken out the laptop to write a quick email, but he hadn't plugged the machine in. It had been sitting on the desk on standby, draining the batteries of any remaining charge.

The screen greyed and dimmed, and another message popped up: *Hibernating...*

No! Catherine rocked the chair and struggled against her bonds as if in an extreme rage she might acquire the superhuman strength to break them. It was no good. The cord cut into her wrists but held fast.

Her rising panic was heightened by shouts from outside. She rocked the chair again and used her feet to ease her way over to the window. The blinds, as always, were closed, but she leaned over and pushed her face into them, squishing the slats apart until she could peer through. A security light shone from high on the gable end of the barn and she tilted her head, trying to see beyond the semicircle of white. There. In the shadows. Toby and Lisa. What the hell were they doing?

She shifted her head again and looked to the right where a stepladder rose towards the huge crossbeam. An awful chill swept over her as she realised Daniel was standing at the top of the ladder. A rope hung loose round his neck and curved up to the beam.

She gave a violent jerk and her head banged into the blinds and thudded on the glass. Lisa glared up at the window. Catherine leaned back and rotated the chair. She threw herself sideways and the chair fell towards the window, the top edge of the high back smashing the blinds. The glass behind the blinds cracked. She rocked again and this time, as the chair hit the window, the glass shattered, and the blind came free from the curtain rail and fell to the floor.

'Daniel!' Catherine screamed, and she saw him turn and face her.

Lisa began to run, heading round the house to the back door. Toby ran too. He sprinted across and shouldered the stepladder. The ladder toppled and Daniel's feet danced off the top step.

Catherine gasped in horror as his hands went up and tried to catch hold of the rope as it snatched taut and tightened round his neck. The ladder crashed to the floor and Daniel swung free, his legs kicking in the air. Toby stepped back, spoke to Daniel, and laughed. Daniel writhed as his hands failed to find any kind of purchase on the rope and then his movements were slowing, his body rotating, his eyes catching hers as he spun slowly before her.

Chapter Sixty-three

It was the next day when I realised the boy was alone in the house. Barney's mum had come round again, armed with a basket of rock cakes and a mouthful of gossip.

'A terrible business,' she said. My ears pricked up, expecting to hear about Will and Red. 'Eleanor in the Post Office told me it was just the pair of them went to London. Well, fancy leaving the little one alone with those two boys to care for him. Somebody braver than me would be calling Social Services.'

I hurried down the drovers' track to World's End Farm and peered in the window. The kid was sitting on the floor of the parlour playing with some toy cars. I went round the back and let myself in, but he didn't seem surprised to see me when I came into the parlour with some bread, cheese, fruit, and a glass of milk. I set the food down in front of him and he ate the lot.

I came back the day after. This time I could smell the boy had soiled himself. I took him to the bathroom and cleaned him up. Gave him fresh clothes and some more food. The same on the day after. A bath, new clothes, food and drink. I hefted a batch of logs in from outside and lit the range to keep the place warm. All the time, he followed me round and, when I made to leave, he took me by the hand and led me into the parlour. He pointed at the window.

I followed his gaze and went across and looked out towards the barn where Will and Red hung just as dead as I had left them three days before.

I guess I hadn't figured it out until then. The little one must have been watching the whole time. He'd have seen me pull the boys from the house and lay them on the ground. Tie a noose round each of their necks. Finally, he'd have watched as I led the horse on and hoisted them boys up one after the other. His brothers swinging there, legs kicking out in desperation, bodies writhing as the last gasp went out of them.

Seeing that could have an effect, I guess, but there was little I could do but leave the boy in the house again. Luckily, later that day Mr Murrin and his wife returned and found Will and Red. Soon there were police officers everywhere. Roadblocks, a helicopter, teams of detectives going door-to-door in every village and hamlet within ten miles of World's End.

Jencks questioned the nipper, but he wasn't much help. He was two years old, so perhaps that was it. Perhaps he didn't have the language to describe what had happened. Folks said he kept saying one thing over and over. 'Pony.' Just that. 'Pony.' Jencks plied the boy with sweets, begged him to try to recall what he'd seen, but he could still only say the one word: 'Pony.'

'It's all he can remember,' Jencks said. 'The bloody pony which was the cause of all this.'

'That's enough,' Mrs Murrin said, and the boy was bundled out of Jencks' reach.

When I heard reports of the interview, I had to suppress a wry smile. The boy was canny. He wasn't talking about the pony which old Murrin had skinned and chopped up, nor the horse I'd used to hang Will and Red. No, he was trying to tell Jencks that it was me who was the killer. The man who'd given him a ride on the big old carthorse back the previous summer.

They moved away after that, the boy and his mother. Far away. I realised I was safe then. Nobody remembers with any sense of accuracy events from their early childhood. The murder of the Murrin brothers would become a part of local history and at some point pass into legend. I would be long dead by then.

The investigation went on for several months and Jencks persisted like a smell which lingers. He kept turning up at our farm, each time with fresh questions. I think he suspected I might be involved, but he suspected everyone. Since everyone but me was innocent, he got nowhere. Eventually, his bosses told him to wind the case down, but he couldn't leave it alone. He pursued various leads outside of his work hours and had a huge corkboard on his living room wall. Pins and bits of string. Dozens of photographs of the crime scene. Pieces of paper with inane jottings.

His unofficial snooping led to the community closing ranks. If he'd been disliked before, now he was detested. And of course the more folks blanked him the more he was sure some sort of conspiracy was taking place behind his back.

It came to a head late in the summer, after Jencks had persuaded his superiors to conduct a drugs raid on a house in the village. The house belonged to Jed Linker and his wife. They had three kids under five and the only drug young Jed took was tea-like in colour and came in a pint glass served at The Crown. Nevertheless, the place was torn apart as Jencks tried desperately to find some evidence to incriminate Jed.

Three days later, Jencks was returning home in the dusk. As he placed the key in the lock of his front door, he was jumped. An unknown number of assailants wrestled him to the ground, secured his hands behind his back, and poured several buckets of pig slurry over him. No one spoke but the message was clear, and when Jencks' wife opened the door to his plaintive cries, those watching from nearby houses knew it had sunk home.

Within a week Jencks had left the village and moved into temporary police accommodation in Exeter. A For Sale *board appeared outside his house, and a while later I heard he'd been placed on long term sick leave. He had mental problems, apparently.*

Then again, haven't we all?

Chapter Sixty-four

The scene played out for Foster in slow motion through a fog of driving snow. He was halfway across the yard as the window in the upstairs room shattered. He saw the woman make for the back door and watched as Toby barged the stepladder. He felt powerless again, the energy draining from him in the same manner as it had when the Murrin brothers had led Helena away.

Then he was head down and charging like a bull, his feet slipping on the snow, but his speed increasing. He covered the distance to the barn like a man a third of his age. Toby saw him coming and tried to aim the gun, but as he bought it to bear, Foster barrelled into him, driving him backwards onto a pile of stone.

Toby lay winded with Foster lying on top, but he shoved Foster off and clambered to his feet. He spotted the gun lying in the snow and staggered towards it.

'Barney!' Foster shouted. He rolled over on his back and tried to rise, realising there was nothing his friend could do about the gun because Barney was standing beneath Daniel. Daniel was trying to balance on Barney's shoulders and hold onto the rope and they were swaying back and forth, Barney struggling to stay on his feet.

'Joe,' Barney said. 'Get the ladder!'

In an instant, Foster considered the options. If he went for the ladder, Toby would get the gun. If he went for the gun, Barney would collapse and Daniel would be strangled by the rope. For some reason Foster thought of what he'd said to Barney earlier. That they would improvise. He remembered he'd mentioned baler twine. A clever bodge with a length of the orange string he always carried had saved the day on countless occasions. String wouldn't be enough now, but the knife he used to cut the stuff might.

Foster rose to his knees. His hand went into his pocket and out came the twine and the knife in a tangle. He stripped off the twine and flicked the knife open. The blade sprung out as Foster brought his arm back.

Then he threw.

The knife hit Toby as he bent for the shotgun. The blade struck him just below his chin, the point penetrating a good three inches into the fleshy area just above his Adam's apple.

Foster was already on his feet, heading for the stepladder. He picked it up and shoved it across to Barney and Daniel. Daniel's feet came down hard on the top step as he lurched from Barney's shoulders and took the weight off the rope. A second later and he'd removed the noose from his neck and jumped down. He rolled to the floor and lay there gasping.

Foster went over to Toby. He too was gasping for air, great wheezing noises spluttering from the open wound in his throat.

'I missed,' Foster said as Barney came over.

'What were you aiming for?' Barney said.

'His hand. Pity about that.'

Barney knelt. Toby lay on his side, half curled like a foetus. His eyes flicked up.

'Huh... huh... huh.' Toby put his hands to his neck. 'Ugh... ugh... ugh.'

'There's a lot of blood.' Barney lowered his head and peered in at the neck wound. 'But you haven't severed the artery. Still, we should call an ambulance.'

'No hurry.'

'Catherine.' Daniel's voice came hoarse and low as he lay on the ground nearby. 'She's inside with Lisa.'

'Bloody hell.' Foster began to move. 'Mouse face.'

Chapter Sixty-five

Catherine slammed the chair back in an effort to break the cord. As she rocked, the chair fell away from the window and tipped over. Her whole body juddered as she crashed to the floor and lay on her side. Outside there was shouting and some sort of commotion. Footsteps hammered up the stairs and the door banged open.

Lisa. The carving knife in her right hand.

'What the fuck are you playing at?' Lisa kicked out, catching Catherine in the stomach. 'You should have done as you were told.'

'Oh God!' An intense pain shot across Catherine's abdomen. She bowed her head. 'Please, Lisa!'

Lisa ignored her and went to the window. She peered out and screamed. 'Toby!'

'What's happening?' Catherine said. She tried to wriggle free from the chair, but she was helpless. 'Please don't kill Daniel.'

'Too late for that.' Lisa walked back to Catherine, the knife raised.

'No.' Catherine tried to shy away. 'Don't hurt me.'

'Stay still.' Lisa slit the cords and Catherine's hands and feet came free. She shook off the bonds and rolled onto her knees. Lisa's arm slipped round her waist and the knife pricked her in the neck. 'Get up. Slowly. You're coming with me as my insurance policy.'

Catherine got to her feet, aware of the blade at her throat as Lisa shoved her in the back.

'Move it. Out onto the landing.'

'Hold it there, lass.'

Catherine felt her heart miss a beat. Joe Foster stood outside the room. He held the shotgun in his hands.

'Who the fuck are you?' Lisa said.

'I'm the friendly neighbour popping round with a cup of sugar and a gun full of lead,' Foster said. 'Drop the knife, sweetheart. I've had this beauty since I was but a young lad, and I can tell you I don't often miss.'

'You're crazy. You're not going to shoot me in cold blood.' Lisa edged forwards. 'I'm a woman, after all.'

'If you knew me better you might not say that.'

'Well, you wouldn't risk hitting Catherine.' Lisa twisted the knife and the point nicked Catherine's skin. 'And if you don't move out of the way I'm going to work this a little deeper.'

'Shush, girl,' Foster said. To Catherine's horror he lowered the shotgun and leaned the weapon against the banisters. He took a step. 'You're just like a stroppy Highland cow I once had. Never let me get near her, she wouldn't. I had to lower my voice and play Grandmother's footsteps. Tippy-toe, tippy-toe, tippy-toe.'

'I'm warning you!' Lisa pressed the knife in harder as Foster edged nearer.

'I'm not listening, lass.' Foster lunged and his left hand swept into the crock of Lisa's right elbow, knocking her arm away.

Catherine rotated free, dropped to the floor and rolled clear as Lisa screamed and lunged at Foster. He put his hand up to defend himself, but the knife caught him across the palm. He stumbled backwards as Lisa changed her grip and stabbed again. Catherine got to her feet as Foster scrambled out the way. He retreated across the landing, but he appeared to be dazed. Then he clutched at his chest.

'Goodbye, old man.' Lisa said, and as Foster stood there defenceless, she stabbed him in the stomach with the knife.

'Joe!' Catherine yelled as Foster collapsed.

'It seems your hero has fallen short.' Lisa raised the carving knife in triumph and bent to stab Foster again. 'You do pick them, Cathy.'

'No!' Catherine lunged for the shotgun. Her hands closed round the stock and she brought it up to bear on Lisa. 'Stop!'

'You haven't a clue how to use that.' Lisa placed the point of the blade to Foster's neck. 'Anyway, you wouldn't dare.'

'That's where you're wrong.' Catherine said.

'I—' Lisa opened her mouth to speak but she never got the chance.

Catherine pulled the trigger on the shotgun. The butt slammed into her chest and the retort filled the air. The blast caught Lisa on her left shoulder and she span round, smashing into the banisters at the top of the landing before toppling down the stairs, bumping over and over until she lay in a heap at the bottom.

Catherine dropped the gun and ran over to Foster. He lay on his back staring blankly, an expression of pain rigid on his face.

'Joe,' Catherine said. 'Hang in there. I'll call an ambulance.'

'You'll need a couple,' Foster said with a whisper. He winked. 'Maybe more.'

'Daniel?'

'They tried to hang him, but he'll live.'

'Thank God!'

'God had nowt to do with it.' Foster gasped for air and his eyelids fluttered. 'But I could sure use his help now.'

'Don't talk, just lie there.'

'Important.' Foster's voice had dropped to no more than a rasp. Catherine bent close. 'Helena Hodgson. You'll find her for me?'

'I will.'

'No!' Foster's hand grasped Catherine's wrist. 'Find her and tell her I'm sorry. I could've stopped it. Stopped everything. No deaths, no misery. Only I was a coward, see? Selfish.'

'That's the last thing you are, Joe Foster.' Catherine kissed him on the forehead. 'In fact, you're the bravest man I know.'

'Thank you.' Foster let out a great sigh, but he gripped Catherine's wrist again. 'I killed 'em, you know? Will and Red. I thought I was putting the world to right, but I never figured on the boy being there to watch them hanged. I can't think what that might have done to him. What trouble I've caused.'

'Shush. Try to keep still.'

'Still, yes.' Foster relaxed his grip a little. He blinked. 'My dog, Jess. You'll have her?'

'I'll take care of her, Joe, don't worry. She'll be fine. Just as you will.'

Foster smiled. His hand opened and fell away and he closed his eyes as Catherine heard footsteps in the hallway below, Daniel shouting out her name.

Epilogue

'He's gone,' DC Taylor said. 'I'm sorry.'

Catherine and Daniel sat on a brown sofa in a small room at the police station. Grey flecked walls. A spread of magazines on a low table. A rubbish bin overflowing with plastic cups. In one wall, a window overlooked a car park, and the morning sun glinted on a number of windscreens. Taylor stood at the door, her thick lips stretched into a flat grimace.

'Apparently he never regained consciousness. I'm sure they did all they could.'

'Yes,' Catherine said. Daniel held her hand. Squeezed. 'Thanks for letting us know.'

'Do you want to know about the other two?'

'Not really.'

'Yes,' Daniel said. He squeezed Catherine's hand again. 'Please.'

'Lisa Paget lost a lot of blood and the damage to her shoulder is substantial. The doctors are fighting to save her arm, but she's out of danger.' Taylor paused, her face lacking any emotion, as if she didn't have an opinion on whether Lisa's survival was a good thing or not. 'Toby Paget hasn't fared so well. He's breathing with the aid of a ventilator, but the signs aren't good. Although the neck wound was superficial his brain suffered from loss of oxygen. At best there'll be brain function impairment and reduced mobility. Needless to say, when and if they do recover, they'll both be facing multiple murder charges.'

'And us?' Daniel inched his head towards Catherine. 'My wife?'

'That's for the future. For now you're free to go.'

'Thanks.'

'One other matter.' Taylor had a hand on the door, but she paused. 'Constable Jencks is under investigation vis-à-vis an assault on Joe Foster. Several officers came forward to say they witnessed the assault and I understand Jencks plans to resign rather than face dismissal.' Taylor opened her hands in a gesture of resignation or apology. 'Just thought you should know.' With that she turned and left the room.

Catherine slumped against Daniel. The news about Joe Foster hadn't come as a surprise. She'd sat with him on the landing, placed a pillow under his head, and covered him with a blanket, but when Barney had clumped up the stairs, she'd looked up and shaken her head. By the time the first paramedics had battled through the snow drifts and arrived at World's End, any hope had gone.

'Come on.' Daniel stood and helped her to her feet. He glanced at the stark surroundings. 'I don't want to stay here a minute longer than necessary.'

They took a taxi back to World's End where they found a police car sitting at the top of the track. An officer waved the taxi past. Inside the house they were confronted with chaos. Slush and mud tramped everywhere. A pool of blood congealed in a brown sludge at the foot of the stairs where Lisa had fallen. More blood in the living room from when they'd carried Toby inside and laid him on the floor. He'd stared up at them, unable to speak, making a horrid gurgling sound as he'd breathed in and out through the hole in his neck.

Catherine went into the kitchen and sat at the table. Daniel made two cups of hot chocolate and they sat drinking them, hands wrapped round the cups as if some of the warmth and sweetness could be transmitted by touch as well as taste. Neither of them spoke for a while. Daniel closed his eyes and sighed. When he opened them again he began to talk.

'I was born Jonathon Daniel Murrin,' he said. 'The man you thought was my father was in fact my stepfather. I'd been aware of that since I was eighteen, but never thought much of it. My mother remarried a year or so after leaving here, so from the age of four my stepdad *was* my dad. When she split from my father, she started calling me by my second name, Daniel. John was my father's name and she didn't want to be reminded of him.'

Catherine leaned forwards. 'Weren't you interested when you found out about your biological father?'

'No. The picture my mother painted of him wasn't a good one. I had no desire to trace him. When my stepdad died, Mum asked me whether I wanted to get in touch with my real father, but I declined.'

'So what happened to make you change your mind?'

'The burglar happened.' Daniel ducked his head. 'That anger. The violence. I realised what I was doing, Catherine, understand? I'd done enough to disable the burglar, but I carried on hitting him. Over and over. Again and again. I just snapped and pure rage came pouring out.'

'Don't, sweetheart,' Catherine said. 'There were no charges, remember?'

'No charges, I know, but I was hurting. Worse, I began to have flashbacks and vivid dreams. I kept seeing this boy sitting alone in a room surrounded by toys and teddy bears. Despite the toys he was crying because he'd witnessed an awful event. I didn't know what that was, but it seemed likely it was some form of abuse.'

'The boy was you?'

'Of course. I knew then I had to find out about my real father and discover if he'd hurt me in some way. Violence begets violence. Abusers abuse.'

'You're not an abuser.'

'No, I'm not, but nevertheless what happened to me as a child could have affected my behaviour as an adult. There could even have been some genetic predisposition that pushed me over the edge.'

'So a year ago you secretly came down here to find out.'

'How did you know?'

'Peter Carmichael. He saw you visiting your father at the hospital.'

'He might have seen me, but he didn't have the full picture.' Daniel's voice faltered. 'You see...'

'Daniel?' Catherine reached out and took her husband's hands.

There were tears in his eyes. 'What is it?'

'I managed to track my father down and I phoned him the week before he jumped from Haytor. I wanted to try and lessen the shock of turning up on his doorstep, but he didn't want to know me. I told him I was coming to visit him anyway.'

'I don't understand?'

'I killed him, Cath. He tried to commit suicide because he was scared of what I would say to him.'

'I thought he had cancer?'

'He did, but it was a long way off terminal. The reality was he couldn't bear to face me. He took the easy way out.'

'And when you did get to see him, what did he say?'

'Not a word. He was unable to speak. I'm not even sure he realised who I was. He died three days later.'

'I'm so sorry, Dan. Why didn't you tell me what was going on?'

'I was stuck in my own head. Confused. I didn't come down for my father's funeral, but a while after I visited his grave. You remember when I was at the movie shoot near Bristol? Well, I bunked off the set for a day and came down here. That's when I discovered about my half-brothers. My father's plot was right beside theirs. I could tell from the dates they'd died young. When I was just a toddler in fact. I realised the trauma and flashbacks had to be related to the deaths of Will and Red, and it took no more than a short search of some local history websites to discover their fate. Up until then I hadn't even thought of World's End, but knowing how they'd died and what had happened, I decided I needed to see the house. When I arrived here, there was a *For Sale* board stuck on a pole. That's when I got the crazy idea of moving.'

'It must have been a shock one moment finding out you had two half-brothers, and the next discovering they'd been murdered.'

'It was, and as soon as I got back to London I went to visit my mother and asked her why she'd never told me about them. She explained to me what had happened, starting with how my father and brothers behaved and how they were hated and despised. Next, she moved onto Helena Hodgson and her father and how that led to the deaths of Will and Red. Finally, she told me about how much she regretted marrying Murrin and that the hangings had been the catalyst for her to leave him. By the time I left her she was ranting and raging, and a nurse had to come and calm her down. The story was a complete mess in my mind, but the idea I'd had about moving began to seem like a solution to everything. Then, two months after my father's death, I received a letter from his solicitor. There was no estate to speak of, nothing of value, but there was an envelope containing some old photographs. The pictures you found in the metal box in my room.'

'Of the barn?'

'Yes, but there was another picture too. It was of me as a child. I was sitting on a horse with my mother standing on one side and a man on the other.'

'I've seen it. Foster showed it to me.'

'Of course. The one I have is a copy. The photo was taken by Foster's mother. I know because there's an inscription on the back which says, "Dear Ellen, thought you might like this, Peggy".'

'Your mother and Joe's mother?'

'Yes. Anyway, when I first saw the photograph I had no idea the man was Joe Foster, but the inclusion of the picture alongside the crime scene images suggested to me that my father believed the man holding the horse was somehow connected with the murder of my brothers.'

'And that made you determined to move down here?'

'Solving the mystery was important and, having seen the picture of Will and Red hanging in the barn, I realised my flashbacks were definitely related to what had happened. However, perhaps what Toby said was also true: I wanted to confront my demons. I wanted to discover if I was made of the same stuff as my father and brothers. I honestly thought living here might both lead me to discover who had killed Will and Red and at the same time let me work through the issues related to what happened up in London.'

Catherine gestured at the room. 'I noticed you didn't have much input when I tried to make the house a home.'

'No. I decided it would be better if you chose the colours and the furniture. That way there was no chance of me reconstructing something from the past that wasn't there.'

'But at some point you realised the murderer was Foster?'

'To be honest, Cath, until you told me he'd confessed as he died, I never knew for certain. I hoped returning to World's End would crystalize my dreams and flashbacks, but after spending a couple of months living here I realised I wasn't going to remember much of what had happened. Parts of it did come back to me though. For instance, I remembered being alone and feeling frightened in the house, but the vision I have of my brothers hanging in the barn comes from the crime scene picture, not from memory. So, while I suspected Foster was involved, try as I might all I could recall was the time he gave me a ride on his carthorse; again, the memory is from the photograph. However, I did guess it was Foster who'd been leaving nasty surprises for whoever lived here, so I left him one in return.'

'The noose in the barn?'

'Yup. He got the message that someone knew what he was up to and stopped trying to scare us.'

'Were you going to confront him or go to the police?'

'Not the police. Not after my experience in London. As for confronting him, I wasn't sure. I spoke with Toby at Christmas and he suggested I should just let it play out. By then, of course, he had his own problems and an ulterior motive. I don't think he had a plan as such, but he could see that knowing my secret might be helpful to him at some point.'

'So you didn't want revenge?'

'For two half-brothers I never met and who, by all accounts, deserved what they got?' Daniel leaned back in his chair. 'No, not revenge, Catherine.'

'I don't understand?'

'There was only one thing I ever wanted from moving here.'

Daniel looked across to the window. Catherine followed his gaze. Outside the low sun bathed the barn in a golden wash.

'Peace,' he said.

***

Joe Foster's funeral took place ten days later. The tiny church resonated with a hundred voices as Father Carmichael led the congregation in a rendition of Psalm 23.

The Lord's my Shepherd, I'll not want;
He makes me down to lie
In pastures green; He leadeth me
The quiet waters by.

Catherine was in floods of tears even before the first verse had echoed off the high ceiling. Daniel clutched her hand and she leaned across and rested her head on his shoulder. They stood in the first pew with Barney and some of his wider family. Foster had no relatives, but even so the place was packed, with some mourners having to stand at the back. Catherine could hardly believe the number of people who'd come.

The service passed in a blur and a handful of Carmichael's words was about all she could remember.

God forgives all and welcomes everyone to the Kingdom of Heaven...

She didn't know if that was true. Was there a place for Joe Foster up there? What about Daniel? Will and Red Murrin? Toby and Lisa, even? A line had to be drawn somewhere, she thought.

When the service was over, the crowd mingled outside in the sunshine. The temperature had risen into the mid-teens as an unexpected band of warm weather rolled up from the continent, promising an early spring. Catherine found herself standing on her own next to a gravestone where a spread of roses poked from a plain vase. Daniel was over near the entrance to the church talking to Carmichael.

'They all realised, you know?' A stout man with a red face sidled across. Barney Weston. 'About what happened at World's End.'

'You mean about Joe?'

'Yes. They knew Foster was in love with Helena Hodgson and it didn't take much to work out who'd hanged those boys. Nobody said nowt though. Nothing. Zilch. I bet if you questioned them now they'll remain tight-lipped. It's tough on your husband, but old man Murrin and Will and Red were an evil trio.'

'Daniel's not like that.'

'No?' Barney cocked his head. 'Praise be for small mercies then, that's all I can say.'

'It was our fault, Barney.' Catherine looked across to where Father Carmichael was listening intently to Daniel. 'If we hadn't moved here, Joe would be alive.'

'Maybe, maybe not. He had a heart condition. He could have dropped down dead while knocking in a fence post or supping a beer with me.'

'Preferable to the way he went though.'

'Perhaps, but Joe was pretty philosophical about life. The stupid bugger would have told you it was for the best.' Barney paused. He tilted his head towards the moor. 'What are you going to do with the farm?'

Catherine turned. World's End and Foster's place lay somewhere off in the distance, invisible in the deep valley. Foster, it transpired, had written down his last wishes before he'd come down to World's End on his rescue mission. He'd willed his farm — minus a field bordering Barney's land — to Catherine and Daniel. There was some doubt to the document's legality, but since he had no relatives, and there was no proper will, it was unlikely to be contested.

'I'm not sure,' Catherine said. 'Not yet.'

'It's funny,' Barney said as a look of profound sadness came over his face. 'I've been ribbing him for ages about the Top Meadow, but now he's finally let me have it, I couldn't care less.'

'I understand. He was a close friend of yours.'

'Since I was a kid.' Barney nodded. 'I've got a lifetime of memories. I...'

He mumbled, unable to speak, but he put out a hand. Catherine ignored the hand and gave him a hug instead.

'I'm alright,' he said. He stepped back, embarrassed, but when he turned to go he smiled. 'Thanks.'

As Barney walked away, Daniel appeared.

'Any particular reason you're standing over here?' he said.

'No. Why?'

'Look.' Daniel gestured at the gravestone and Catherine read the name and the dates and the eulogy.

Taken by the angels.

'I didn't realise.'

'Stephen Hodgson, Helena's dad.' Daniel knelt and rearranged the roses. 'These are fresh. A few days old at the most.'

'Who brings them?'

'Helena.' Daniel stood. 'A bunch every month without fail, according to Carmichael.'

'She lives locally?'

'Cornwall apparently.'

'Do you suppose Foster knew?'

'I don't see how he couldn't have known. Someone in the village must have seen her if she's been coming here for the past thirty-five years.'

'Poor man. Imagine having that hanging over you for half your life.' Catherine turned from the grave. 'I promised Joe I would track Helena down and deliver his message.'

'I can't imagine she'll be pleased to see you. Not seeing as you live at World's End and are married to a Murrin.'

'No, but I'm going to do it nonetheless.' Catherine looked towards the church. 'What did you make of the sermon?'

'That we're all sinners but we can all attain redemption?' Daniel snorted and cast a glance towards Father Carmichael. 'Crap, to be honest.'

'Foster asked me whether I believed if people were born evil or if they were made that way.'

'When was this?'

'Right before he showed me the picture of you on the carthorse. I think he was weighing the evidence against you.'

'What was his verdict?'

'He never said. I guess the fact he showed up to rescue you means that, on balance, he decided you were a victim of circumstance.'

'And what about you?' Daniel smiled.

'I'm agnostic.' Catherine smiled back, but she wanted to make a serious point. 'Toby and Lisa had no connection to World's End and they weren't genetically related to the Murrin family. Nor, as far as we know, did either of them ever witness anything as shocking as you did in your childhood. Despite that they murdered Gemma and her baby and Joe Foster.'

'Which means what?'

'I don't know.' She shrugged, depressed there wasn't an easy answer to any of what had happened. 'The only conclusion to draw is we're not bound by history. We make our own choices, for better or worse, for good or evil.'

Daniel stared at Catherine. He didn't appear to have caught her mood or followed her line of argument. He didn't seem to understand that in a single sentence she'd both forgiven him and condemned him. Never mind, she thought. Perhaps she'd been the one who'd needed to hear the words as a confirmation of the way she felt about him.

'Well, my choice now is we should be off,' Daniel said. The crowd was thinning and several people were casting glances in their direction. 'I wouldn't want to outstay our welcome with the locals.'

'You *are* a local.'

'I guess I am. Or rather we are. At least for now.'

'What's that supposed to mean?'

'We have to decide whether we're staying here or not. You've been itching to get back to London and all the while I've ignored you. It's time for me to stop being selfish and let you make the choice.'

'And you won't hold it against me if I want to move away?'

Daniel paused as if he wasn't quite sure how to answer. He leaned in close and kissed her on the cheek. 'No, I won't.'

Back at World's End, Catherine went out onto the rear patio and sat in a garden chair. She felt a little dizzy and nauseous after the funeral, but the sun warmed her face and a breeze teased at her hair. The air smelled fresh and at the side of the house the brook gurgled and bubbled. She opened her eyes and looked out across the moor. An ash tree wore a tinge of green and a swathe of daffodils painted a yellow streak over a grassy bank. Birds flitted low across a nearby field, their calls drifting to her on the wind. As Daniel had said, spring often came early in this part of the country. Had he been right about World's End too?

She realised there was still a possibility this was heaven, their forever place. What had happened in the last few days, what had happened decades ago, couldn't change the here and now. In fact it did the opposite, reinforcing the importance of the present and of what was to come. Daniel had said it was her decision. They could sell the house and Foster's farm and move back to London. They'd have money to spare. All her worries about living out here would be gone. No more dark, silent nights. No more memories.

Beside her Jess stirred. They'd taken Foster's dog even though Barney had said he'd have her. It had been a promise to Foster after all. Catherine put out a hand and caressed the top of the dog's head. If they moved, what would become of Jess? It was silly to worry about that, but she did. She'd been surprised the dog had shown no signs of missing Foster or pining for life back at the farm, but she figured that was because animals lived in the moment. They remembered people and places and events, but as for having regrets, or feeling sadness, self-pity, or guilt? No, those were human frailties. Perhaps there was a message in that, Catherine thought. A message to take forward into the rest of her life.

'Do you want a cup of tea?' Daniel came out from the house and stood by her. He reached down and stroked the dog. 'Or perhaps a glass of wine?'

'Neither,' she said. She glanced at the sky. 'I feel a bit odd. I guess it must be the heat. We're not used to it.'

She rose from the lounger and followed Daniel inside. As he set the kettle to boil, she drank a glass of water and went upstairs. She lay on the bed, hoping the nausea would go away. After a while she got up and went to the bathroom. She retrieved a small packet from her side of the bathroom cabinet and sat on the toilet. A minute later she was done, and she peered down at the object in her hand until the indicator line appeared alongside the control strip.

'Blue. Well that figures,' she said. As she realised the enormity of the situation, her heart caught in her mouth. 'Oh, shit.'

At that moment the door opened, Daniel framed in light. For a second he appeared confused. Then he walked in and knelt beside her like a suitor from a more chivalrous time. He looked at the blue line.

'Bloody hell,' he said. He raised his head. 'But amazing, right?'

'Yes.' Catherine clutched the pregnancy tester tight in her hand, as if the blue line was a physical manifestation of the baby. 'Are you sure you're OK with it?'

'Of course. More than OK. I'm delighted. Ecstatic.'

'Good,' she said. She closed her eyes, feeling lightheaded, speaking without thinking. 'I want to stay here too. At World's End. I want to put things right.'

'That's fine by me. We'll make it work.'

'You promise?' Catherine opened her eyes and looked at Daniel's face. Black pupils surrounded by a deep pool of shimmering blue and a smile she couldn't read.

'Yes,' he said.

Author's Note

The winter of 1981-82 was a bad one, but not as severe as 1962-63 when some parts of Dartmoor were cut off for weeks. Helicopters were used to ferry food and animal fodder and in places the snow lay on the ground from Boxing Day until early March. Other parts of the UK were hit too: the sea off the coast of Kent froze a mile out into Herne Bay, and the average temperature in England for January was minus two degrees Centigrade — the coldest month since 1814. For my purposes, 1962-63 was too far in the past, so I used a little poetic licence and transposed the extreme weather forward two decades.

Until recently, the thought of another winter like the one of 1962-63 would have seemed the stuff of fiction, but in March 2018 the so called 'Beast from the East' met a storm pushing up from Western Europe. The UK experienced a spell of very harsh weather with the Met Office issuing a Red Warning (meaning a danger to life is likely) for parts of Devon. Heavy snowfall and gale force winds caused drifts up to two metres deep and many communities were cut off. This time though, the cold snap lasted just a few days, and soon heavy rain washed the snow away.

World's End Farm is, of course, a creation wrought from my imagination. However, if you take a trip to the remoter parts of Dartmoor, you can still find farms like World's End or The Steddings. They tend to be nestled in deep valleys, accessed along rough tracks, and surrounded by a motley range of stone barns, decrepit outbuildings, and rusting farm machinery. As you approach one of these places, you'll spot a barking dog keen to chase you away and — if you linger — Joe Foster might emerge from behind a building, shake his fist, and reach for his gun.

Should you see him, send him my regards.

About the Author

Mark Sennen was born in Surrey but spent his formative years in rural Shropshire where he learnt to drive tractors and worm sheep. He has been a reluctant farmer, an average drummer, a failed Ph.D. student and a pretty good programmer. He lives, with his wife, two children and a rather large dog, beside a muddy creek in deepest South Devon where there hasn't been a murder in years.

Web: http://www.marksennen.com
Twitter: @marksennen

Also by Mark Sennen

The DI Charlotte Savage Series

Touch
Bad Blood
Cut Dead
Tell Tale
Two Evils
The Boneyard

Printed in Great Britain
by Amazon